THE ROOM OF THE DEAD

M.R.C. KASASIAN was raised in Lancashire. He has had careers as varied as a factory hand, wine waiter, veterinary assistant, fairground worker and dentist. He is also the author of the much-loved Gower Street Detective series, five books featuring personal detective Sidney Grice and his ward March Middleton. He lives with his wife, in Suffolk in the summer and in Malta in the winter.

Also by M.R.C. Kasasian

THE GOWER STREET DETECTIVE

BETTY CHURCH MYSTERIES

THE
ROOM OF
THE DEAD

A *Betty Church* MYSTERY

M.R.C.
KASASIAN

HEAD
of ZEUS

First published in the UK by Head of Zeus Ltd in 2019
This paperback edition published by Head of Zeus Ltd in 2020

9 7 5 3 1 2 4 6 8

A catalogue record for this book is available from the British Library.

ISBN (PB): 9781788546416
ISBN (E): 9781788546386

Printed and bound in Great Britain by
CPI Group (UK) Ltd, Croydon CR0 4YY

Head of Zeus Ltd
First Floor East
5–8 Hardwick Street
London EC1R 4RG

WWW.HEADOFZEUS.COM

For
Tiggy, always loved,
and
Betty, sadly missed.

COFFEE IN THE ICE AGE

Jimmy was reading yesterday's *Express*.

'Anything interesting?' I was struggling with my torn-out crossword that morning, but too proud to admit it was beating me.

'Nothing much.' He rustled through the pages. 'No sport.' There was not much of anything being played those bitter days of January 1940. Apart from the government's discouragement of crowds for – so far – unfounded fears of mass attacks by the Luftwaffe, the weather was the worst in living memory. We had had no snow yet but temperatures had dipped to 36 degrees below freezing in some areas and Suffolk certainly felt like it was one of them. Today was a little warmer, though, and with the benefit of our overcoats and a wood stove we were able to sit comfortably in the wheelhouse of *Cressida* and gaze over the bracken-crusted white and the river, every ripple solidified in mid-flow as if time itself had been turned off as an energy-saving measure. 'And not much war either.'

Captain Carmelo Sultana was out collecting kindling from Treacle Woods. He had built *Cressida*, his permanently landlocked ship, on the tiny island of Brindle Bar in the Angle Estuary and his land had been denuded of fallen twigs and branches long ago. Jimmy and I had both volunteered to go scavenging. None of us liked doing it because the woods sloped up sharply and were overgrown with gorse and brambles but the Mad Admiral – as he was known locally – insisted on taking his turn.

Jimmy folded the paper neatly, something he was always telling me women couldn't do. He was on a twenty-four-hour leave and, being stationed at nearby Hadling Heath aerodrome, it was an easy journey to visit us in what was now almost his home.

'Maybe there won't be,' I conjectured. 'Perhaps Hitler will be satisfied with Austria and Czechoslovakia and Poland.'

Jimmy peered at me. He had grown up a lot in the few months since he had rejoined the RAF. The moustache alone had added a few years to him and the severe burning of a friend in one of their squadron's few encounters with the enemy had chipped away at his boyish notions about the romance of aerial combat. 'You don't believe that.'

'No,' I admitted. 'I think we're allowing him to consolidate his position and build up his forces while we sit waiting for him to make the next move.'

'It's those poor sods at sea I feel sorry for,' Jimmy said. 'At least I have a sporting chance of fighting back up there. If you're a stoker in the bowels of a merchant ship, all you can do is shovel coal and pray the next torpedo isn't aimed at you.'

'If four down is *LEGEND,* that means *ICARUS* must be wrong,' I said loudly.

'What the—' Jimmy followed my gaze as his Great Uncle Carmelo appeared on deck.

The captain had enough to worry about with his son, Adam, being posted abroad on what we were told was hush-hush business.

'Madonna, it is half cold.' Carmelo shut the door smartly behind him to keep the heat in.

'Did you get much?' I asked.

'A sackful, but it is all wet.' He tugged off his gloves to warm his hands at the stove. 'There is anything left?'

I poured him a mug of coffee from the pot we kept simmering. 'I'd better get going.'

My heavy blue coat hung over the back of a chair, as close as it could to the heater without getting singed.

'Want me to take you?' Jimmy dropped the paper on to the polished floor by his chair, forgetting how the captain hated such slovenliness.

Jimmy had acquired a Norton motorcycle, which was nearly as old as him but – as he was fond of demonstrating – still capable of travelling at terrifying speeds and I was torn between the thrill of rushing air and a desire to see the day out without losing any more limbs. My left forearm bobbed sullenly in a jar of formalin in my cabin.

'I need my bike.' I wrapped a scarf around my neck and put my coat on over my East Suffolk Police Inspector's uniform, struggling one-handed to tuck my blonde hair into my green woollen hat and pulling it over my ears, mortally wounding yesterday's perm. My helmet would be slung over my shoulder until I went on duty. There isn't much heat insulation in a metal bowl.

'I'll come down and feed the rabbits.' Jimmy zipped up his flying jacket, oblivious to how envious I was of that thick sheepskin lining. 'If they haven't frozen solid in the night.'

'They are warmer than we are.' Carmelo was now defrosting his fingers on his white enamel mug.

We had raised the rabbits' cages off the ground and given them thick straw to burrow into.

'Bye, Carmelo.' I kissed the man who would have been my father-in-law on the cheek.

'Take good care,' he warned. 'The path is as an ice rink.' He had never seen snow or ice until he left his native Malta as a youth but he was more than making up for the latter now.

'I will.' I grabbed my gas mask and followed Jimmy out, reluctantly braving the East Anglian region of the Arctic Circle.

3

MRS PERKINS AND THE PRANCING PONIES

The most difficult part of the journey was, as always, the first. The wooden steps down the side of *Cressida* were slippery with frost and the ground was hard as iron in that bleak midwinter, every ridge or divot now an invitation to lose my footing.

For the first time I could remember, the River Angle was solid enough to walk over. Jimmy had helped Carmelo and me break the ice away and beach the rowing boat so now I made my way towards the bank, sliding my feet like a ski-less skier on to the small crescentic bay imaginatively known as Shingle Cove.

Mrs Perkins, our biggest and blackest hen, saw me and charged, skittering after me like a terrier wanting a walk, but Jimmy caught her and put her, struggling impotently and squawking indignantly, into one of the rabbit hutches. I didn't give their inhabitants names because – cute twitchy noses and whiskers or not – they were dinner.

'Bye, Aunty.' Jimmy tried to kiss me on the mouth and succeeded but I pulled away, though probably not as quickly as I could have. I had never actually married his Uncle Adam so, as long as that was as far as things went, I saw no harm in it. He was a good-looking young man, tall and athletic with fashionably tousled brown hair and sapphire eyes. If only he had had the sense to be born a decade and a half earlier, I thought as I prepared to trek out across the ice.

I glanced across the inlet and up the wide clearing towards

White Lodge, Dr Edward 'Tubby' Gretham's home, standing at the top of Fury Hill, grey smoke swirling out of one of the six chimney stacks. That would be coming from the kitchen range.

'What the hell are they doing here?'

'Who?' Jimmy shielded his eyes.

I didn't answer immediately because I hoped I was wrong, but the two gangling figures in blue were unmistakeable even from that distance.

'The Grinder-Snipes,' I breathed.

The constables were making their way down the middle of the clearing, picking through the clumps of grass that had been a lawn until Tubby decided it wasn't worth the effort of mowing, and even from a hundred yards away I could hear them squealing as they clutched each other's arms.

'Are they actually policemen?' Jimmy asked incredulously.

I had told him of the twins' existence but very little else.

'Just about,' I muttered.

Algy, I think, though it was difficult enough to tell them apart even close-up, slithered over on to his back, legs flailing in the air like a demented cyclist.

'Ohhh, Algernon,' Sandy confirmed my identification, 'are you oreet?'

'Dohhh but I'm all shaken up, Lysander.'

It was embarrassingly impressive how their voices carried through the still air.

'Oh, you poo-ah little gooze.' Sandy dusted his brother down.

'Why don't you go in and have a nice hot coffee?' I suggested to Jimmy.

'Oh, I'm having far too much fun out here,' he assured me.

Somehow the twins stumbled and tumbled down to the opposite bank.

'Cooeee.' Algy waved his left arm.

''ello.' Sandy followed suit, though they were both right-handed.

''ello, mam.' They waved their right hands. 'It's uz.'

'I think you could have worked that out,' Jimmy grinned.

Oh, good grief, I thought, and said quietly. 'Go inside, Jimmy.'

'What, and miss this?'

I could have ordered him, saying that it was official business, but he would have known as well as I that the civilian police have little authority over military personnel and, anyway, we didn't have that kind of relationship. 'Please.'

Jimmy shrugged. 'OK,' he muttered and turned back towards the boat.

'What do you want?' I demanded.

'Ohh, a nice 'ot mug of tea would be luvleh.' Sandy cupped his gloved hands in a mime of receiving one.

'And a Chorleh cake.' Algy rubbed his stomach in big circles.

I tried again. 'What have you come for?'

'For you...' Algy began.

'Mam,' Sandy finished.

I was growing tired of shouting our conversation.

'You'd better come over,' I sighed, and the twins looked at each other and then at me and then again at each other doubtfully.

'Over?' they queried.

'Here,' I confirmed.

'Oh.' They came through a patch of tangled ivy, raising their legs like ponies stepping over low fences until they got to the river's edge.

'It's frozen solid,' I assured them.

'Ohhhh,' they tremoloed, dabbing the ice with the toes of their boots. 'Mam.'

'This is ever so...' Sandy warbled.

'Scary,' Algy hissed.

'Stop it,' I scolded, all too aware that Jimmy and the captain could see them from the wheelhouse if they were looking – and they would be. 'Police constables do not hold hands.'

'Not even if one of them is blinded and they are escaping a burning building?' Sandy enquired.

'Well, *then*, perhaps.'

'Onleh per'aps?' Algy asked in astonishment. 'What if one of them is sliding off the edge of a cliff and the other has 'old of 'im?'

'Well, then, as well, and I suppose it would be sensible if you were worried about falling through the ice...'

'Through...' Sandy gasped in horror.

'The ice?' Algy was equally aghast. 'Oh, we never thought...'

'Of that.' Sandy gulped, his Adam's apple disappearing under his pointy dimpled chin only to drop halfway down to his collar again.

Algy's apple bobbed like this was a Halloween party. 'Our dad wouldn't be 'appy.'

'Oh, for goodness' sake,' I said. 'Wait there.'

The constables looked at me and Sandy took the lead.

'For how...'

'Long?'

'Until I get there.' I stepped down on to the river, staying close to the rope that the captain had fixed across the inlet so that we could pull the boat from the opposite bank when the water was flowing. *Please God don't let me... My* feet shot out... *slip*. I snatched at the rope. It sagged and I did a high kick that would have had me in the front row at the Folies Bergère.

'Ohhh, mam,' they yelled as I managed to steady myself.

I said please, I scolded God; but like any man, if God is ever sorry, he will never admit it. I gave up trying to walk with dignity and went back to sliding, an inch at a time.

'What is it?' I demanded when I reached the other side.

'A rope,' they told me in unison.

'Why are you here?' I tried again, praying they did not think I was being philosophical. They had once gone into a duet as long as anything by Wagner in answer to my asking *What's it all about?*

'There's a man,' Sandy informed me.

'Onleh there int,' Algy pointed out.

'Well there is,' Sandy insisted. 'Onleh we don't know where 'e is.'

'Mind you,' Algy tugged at his chin as if it sported a goatee. 'We didn't know where 'e was before.'

'I suppose that's...'

'So,' I said in unison with Algy, but for a different reason.

'She can't do that,' Algy muttered indignantly. 'Complete our—'

'Sentences,' I broke in just to prove I could and they pulled back in shock. 'So,' I began again, 'we have a missing man?'

'Oh no, mam.' The twins slapped their legs – their own for a change – in amusement.

I could have done that for them, and much harder.

'We don't 'ave 'im.' Algy shook his head.

''cause 'e's...' Sandy explained because the entire concept was obviously too complicated for me, '...missing.'

THE DIGNITY OF OSTRICHES IN THE PROMISED LAND

There are many reasons why the British police are not armed, even in wartime, and one of those reasons is so that senior officers are not given the means to gun their juniors down.

I breathed slowly in and out in a way that is supposed to calm you down but never does.

'Who...' I began.

'Is?' they broke in to show me I was not the only one who could do the completion trick. 'Mr Orchard,' they answered my half-question.

Oh good grief. I knew Garrison Orchard. He used to sell very fine kippers before his smokehouse burned down in non-suspicious circumstances.

'Have you looked in his allotment shed?' I asked wearily and they pulled their lips down in as perfect unison as if they were puppets on the same string.

'We don't like loooking in sheds,' Sandy confessed.

'You never know what you might find in them,' Algy explained.

'Well, you might have found Mr Orchard,' I suggested. 'He's always wandering off and nine times out of ten he's pottering in there and has forgotten the time. Where did he go missing?'

The twins exchanged we've-got-a-right-one-'ere looks.

'If we knew that...' Sandy said.

'We would know where 'e is,' Algy told me ploddingly.

I tried again. 'Where did he go missing *from*?'

'We don't...' Sandy chewed that one over.

'Know,' Algy said.

'Where was he last seen?' I stamped my boots to defrost my feet and they backed away.

'But we don't know,' they chorused.

'Then how do you know he is missing?' I stamped my feet for a different reason.

'Because,' Sandy said as Algy genuflected to tie his brother's shoelace, and I was beginning to think he thought that was sufficient when he added, ''is daughter told...'

'Uz.' Algy wobbled in his attempts not to kneel in the snow.

This was worse than extracting teeth, and I should know because I had watched my dentist father do it often enough and even lent a hand when the patients were anaesthetised.

'Just come with me to the station,' I snapped.

'Just?' Sandy queried. 'Is that all we 'ave to do?'

'Then can we tekk the rest of the day off?'

'No and no,' I replied and shooed them up the path like you might if you were trying to round up a gaggle of geese.

'I think she got out of bed the wrong side this morning,' Sandy remarked, apparently under the illusion that I had been struck stone deaf.

''ammock,' Algy corrected him.

'I am not!' Sandy bridled.

'No, they sleep in 'ammocks on ships.'

'Well, she got out the wrong side anyroad.'

'Shush. She'll 'ear you,' Algy warned.

'No, she won't,' his twin assured him. 'Sound can't go backwards down inclines.'

I left them with that illusion. I know that listeners hear no good of themselves but occasionally they hear something useful.

'That's sheep,' Algy objected. 'They can't swim backwards in water.'

Time, I decided, to drop a gentle hint that I could hear them. 'Stop talking drivel,' I barked.

'Ohhh, mam,' Sandy wailed, 'but we don't know how...'

'To talk anything else,' Algy concluded, and I could not find it in my heart to contradict them.

Eventually I managed to herd the Grinder-Snipes through Treacle Woods and over the brow of Fury Hill to where the path crossed Smugglers Way, an old track running from the cliffs. Here we had a view the envy of anyone who liked views, and I did. There weren't many of them in our part of the world.

Suffolk is not renowned for its mountains. If Great Wood Hill near Newmarket is the Everest of the county at about 400 feet, Fury Hill is its K2. On a clear day such as this I could see the great flatness of the drained fens stretching inland to the south and west. The River Angle curled lazily below me with the prosperous resort of Anglethorpe across the water to the north. To the east was Sackwater, its Victorian dreams of rivalling Felixstowe never realised. Even its greatest glory, the pier, was not much more than a stump since storms, a fire and the sappers had taken their turn in damaging it. Sackwater was my parents' home town and, much to my chagrin, my last posting had made it mine again.

I had left my bicycle at the top of the path in an old gamekeeper's hut, though there had been no game worth keeping this side of the Great War.

We paused to catch our breath.

'Oh, mam,' Sandy whinged, 'it looks ever so...'

'Far,' Algy – never a man to be left out of a whinge – joined in.

'That is only,' I pointed towards our destination like Moses showing the Israelites the promised land, 'because it is.' And down we trudged, my constables first, so that they might hear but they couldn't see me slithering about with all the dignity of an ostrich on roller skates.

4

THE GREAT EXCITEMENT AND
THE SPANISH LADY

The first time I saw Sergeant 'Brigsy' Briggs asleep behind the desk in Sackwater Central Police Station, I thought he was dead. Today, even wide awake and slurping on his brown mug, the likeness to a corpse was still striking. Brigsy's skin was grey and blotchy and had sunken into his face as it would on a man settling comfortably into the first stages of decomposition. There was a warmth in Brigsy's eyes, though. It came from his heart. He was more dependable than I first gave him credit for and he made a good mug of tea when we were alone on late shifts at the station.

'Mornin', madam,' he greeted me and I was glad he hadn't said *good* because it wasn't especially so far. Brigsy leaned his sparsely tufted head back and yelled, 'Tea for the inspector.'

'Which one?' Bantony's voice came from the back room.

'The one whose tea you don't do anything nasty to,' I called back, having witnessed the fury of my unesteemed colleague Inspector Sharkey at discovering salt as one of the more pleasant things his beverage had been laced with.

'And for uz,' the twins chorused.

'Get yer own.' Bantony came through with my white enamel mug. 'Oy ain't a bleedin' nippy.'

I had to admit that Constable Bank-Anthony did not look much like a Lyons tea shop waitress. He was quite a tall man, well-built and, with his black hair Brylcreemed back and razor-parted, he was almost as good-looking as he thought he was – if you like spivs, which I don't. The daughter of his old chief constable in Dudley clearly did. It was she who had persuaded Daddy not to sack Bantony – for how his fear of blood interfered with his duties and his love of the ladies interfered with theirs – but to have him transferred here. Policemen or women don't usually change forces but Sackwater was so desperate for reinforcements after the exodus to Anglethorpe that it had become a sort of Botany Bay for unwanted officers, including myself.

'Button your collar,' I instructed, mainly to divert him from an appreciative leer at my calves. But Bantony was not so easily distracted and was quite capable of performing both tasks at once.

'Right.' I plonked my helmet on the desk. In peacetime inspectors don't wear helmets but a peaked cap would offer little protection against whatever Goering's boys were planning to deposit on us. 'Where and when was Garrison Orchard last seen?'

' 'spector Sharkey take the details just before I do arrive.' Brigsy leafed through his incident report book, though he hardly needed to bother. Since the so-called Vampire Murders in the autumn there had not been much to write in it. Even the great excitement of an attempted break-in at the vicarage through the pantry turned out to be a faulty window catch. 'His daugh'er, Miss Georgina...' He screwed up his eyes.

'If she is still a Miss, I think any of you can have a guess at her surname,' I suggested, while Brigsy struggled with his wonky wire-framed specs to read his superior's inky scratches.

The twins looked at each other blankly.

'Oh, I don't think...'

'Weh can,' Algy concluded.

Why are you doing this to me? I turned to Bantony. 'You tell them.'

Bank-Anthony eyed me suspiciously. 'It's a trick question, isn't it? Loike those ones about moy father's brother being moy son's cousin's 'usband's uncle.'

'No,' I said. 'It's simple.'

'Miss Georgina Simple,' the twins said, then alternated, 'That's – a – strange – name.'

'Miss Georgina Orchard,' Brigsy deciphered, and I was not sure if he was telling them or announcing her, for the front door swung open and it was like that scene in *The Plainsman* when Gary Cooper goes into the saloon – or am I thinking of John Wayne in *The Big Trail*? Anyway, the room fell silent to watch the stranger make her entrance.

This was no stranger to me, however. Georgie Orchard and I had been in the Girl Guides together until I was cashiered.

'Oh Bett—' She stifled my name. 'Inspector. Thank goodness you're here. I am so worried about my father. Around seven o'clock I popped out to get a loaf from Twindles' and when I came back he was gone and he hasn't been seen since.'

In one sentence Georgina had given me more information than half of the Sackwater police force had managed to cobble together since the Grinder-Snipes had skittered into my day the best part of an hour ago.

'Where have you looked?' I asked them all.

'Can't leave my desk.' Brigsy smoothed the gritty smudge on his top lip that almost served as a moustache. He was right, of course. The station had to be manned at all times. You never knew, we might have a crime to cope with.

'And we 'ad to loook for you.' The twins quailed under my gaze. I was getting quite good at quailing men and only wished I had had that skill in my younger days.

'Both of you?' I challenged, uselessly I knew, because Siamese twins could not have been more inseparable than this identical pair.

'Yes,' they assured me fervently.

'But if you'd checked the rota, you'd have seen I was on my way here anyway,' I pointed out.

'Oh,' they said usefully.

'And you?' I quizzed Bantony, who looked like he would like to run more than his eyes over my friend. I am tall but Georgie was taller and more athletically built, with thick wavy black hair that Vivien Leigh might have been proud to swish around Tara. Also, Georgie was golden tanned, partly from a passion for tennis but mainly from a Portuguese grandmother, causing locals to refer to my friend, not wildly inaccurately, as 'the Spanish Lady'.

'Oy looked everywhere.' He took his eyes reluctantly off the newcomer and cast them around the waiting room like he was still searching.

It was then that the door burst open.

'Oh, hello, Boss,' Constable 'Dodo' Chivers sang out. 'I'm as tired as a typewriter. We have searched absolutely everywhere.'

'But no joy,' Constable Rivers hobbled in behind her, massaging his right kidney. Rivers was a martyr to his back and we were martyrs to his whinging about it. The idea of him feeling anything approaching joy was bizarre to say the least.

'Right,' I said. 'Miss Orchard is coming to my office now and while we are there, you will all write down exactly where you searched and not one of you will use the word *everywhere* even once in your account.' I set off down the corridor. 'Oh, and Miss Orchard would like a cup of tea.'

'With one sugar, please,' Georgie called over her shoulder as she followed.

'Oy'll do that,' volunteered Bantony, who usually had to be treated very cruelly indeed before he would put the kettle on – always the perfect gentleman until he got the opportunity not to be.

5

LISA SAND'S FOOT AND THE COLOUR OF CAPILLARIES

shut the door, settled Georgie into a chair and perched on the edge of the desk so I could take her hand.

'What was your father wearing?' I asked, because he had wandered off on Boxing Day in his pyjamas and slippers.

'He took his coat and scarf and hat,' she told me, 'but I don't know if he put them on.' Georgie's grip tightened. 'Oh Betty, it's so cold out there.'

'Where have you looked?'

'Everywhere,' Georgie told me, 'that I can think of,' she added hastily. 'He often goes to Mum's grave or the park where they used to feed the ducks. He likes to walk the cliffs in the summer but I can't think he'd go up there in these conditions.'

'I'll send a man to look,' I promised, calculating who had annoyed me most in the last few weeks. 'Anywhere else?'

'He enjoys a half and a game of dominoes at the Unicorn but that's closed until lunchtime. I went to the bowls club. I ran down the alleys. Oh Betty, it's been three hours now.'

'I know your father's mind tends to wander,' I told my friend, 'but he's still strong. He lifted that crate off Lisa Sand's foot last month,' I reminded her, omitting to mention that he had knocked it over on to her foot in the first place, 'and not many men half his age could have done that.' I stood up, still holding Georgie's hand. 'The best thing you can do is go home and wait for him.

Nine times out of ten, people who wander off wander back again and he will need you there.' I let go of her. 'Let us know if he does and we will let you know the moment we hear anything.'

Georgie puffed out her cheeks. 'Do you think he'll be all right?'

All at once she was a child looking to her mother for comfort, but I could not bring myself to raise her hopes. I had been cold enough just getting to work so I dreaded to think how Garrison Orchard was coping.

'We will do everything we can,' I promised, because that was all the hope I could offer.

I saw Georgie out and as I went back to my office, Sharkey came out of his, fag-end wedged between yellowed fingers, eyes red-capillaried like he had been bathing them in the Scotch he stank of. I knew he had manned the station overnight but his clothes looked like he had slept in them and badly, which was probably the case.

'Are you going to help look for Mr Orchard?' I asked. We rarely bothered with pleasantries.

'Have helped,' he told me huskily. 'I logged it.'

We all had to take our turn at nights but I knew that Old Scrapie resented doing what he regarded as menial tasks.

'And that's it?'

Sharkey stubbed his cigarette out on the lino with his toe.

'That's it,' he agreed and ambled past me. 'Got better things to do than rush around the county after silly old fools.'

'Takes one to find one,' I murmured as I went on my way.

An old man stood in the lobby. Somebody had given him a mug – Georgie's tea, when I thought about it – and he was shivering so violently he could hardly get it to his lips. Brigsy reached across and guided his hands.

'Hello, Mr Orchard,' I greeted him in relief. 'We've been looking for you.'

'*We?*' Rivers muttered indignantly.

'Oh, Betty!' Mr Orchard slopped most of his tea down his sleeves. 'Thank the good Lord it's you. Georgina went missing this morning and I can't find her anywhere.'

'I think I can help you there,' I smiled.

'A thin can hell pew?' Garrison Orchard cupped his ear in puzzlement.

'Constable Rivers will run out and fetch her,' I shouted.

'Fletcher?' He shook his head confusedly.

'*Run?*' Rivers and his colleagues echoed in disbelief.

'Walk briskly,' I compromised foolishly, for Mr Chamberlain had taught the world the dangers of making concessions.

6

THE RETURN OF THE ALBATROSS

When I arrived the next morning, the men were doing what police officers do best – drinking tea. The twins were leaning with their elbows on the desk top and pinching their white china cup handles between thumbs and forefingers as if enjoying cocktails at the Ritz.

'Oh, but it was ever so exciting looking for Mr Orchard,' Dodo was telling the assembly. 'Rivers and I had to peep into a coal bunker and I thought I saw a rat but Inspector Church told me they do not exist.'

'I did not,' I started to protest, but found I couldn't humiliate us both by pointing out that I had told her there was no such creature as a *ratty* when she had seen an old tennis ball floating down a gutter and shrieked the word out. It would only reinforce their all-women-are-silly creed.

'Ooohhh,' Dodo plonked her hands on her hips.

This, I calculated, was the time to change the subject.

'I wonder if the government will introduce food rationing,' I speculated, to general dismay.

'They can't do…' Sandy said.

'That,' Algy chipped in. 'We would 'ave ter watch what we…'

'Et.'

'They'll ration the air we breathe, I do believe,' Brigsy forecast gloomily.

'Oh dearie me!' Dodo exclaimed. 'But what happens if I lose my ration card and run out of puff before my new card arrives?'

'Don't you worry about that, Dodo,' Bantony reassured her. 'Oyl give yow some of moy air.'

'Oh,' Constable Chivers put her hands together like she was about to lead prayers, 'but how will you do that, Constable Bank-Anthony?'

'Come to the cells and Oyl show yow,' he offered gallantly.

'You will not,' I said firmly as Constable Box came in.

'Oh, Boxy,' Dodo cried. 'You look positively gelid.'

Box stamped his snow-shoe-sized boots, showering dirty slush over the dirtier floor. 'Good job my missus int 'ere to 'ear you say tha',' he said.

'But where else could she be to hear me say it?' Dodo puzzled.

I shook my head but their nonsense still swirled around my brain. 'You're back early,' I commented. Even though we were working shorter stints on the beat because of the weather, he still had another hour to go.

'I come for urgent reinforcements,' Box declared as he stomped towards us. 'Any tea left, Constable Bank-Anthony?' he asked, bringing a new definition of the word *urgent* into our workplace.

Bantony shook the pot. 'No,' he said, though we all heard the sploshing. He and Bantony had had a falling out and I had not yet troubled to find the cause. It was hardly worth it when they might be best of chums the next day and then mortal foes the day after that.

'Then you had better make him a fresh one,' I said.

'Might be able to squeeze one out of this,' Bantony muttered and stomped into the back room to get his colleague's mug.

'Why do you need help?' I asked Box.

'It's old Mrs Young,' he told me, shaking his cape like a matador goading a bull.

Mrs Young had been old Mrs Young since I was a child. Ancient Mrs Young might be a more accurate title now.

'What is?' I sipped my tea. It was hot and strong, as I like it, but the milk was on the turn.

'She do be complainin' 'bout her neighbours, she do,' Box told me. 'She say they be passing messages to the enemy.'

'What, the Harrisons?' I asked in surprise. Reg Harrison was as English as they come. You could hardly see his house for flags on Empire Day.

'No, Boss, the Germans are the enemy,' Dodo told me helpfully.

I ignored her. 'Have you spoken to them?'

'I hope not,' Dodo put in. 'Fraternising with the enemy is treason.'

'Wellll, it do be a bit awkwish.' Box's parsnip complexion turned radish. 'It do,' he repeated.

'One should never be embarrassed to confront traitors,' Dodo informed her colleague. 'It is they who should hang their heads before the executioner does it for them.'

'Why?' I put up my hand in a stop sign. 'And that question was aimed at Box.'

'Well, Mr H take agin me at the summer fair,' Box confessed. 'I see Mrs H coming out the tent with a rabbit pie and say *I wouldn't mind a bit of tha'* and he take it all wrong. Trouble is...' Box coughed '...Mrs H think so too, ever since I see her unmentionables on the line and it be startin' to rain and I told her she had better get them off.'

'If they were unmentionables, why did he mention them?' Dodo wondered to the ceiling. She had got into the habit of addressing inanimate objects.

'Trouble is,' Box admitted ruefully, 'Mrs H invite me in to help her and Mr H do be at work so I be affeared to be with her alone.'

'She couldn't hurt you, a little thing like that,' Brigsy reassured him.

'No, but Mrs Box could,' Box assured him. 'She has a fearsome way with a rollin' pin, she do.'

I wondered briefly if that was why my constable's face was so misshapen. It didn't seem so much to have lumps and bumps as to be constructed of them.

Box sniffed his beverage appreciatively. 'Taste better sour, it do,' he declared, and rolled it around his mouth like he might a fine wine or, in his case, a good pint of Tolly Cobbold bitter.

I went down the left-hand corridor.

Sharkey's door was ajar and he was lounging with his feet on the desk in a fug of smoke. He stubbed out his cigarette into a pile of dog-ends.

'Got any more doddery old fools to look for, Church?'

'I did,' I told him, 'but I've just found him.' And went into my office for my coat and helmet and a quick drag on a roll-up. Everyone except Dodo smoked but I never really liked doing it in front of the men.

Box was still savouring his tea when I went back to the foyer.

'Come along, Constable,' I urged and shooed him to the main door, where he stood back. I stopped. 'Do you hold the door open for Inspector Sharkey?' I had never seen him do so.

Box huffed. 'More than my life's worth.'

'Then don't ever do it again for me.'

'But…' My constable stood uncertainly.

'I am sure you are a credit to your mother,' I said sternly. 'But you should know by now I will be treated the same – no better and no worse – than he is.'

'I don't think you want 'xactly the same, ma'am,' Box warned, and his voice dropped confidentially. 'It's me wha' put tha' mustard powder in his tea last week. Just between ourselves,' he ended worriedly.

The cold air hit my face like iced water.

'Try that on me and I'll pour it over your head.'

And Box chuckled, 'Tha's wha' he do.'

'It's part of the inspector training,' I said as we marched out of the forecourt on to the pavement.

'What else do they teach you?' He grinned uncertainly.

'How to watch what I tread in,' I replied and his brow wrinkled.

'I don't know wha'…' He looked to where I was pointing. 'Oh, blast it – blast those blasted dogs – excuse my language – oh sorry, ma'am. I s'pose it's all right to curse in your presence too.'

'No, it is not,' I said primly, though I would hardly have noticed his expletive if he hadn't pointed it out.

We turned down Bath Road. At one time this had been a happy place for me, visiting my friend Etterly Utter, but then she climbed into the hollow of the King's Oak – or the Desolation Tree, as some called it – and was never seen again. There had been a bloody murder in Bath Road too, just after my return to Sackwater. But everything looked peaceful now.

A plane droned overhead but I couldn't see it properly. The winter sun was low and shining straight in my eyes and I wished I could wear sunglasses, but regulations, always keen to make life difficult, forbade the wearing of any type of spectacles on the beat. I had known a few policemen who would have benefited from them, though.

Box made a shade with his huge hand and tipped his head back.

'Lancaster,' he diagnosed. 'My boy Leonard do have a-nidentification chart with pictures.'

We had an identification chart with pictures at the station, too, but it was obviously a poor effort compared with his boy Leonard's.

'I wonder where it's been?' I squinted. It was heading inland.

'Bombing Jerry, I hope.' Box raised his arm. 'And here come the others.'

There were five more smudges creeping down through the clear sky, wings outstretched like great grey albatrosses.

'I'm just glad they're coming back safely.' I lowered my head.

'We can cut through here.' Box pointed to Armadillo Alley and I smiled. I had been born on those streets – on the top floor of a bus, to be precise, my mother having boarded it while my father rushed about uselessly for a taxi – and I had played in those roads for years, but I knew Box meant well in directing me.

We made our way down the flamboyantly named passageway and came out on Spice Lane.

Box chuckled. 'Funny we be lookin' for spies on Spice lane.'

'Is it?' I asked a little sourly, because I had wanted to make that joke and it worked better the way he pronounced *spice*.

The front door of number six, the middle of three houses, opened a crack and a voice piped, 'Oh, I thoughted it was you.' And Shirley Temple – as I had dubbed her when she came into the station to report a *losted* button – came trotting into the road. 'My name is Slyvia and I is having my birfday party,' she told me excitedly. 'Would you like a slice of cake? It's...' Her big blue eyes sparkled with the magic of her next word, 'choc-o-lit.'

'Can I have a piece?' Box grinned hopefully. He was a big man forever on a mission to make himself bigger, but it was astonishing how fast he could move when he flew at me.

7

THE LEATHER LOAF AND THE RUBBER STACK

've never been hit by a train but I imagine it must feel very like this did and I was vaguely aware, as I collapsed on my back underneath him, that Box was not the only thing flying at that moment.

'Ma'am?' he shouted through the cotton wool in my ears and above the clanging of church bells, the untuned sort they have in Malta. 'What's happening?'

I tried to push him off me but it was like being under a felled tree.

'An explosion,' I managed to yell in his ear, which I wasn't happy to find myself nuzzling. 'A bomb from that plane, I think.'

''n'explosion?' Box marvelled, and I must have made quite a comfortable mattress for he seemed settled down for the day. 'Well I never.'

'Get off me.' I pushed and he half-rolled away to sit up with his back to me like we had just had a cuddle and he was now in a bit of a mood because I had stopped him going too far.

Box swivelled round. His face was blackened and his tie askew and I automatically reached up to straighten it. We had landed on the road. When I was a child I had thought it would be wonderful if we could fly and I'd just found out that it wasn't.

'Help me up,' I said – it was the least he could do after we had been so intimate – and Box struggled to his feet before offering me a giant paw.

I glanced down. My skirt was filthy and I could say goodbye to my stockings. I rubbed the grit out of – that is, into – my eyes.

All three houses of the terrace had been damaged. Number four, to the left, had collapsed completely and was no more than a hill of bricks and shattered timbers. Number six, next along, had lost its adjoining and front walls and the roof was tilted down forty-five degrees sideways towards number four. Number eight didn't look too bad except most of its slates had slipped, baring the rafters.

The windows of every house I could see on that side and across the road were smashed and curtains fluttered through some of the frames. And the road between was ripped up into a ragged tarmac rim around a crater maybe ten foot across and three times as long.

A fire engine bell was clanging.

Box helped me over two paving stones tilted up into a tent and I sagged straight down again on to a convenient empty beer crate, vaguely wondering where that had appeared from. My right knee had been gouged by something and was starting to complain bitterly.

'Allow me, ma'am.' Box disentangled a splinter of cream-painted wood from my hair, threw it away and handed me a filthy squashed leather loaf. It took me a moment to recognise my handbag.

Blast. That was nearly new. I put it down and took hold of his shoulder. 'Please tell me you can hear that bell.'

'Have to be deaf not to.'

I tried to organise my thoughts. 'Shirley Temple!' I cried. She had come from the middle house.

'She's hallucinating,' a man's voice said from somewhere behind me.

'No, the little girl.'

Box rubbed the nape of his neck. 'Can't catch no sign of her.'

I tried to stand but my legs had had several more pints of beer than the rest of me.

Box put out an arm and between us we heaved me to my feet. 'I could use a few aspirins.' I tested my balance. 'Or a shot of Johnnie Walkers. You can let go now.'

Somehow Box had his arm around my waist and was looking very embarrassed about it. He let go cautiously but took my good elbow to help me off the pile and on to the kerb.

I tried to reorganise my thoughts.

'Have you seen the little girl?' I found myself asking a wiry ambulance man in his brand-new uniform with nicely creased trousers already frayed around the knees.

'Never you mind about that, miss,' he tried to soothe me. 'Just get yourself over there to the medics.' He pointed to an ambulance on the junction with Montague Road and was about to signal to the two men standing beside a stretcher propped up against their vehicle when I said, 'We must find her.'

'All under control, miss.'

'Inspector,' I corrected him and stumbled over the torn-up paving slabs towards the terrace.

Two ARP wardens and half a dozen workmen were shovelling debris away from the front of number four and, in all the confusion, I was impressed by their calm and the speed with which they'd got to what must have been their first real emergency.

A nurse stepped up and took a look at my head. 'We need to get you to hospital.'

'Later.'

'Now.' She wagged her emergency kit with a green cross on the lid as a badge of unquestionable authority.

'N'inspector Church don't take no orders from no one,' Box

told her proudly, if ungrammatically and inaccurately, and I stumbled away.

The house was filled with rubble, broken timber jutting through clouds of thick choking dust. The men heaved a heavy beam out of what would have been the front sitting room and a shower of bricks rattled down. The front door lay across the pavement and they were about to clamber over it when I put out my arm.

'Wait.'

'What is it?' Box asked, peering over my head.

'That door moved.'

'Course it moved,' a workman explained in exasperation. 'I had my foot on it.'

Box – with greater faith in me – bobbed, knees cracking, to peer under it. 'Give me a hand,' he said and three of them heaved at the top end, hinging the door up and cascading bricks and cement over their feet.

'By George, she's right,' a warden exclaimed, as if the very idea of me being correct was astonishing. 'Put your back into it, boys.'

The men all strained and stepped forward, forcing the door up halfway. *Slyvia*, as she had called herself, was lying prone, facing to her left, her legs towards the house, her only visible eye closed. She was coated head to foot in ashen dust, like one of the bodies they discovered in Pompeii.

'There's someone else here,' a woman shouted.

'I can hold the door,' Box told the men and they hurried off to number ten, two of them bearing shovels.

The nurse hurried forward and crouched to check the little girl's pulse.

'She's alive,' the nurse announced.

'We need to get her out,' I said.

29

'No, we mustn't move her. She may have a broken back.'

'She may have a broken everything if the house collapses,' I argued.

I seized Sylvia under her armpits but her feet were stuck. Box adjusted his grip, went on one knee in the broken glass and rose, straining with all his considerable might, to wrench the door higher and swivel it on to one corner. 'Got it.' Box's face was purple in a shade you don't really believe faces can go.

'Can you hold it?'

'Damn me if I don't.'

'Watch your language,' I scolded automatically and knelt under the door to check the little girl before I pulled again. I tossed a couple of red quarry tiles off her ankles, slipped my stump as far as I could under her shoulders and my right arm under her legs and lifted her free.

'OK.' I stepped back and Box, with a gasp of relief, let the door crash back, creating a miniature dust storm to join the rolling clouds.

'Pretty little thing,' he cooed and her eyelids fluttered apart. 'Thank you ever so very much,' she whispered croakily. 'But I'm not likkle,' she added crossly. 'It's my birfday.'

She must have been light but she felt as heavy as my constable in my unsteady state.

I stroked the hair from her face. 'Are you all right, darling?'

Box opened his mouth to reply before he realised.

'Get back all of you,' an ARP man bellowed. 'That chimney is on the move.' I glanced up. The whole stack was swaying like it was made of rubber.

I thrust the little girl at Box. 'Run. And that's an order.'

Box hesitated. 'You too, ma'am,' he called as he scrambled away.

'Look out,' somebody yelled and I scuttled sideways as the

chimney pot came crashing down to where we had just stood, shattering in a deluge of masonry, chunks of mortar flying up but not one of them hitting me except for a few bits the size of gravel.

'Thank you, God,' I said aloud as the world sailed up and away.

'Oh Lord above, ma'am,' Box said. 'Are you all right?' His face was over mine, white with dust and anxiety and fading into an impenetrable night.

8

THE WELLS OF WATER AND DARKNESS

For a moment I was back in Balluta Bay, sunbathing on the rocks with Adam. But what was my constable doing there and why was he so grubby?

'You've had a fall, ma'am.' Box had his hand behind my head and was lowering it carefully and I was dimly aware that he was touching me. Constables are not supposed to do that. 'You stepped back into the crater.'

'Oh, for goodness' sake.' This was the sort of thing I would despair at Dodo or the Grinder-Snipe twins doing.

'You were out cold.' My constable's eyes clouded. 'I was startin' to think you were...' He didn't need to say the word but he did. '...dead.'

I was lying on my back, propped up by rubble, lots of jagged bits sticking into lots of tender bits, the air thick with blasted fragments.

Box was lifting something quite heavy off my stomach and tossing it aside.

Somebody had left the bath tap on. I could hear it running and my feet were getting wet. 'Where is she?'

'She's in an ambulance.' He cradled my head as gently as he had the little girl's.

'Help me up.' Something was stopping me. 'And don't give me any of that lying still nonsense that we give the public.'

Box looked doubtful. 'I don't think I can, ma'am.'

I raised my head and a lightning bolt jolted through it. I saw it flash and heard it crack.

'Blow that.' I struggled to get on to my elbow but my right arm was being squashed. 'What's happening?' I was suddenly aware that I was lying in a pond.

'Burst water main,' Box informed me.

A blurry woman drifted by high above me. She was carrying a chair, or a dog, or something.

'Then you had better help me out.'

Box nibbled his upper lip. 'Bit tricksy, ma'am.' He sampled his lower lip like he was comparing flavours. 'Your right arm do be trapped.'

'I can feel that.' I was getting cross now. Why did I have to tell them everything? 'Untrap it immediately.'

I could still hear emergency bells.

'By the gas pipe.' Teddy Moulton the bookseller's face appeared high over the edge of the crater, crowned by an ARP warden's helmet, the strap twisted under his chin in an annoying way.

'Then get it off me.' The water was up to my waist now.

Box pulled, his neck muscles fanning out so much I thought his collar would burst. 'Won't shift, ma'am, and there's a concrete block behind it.'

'The side of the crater collapsed and a lot of rubble fell in with you,' Teddy explained as patiently as he had Cartesian dualism once, when I hadn't even asked. His discourse was of rather more interest this time, though. 'They got most of it off but it twisted the pipe.' He sucked on his Falcon pipe, sensibly unlit. 'Lucky you weren't crushed, Inspector.'

More silhouettes were appearing above, like vultures gathering over an injured goat.

'Where is the nearest stopcock?' I shouted to them.

'Burst the wrong side for that.' A fat figure in a bowler hat leaned over. 'This is the backflow.'

'I've sent a boy to the water company,' somebody else said.

A fireman leaned over, his helmet glinting like an ancient Greek warrior's on the bloodstained plains of Troy. 'Hurry up with tha' pump,' he bellowed and a thick hose drooped over the rim and down into the rising water.

I could hear the motor going and a gurgling sound and then the motor stopped. 'I told you to get tha' fixed,' the fireman bellowed.

'I did fix it,' his colleague whined.

'Well, fix it so it works next time.'

'Buckets,' Box suggested as the water rose to my chest. 'Lots of them and quick.'

'Cut the pipe,' a woman suggested.

'There's a fire in tha' house,' the fireman told her. 'If the gas do get to it, you'll blow half the town up.'

'You'll have to chop her arm off,' a man said. I knew that voice. It was my old chum Sharkey. He had a knack of turning up at the worst possible time and I could only imagine the satisfaction he got from giving that instruction. All the influence in the world could not keep me in the force if I had no hands.

'You will *not* cut off my arm.'

'Only the hand,' Teddy bargained on my behalf.

'Leave my f— blasted hand alone,' I shrieked.

'Mind your bloody language,' a woman scolded. 'There's a little boy here... even if he do be dead.'

A little boy? Oh God, why do you allow these things. I seemed to remember Sister Millicent rabbiting piously about free will but it seemed a pretty flimsy excuse to me. If I did half the things God did, I would have been sent to meet him years ago.

Box was hurting my neck in his efforts to keep my head above the surface.

'Pass me an axe,' he called.

'Don't!' I yelled, but it seemed that Box outranked me because the fireman handed one down.

'You will not use that axe, Box,' I yelled. 'And that is an order.'

For some reason, Box was taking his cape off. It was hardly hot work, crouching in that near-freezing water.

'Do it, man,' Sharkey urged.

'No.' I waved my stump uselessly at him and wriggled my right arm violently, but it was stuck solid. I didn't want to die but I was damned if I would lose my right hand too. But then I could hardly let them risk the lives of everybody else.

The phrase *horns of a trilemma* drifted uselessly through my thoughts.

'Need to let go of your head now, ma'am,' Box said with a calm authority I had never known he had. 'Hold your breath.'

He let go of me and I strained to keep my head up but the water was flooding over my chin now and slopping up my nostrils and into my stupidly open mouth.

'I'm sorry, ma'am,' I think he said, but I was too busy coughing to hear him properly. I saw the axe rise as the water closed over me but I couldn't do anything except toss my head wildly and arch my body and heave and thrash my legs. I managed to get my head up briefly for a gasped choking breath and saw the blade, huge and hurtling towards me. I wasted that last gulp of air on a yelp. My head fell back. The axe came down and there was nothing but pain and my chest filling with water and the light being dimmed very quickly.

Was this what death was like – the welling up of darkness and nothing more?

9

REFEREES AND THE PISCINE QUALITIES
OF DESIRES

There was a pain in my head and both my arms and a loud whistle like a dozen angry referees with inexhaustible breath. I opened my eyes and wished I hadn't, not just because the light hurt them but also because the first face I saw was Sharkey's. It wasn't an unpleasant face – well proportioned, if a little grey, teeth that were straight, if also a little grey, and hair that should have been a little grey too but was soot-black. It was the owner of that face who was unpleasant. At least, I considered, I could not be dead. Old Scrapie, as he was unaffectionately nicknamed, would not be going to heaven and I didn't think I had done anything bad enough to merit eternal damnation – yet.

'Awake, are you?'

The referees were calming down except for one, who was still very agitated.

'No, I always sleep with my eyes open.'

'You're a very lucky girl,' he told me, and the last referee gave it a rest.

'I may be lucky but I am not a girl,' I told him, wondering if I sounded like my godmother, the famous personal detective March Middleton, and rather hoping I did. 'So why am I lucky?'

The memory hit me, my arm trapped, his incitement to chop it off, Box wielding the axe.

I raised my arms. The left was still a stump – I had had a

half-formed fleeting ridiculous hope that I had dreamed that – and the right was bandaged but intact. I asked my fingers to wiggle but they did not wish to oblige.

'But—' I tried to rub my brow but the bandages were too stiff at the elbow.

'Box chopped the gas pipe,' Sharkey told me in disgust. 'Could have blown the whole pigging town up.'

'Then why didn't he?'

My fellow inspector shrugged. 'Managed to plug it with his cape.'

'So that was why he took it off,' I realised. 'And you told him—'

'To chop the pipe off,' Sharkey broke in with a defiant curl of his lip and I didn't have the energy to uncurl it.

'How long have I been out?'

'Two days.' The Shark informed me. 'They injected you with morphine.'

I had an image, too vague to be sure if it was a true memory, of being lifted out and laid on a stretcher.

'The little girl,' I remembered and Sharkey sniffed.

'Concussed,' he said. 'But she'll be all right.'

'And her family?'

'Still being dug out of the rubble, what's left of them.' Even Sharkey had some human feelings. He looked down and swallowed. 'All dead.' He took a breath. 'Both parents. Sam, her little brother – he was blown clear unscathed, must have been the shock wave. Uncle and aunt. Even her dog. The verger found her father's leg in the graveyard – only identified it by his shoe.'

'Where is she now?'

'In the next room.'

'Has she been told?'

Sharkey nodded. 'Matron had to tell her. She was asking for her parents.'

'And...' This was a stupid question, I knew, but I couldn't think of another way to phrase it. '...how did she take it?'

'Very calmly.' Sharkey rubbed the bridge of his nose. 'I wasn't there but I was told she didn't believe it.'

'It's a lot to take in and she was probably doped up, too,' I speculated. 'Do you know if she has any other relatives?'

'We're still looking into that but she says not.' Sharkey grimaced.

'What's her surname?'

'Satin.'

'There's a Danny Satin who runs the fish and chip shop,' I remembered. 'I wonder if he's related.'

'Uncle,' Sharkey said. 'They pulled his body out this morning.'

'Oh, for God's sake—' I took a breath. 'Is Box all right?'

Sharkey snorted. 'Few cuts and bruises and terrified of what you'll do to him for misidentifying a Dornier bomber.'

I was not going to tell my colleague, sympathetic as he seemed at the moment, that I had thought it was a Lancaster too.

'He saved my life.' I tried to shrug but my shoulders were too stiff.

'As if he hasn't got enough to feel guilty about,' Sharkey said and lit a cigarette.

He didn't offer me one and I was not going to ask. I struggled to a sitting position.

'Where d'you think you're going?' He watched me with derision.

'To see Sylvia.'

'No visitors allowed,' Sharkey told me, and I managed a quarter-shrug.

'Since when have you or I only done the things we were allowed to do?'

38

It didn't feel right to lump us together in the same category and I wished I hadn't said it, but as Pooky, my parents' old maid, used to tell me, 'If wishes was fishes we'd run out of dishes.' Whatever that was supposed to mean.

10

THE PATIENCE OF PATIENTS AND THE WOUNDING OF STONES

I told Sharkey to leave. My nightdress had risen and I was not going to give him a viewing of anything above my knees. My legs were stiff and when I looked down I saw that they were cut and what Tubby liked to call 'contused'. I put my bare feet on the cold lino floor and stabilised myself on the side table, waiting to feel steadier. It was a bit of a wait and I have never been the most patient of patients. I swayed, let go of the table and tottered out of the door.

My room was at the end of a long corridor with doors on one side only, so it didn't require too many of my professional skills to work out which was the next room that Sharkey had referred to.

The door was slightly ajar and swung silently when I pushed it wide. Sylvia Satin lay on her back, her head resting on a white pillow, her golden locks radiating like a halo around her pale little face. She had two black eyes, a bruised button nose and small abrasions on her forehead, but she seemed to be sleeping peacefully. There were two beds in her room and the one to her left was empty and had been stripped, with the blankets folded at the foot. I sat on the edge of the mattress and looked at her. She was breathing through her mouth, her bow lips parted like she was trying to whistle.

A nurse walked by, presumably on her way to see me. She stopped, revolved ninety degrees and marched into the room. I had seen her before and she still reminded me of a pug with her little projecting lower teeth and short-muzzled face.

'What on earth are you doing?' the nurse demanded, ignoring my shush signs.

I had not liked her the last time and I actively disliked her now.

'Not so loud,' I whispered urgently, but Sylvia jumped awake.

'She is not to be disturbed,' the nurse scolded, as if I was the naughty girl at the back of assembly.

I would argue another time about who had disturbed the patient.

Sylvia looked about her. 'Oh hello, nurse,' she said weakly and her head turned towards me. 'Hello, nice police lady. I'm Slyvia.'

The nurse sneezed backwards.

'How are you feeling?' I asked and Sylvia looked puzzled. 'Why am I in bed, Mummy?' She struggled to sit up. 'I want my daddy.'

I hurried over to take her hand and a doctor rushed in to take her other hand, but the comfort he was giving her came through the bore of the needle he was sliding slickly into the blue thread just below the crook of her elbow.

The nurse looked across at me with all the righteous fury that people usually manage to muster when they know something is their fault, but I was not going to stand there and be lectured by a miniature mastiff with a starched hat so I limped away.

'Go to your room,' she yapped at my heels.

I had intended to do so but I swung right instead of left, wrenching something that didn't like being wrenched in my side, and staggered away.

Three corridors later I found myself at the hospital chapel and went in. One of Macbeth's witches was attacking the flagstone

41

floor with her besom broom. She huffed when she saw me and marched off. Had she been told to leave worshippers in peace?

'You don't have to go,' I hastened.

'Yeah I do,' she replied. 'Can't bear people wailing and gnashing teeth. Makes me go all chronological.'

Whoever had offloaded that last word on the old crone had seriously misrepresented its purpose to her, but she used it with such rancour that I was almost prepared to believe it meant whatever she thought it did.

I tried to pray but I couldn't. I was disgusted with God and, anyway, it was a bit late to ask him to intercede now. I looked at the stained-glass window to make me feel more spiritual but could only think of the fuss Pooky would create if she was asked to clean it and what a smeary mess she would make of the job.

Sister Angela at Roedene Abbey often told of the man who was about to defenestrate himself who chanced upon a Bible, which he somehow knew was left by his guardian spirit. He opened it to find his faith restored and set off to take the word of the Lord to those darker and, therefore, less fortunate than ourselves.

I sat at the back and picked up a King James. The spine looked almost as damaged as mine felt when I tried to sit up. *And thou shalt eat the fruit of thine own body, the flesh of thy sons and of thy daughters*, I read.

I flicked through a few more pages.

He that is wounded in the stones, or hath his privy member cut off, shall not enter into the congregation of the Lord. This was hardly more inspiring, unless the *He* referred to my good friend Sharkey.

So much for Deuteronomy. I jabbed my finger randomly on a verse in Judges.

And the haft also went in after the blade; and the fat closed upon the blade, so that he could not draw the dagger out of his belly.

This was a little too much like the murder of Captain Hustings, which I had investigated on my old beat in Bloomsbury. I had lost a good colleague in capturing his killer.

I closed the Bible and my eyes and prayed that Sylvia would have a relative to save her from the orphanage, but God is the ultimate husband behind a newspaper – you can chatter away and think you hear some sort of response but can never be quite sure if he's listening. Today, though, for the first time in years, my prayers were answered. I was on my way back to my room when I saw him – a kindly looking gentleman in his fifties, I judged, standing at the side of Sylvia Satin's bed and gazing at her tenderly.

'Harrold Schofield,' he introduced himself with a hint of a bow. 'Uncle Harry to little Sylvie.' He took off his steel-rimmed spectacles to wipe his eyes with a handkerchief almost big enough to cover the average tea tray. 'I must be her only relative now.'

Harry Schofield was quite a well-spoken man, though I did not think he was born to that accent. He squeezed his lips hard together.

'You were not at the party?' I hoped that didn't sound too much like a police interrogation.

'Couldn't make it,' he told me, his eyes never leaving his niece. 'I live in Great Yarmouth and it would have been a day off work.' He exhaled unsteadily. 'Be taking a few of them now, I suppose.' He stroked Sylvia's cheek with the back of his fingers. 'Poor darling,' he whispered. 'I can never replace your family but I shall do everything I can.' His voice broke and I touched his arm, but he hardly knew I was there any more. So, an hour or more after I had been commanded to, I returned to my room. Harrold Schofield was not the only one who knew how to cry.

11

THE TWELVE-TOED CAT AND
THE PARTING OF PARENTS

Toby Gregson came attractively crumpled as usual.

'You made the front page,' he told me, brandishing a copy of the *Sackwater and District Gazette*, of which he was editor, reporter, photographer and many other things.

This was no great achievement as their previous star subject had been a twelve-toed cat, but there I was, blackened with smoke and dirt, my helmet lopsided, standing in the rubble. It was not a look I would cultivate in future but I was cradling Sylvia Satin and she, even unconscious, made the picture look wonderful.

'I didn't know you were there,' I said.

'It was me who called *look out*,' he told me.

'Lots of people kept calling *look out*,' I said. 'But nobody said they meant me or warned me what to look out for.'

Toby raised his hands in protest. 'Sorry I didn't have time to shout *Oh do please have a care, Inspector Church. You appear to be unaware that you are running backwards into a crater*.'

'I take your point,' I conceded, and had another look. 'It's a very good photo.'

'I'll get you a copy,' he promised, perching on the edge of the bed.

'Any other news?' I asked my favourite newshound.

'No,' he yawned. 'In fact, it's been so quiet I've started a detective story.'

'Oh yes? Who by?'

'Me. Are you in pain?'

'A little,' I admitted, but didn't tell Toby that he was adding to it. A successful crime publisher could not have been inundated with more whodunnit plots in the course of a career than I was by the public – evil twins being a favourite device. Tubby Gretham had given me at least half a dozen versions of that one.

'Oh dear.' Toby patted my hand as you might calm a hysterical child and, having relieved my distress entirely, continued with, 'It's different to all the others.'

All the others always are.

'In that it's told from the point of view of the condemned man,' he continued. 'I was thinking of calling it—'

'The Condemned Man,' I broke in rudely, but visitors were supposed to be pampering not torturing me.

Toby sat up. 'Actually, that's a lot better title than I'd thought of. I was going to call it—'

'Save it for the next book,' I suggested and he could not help but catch my tone that time.

We fell into one of those awkward silences that hospital beds are so skilful at creating. I cleared my throat and, after a decent interval, Toby cleared his.

'I brought you a couple of bottles of beer,' he said just as I was nodding off and I perked up immediately. 'But matron heard them clink and confiscated them.'

'She'll probably drink them herself,' I predicted.

Far away a woman's voice was warbling *Sally, Sally, pride of our alley.*

'Sounds like she's started,' Toby chuckled.

I didn't remember saying he could hold my hand but then I didn't remember trying to pull it away.

*

45

Dodo came to visit for the second day in a row.

'Everything is going really well at work,' she assured me, dumping a heavy carpet bag on my shins. 'In fact, we were just saying how smoothly things go without you.' This was slightly less reassuring.

'Are you saying I disorganise things?' I asked very grumpily, because I had been having a lovely dream about sailing in a yacht with Spencer Tracy plus I had a splitting headache plus nobody wants to be told they are not missed.

'Oh, of course not, Boss.' Dodo gave me a playful punch on my bruised shoulder. 'It's just that all the men commented that we never have any murders when you are not around.'

'Are you saying I commit them or incite them?' I struggled to plump up my pillow with one stump and one bandaged arm.

'Oh no, Boss,' Dodo laughed, and I steeled myself for another assault. 'You taught me better than to actually accuse somebody until I have proof.'

What? Was I going to return to find myself under investigation for crimes I had solved?

'Did you find anything out about Harrold Schofield?' I asked, certain she would have forgotten.

Dodo chewed a fingernail and I was just about to tell her it had been a simple enough request when she said, 'Indeed yes. Mr Schofield is Sylvia's uncle. He is a bachelor of good repute and works as a manager on the Wherry Railway.'

'Well done.' I smiled at the grown-up way she had delivered her report.

'Thank you Wherry much, Boss.'

I let that pass. 'Anything else?'

'Mr Schofield,' Dodo recited carefully, 'took guardianship of a deceased neighbour's child and was a devoted second father to him and was devastated when the boy died of a fever.' Dodo took a breath.

'Oh, how sad,' I commented.

'How *exceedingly* sad,' Dodo corrected me.

'What's in that bag?' I asked. *Something to eat,* I hoped, *or even something to read.*

'A present,' Dodo smiled, 'for Inspector Sharkey for saving your life.'

'What?' I gasped in disbelief.

'I cannot tell you,' Dodo put a hand on the bag like she thought mugging was another of my vices.

'No, I meant what on earth made you think he saved me?' I punched the pillow.

'He did,' Dodo said simply. 'Boxy was going to chop all your limbs off until Inspector Sharkey intervened.'

'And does Box agree with that story?' I asked incredulously.

'Boxy has been off sick too,' Dodo said.

'Nobody told me that.'

'We didn't want to worry you.' Dodo chewed her lower lip. 'He stubbed his great toe and there's a serious risk...' She swallowed noisily. '...that he will lose the nail.'

'You could have broken that a little more gently,' I said sarcastically.

'Oh, but I did not break it,' Dodo protested, 'and neither did Boxy.'

I would deal with Sharkey when I returned to work, I decided, giving up on my plumping attempts.

'Allow me, Boss.' Dodo, seeing my struggles, whipped the pillow away, letting my head clunk back, and put it behind herself as a cushion.

*

'It's not very convenient,' my mother greeted me on my return to Felicity House.

When I first returned to Sackwater I discovered they had given my room to a trial run of evacuees and, when these were taken away, to Dodo.

'But you have eight bedrooms,' I pointed out and not for the first time.

'It would be very awkward for dear Dodo, living with her inspector.' My mother wrung her hands like old dishcloths.

'She would love me to live here,' I objected. 'She's always saying so.'

'If indeed that is the case it is because dear Dodo is too frightened of you to say otherwise.' My mother pulled her hands apart like they were gummed together.

The surgery door opened and my father came out.

'Good afternoon.' He shook my hand. 'Oh, Betty, it's you. Why didn't you say?'

'I didn't know I had to,' I said, nonplussed.

'The sun was in my eyes.' He shaded them to demonstrate the blinding power of the light creeping weakly into the hallway.

'You come so rarely it's not surprising your poor father didn't recognise you,' my mother said, obviously unwilling to let me let his error pass.

'I was here the day before my accident,' I reminded them.

'Oh, it makes my blood run cold to think of that.' My father shivered. 'To think little Dodi-pie might have been with you and got injured.'

'Well, she wasn't,' I snapped.

'You sound as if you wish she was.' My mother folded her arms under her bosom – one of her few generous features.

'After all the times she's stuck up for you against us,' my father chipped in.

A familiar figure approached the stained glass of the front door. A key scratched, clicked in after several attempts and the bolt jumped back.

'Hello, Mumpsywumpsy and Poppsywopsy,' Dodo trilled.

'Hello, Dodikins,' my parents gushed, stepping in front of me like I was something shameful.

My father used to call me *Bettyboo*. I never liked it but at least it was a term of endearment.

'Oh, you're home early,' he beamed.

'I sneaked out, but please do not tell your beautiful daughter,' Dodo confessed. 'Oh, but whose is that suitcase?'

My parents parted reluctantly.

'Oh hello, Boss,' Dodo beamed, apparently unaware that I had heard her confession. 'Have you come to stay?'

'No, she has not,' my parents chorused.

12

STOLEN PROPERTY AND THE MAN FROM
DAFFODIL LANE

S t Hilda's Church must have been one of the oldest buildings in Sackwater – built over seven hundred years ago, Adam always described such buildings as *stolen property*. In his eyes, St Hilda's had been a Roman Catholic church for two centuries before Henry VIII's gonorrhoea-induced difficulties in producing an heir led him to seek an illegal divorce, break away from the mother church and confiscate all of her possessions. I had heard much the same things at Roedene Abbey but never really shared the nuns' sense of outrage. After all, I was one of those filthy Protestants they loved to rail against.

I was a little late for the funeral and the six coffins had already been lined up in front of the altar rail. The church was packed and I sat at the back, tripping over the jutting base of a font, impressed and dismayed at how loudly my clumsiness clattered over the murmured devotions.

I had glimpsed little Sylvia Satin as I came in. She was perched on a front pew, her legs not reaching the floor, next to her Uncle Harry. She turned to see what the commotion was about and gave me a friendly wave and I raised my hand in acknowledgement to more clicking of tongues than if I had roared out *Hello, darlin', how's tricks?*

Sylvia looked very sweet in her black dress and matching Alice band and she gave me a little smile with that wave. Either she was still doped up, I decided, or did not really understand or believe what was happening.

The vicar, Reverend Heath, was asking us to pray for the souls and, though I knew the numbers, I was still shocked by his list – Sylvia's parents, Geoffrey and Jillian Satin; her younger brother, Wilham, known as Willy; her Uncle Daniel and Aunt Mabel Satin; her Uncle Horace Worbrow.

'And Rusty,' Sylvia piped up and Reverend Heath stumbled over the eternal rest he was about to beseech the Lord to grant them.

'Who?' He eyed the coffins, worried he might have missed somebody out, and a lady in the pew behind Sylvia half-rose.

'Rusty do be Sylvia's pet dog, Vicar.' She was a short skinny woman with milk-bottle lenses in tortoiseshell frames curtained by a black veil hanging from a flat velvet hat. 'But he do get killed too.'

The vicar looked peeved by these interruptions.

'Well, we don't have funeral services for animals.' He turned a page back in his Book of Common Prayer. 'Eternal rest,' he restarted, with a devoutly Christian lack of concern for the wailing child before him.

'Shouldn't be here, tha' child,' Mrs Whestle declared loudly.

'No, she shouldn't,' I agreed softly. 'But then her family shouldn't be dead.'

'Shush,' a pock-faced woman in brown with a black armband told me crossly, because my quiet tone was more distracting to proceedings than either of their strident contributions.

Harrold Schofield sat bolt upright, facing forward. Why is it that even the nicest of men can be stuffed shirts? A woman would have put an arm around her niece and tried to reassure her. Men usually hope that emotions will pass away.

The rest of the service went as expected. The vicar had been acquainted with the family. Jillian, Sylvia's mother, had helped with flower arranging. Geoffrey, the father, was a mechanic and had repaired the vicarage lawn mower and the vicar's Riley Nine, rather a sporty car for a vicar, people carped, as if he would do his job better in a Tin Lizzie.

Reverend Heath trotted out the usual stuff about the deceased sleeping until the last trump and narrated the whole of Henry Scott-Holland's poem:

Death is nothing at all.

I have only slipped away into the next room.

He began and I could only pray that this was true.

The coffins were put in the ground and since St Hilda's only had two sextons, the process was painfully protracted.

I found myself next to the little woman who had explained about Rusty.

'Mrs Josie Whitehouse,' she introduced herself, 'a close family friend.'

But not so close as to be at Sylvia's birthday party, I thought unkindly.

'I was on my way to the party but I got delayed by the plumber,' she explained, as if she had peered with her magnified eyes into my mind. 'Otherwise I'd be down there now.' She nodded towards the six mounds beside their unfilled holes.

Sylvia came trotting up. 'Hello, nice police lady. Hello, Aunty Josie.' She gave Mrs Whitehouse a hug.

'Hello, darling.' Mrs Whitehouse stroked her head affectionately. 'Don't you goo worry 'bout Rusty. A kind warden take him to lay in the pine woods. He love it there, dint he, sweetheart?'

Sylvia nodded vigorously as Harrold Schofield came along.

'Inspector,' he greeted me. 'I hope you are well.'

'Quite well, thank you,' I replied. There was an aloofness in the man that I had not sensed at our previous meeting and I did not feel like telling him that I was still having problems. Was this how he remembered me looking when we met? My face wouldn't have been much worse if I had been trying to separate two tomcats who were fighting on my shoulders.

'Hello, Harry,' Josie said. 'It's been a while.'

'Indeed,' he said tersely as Mrs Heath, the vicar's wife, came and took Sylvia off by the hand.

'How are you and Sylvia getting on?' I asked him.

'Quite well,' he replied a bit stiffly, and I wasn't sure if he was mocking my reply to him. 'Do you know of any reason why we shouldn't?'

'No,' I replied, a little taken aback by the oddness of his question. 'I just wondered, with you not really knowing each other.'

'Oh, but we understand each other very well now,' Harrold Schofield assured me coolly and called out, 'Come along, Sylvia. We have a long journey ahead.'

Sylvia pouted and traipsed, dragging her feet back towards him.

'I don't like her talking to all these people,' he told us and took his niece away.

'*These people!*' Mrs Whitehouse quoted indignantly. 'They're the ones she has known all her life.'

'How do you know him?' I asked.

'Used to live down Daffydil Lane, he did. Never like him, I dint. Never trust him neither. All airs and graces now he do got a n'office and a secret'ry.'

'Was that true about the dog?' I watched Sylvia clamber into the front passenger seat of a yellow Austin Seven.

'Oh yes,' she assured me. 'That bookseller do it.'

'Teddy Moulton?'

53

'He's a good sort.'

'He is,' I agreed and Mrs Whitehouse buttoned up her coat, which is as effective a way of ending a conversation as I know of.

I exchanged words with the vicar and his wife and a few other people, some I had known most of my life.

'A terrible thing,' Reverend Heath told me, as if I hadn't realised, 'but one that strengthens my conviction that we are fighting God's war.'

I didn't argue. What was the point? I just wished that God would fight a few of his own.

13

THE WIZARD AND THE WAITER

M r Hiltrop, the chief surgeon at the Royal Albert Sackwater Infirmary, had told me I would not be back on duty for at least six months and Tubby Gretham had firmly agreed with him. Most convincingly, my body heartily agreed with them both. It was battered and bruised with innumerable cuts, mainly, I was told, from the amount of broken glass that had found its way inside my uniform with more skill than most men had managed.

Most worryingly, my fingers still felt numb. I could only move them stiffly and they already had to do more than should have been expected of them.

Living in Felicity House was far more exhausting than being on duty, though. My parents' relentless carping at me and each other was almost as stressful as their lodger's relentless cheerfulness. Who comes down to breakfast on a dark winter's morning singing the Munchkins' songs? Dodo did, celebrating being part of the Lollipop Guild at the top of her voice. Where she had heard it, I had no idea. *The Wizard of Oz* had not even been shown in Suffolk yet. Perhaps her father, Chief Superintendent Frederick 'Fido' Chivers, had treated her to a trip to London. If so, I was surprised she hadn't mentioned it.

What really propelled my earlier return to Sackwater Central, however, was a visit by Superintendent Vesty.

'Thought I'd see how your young lady is,' he told my father just as I was starting to hobble down the stairs.

'I am quite well, thank you, Superintendent Vestry.' My mother bobbed a little curtsy.

I had given up trying to correct her pronunciation of the Super's surname.

'He means Dodo,' my father explained with a scowl. Vesty was an ex-patient who had declined to pay when my father extracted an upper instead of a lower tooth and my father, whose memory was not always good, never forgot a grudge – especially if it was against himself.

'Good morning, sir,' I greeted him from the bottom step.

The superintendent touched his forehead where the skin was sunken into a rectangle. He had lost part of his skull in the Great War and it had been repaired, Brigsy had told me, with a stainless-steel plate.

'I am so sorry, Superintendent Vestry.' My mother bowed her head. 'She is always interrupting.'

I took my superior officer into the waiting room. We were unlikely to be disturbed there. Vesty declined my offer of a ripped chintz chair and stood by the fire in the forlorn hope that the clinker might give a little warmth. There was a lovely lacy pattern on the window – of frost.

'Sharkey tells me you are taking retirement,' he began and I was just about to explain that Old Scrapie was a three-faced lying toad when my superior added, 'and I have come to request that you do.' Vesty cleared his throat. It was a long process and I was just about to take that seat myself when he finished clearing and said the best word I had heard for a long time. 'Not.' I cleared my own throat to explain that I had absolutely no intention of quitting, but Vesty was fanning his hand like a diner dismissing an overly attentive waiter. 'The men were hopeless before you came.' He bent sideways so suddenly I thought my chief was collapsing, but he grasped the poker and raised it like a warrior in one of those last-stand paintings so beloved by empire builders.

I rather thought the men were still hopeless but Vesty swung away to plunge his weapon into the heart of the fire, scattering dying embers on to the hearthrug but producing no discernible heat.

'And none of them can stand up to Sharkey when you aren't there.' Vesty thrust the poker back into its old iron sheath. 'At least reconsider.'

'I—'

But Vesty brushed my protest aside. 'Think it over,' he implored so piteously that if I had already handed in my resignation and booked my wedding, I would have cancelled them both. 'Well.' He tugged his right earlobe. 'I must not detain you any longer.'

'I—' I tried again but he was back in the hall.

'To give the men their dues,' Vesty took his cap off the rack and opened the front door, 'they were very helpful when it came to clearing your office.'

That settled it.

'I shall be back after Easter, sir,' I promised and Vesty treated me to a rare smile.

'That's the spirit.' He tipped his cap with his swagger stick. 'It's British pluck like yours that keeps Jerry cowering behind the Maginot Line.'

I rather thought the line had been built for us and the French to cower behind but my super, being an ex-military man and a hero of the Battle of Ypres, no doubt knew best.

I returned to my room.

My darling Adam, I began, but that was as far as I got. It was not just the trouble with my hand that stopped me writing any more.

*

'If you are well enough to return to work, you are well enough to go back to your boat,' my mother reasoned and I nearly asked why they both hated me, but I had a terrible suspicion that one of them would give me an answer.

14

BLEAK AND NOT SO BLEAK HOUSE

I had not been looking forward to last Christmas. The thought of another round of charades with my father doing *Bleak House* merely by grimly pointing to everything around him had not been an enticing one. Dodo, I felt sure, would be beside herself with excitement and sneaking into my room with a stocking and expecting me to do the same for her. I loved Christmas – or at least the idea of it – but years of experience had turned me into Ebenezer at his Scroogiest.

Captain Sultana had been invited by Jimmy to be his guest at the officers' mess and at least had the prospect of some fun but, as it turned out, they and all of us in Felicity House were struck down by the 'flu. My infection, my mother diagnosed, was not as serious as everybody else's and so I was called upon to nurse them and I doubted Florence Nightingale ever had more demanding or less grateful patients.

February 10th was Carmelo's birthday and also the feast of St Paul in commemoration of the apostle's shipwreck on the coast of Malta, an important event in the land of the captain's birth, so we decided we would celebrate both on the boat. He would bake our biggest rabbit and I would cheat and buy a cake. Tubby and Greta were having none of that, though. They had been ill too and so we would celebrate the birthday, St Paul's and a belated Christmas simultaneously with them.

Jimmy was supposed to be on duty that day but then he went and sprained a wrist playing rugby after dinner in the mess. So the three of us made our way up to White Lodge for the day with a bottle of Captain's limoncello and a tin of his delicious *mqarret* rolls baked with the very last of his figs. I took brandy – which my father had protested vehemently but falsely was his – and my attempts at mince pies, with which I had foolishly declined any offers of assistance. Jimmy brought champagne, which he promised me he had paid for, and a huge ham, which he insisted he had won in a raffle.

'So long as we don't get the snowdrops swarming aboard,' I warned. The snowdrops were the RAF police and Jimmy had told me before about their interest in the pranks he and his fellow officers engaged in.

Greta had roasted a goose with piles of vegetables and steamed a football-sized pudding. She accepted my meagre culinary contributions with great grace and put them in the pantry *for later.*

After dinner we all joined in the washing-up before going to the sitting room to play charades, Jimmy – who had suffered it one year – persuading me to re-enact my father's shenanigans, which, after all our alcohol, was breathtakingly hilarious. Then Tubby had us all singing from *Top Hat* and *42nd Street* round the piano, drowning the rest of us out and proving that while he could play a tune, he couldn't hold one.

'How did you sprain your wrist?' Greta asked Jimmy.

'I'll show you,' he offered.

'Please don't,' I begged but he was off, leaping over the coffee table without – thank heavens – damaging anything except when he landed and sprained his other wrist.

'Shall we listen to the news?' Tubby suggested after he had bandaged Jimmy up, but he was unanimously voted down. We had had good news before Christmas with the scuttling of the *Graf Spee* – Captain Sultana being especially happy that we had not lost any more men or ships after the Battle of the River

Plate – but there had been too much bad news about our own shipping ever since and we all knew there would be plenty more of that to come.

Instead we slumped on ancient sofas with our brandies while Greta read us a ghost story by M. R. James, but I don't think she had got much beyond the first couple of pages before all of us – including her – fell asleep around the crackling fire.

After two months of inactivity I was teetering on the brink of insanity. I went for long walks in the surrounding countryside and through the town. Spice Lane was still partially cordoned off. The council had finished the Luftwaffe's demolition work on number six, Sylvia's family home, and the two houses either side, but made no attempt to clear the rubble from the site. The road itself had been repaired quite quickly but several properties had developed cracks and were shored up by old railway sleepers and scaffolding. Four across the road were uninhabited now.

February had been dull but dry and we were getting quite used to that and even thinking of casting a clout before February was out, but it saved us the trouble by getting very cold again. Then, as if it wasn't in short enough supply already, paper was rationed.

March was dull as well but, just for a change, it was wet. At least I could go back to *Cressida* and augment the new meat rations with our own livestock.

I went back to work. There were no celebrations. Dodo had a week's leave and had gone to stay with her father. Brigsy welcomed me with crinkled eyes and a big mug of tea – an enamel one.

'Your china one broke itself,' he explained, 'and I promised the twins not to tell you how.'

Sharkey circled me, shark-like, and said, 'You don't look fit to be on duty.'

'Neither do you,' I told him cheerfully. 'But then you never have.'

We had thought it bad enough in December with the ice and fog but then came the snow and, just to cheer us up, the government introduced rationing of butter, sugar, bacon and ham. Then came more snow. I had never seen so much of it and I had been around most of the century. It came heavy and it drifted and I was forced to move back into Felicity House, the police station being less well heated inside than out. The captain took a room above the Anchor Inn. The Grethams offered him a space but White Lodge was much draughtier than *Cressida,* and a pub with convivial company, unlimited alcohol and an inglenook fireplace suited Captain Sultana very well indeed.

'I am requisitioning accommodation in this house by authority of the Home Office.' I presented my father with an unfilled summons for not having a dog licence and he glanced at the official letterhead, too stubborn to admit that he needed spectacles.

'Well, that seems to be in order,' he conceded.

'Let me see that.' My mother held out both hands as if about to receive a ceremonial mace.

'I think my daddy can read a requisition order.' I snatched the form back and folded it up.

'She called me *Daddy.*' My father touched his cheek as if I had just kissed it and so I did. 'Oh yuck,' he said and wiped it away.

Even my return to work, I found, did little to relieve my boredom. We had no crimes. Well, no proper ones.

The Case of the Stolen Wheelbarrow made page three of the *Gazette* and occupied us for the best part of a morning until the owner remembered he had left it in the woods when he was collecting leaf mould. We had an unprovoked assault on a gentleman's outfitter by two masked men but the *victim* confessed on questioning that he had fallen downstairs drunk and been terrified to admit it to his teetotaller wife. We also had seven sightings of German paratroopers, of which four were unexplained, two were scarecrows and one was a goat. We had a German submarine – though I was never clear why that was East Suffolk Constabulary business – but, having nothing else to do, we satisfied ourselves that it was an old bathtub and I could only hope the Germans didn't have anything so skilled at negotiating its way through the Royal Navy's minefield.

But, like the weather, life in Sackwater had reverted to what it had always been – dull, dull and dull.

I tried teaching the men to sharpen their observational powers by getting them to remember details of people who came into the station or who we walked past on the street, but after the twins described a burly bearded seaman five minutes later as a pretty young lady, I gave up.

Then April came and, surprisingly, it was dull.

'Oh Lord, make something happen,' I prayed, but prayer is a monkey's paw. You have to be very careful what you wish for. In fact, you would be best throwing it straight into the fire.

15

THE POTTER AND THE TURTLES

went for yet another walk. Officially I was patrolling. Inspectors don't but I did. It was either that or go mad and massacre the entire station. I would spare Superintendent Vesty, I decided, and I would save Sharkey until last so I could kill him at my leisure. Somewhat cheered by this thought, I set off.

We had had three dry days in a row, which felt like something of a record, and the sun was actually making a brief, self-deprecatory appearance. A woman was walking down The Avenue holding the hand of a child.

'Sylvia?' I shaded my eyes against the low light.

'So it *is* Sylvia,' the lady said in mock indignation and nudged her little companion. 'You told me it was Slyvia.'

'That's right,' Sylvia agreed, 'Slyvia.'

She was in some odd shapeless woollen dress far too big for her. Was this how her Uncle Harry saw fit to clothe her? I would have a few words with him.

'Good morning, Inspector,' the lady said and I recognised her as Lizzie Longhorn, who had made quite a name for herself in the twenties with her pottery but was now, I thought, largely forgotten in fashionable circles. 'I found this young lady in our pond and had to fish her out.'

Lizzie must have been about my age but she had her black hair kept long in a bright blue ribbon to match her swishy floral dress. She had very clean-sculpted features and a longish face like a Modigliani painting, only prettier.

'I goo visit the turkles,' Sylvia declared.

'We have a pond,' Lizzie explained, 'with some rocks in the middle. You can see them from the road through the hedge.'

'They is toytoysis what can swimmed only I felled in and I can't swimmed and a nice man-lady do pull me out.'

'Tony found her,' Lizzie explained. Antoinette was Lizzie's live-in companion and her fondness for wearing men's clothes, especially tweeds, did nothing but fan rumours about what that companionship involved.

'And this nice lady do gotted me dry,' Sylvia told me earnestly, 'and the man-lady give me hot milk with skin on. I dint like skin.' She curdled her mouth. 'It's yucky.'

'I shall make sure she never does it again,' Lizzie promised with a smile.

'And the man-lady is very silly.' Sylvia stamped her foot. 'She putted my pretty dress in the fire.'

Sylvia wrinkled her forehead furiously.

'It was an accident,' Lizzie assured me, though I was hardly likely to make an arrest. 'Tony hung it on the rack and it caught alight. It's frightening how inflammable clothing can be.' She shuddered. 'Just as well Sylvia wasn't in it.'

'How long have you come back for?' I asked Sylvia.

'For ever,' she told me with a defiant tilt of the head.

'Has Uncle Harry come back to live here?'

Lizzie was shaking her head warningly. She had obviously had this conversation already.

'No.' Sylvia's lower lip trembled and her big blue eyes glistened. 'He do send me away for ever.'

'But where are you living?' I asked in shock.

'With Aunty Josie,' Sylvia told me, swinging on Lizzie's arm.

'I'm taking her there,' Lizzie told me. 'Unless you would like to.'

'You take me,' Sylvia cajoled.

'You seem to have acquired a new best friend,' I told Lizzie.

'And an expensive one,' she grimaced. 'I shall have to get the pond fenced off now – the next child might not be so lucky – and I feel honour-bound to stop off at Jenny's and get this young lady a new dress.'

'Well, I'd better let you get on with that,' I laughed and off they set towards the town.

'A blue one like yours?' Sylvia skipped beside her.

'We shall see,' Lizzie promised in the way that adults have of promising nothing.

I continued along The Avenue. It was probably none of my business, officially, but I would call in on Josie Whitehouse later. It was a big mistake choosing this route, I reflected regretfully. Every step I took carried me further from the centre of Sackwater and the prospect of a coffee or a cake. And I used to scold my men for not planning their beats more carefully.

16

THE GORINESS OF HADES

t was not until after I had reached the end of The Avenue and was turning left down Dove Lane that I saw our black Wolseley Wasp coming up alongside. This was officially the station car but since nobody else except Vesty could drive and our super had his own vehicle, Sharkey found all sorts of excuses to use it on official business.

'Inspector Church.' He wound down the window, crawling along beside me like he was trying to negotiate terms for a good time.

'Inspector Sharkey.' I kept walking. 'What brings you here?'

'Off to see Box,' he told me.

'Didn't have you down as a ministering angel,' I remarked.

He had only visited me in hospital in the hope of being able to gloat.

'Going to catch the lazy sod out,' he explained.

'I don't think he's malingering,' I said.

Box's bruised toe – so much ridiculed by the men – had got nastily infected, Tubby had told me, and the whole foot was badly swollen.

'What? For a stubbed toe?' Sharkey mocked.

'What a coincidence.' I mentally rewrote my already vague plans. 'I'm on my way to see him too.'

'Going the wrong way,' he told me.

'There are no wrong ways, only different ways,' I replied, as if that meant something.

'Bollocks,' Sharkey said succinctly, if somewhat inelegantly. 'Hop in then and I'll give you a lift.'

I would have preferred to walk but decided it might be sensible to be there the moment he confronted our constable. I didn't want Sharkey pretending he had seen Box kicking a football in the road.

I slid in – my colleague watching with interest as I demonstrated how little encouragement my skirt needed to rise up my legs – and sat as far from the gearstick as I could. I had been caught like that by Father Farthing when I was fourteen and was surprised that he needed five gear changes just to set the car in motion.

Sharkey shot off. I had never quite understood why men think pressing an accelerator hard impresses a woman. Are men impressed by women's aggressive approach to sewing machine pedals? If they are, they hide their feelings with more skill than I would have given them credit for.

I opened my handbag and pretended to be engrossed in looking for something. If he wanted to show off, I was not going to be his audience.

Sharkey's effort was rather wasted anyway because he had to demonstrate almost immediately how he could also press the brake pedal hard and turn the wheel hard to swing hard left into Fendale Road, and now he was stamping hard on the clutch. Was there nothing this man could not do? I wondered, finding a small screw in a side pocket of my bag and wondering where it had come from. Suddenly Sharkey was slamming the brake on so hard I had to grab the glove box to prevent myself exiting via the windscreen.

'Shit,' we both cursed.

'What the hell—' I began.

'What the bloody hell?' He outdid me that time.

A man was staggering drunkenly in front of us.

Sharkey rammed the gearstick into neutral, though the car had already stalled, and flung open his door to jump out.

'What the bloody hell are you playing at?' he raged, a very limited range of expletives by his standards indeed.

The man quarter-turned towards him, stopped, then stumbled clumsily backwards, and I saw that this was Reverend Heath and that he was not intoxicated after all.

scrambled out.

'Reverend Heath!' I hurried around the front of the car but the vicar was tumbling away from me, clutching his chest.

Was he having a heart attack? He had his back to me again.

Sharkey got to him first. But the vicar dodged away with an agility that might have got him into any half-decent rugby team if he had stayed on his feet. He stumbled to one knee but managed to get up into a crouching jog, heading back up the road away from us.

A young mother was coming along the pavement, proudly pushing a new pram.

'Here, what you doin'?' she demanded as he grabbed the side and nearly tipped her baby carriage over. 'Get off!' She righted her pram and peered solicitously inside.

Reverend Heath let go and staggered on but we both caught up with him easily. He was slowing and breathing hard. A doe's foot projected bizarrely from his waistcoat on the left side on his chest, near the middle.

'Oh shit,' Sharkey said, still at a loss for a new oath. 'He's been stabbed.'

'With a paperknife,' I chipped in.

The vicar stopped, straightened up, peered down and grabbed hold of the furry handle with his right hand.

'Don't pull it,' I warned, but Reverend Heath was beyond listening. He had a firm grasp and was not about to let go.

'Crikey!' the reverend exclaimed, very mildly under the circumstances.

The mother saw it too now and screamed and the vicar gazed over in surprise.

'I didn't mean to upset her,' he told us sorrowfully, and pulled.

I tried to stop him with my hand over his and Sharkey took a strong grip on the vicar's wrist and it might not have been so bad if we hadn't, but you have to try. Reverend Heath kept pulling and, in his efforts to overcome us, he was wiggling the blade side to side now.

'Ouch!' the vicar cried as he wrenched and twisted the handle.

But he never got that knife out. That would be Tubby Gretham's job soon enough. The wound must have widened as the vicar raked the blade side to side, though we could not see it through the waistcoat. We saw the blood, though. It gushed in pulsing torrents. There was a sudden yelp and a faint whimper and that was all. I doubt we had managed to lower Reverend Heath to the tarmac on his back before he was dead.

'God bless you,' I said in the hope that he could hear me, but Reverend Heath was gone, leaving us to clear up the gory mess he had left behind.

'My case,' Sharkey said in much the same way as a child bagsies the last iced bun.

'Take it,' I said bitterly and stupidly, 'you walking pile of...' I tried to control myself in front of a man of the cloth. '...mess,' I ended feebly and stood up.

The woman rammed her fist into her mouth.

'Is he?' she asked.

'I'm afraid so,' I told her.

'Was he a Nazi paratrooper?' she asked, because we had all

read about how they disguised themselves as nuns or clergymen. 'Is that why you killed him?'

'My colleague will explain,' I told her and leaned over to see her baby gurgling gummily, dribbly and happily. 'It's his case.'

18

STRAY DOGS AND THE TURKISH MOSAIC

A middle-aged woman emerged from the house opposite.
'I was a QA in the war,' she told me – funny how people still referred to the last war as *the* war. 'Is there anything I can do?'

'I'm afraid you're too late,' I told her, but she raised her chin and said, 'A Queen Alexandra's Royal Army Nursing Corps Principal Matron is *never* too late. The departed are as much in need of care as the living.' And, having been through the Great War, she would have seen a great many of the former.

'This is a crime scene,' Sharkey told her. 'Don't touch anything.'

'Does a murder victim deserve no respect?' she asked and went back to her house, leaving him to ponder over that one.

'I think we know enough about how he died without having to worry about disturbing the body,' I said quietly.

Men, like stray dogs, respond better to soft words.

'I suppose so,' he conceded and I wondered how Sidney Grice or March Middleton would have reacted. They would have wanted to scrape the dust from his suit into thirty different envelopes, labelled according to exactly where the sample was taken from, but crime was so much simpler and so much more complicated in the days of the first Empress of India.

The old QA went back to her house and returned with her arms full of grey blankets. She knelt on one, straightened out the corpse and crossed his arms.

'Don't touch the knife,' I warned and she looked at me with something verging on mild amusement.

'Do you really think,' she asked as she laid a blanket over Reverend Heath, 'that I am that bloody stupid?'

We left the QA to guard the body. Mrs Blender-Dyer, she said her name was, and I realised she must have been the widow of Admiral Blender-Dyer, hero of the Battle of the Atlantic. Principal Matron was the equivalent rank of Lieutenant-Colonel, yet she was not too proud to kneel in the street and be bossed about by two local coppers.

'And keep your eyes open,' Sharkey instructed her. 'There could be a maniac on the loose.'

'There could indeed,' Mrs Blender-Dyer agreed, ironically, I thought.

'He came from somewhere over there.' Sharkey peered up and down the street.

'The vicarage, perhaps?' I suggested.

'I thought that was next to the church.'

'No, that's the Old Vicarage. This is the new one.'

We walked briskly towards it, four houses up the road.

The church authorities had sold the Old Vicarage rather than repair and maintain a vast mansion built for the alarmingly large Victorian families and their legions of live-in servants. The new one, cleverly called 'The Vicarage', was merely huge – also Victorian, but designed for less fecund occupants with no need of a fourth storey or mock-defensive turrets. Reverend and Mrs Heath had two independent adult children and would be lucky to have a live-out maid in these days of austerity.

The front door was wide open and we stopped just outside it.

'He could still be in there,' Sharkey muttered.

'Hello,' I called out. 'Is anybody home?'

Nobody replied.

'What?' Sharkey mocked. 'You think the murderer is going to give you a cheery reply?'

'Mrs Heath might be in there,' I suggested, 'and not even aware of what has happened or have been stabbed as well.'

'One way to find out.' Sharkey stepped into the hallway, the floor tiled in a sort of Turkish mosaic and walls papered in something that made me feel dizzy. 'Police,' he yelled. 'We are coming in.'

19

BLOOD ON THE FIREPLACE, BLOOD ON THE SILL, THE CREEPING WOMAN AND THE LURKING MAN

The doors to either side of the entrance hall were shut except for one at the back left, which was wide open.

'I'll take that,' Sharkey volunteered. 'You check out the other rooms.'

There was a smeared handprint on the wallpaper and I was just about to draw it to my colleague's attention when he said, 'Bloodstain. I'm surprised you didn't notice that.'

'I'm surprised you think I didn't,' I replied, aware of how feeble that sounded.

'Yeah, right,' he sneered.

'And on the inside of the door,' I counter-attacked.

'Of course,' Sharkey said, dismissing the very idea that it might not be, and selected a stout walking stick from the umbrella stand, grasping it like a cudgel, leaving me with a pretty frilled rolled-up parasol.

'Not even handy if they have a leaking ceiling,' I grumbled as I held it out rapier-style and went to the front left door.

Sitting room – very chintzy, fading nicely. Next, a music room – that is, a baby grand piano with Schuman on the stand. Everybody did that. There would probably be Gilbert and Sullivan in the mahogany cupboard. I doubted the Heaths were admirers of Fats

Waller. A dining room, long lacquered table and a substantial sideboard with an asbestos mat to protect it, but no more bodies and no lurking lunatics slavering in the corners, not even in the back right-hand snug with its cosy armchairs by the uncosily unlit fire, nor in the kitchen with its ancient gas stove. There were battered pots hanging from hooks here, tarnished copper jelly moulds on a pine shelf and, of most interest, a row of wooden-handled knives displayed in a rack. Why use a paperknife, I wondered, when there was such an array of lethal utensils to hand? The meat cleaver alone could have been used to slaughter an ox.

I joined Old Scrapie in the back room – a large study with a big oak desk, the high-backed chair placed in a bay so its occupant would look out through one of the four long sash windows over a dense shrubbery into the large, well-stocked garden.

'Anything?' I asked, propping my parasol against the wall.

Sharkey had laid his stick on the desk.

'Some blood on the fireplace and the hearthrug,' he pointed. 'Not much, but then there wasn't until the silly bugger ripped himself.'

The rug was rucked up.

'There's a smudge on the window sill,' I said.

'I've seen that,' he said unconvincingly. 'And a bit on the door handle on the inside,' he suddenly realised. 'Take a look upstairs.'

I did – five beds and an attic, all in good order. Sharkey came out of the cellar as I returned.

'Nothing and no one,' I told him.

'Same,' he said, clearly disappointed.

Personally, I would prefer not to confront a knife-wielding homicidal maniac but, for all his faults, Sharkey was no coward. Besides, it saved a lot of detective work and even more paperwork if he caught the killer literally red-handed. Also it gave him a chance of being promoted, bestowing authority to him over me.

We went back into the study.

'Know what I think?' Sharkey didn't wait for an answer in case I came up with the right one. 'Accidental death.'

'How so?'

'Obvious,' he told me, and I hated it when people did that because it wasn't at all obvious to me. 'No sign of a struggle or a forced entry. Tripped on the hearth rug and stabbed himself. They're bloody lethal, some of these paperknives. I bet, when we get it out, you'll find it's got a point like a stiletto. See that?' he showed me triumphantly. 'A part-opened letter on the desk.'

'Have you noticed,' I asked, and knew, the moment the words left my lips, that he would tell me he had, 'the blood is all clotted.'

'Course I did. So?'

'It seems quite quick to me,' I commented, 'especially in these temperatures.'

There was no fire in the grate and the study was distinctly chilly.

'Different people's blood clots at different times,' Sharkey maintained.

'Where did you read that?' Something caught my eye outside.

'It's a well-known fact,' my colleague asserted, which people always say when they haven't an imperial ounce of evidence for their statements.

'I'm just not convinced,' I said, and Sharkey huffed just enough to let me know what a silly woman I really was.

'You're a believer in reconstruction,' he said, having witnessed a lecture I gave to the men in the wretched hope of getting them to start doing it. 'Right.' He grabbed a wooden ruler off the desk and an unopened envelope. 'I'm opening this letter.' He mimed the action. 'And while I'm walking about, I trip.' He stumbled theatrically over the edge of the rug, then genuinely tripped over his own feet, cracking his head on the carved wooden mantelpiece with a highly satisfactory thud. 'Oh, bloody shit,' he swore, rubbing his brow vigorously.

'Now you've rucked it all up,' I complained.

'What?' He kicked at the rug hem furiously. 'It was bloody well rucked up when we arrived.' He crouched.

'Don't!' I cried in exasperation, but my colleague did. He pulled the edge of the carpet to straighten it.

'Happy now?' he demanded.

'No,' I sighed, 'because now we can't tell if any of the blood was under the folds.'

'So what?'

'So we could work out if the carpet was bled on before or after it was rucked up.'

'You're the one who's rucked-up,' Sharkey stormed, but we both knew he had destroyed a possibly important source of evidence.

'Also,' I pointed out, 'when you tripped, you didn't stab yourself with the ruler. You shot both hands out to break your fall.'

'I have lightning reflexes,' Sharkey told me coldly. 'That old man wouldn't have.' He sniffed so long and so loudly I thought he had detected some olfactory clue – a rare perfume, perhaps, that would incriminate an exotic female foreign agent – but he was just sniffing. 'I'm going to the station for reinforcements,' he muttered and stalked out.

Something caught my eye again and I realised that it wasn't something at all. It was someone. There was a man lurking suspiciously – because there is no other way you can lurk – in the shrubbery.

I considered my options and they were few. Pretending I hadn't seen him and sneaking away was available to me. Alternatively, I could open one of the sash windows and bellow *Halt! Police!* and the average law-abiding citizen would do as he was instructed. The problem with that was that some non-average law-abiding citizens would senselessly panic and run while the average law-breaking citizen would sensibly panic and run, and by the time I could have scrambled over the sill and down into the garden, whoever had decided to scarper could have done so.

On the whole, I decided, law-abiding citizens do not skulk in shrubberies outside the window of a room where a murder has quite possibly just occurred. It did strike me as a bit odd that he had his back to me and so was not trying to look in and also that he was joggling his head about in such a way that few people could have failed to notice him.

I hurried to the front door. Sharkey had shut it behind him and it had an odd fiddly lock that was sticky with blood and difficult to manage one-handed. I doubt it delayed me more than ten seconds but ten seconds gives a man quite a good start in a race.

Assuming he hadn't seen me, I might still manage to take him unawares. I crunched over the gravel as quietly as I could – which was not very – along the front left and around the side of the house, pausing to open the iron side gate, being careful not to clink the catch and creeping along the paved path to the back of the house.

I saw the man the moment I stepped on to the lawn. He was emerging from the shrubbery now and holding an enormous knife, the blade curved up scimitar-like to a wicked-looking point. And he was coming straight towards me.

20

A BRIEF HISTORY OF IMPALEMENT

stopped dead in my tracks – possibly not the cleverest of moves. If you are going to tackle a man armed with something that could cut you in half, you need to go headlong at him, your only hope being that he will be taken off balance, but I was completely unarmed. I hadn't even thought to snatch up the parasol – for all the good that would have done me.

'Halt,' I commanded, a lot more forcefully than I felt, and I held out my hand the way I was trained to stop traffic. There was a time I could do that without even trying.

The man stopped. He was not especially big but his knife was.

'I int done nothin',' he protested in the way that people who haven't not done anything always do.

'Put your weapon down on the ground,' I ordered.

'I int got no weapon,' he protested.

He had on an old sagging jacket and even older corduroy trousers tied at the waist and both ankles with that horrible hairy brown string, the sort that makes you itch just to catch sight of it.

'Put it down now.'

The man took a step towards me, waving it menacingly.

'It's just a billhook,' he told me.

'I know what it is,' I lied. 'Put... it... down.'

The man pulled the corners of his mouth down like he was telling a friend *We've got a right one here* and tossed the knife on to the grass to land alarmingly close to my feet. I wondered briefly if I could still have kept my job without them.

'Who else is here?' I asked. It plants the idea in people's heads that you know they are not alone if you ask that, rather than if they are.

'No one,' he insisted, then mouthed to his invisible accomplice, *We've got a right one here.*

'What are you doing?' I asked.

'Prunin'.' The man flapped an arm towards the bush and a small pile of lopped branches beside it on the lawn. 'I trimmed all that rhonydedron,' he added defiantly.

And then it clicked, what should have clicked right from the start, even if only from his clothing and the mud on the knees of his corduroys. This man was the gardener.

'What's your name?' I demanded.

'Gervil Fisher.'

What few teeth I glimpsed were twisted and what they lacked in enamel they made up for in tartar.

'Where do you live?'

A female blackbird came bouncing towards Mr Fisher, presumably used to him being a source of worms and bugs when he dug the ground.

'Thirty-eight Delhi Terrace.'

He dipped to pick a piece of gravel off the lawn.

'Who lives at number forty?'

'Joe and Beatty Polter.' His answers came too pat to be invented on the spot.

'How long have you been here?' I asked, adding, 'today,' before he gave me his autobiography.

'Two hour,' he replied without hesitation. 'Clock be at ten when I come and it be at twelve now.'

I glanced up at St Hilda's, two streets away.

'Have you seen anyone?'

'Not a soul,' he told me, ''cept tha' thrush.' It didn't look like anyone had bought him an avian identification chart recently.

'And nothing unusual in the house?'

'Never look in,' he insisted. 'Mrs Heath do sack the last man for that, she do.'

'And you didn't hear anything?'

''cept him singing his little heart out.' Gervil Fisher smiled fondly, if foully. 'He love me, he do.' The gardener's hand whipped forward. 'But I hate him,' he said, his stone just missing the blackbird and clattering into the side of a stone sundial with such force that a more accurate throw might have taken her head off, 'I do.'

The blackbird hopped closer.

'I have some very bad news,' I announced. 'Mr Heath has died.'

Gervil Fisher paled.

'Oh my good maker,' the gardener crossed himself. 'I can't hardly belief that.' He swayed his head side to side incredulously. 'Who goon pay my wages?'

'I'm sorry but that's nothing to do with me.' I ushered him out through the side gate. 'You will have to come to the station tomorrow morning to make a statement.'

Mrs Heath was coming up the street now with Mrs Blender-Dyer and I wondered who was looking after the body now.

Gervil Fisher caught sight of her and hurried over. Surely he would not be so insensitive as to worry her about his wages at a time like this? He scooped the flat cap off his head.

'I am so dretful sorry,' he consoled her, 'that your poor late husband forget to pay me last week.'

'Go away,' Mrs Blender-Dyer said so fiercely that the gardener visibly crumpled before he slunk away.

'Miserybold uddercats,' he muttered, probably about the three of us.

I turned to Mrs Heath.

'I am very sorry,' I said, as if that would give her the slightest consolation. Sharkey was getting out of his car grimly with the Grinder-Snipe twins and Rivers. It was difficult to know which of them he detested most and it was even more difficult to blame him. 'This must be a terrible shock,' I said rather obviously, and I wondered why we do that – tell people how they simply must be feeling.

'Well.' The vicar's newly widowed widow wiped the corner of her eye with a brown glove. 'I can't say it's altogether a surprise. He was always messing about with that knife. I warned him – it had a point like a stiletto.'

Sharkey heard that as he locked the car. I had a mongrel called Elcsar once and she was highly alert, but she never pricked her ears as sharply as Old Scrapie did his.

'I wouldn't be surprised if he tripped over that hearthrug,' she continued. 'He was always very clumsy on his feet. Ladies used to dread dancing with him. I always refused.'

'Have you spoken to Inspector Sharkey?' I asked as casually as I could.

This sounded not so much like coaching a witness as writing a script for one.

'Not yet,' she said, but from the ill-concealed smirk on my colleague's face, he was very much looking forward to having his diagnosis proved. If anybody at all agreed with him, he must be right.

'Was your husband very accident-prone?' I asked.

'Oh, very,' Mrs Blender-Dyer assured me. 'Why, after you left the funerals, Inspector, he stepped back into an open grave.'

'He was rather an imbecile,' Mrs Heath agreed.

'Can't imagine anyone stepping back into a hole. Can you, Inspector Church?' Sharkey asked me, so innocently I rather wished I could step into a deep one now – or better still, push my esteemed colleague into it and start shovelling the contents back over him.

'There does not appear to be a great deal we can do,' March Middleton commiserated over the phone that evening. 'If he had not have done all that to the rug, even a couple of photographs with it undisturbed then straightened would have illustrated your point satisfactorily. And what you say about the way Inspector Sharkey tripped with the ruler usually holds true but I *have* known people to fall on their knives accidentally.' She chuckled. 'Edward stabbed himself in the calf with his ceremonial sword once.'

I laughed. Edward had been Aunty M's first fiancée but he had died twenty years before I was born. From the stories she told, he sounded a lovely man but, quite honestly, a bit of a twerp. She had loved him dearly and mourned him for years but then she found a deeper love and never stopped mourning the loss of that even though she found love later, a third and final time. I was beginning to wonder if I had ever really known it. The last time Adam wrote, I had waited until the next day before I bothered opening his letter. It would only be another lecture about how I should give up my career for him, whereas he had been outraged when I asked if he would do the same for me. Policemen are encouraged to settle down with a wife but policewomen are forbidden to marry. We might do embarrassing things like have babies. Also, no man could be expected to see his wife in a position of authority.

I should reply, I knew, and I would. It was just knowing how to say what I knew I must say.

21

FRED AND GINGER AND REX
THE VERY BRAVE DOG

There was a sea mist at the bottom of High Road East. It hovered, undecided if it could be troubled to creep any further into town. Many a visitor did that as well. A foghorn mooed mournfully out to sea.

'Goodness.' Dodo clapped her hands together as we went by the ramshackle pier pavilion. 'It is as chilly as a cactus. Where are we going, Boss?'

'Along the promenade,' I told her grumpily as the black ocean slopped against the sea wall, spraying us even on the other side of the road. We passed the Royal George with hardly a glance. It surprised me the hotel kept open. It had had few customers in the best of times and this was the worst of times, with the war and memories of the ghastly murders we had investigated there shortly after my return.

The wind was getting up more now, almost what March Middleton might have termed a *tempest*. No doubt she or her guardian, the famous personal detective Sidney Grice, could have deduced something very clever about the old woman hobbling towards us wrapped in a brown coat and woolly hat, her face swathed in a grey scarf, but try as I might, I couldn't.

'Marnin',' she greeted us. 'My word but it's rafty.'

'What does rafty mean, Boss?' Dodo asked me as the old woman went on her painful way.

'Raw,' I replied.

'Raaarrrr.' Dodo slashed the air with pretend claws.

'No,' I explained. 'Raw meaning cold.'

'Did you notice something about her?' Dodo asked as we crossed over.

'Several things,' I replied warily, because senior officers cannot admit to being less observant than their juniors. It would be like the pope saying *Correct me if I'm wrong*. 'What did you notice?'

'She was very old,' Dodo told me with great satisfaction.

A sudden gust had us both sidestepping with synchronised steps that Fred and Ginger would have been envious of.

I glanced at a couple holding hands in one of the thirteen promenade shelters and wondered if I would ever be half a couple again.

'Anything else?'

'No,' Dodo replied simply. Her voice rose an octave into the shrillness that she called singing. 'Oh I do like to be beside…'

'Be quiet,' I snapped.

'The seaside,' she whispered, gazing at me like a fawn caught in a trap.

We stopped by the statue of Rex, the terrier who had dived off the pier and saved a baby's life. The baby was in her sixties now. We stopped to pat Rex's head. Everybody did and the stone was getting worn.

'What happened to her, Boss?' Dodo asked.

'His owner sold *him* to a showman who got people to pay to watch him jump off the pier again. He was not so lucky the second time.'

Rex had been badly taxidermied and stood lumpy and unsteady on a little stage in the Sackwater Museum with a ridiculously long varnished tongue dangling out of the side of his mangy mouth, staring glassily at the two-tailed Siamese cat aloof in a glass case nearby.

'Oh for goodness' sake,' Dodo said crossly. 'Why on earth would anybody steal a shop dummy?' Even as Dodo's non sequiturs went, that was one of the non-est.

I followed the direction of my constable's gaze back to the shelter.

'They are real people,' I said, forgetting that, while most people look at whatever they are talking about, Dodo Chivers was definitely not like most people.

'No, there, Boss.' Dodo waved her arm towards the horizon, sweeping about like she was trying to polish it. 'Or at least it was there.'

There were no boats in sight but you could have hidden half the German Navy a mile or so out in the fog. I scanned the beach. An eddy of wind wafted the mist away and then I saw it too. Beyond the tangled bails of barbed wire stretched between the concrete blocks to delay the imminently expected invasion, somebody was lying on the shingle, slightly propped up against a timber groyne near the water's edge. It looked like a man but it was too far away to be certain.

'I don't think that's a mannequin.' I shaded my eyes.

'It is not a very feminine way for a womannequin to dress,' Dodo reasoned.

The figure seemed to be in a greatcoat with trousers but, at thirty yards or more in those conditions, it was difficult to tell.

'Run back to Felicity House and borrow my father's binoculars,' I ordered. 'They should be in the hall table.'

'Shall—' Dodo began and I just knew that whatever she was going to ask would be stupid.

'Just go and get them,' I snapped.

'Yes Boss.' Dodo saluted and I did not think she was being

sarcastic but I was not so sure when I heard her mutter as she sauntered off, 'Would it have hurt to say *please*.'

'Yes, it would,' I called, resisting the urge to say *get your skates on* and give her the opportunity to explain that she did not have any skates to get on and couldn't skate anyway. 'And get a move on.'

I screwed up my eyes in an effort to sharpen their focus but the mist was rolling back up the beach, parting briefly every now and again to give me a tantalising glimpse. I had seen a few dead bodies in my time and I was fairly certain that I was seeing another one now.

22

DEATH WEARS TWEEDS

I paced up and down the promenade, partly to keep warm and partly in the hope that a different angle might give me a better view. It didn't. The figure was not going anywhere, I decided eventually, but the couple in the shelter might be, so I strolled over.

'Good morning,' I greeted them.

The couple could not have jumped more if I had sneaked up behind and fired a starting pistol.

'You affritted us,' the girl explained after they had screamed in a unison that boded well for their future relationship.

'Sorry,' I said. 'I thought you saw me approach. Have you been here long?'

The girl clamped a hand over her young man's mouth. 'Don't answer that.'

'I'm not accusing you of anything,' I hurried to explain.

'Good.' She clutched her handbag. ''cause we int done nothin'.'

Here we go again, I thought.

'Bug-roff,' came muffled through her fingers, 'copper,' came more clearly as he twisted his head away.

The girl rounded on him. 'Shut your gobhole. She dint know nothin'.'

I hadn't known that there was anything to know until that moment, but I did now.

'Right then.' I stood as tall as I could without going on tippy-toes and looked sternly down at them. They were little more than children really. 'You had better come clean or it will be the worse for you both.'

'We int done nothin',' the girl reasserted.

'Perhaps you would like to discuss what you *int* done at the police station,' I suggested, focusing my attention on her companion because, in my experience, boys almost always crack first.

'It was just a joke,' the boy mumbled. 'Stupid old sign anyway.'

I turned to look at it. *No Danger Keep On Beach* was pencilled over the words so faintly that I could hardly read the changes. I suppressed a smile, remembering how Hervey Stronburrow from up the road used to think it the height of hilarity to insert an *I* between the words of *To Let*.

'Damaging government property.' I brought out my notebook and he winced. 'Aiding the enemy by defacing war notices.'

The boy shrank back. 'My mum will lather me.' This prospect seemed to terrify him far more than the threat of penal servitude.

'Clean it up,' I said. 'And don't let me catch you at it again.'

'At what?' Dodo asked breathlessly. 'No.' She tipped her helmet up and it slid down the back of her head. 'Let me guess.' Dodo wiggled her tiny nose. 'They don't look like murderers but then murderers rarely do.'

'Got the binoculars?' I asked, suspiciously eyeing the leather tube hanging around her neck.

'Well, sort of.' Dodo tapped it. 'But then I thought with you having bits missing, this might be easier.' She unclipped the lid and, as I had suspected, slid out my grandfather's old telescope.

'Well, it isn't,' I told her.

She parried my blow and countered with one of her own. 'I used my initiative. And you are always telling me to do that, Boss.'

'I lost my lower arm, not my eye,' I reminded her crossly and Dodo wiggled her nose. 'Give it to me.'

I held out my hand and Dodo reluctantly complied.

We walked back to the statue. 'What took you so long?'

'I was as quick as Quink,' Dodo retorted.

'Your breath smells of tea.'

'Only because Mumpsy was up and insisted I had something to warm my insides.'

I had had words with my parents before about making their lodger late for work. They had never worried about me going out with no breakfast, even in the worst of storms.

I raised the telescope but it was hopeless. The images bobbed about like we were in a rowing boat in a storm and I couldn't adjust the focus one-handed.

'Elongate it,' I commanded and Dodo pulled the eyepiece out as if she was extracting a fuse from an unexploded bomb. 'Turn away.'

Dodo blinked. 'What are you going to do, Boss?' she asked nervously, because I was forever playing pranks on her.

'I need your shoulder to steady the telescope.'

I was never very good with telescopes even when I had my full quota of limbs. They never point exactly where you think they will and they won't hold still. I trained it down from the charcoal-smudged sky, the horizon hidden by the fog and the black sullen sea. Tethered mines bobbed spikily and evilly in the distance. I found the water's edge and the shingle and scanned side to side.

'Just as I thought.' I struggled to hold steady. 'It's a man.'

There wasn't much more I could say for the time being. His hatless head was turned away and his hair was greyish and I couldn't see his hands. He had a putty-coloured coat on and brown trousers and shoes.

'What?' Dodo was incredulous. 'Who goes sunbathing in this weather? ... And how on earth did he even get there?' She cupped her hands into a megaphone and yelled, 'Can't you read? The signs say *Danger Keep Off Beach*, except one of them that's been vandalised.'

'I don't think he is sunbathing,' I said.

'What then?' Dodo demanded. 'If you are signalling to an enemy submarine you will be in very serious trouble,' she bellowed, adding after a pause, 'indeed.'

'I think he is dead,' I said.

'Dead?' Dodo repeated, because people always do. 'What did he die of, Boss? How did he die? Why, Boss? When? How? … Oh, I have already asked that.'

'He must have been washed ashore. He couldn't have scrambled through that barbed wire and the beach is mined.'

'This sounds like a job for the army,' Dodo said, sensibly for a change until she ended, 'with a tank.'

'The sappers might be a better bet,' I suggested.

'And they have a camp near Tringford near Stovebury near Slackwater in Suffolk do they not, Boss?'

I had given up telling her we lived in Sackwater. Slackwater was a much nicer word, she had decided, so Slackwater, for her at least, it was.

'Yes,' I said.

'But how shall we get there, Boss? Neither of us can drive. Shall we go to Slackwater Central Police Station and ask Inspector Sharkey to take us in the police car? Please say no. He will only spoil our fun.'

She had a different idea of fun to mine.

'No,' I said, because I sort of agreed with my constable. I wanted to keep Old Scrapie out of this as long as possible. He would only try to steal any credit there was to be had or apportion any blame if things went wrong.

'Shall we proceed by charabanc?'

'The next bus to Tringford leaves in about...' I checked my watch. 'Two days.'

'Shall we ask Daddykins to chauffeur us in his motor car?' Dodo skidded sideways and clutched my empty sleeve to save herself.

'My father's car is on blocks for the duration,' I reminded her. 'And *we* are not going anywhere. I am going to use his phone and you are staying here to guard the body.'

'Oh!' Dodo shrank away from me. 'You think it might rise up and attack me like Frankenstein's monster in the film *Frankenstein*?'

If only, I thought, but only said, 'No. I am thinking about members of the public.'

'Oh!' Dodo unshrank towards me. 'You think somebody might try to steal it like Dr Frankenstein?'

'No, but we cannot leave a body unattended for people to come across.' And before she could question how anybody could get to the body, I added, 'We don't want anybody to see it.'

'Oh.' Dodo tapped her nose in a way that was supposed to look conspiratorial but looked more like she was dabbing it with ointment. 'Because it is our secret.' She raised her voice. 'And no funny business.' She lowered her voice to a whisper. 'Just in case he is pretending, like that man in *Death Wears Tweeds*.'

I didn't answer. It sounded like Death had more sense than any of my constables.

23

THE CLASSIFICATION OF MONSTERS

When I was twenty-one I was given a key to the door of Felicity House. It was not an especially proud moment as I lived and worked in London by then, but it had been a humiliating one when I was made to give that key back for Dodo.

'What kind of a monster are you?' my mother demanded as she admitted me. 'Leaving that poor child outside alone in this weather.'

'Constable Chivers is a police officer,' I reminded my mother. 'We do not take children on the force.'

This was clearly not the answer my mother wanted because she ignored it.

'Oh, the poor little waif.' She hugged herself.

The surgery door opened and my father emerged into the hall. 'Oh.' His face fell. 'I thought it might be dear Dodo.'

'Good morning, Father.' I kissed his cheek and he winced like my chin was bristly. 'No patients?'

He rarely had any these days, word having spread about his poor skills and worse manner.

'Not yet,' he agreed cheerily, 'but I am expecting a family of six in...' He brought his wristwatch up and dipped his head until the two were about four inches apart. '...eighteen minutes.'

'Can't you see the time any further away than that?'

'Of course he can,' my mother railed at me. 'He can see the town clock from hundreds of yards away.'

'They have just moved into the area and they were going to go to Bradley Court.' My father rubbed his hands. 'But then they found out that I am more expensive and realised I must be better.'

Until recently my father had been the only dentist in Sackwater, although Mr Crab, the chemist, did extractions in his back room, so the arrival of two young, modern and – by all accounts – pleasant dentists did not so much hit my father's practice as bludgeon it almost to death.

'Can I use the phone?' I asked, suddenly the little girl wanting to invite Georgie Orchard to play tennis.

'What for?' my mother asked suspiciously.

'To bake a cake,' I replied.

'You want to rein in that sense of humour,' she scolded.

My fellow officers would probably tell her that I had not only done so but put it in the stable, bolted the door and swallowed the key.

'It's police business,' I said.

'Oh,' my mother said, 'aren't we the important one?'

'I have to pay for that phone.' My father stepped in front of it like he was sheltering a small child from a rabid mastiff. 'And a patient might be trying to get through.'

'I shall reimburse you,' I promised. 'And I'll be quick.'

'Be sure you do and be sure you are,' my father said, like it was a proverb and therefore wise.

He stood reluctantly aside to let me get the phone book out of the drawer and leaf through it.

'I haven't got all day,' my mother complained and stomped towards the kitchen, though she had all day every day as far as I could tell.

I dialled the operator and Maggie answered with a very grumpy, 'What?'

I had probably interrupted her knitting. She had provided

half our merchant navy with balaclavas before being told they had to have eye-holes.

'Tringford twenty-four please,' I said, imagining sailors groping blindly along decks and crashing into each other.

Maggie groaned resentfully at the onerous task I had imposed on her.

'Twenty-four?' she queried.

'Tringford,' I confirmed.

'Putting you through now, caller.' There followed a lot of grunting and huffing, the sort of noises you might make if you had to drag a piano upstairs by yourself with somebody below trying to haul it back down again. When Mabel Knutty ran the exchange, I used to go and sit on her knee and she would let me connect callers. It involved inserting the right jack into the right hole and was probably less strenuous than raising a cup of tea.

There were a few faint clicks, a whir and then a ringing. The latter went on for quite a while and then there was a loud click and a throat clearing and a, 'Tringford Camp, Captain Sweep speaking.'

'Sooty?' I said in surprise. Everybody called him that. 'It's Betty Church. Are you on phone duty?'

'Bouncy!' he exclaimed. This was his nickname for me and I did not especially care for it. 'Just happened to be passing when it rang. How's tricks?'

'Well, I'm ringing in my police inspector role,' I told him. 'There's a man's body on the beach,' I said to Sooty Sweep, and I thought I heard Maggie gasp. 'And we can't get to him because of the barbed wire.'

'Stout cutters will deal with that,' the captain breezed. 'I'll send a man over.'

'And there's the mines,' I reminded him, not that I needed to.

'Ah yes, I'd forgotten about those,' he said, because I had needed to after all. 'That could be tricky.'

'If they weren't, I wouldn't have rung you,' I said.

'Ah yes,' he said again. 'And, if one goes up, the whole lot will and then it'll be a fond farewell to Sackwater.'

'Well, that wasn't very bright,' I commented.

'Ministry orders,' Sooty said in that horrible faux-mysterious way people do when you just know they are tapping their noses. 'Mind you, it's all hush-hush. Hope that old hag Maggie isn't listening in.'

'So can you deal with them?' I asked, knowing full well that she would be.

'I am a Royal Engineer,' Sooty declared and I could almost hear him tossing his long black mane like a stallion. 'And we can deal with anything.'

He hadn't dealt very well with Georgie saying she didn't want to go out with him but I thought it best not to mention that.

'Leave it with me,' Sooty proclaimed as grandly as if he were on a one-man mission to assassinate Hitler. 'Let me see. It's ten past eleven hundred hours. The chaps will need their lunch and then they need to let that go down. We should be able to make it for fourteen hundred hours.'

'Three hours' time,' I seethed.

'See what you mean,' Sooty said soothingly. 'Best make it fourteen thirty.'

'Cheeky puppy,' Maggie fumed after Sooty had hung up. 'Old hag indeed! I *never* listen in.'

'I know you don't,' I assured her. 'Can you put me through to Sackwater Central Police Station, please?'

Rivers answered.

'Come down to the promenade immediately,' I instructed him. 'I have a job for you.'

'The promenade, ma'am?' Rivers gasped like I had told him to enter a snake pit naked. 'Tha' wind do dretful things to my back, it do.'

'Nothing like as dretful as I will if you are not here in ten minutes.' I had put the phone down before I realised I had not told him exactly where *here* was. The promenade was nearly a mile long. Still, I decided, the walk would do him good.

24

THE QUEEN OF THE MAY AND MR CAPONE

returned to find Dodo chewing contentedly on a sweet.

'I found five in my jacket pocket,' she announced, like this was the most important event of the day.

Rivers hobbled along the prom, staggering about in what was now a fresh breeze like it was the roaring forties and clutching his kidneys as if they would burst out of his much-bandied back if he let go. I gave him his instructions, which were to stand there and keep members of the public away. Dodo, being kinder, gave him one of her sweets but didn't offer me one.

'I can't stand out in this,' he whinged.

'Good,' I told him. 'Because I want you to patrol up and down.'

'Farewell.' Dodo waved and seemed about to blow him a kiss but was actually wiping a smudge from the tip of her button nose.

We turned up High Road East in silence, by which I mean I was silent. Dodo had yet to discover how to be so.

'This is one of the best days ever, is it not, Boss?' she burbled. 'A mysterious corpse and almost half a dozen toffees with hardly any fluff on them, what more could a girl ask for?'

'If I come across a girl, I shall make enquiries,' I said, lengthening my stride in the hopes that she would get breathless trying to keep up but not trip over a kerbstone. She had done that on more than one occasion and it does little for the image of the force for an officer to be seen sprawled like a drunk and disorderly face-down on the pavement.

'Oh.' Dodo shortened her step but speeded her pace so that

she was shuffling along beside me like the clockwork Chinaman I had once before Pooky smashed him with a poker, thinking he was a rat in the shadows. 'But there is a little girl over there, Boss.'

And so there was – *the* little girl – Sylvia Satin – though I hardly recognised her at first. She was swaddled as almost everybody was in an overcoat, gloves and woolly hat, walking with her *Aunty* Josie Whitehouse down Tennis Court Road.

'Sylvia,' I called softly and both of them swivelled towards me.

'It's the nice police lady,' Sylvia told her companion.

'And Inspector Church,' Dodo added as we crossed the road.

'I hope you haven't jumped into any more ponds,' I smiled and Sylvia frowned crossly.

'I didn't jumped, I felled,' she corrected me with great dignity.

'We goo to the grave,' Mrs Whitehouse said when we had caught up with them and, sensing my concern, added, 'Sylvia do ask to.'

'Hello,' Dodo said. 'I love fluffy things, especially bunnies. Do you?'

For a moment I thought my constable was talking to Mrs Whitehouse but she was bent over Sylvia, who nodded vigorously. 'So does me. Do you like furry things?'

'I love teddy bears,' Dodo said, 'but I think real bears would be dangerous and scary.'

'I goo see a real bear in a picture book,' Sylvia told her, 'and he was ever so fierce.'

At last Dodo has found somebody of her own age to talk to, I thought unkindly as they walked hand-in-hand ahead of us.

'What happened in Great Yarmouth?' I asked quietly.

Mrs Whitehouse grimaced. 'Uncle Harry int all he's made out. He say Sylvia is a spoiled...' – she dropped to a whisper – '...brat. She dint say much but I do believe he is overly strict with her. I think he slap her more than one time.'

After my first meeting with Harry Schofield, I would have been incredulous at that accusation. After the funeral I was not so surprised.

'Oh, for goodness' sake,' I murmured, 'after all she's been through, he might have made some allowances.'

'Know what I think?' The woman sniffed. 'I think Harry Schofield belief Sylvia is comin' into money. Geoff, her father, always claim he own his house but I happen to know Mr Smart owns all tha' row and the one opposite.'

'Crake Smart?' I queried and she nodded.

Crake was Sackwater's answer to Al Capone. He had made his money running a protection racket and was rumoured to control a couple of brothels. I did not know he had moved into the property market but I would not have wanted him as my landlord. He was unlikely to be sympathetic to late payers.

He was also somebody that I wanted for the murder of his son's girlfriend.

'So when he find Sylvia int comin' into the house and there's no insurance money, he send her packin'.' She breathed fiercely. 'Turn up bold as brass, he do, and say, *I've had enough of this. You take her or she goo in an home.*' We almost caught up. 'So I take her,' Josie Whitehouse concluded simply.

'But you're not a relative, Mrs Whitehouse?'

'Just a family friend,' she told me, 'but he do say if I want guardianship, he won't stand in my way.'

'And do you?'

'If there int nobody else.' Josie Whitehouse's voice fell. 'I'd die before I see her in an orphanage.' She spoke so softly now I could hardly hear her. 'And I'd kill any man or woman who tried to put her in one.'

There was such vehemence in those words that I did not

doubt for one moment that Josie Whitehouse meant exactly what she said.

Dodo and her new friend were waiting at the gate.

'What is your favourite colour?' Sylvia was asking. 'Mine is pink.'

'Mine too,' Dodo assured her, but both of them fell silent as we passed through the gate.

St Hilda's cemetery was the oldest of the five in Sackwater. We didn't really need that many but people can't be expected to share a graveyard with anyone who has a different opinion on how you should break bread and whether water can be holy. Sea air is corrosive and the older stones stuck out like partly sucked Fisherman's Friend lozenges, their inscriptions long since eroded, the names of deeply loved ones lost for ever. The far end was Victorian at its most Victorian – elaborate marble vaults for the gentry to decompose in comfort, statues of lichen-caked angels on sentry duty or women grieving, their faces eaten by the elements.

The Satins' graves were still simple mounds of earth, beneath which whatever bodies and body parts could be collected were laid to rest. There were no stones yet and I wondered if there ever would be. It didn't sound like Uncle Harry would be funding any.

'There they are, darling.' Josie put an arm around her unofficial ward and Sylvia turned her face up in surprise.

'Where, Aunty?'

'They are sleeping under here,' Josie said uncertainly and Sylvia tossed her golden hair.

'No they int.'

'I think they are,' Dodo said gently and Sylvia rolled her eyes.

'Then you are very silly,' she told my constable sternly.

Out of the mouths of babes and sucklings comes much wisdom, I thought, and saw those big blue eyes looking curiously into mine.

'Do you know where they go, nice police lady?'

Sister Millicent and her brood at Roedene Abbey had spent eight years teaching me the answer to that. They had been wrong about a lot of things but I was hoping more than ever that they were right about this one.

'They must be in heaven now,' I told her with as much conviction as I could muster.

Sylvia blinked slowly and crinkled her freckled nose.

'You int much of a liar,' she told me sternly and skipped away, dancing around an obelisk as if it was a maypole and she was the queen of the May.

25

PRESTIDIGITATION AND
THE PROVENANCE OF SCARS

t was nearly four hours after my phone call before a Bedford truck trundled along the prom, camouflage-painted with a canvas-covered metal frame at the back. It ground to a halt and the front passenger clambered out, swagger stick under his arm.

'Don't normally come out for these things but seeing as it's you…' Sooty Sweep saluted flashily and dropped his voice. 'Far too dangerous but these chaps, they're mad – don't you know? – absolutely thrive on it.'

The last time we met, Sooty had told me I was too pretty to be a policewoman and I told him he wasn't pretty enough for the army. We drank a lot of whisky that night. I hadn't had enough not to push him away when he tried to get his hands inside my dress but he had had enough to fall over and hit his face on a telegraph pole. I half-dragged him to the Royal Albert Sackwater Infirmary where he had eight stitches and a good telling off. The next day he went to Chatham and I to London. We wrote to each other sporadically but it wasn't so much that things fizzled out as we never lit the touch paper. Sooty got married soon after that and soon after that he got unmarried.

Two men jumped out of the back. The older one, carthorse-like with his slow, heavy frame, was wielding long cutters. The younger one was more frisky, like something you might back each way at Doncaster if the going was soft.

'How are they triggered?' I asked and ignored Dodo's, 'The men are triggered?'

'Magnetic and pressure,' he told me.

'So if enough shingle shifted on top of one...' I wondered and Sooty threw his hands up in the air.

'Boom!' he laughed.

This was a new, devil-may-care Sooty that I had never come across before and I found it rather attractive. He looked better with a short back and sides as well, rather than the massive mop he used to sport.

'Gracious!' The same old mortifying Dodo leaped backwards into the older sapper, making him go *ooff* and clutch his middle.

The younger sapper whinnied and his lips curled back as if to take more hay.

'The thing about wire is that if you just snip it, it can spring back and, being razor wire, rip half your face off in the process,' Sooty explained. He still had a white scar on his cheek and, no doubt, told the girls it was a war wound.

'Is that what happened to you?' Dodo asked.

'Something like that,' he lied unashamedly. 'Okay, chaps.'

The men vaulted down off the pavement, landing quite heavily and very heavily on the shingle respectively. The young one held the wire in thick leather gloves. The older one snipped and the wire pinged apart. The young one carefully let the two parts relax.

'But what about the mines?' I asked.

'Leave them to me.' Sooty produced a ball of string and tied one end around Rex's neck.

'He will not go walkies,' Dodo warned.

Sooty gave her that puzzled look that most people give my constable and climbed down the three foot or so of sea wall, trailing the string after him as he joined his men. They had cleared a low tunnel through the first roll of wire and he went through it on his hands and knees, poking in front of him with his swagger stick. He stood on the other side. 'Righty-ho, men, be sure to follow my trail.'

The sappers bent over and trod cautiously after him, keeping close to the string. The fog lifted for a moment and I saw a flock of seagulls wheeling, swooping and landing, wings outstretched, on the head and shoulders of the man.

'Should we not be taking shelter?' Dodo called nervously.

Sooty laughed. 'You'll need to take shelter in Cambridge if this lot goes up.'

'Oh, but that is a long way.' Dodo tugged anxiously at the pink woolly fingers of her pink woolly gloves.

'You can go to the Grand if you like,' I told her. 'They have a shelter in the back garden.'

'What, and desert you, Boss?' Dodo said stoutly. 'Never.'

Sooty was on his knees poking about again. 'Hold it.'

'Hold what?' Dodo asked, gripping my sleeve in both hands.

'He was talking to the men,' I told her. 'Let go.'

She looked down in surprise and released my sleeve as you might let go of a boa constrictor's tail.

Sooty was parting some pebbles with his bare fingers. 'Okay,' he said, just loudly enough for us to catch his words, and planted a little red flag, the sort you put on sandcastles after you've flooded the moat. 'Give that a wide berth, men.'

He mopped his brow with a handkerchief. Things seemed to materialise in his grasp and disappear just as mysteriously.

The men edged around his flag and set to work on the next tangled bale.

'Goodness, they are so brave.' Dodo clapped her hands. 'They should be given medals.'

Or court martialled for planting the damned things in a

residential area in the first place, I pondered, but only mumbled, 'Indeed.'

There was one more bale and two more flags before the way was cleared to the water's edge. Sooty hacked his way through the birds with his swagger stick and they scattered with resentful shrieks. He stood over the body and made a megaphone of his hands.

'I do that,' Dodo reminded me, 'sometimes.'

'Well, he's dead all right,' Sooty called. 'If you follow the string and avoid the flags you should be perfectly safe.'

'Indeed,' I muttered again and climbed down on to the beach.

'Oh, give me a paw, please, Boss,' Dodo begged. 'I am only tiny.'

That much was true. Dodo was well under regulation height and weight but had cheated her way into the force.

I gave her a hand down and scrambled with as much grace as I could – that is, not much – towards the men where they stood looking at the body. It was a solidly built man, his hair not as grey as I had judged through the telescope but more gingery, and it was frizzled like I had ended up with once when Veronica Shrimp overheated the curlers in her salon. It took forever to grow out and she burned my left ear in the process.

The dead man wore a heavy putty-coloured mackintosh, the belt tied at the waist, a brown sweater, trousers and shoes. There was seaweed – bladderwrack, I thought – draped grey-green with swollen nodules around his neck, like one of those wreaths you see pictures of visitors being adorned with in Hawaii.

His face had the colour and pocked texture of unbleached tripe but was not too badly decomposed at first glance. The worst damage appeared to have been wreaked by the gulls. Chunks of flesh had been torn out of his cheeks and his moustached upper lip had been half ripped away, giving him a lopsided grimace as if he could still feel pain.

Most horribly of all, the dead man's eyes had been pecked out, leaving two black craters to stare unseeingly across the ocean, an off-white cord dangling in the back of the left socket, the remnants – I supposed – of the optic nerve.

'Must have been in the sea a good few weeks from the state of him,' Sooty judged.

'I wouldn't have thought so,' I disagreed. 'I'd expect him to be more bloated if he'd had prolonged immersion in salt water. I've seen bodies fished out of the Thames Estuary, rotting and so eaten by eels and dogfish you would hardly know they were human.'

'Lovely,' Sooty commented queasily.

I tugged up the dead man's left sleeve. At first I thought he was wearing an old driving glove but then I realised the ochre wrinkling was his hand. His wristwatch was the sort of thing officers bought for the trenches when fobs fell out of favour. The hands would have stopped for Sidney Grice or March Middleton, giving them a time of death, but this one was ticking away merrily. *Blast you, for your excellent workmanship, Williamsons of Coventry*, I thought, but at least it backed up my theory. Few watches would have stayed wound up for more than a couple of days at a push.

Dodo bent over, seemingly unaffected by the powerful fusty fetor, her face almost close enough to the dead man's to have kissed him.

'He looks a bit like Sylvia Satin's daddy,' she declared, 'only much older and yuckier and with a wonky nose. I saw his picture in the *Sackwater and District Gazette* after he was blown up.'

'They showed him after he was blown up?' Sooty asked in disgust.

'No, they showed him before he was blown up after he was blown up,' Dodo explained.

'We need a stretcher,' I said.

'Well, we don't have any,' Sooty shrugged. 'We're sappers, not ambulance men.'

'Why are you called sappers?' Dodo enquired, standing so suddenly that she nearly smashed her head into the nose of a soldier who was trying to get a look over her shoulder.

'It comes from the French *saper*, to undermine walls to make them collapse,' Sooty explained.

'Well.' Dodo put her fists on her hips. 'That sounds very dangerous and I suggest you stop it immediately.'

'The hospital should be able to lend us one,' I suggested.

'Right, men,' Sooty ordered. 'Nip to the hospital and get one.'

The older of the two put his hands out like he was comparing the weight of two parcels.

'Dunno where it is, sir.'

'Nor me.' The younger man ran an eye over Dodo. 'P'raps this young lady can show us.'

'I am not a lady,' Dodo corrected him.

'All the better,' he winked and they set off back the way we had come.

'It would be safer to walk on a breakwater,' Dodo said as she hopped up on to a wooden groyne. The shingle had heaped almost to the top of it on the northern side.

'Get down,' I told her and she did, but not in the way that either of us planned. Dodo wobbled, toppled and fell, crashing sideways on to the shingle.

I ducked, because that would definitely have saved me if a mine went off.

'Oh,' Dodo howled, covering her face. She took her hands away one by one, opening her eyes likewise. 'Oh,' she breathed. 'I have not been exploded after all.'

'Dashed lucky,' Sooty told her. His eyelids, I noticed sceptically, had hardly been batted. 'But best just follow the string, old girl. And look out for the flags.'

'I shall look out for the flags,' Dodo called back and trotted after the two privates.

'You crummy fraud,' I murmured in Sooty's ear.

He didn't even bother looking indignant but grinned boyishly. 'Well, you couldn't expect us to announce to the world that the beach isn't really mined,' he whispered back. 'And we didn't have any to waste on a dump like Sackwater.'

26

THE JACKDAW AND THE HEDGEHOG

quite like searching people. You can't be a police officer and not be nosy. And it's surprising what some people carry. I have come across a baited mousetrap in a man's breast pocket and a decaying jackdaw in a housewife's handbag.

This man was rather more prosaic. He had a clean, if soggy, pressed and folded handkerchief in his right trouser pocket and a Yale house key in the left.

A crab scuttled crabwise from under the dead man's back and I wondered if it had been feeding on him too. It depressed me to think how we all become a larder for the lowliest of creatures.

There was a leather wallet inside his tweed jacket and inside that was a one-pound and a ten-shilling note; a creased photograph of a rather striking middle-aged couple, the man with frizzy hair; and one important document – an ID card. The ink had run a bit but still blurrily identified him as Grevan Martin Eric Bone of Harvest Mansions, Sea Road, Sackwater, male aged seventy-two, a retired clockmaker and married. There was also a penny bus ticket dated a week ago.

In the jacket I found all the accoutrements of a pipe-smoker – a soft pigskin tobacco pouch with sodden ribbons of what smelled like whiskey flake; a box of Captain Webb matches, the heads rendered useless by immersion; a pipe-knife with a flat end for tamping; and a hedgehog, a spiky metal acorn with a handle for reaming out the pipe bowl. Everything you might need except the actual pipe. From the remnants of dottle in the outer breast pocket, it would habitually have been stored in there.

He had on a brown sweater and under that a white shirt with a plain blue tie. Obviously, he would be stripped and searched more thoroughly at the mortuary.

'I think that's all I can do here,' I said as Dodo returned, weaving carefully back to the waterfront and leading the two sappers with a canvas stretcher flapping between them.

The two sappers took hold of the body by the coat at one end and shoes at the other and heaved him on to the stretcher with obvious and understandable distaste.

'Hold it.'

I looked up to see Toby Gregson crouching on the pavement, armed with his camera. Sooty turned to show his scar and jutted his chin. The two men grinned like they were on their annual holidays, Dodo put a hand to her flaming thatch and I chose that moment to sneeze.

'Lovely,' Toby waved. 'We'll get another without the corpse when you get back.'

'Actually,' Sooty remembered, 'this is a military zone and it is an offence to photograph it without written authorisation.'

'Mr Gregson is a police photographer,' I bluffed because, although he had helped us on a number of occasions, Toby had no official standing.

'Still a civilian,' Sooty objected, going all military on us.

'Perhaps I could get one of you standing up here and staring out to sea, Captain,' Toby called, unrepentant at the number of wartime regulations he was transgressing. 'Courageous Royal Engineer, guarding our coast, that kind of thing – perhaps a bit about how you were wounded.'

'Oh, I can help you with that,' I murmured but Sooty was

pushing ahead, scrambling through the wire and oblivious to having trodden on one of his own red flags.

'Don't like to boast.' Sooty straightened his battle blouse as he hurried towards his appointment with fame and glory.

27

A CIGARETTE AND ONE PIPE PROBLEM

recognised the voices as I opened the door. Sharkey was leaning on the desk with one elbow like he was waiting for a pint at a bar.

'Well, you don't sound very British to me, chum,' he was telling Captain Sultana.

Captain was puce and clenching his fists at his side.

'Is there a problem?' I asked, shutting the door behind me.

'*Għala zobbi*. I got a letter this morning telling me to report here,' the captain told me, 'and this *ħanżir* tells me I am not British.'

'Who you calling a hand's-ear?' my colleague challenged. 'And what's it mean?'

'Who are you calling chum?' the captain retaliated.

'*Ħanżir* is Maltese for gentleman,' I lied before the captain revealed that it meant *pig*.

'We had reports of a suspicious-looking man with a German accent,' Sharkey told me, 'and when we picked this character up, he refused to show his papers and said his name was Raison.'

'Sultana,' Captain shouted. 'I send the card back because they are misspelling my name.'

'I can vouch for this gentleman,' I told my colleague. 'He is Captain Carmelo Sultana and has been a British citizen since before you were born. He served in the Royal Navy in the Great War and was decorated three times for bravery.'

Sharkey clicked his fingers. 'He's the geezer you live on that boat with.'

I was not going to trouble to explain our relationship to Old Scrapie. He would put his own grubby interpretation on the arrangement whatever I said.

'And while you are here, Captain,' I said, 'if you would like to come to my office, you might be able to help me with my enquiries.'

'Madonna! How do you work with that man?' The captain asked when I had installed him in a chair with the door closed.

'As little as possible.'

I rolled a cigarette while my visitor lit his pipe. Some people complain about the smell of a Navy Flake. It is soaked in rum and molasses and gives off a heavy smoke but I love it. It reminds me of my maternal grandfather, a sometimes foolish but always kind man.

'We found a body on the beach this morning,' I announced. 'Could it have washed ashore from a boat?'

The captain puffed thoughtfully. Men always look wiser with a pipe and I suppose that is why the habit is so frowned upon for women. You can't have them looking clever. It would fly in the face of nature.

'It is not likely,' he decided. 'A boat would have troubles getting close with the mines.' That minefield was not a fantasy, I knew. 'And there are wires across the bay to stop surface vessels or submarines getting to the shore.'

'He can't have got through all that barbed wire on the beach.' I sucked on my cigarette, wondering if I looked like Joan Crawford in *Chained* when she smoked a Lucky Strike and deciding I probably didn't. The captain with his long pigtail and luxurious beard would have made a very unconvincing Clark Gable.

'Even when the tide is coming in, the currents sweep southwards,' the captain pointed out.

I knew that from the way the shingle heaped against the

groynes and from paper hats and picnic remnants that drifted down from Anglethorpe on to our shore.

'What if he fell from the cliffs?' I suggested. 'He would be on the shore side of the wire and north of the beach.'

The captain puffed and pondered.

'I will make a sailor of you yet,' he smiled with crinkled eyes and I simpered foolishly because Captain Sultana knew of no greater compliment than that. 'I had a letter from a major in Adam's regiment,' he announced. 'He cannot tell me where my son is but at least I know that he is alive and well.'

'I'm glad,' I said, aware that Carmelo was watching me closely and that he must have been wondering – why would I not be?

28

THE TWENTY-NINE STEPS

Harvest Mansions was a rather grand name for a nondescript block of flats and a rare example of Sackwater's brief and unenthusiastic flirtation with modern architecture. What was supposed to be art deco, however, was an ungainly cube of grey concrete with disproportionately large flush-fitted steel-framed windows.

Inside was even less inviting, the plain plastered walls stained by years of condensation in the ill-ventilated lobby and a concrete stairway going up at the back on either side. If this was a prison, I thought, the Howard League for Penal Reform might have campaigned to improve it. A central board pointed in alternate directions with numbers at the blunt end of each arrow. I followed the one for apartment five and trudged up. Fourteen steps led to a landing with a door at each end and another fourteen took me to the top floor, a stiff metal door and a short corridor.

A tall elegant elderly lady answered my ringing the bell and I recognised her at once from the photograph in her husband's wallet, though obviously she was older and her face had been whitened by a heavy application of powder.

'Mrs Edwina Bone?' I asked and she bowed her head in acknowledgement.

'You must be Inspector Church.' She furrowed her brow. 'Your sergeant didn't tell me you were a woman.' She tossed her unnaturally auburn hair as if it had been her achievement. 'Good for you.'

'I didn't have much say in the matter,' I observed and she quarter-smiled.

'I meant your rank,' she said. 'As you well know. If anything worthwhile is come of this wicked war, it may be that our sex gets the recognition it deserves and men realise they need us after all.'

'I seem to remember being told that last time.' I shook her hand warmly.

'I have a feeling we will not go back to our kitchen sinks quite so easily when this one is over,' Mrs Bone forecast with greater faith than I possessed. 'Come inside, Inspector.'

I stepped into a small internal porch and she opened the inner door and our world was instantly transformed. Those windows, so uninspiring from outside, filled the room with clear morning light.

'Eric loved the view from here.' Edwina Bone waved a hand towards the ocean and, seeing my slight puzzlement, explained, 'He hated being called Grevan.'

Personally, I never saw the attraction of the sea around England. When Adam took me to meet his family in Malta, the Mediterranean glittered in every shade of blue and dazzled us with silver shafts of sun bouncing off the surface. The North Sea is cold and stormy and varies from brown to black and if it's lightened with white crests, that's because it's rough.

'I am sorry we had such bad news for you,' I said.

Superintendent Vesty had preceded me to break it to her. He had played golf with Eric Bone apparently and knew Edwina from their annual dinners.

'I believe you risked your life to recover his body,' Mrs Bone said and I could not deny it without breaking the Official Secrets Act, besides which, we thought we had at the time.

'My constable came with me,' I told her because Dodo at least deserved some credit for that. 'It was difficult to see in the mist so we were hoping your husband might still be alive.'

Mrs Bone guided me into an armchair and sat in another, facing mine at an angle so we could still look out.

Give me a country view every time, I thought with half an eye on the bleakness.

'Poor Eric,' she said. 'He was in the war, you know.'

'He must have been too old to have been conscripted,' I calculated.

Eric Bone, I knew from his identity card, was seventy-two, which would have made him forty-one before the Great War even began.

'Eric volunteered and only then because our Peter did,' Mrs Bone told me sadly. 'He had some foolish notion that he could protect Peter but in the end it was Peter who died, carrying his wounded father to safety.'

'Oh, how awful.'

Mrs Bone inhaled deeply. 'Eric never forgave himself. He never spoke about it but I would hear him talking to Peter in the night, weeping and saying *I told you to leave me, son*.' She breathed out through slightly parted lips. 'That is why we bought this place,' she said.

'I'm not sure I follow you,' I said. Being built in the twenties, the apartment could not hold memories of Peter for them. Or were they trying to escape those?

'Eric was buried alive,' Mrs Bone said. 'Ever since then he had a terror of being trapped. With these big windows and the open views, he felt safe. We never closed the curtains and he kept a lamp on by the bed. Then came the blackout. We had to comply, of course, but Eric would get panic attacks and have to look out of the window. Sometimes he forgot to turn the light out first and he was virtually accused of signalling to the enemy but Ian Vesty sorted that out for us.'

'Have you any idea how your husband ended up on the beach?'

'Well, he couldn't swim and he hated boats,' Mrs Bone told me. 'But Eric liked to walk up to Jacob's Point and I can only assume he fell off the cliffs.' She patted her hair. 'But how he managed to do that I have no idea.' She plucked at her brow. 'He knew that they are undermined in places and never left the path.'

'Do you think it possible...' I hesitated.

'That he jumped off?' Mrs Bone completed my thought. 'No, Inspector, I do not.' She sat up very straight. 'Eric was a devout Roman Catholic. He believed that suicide was a grave sin and that he would go to hell. The one thing my husband lived for was the hope of him and me being reunited with Peter in heaven. No matter how unhappy Eric was, he would *never* have killed himself.'

My next question was even more difficult.

'I have to ask you this, Mrs Bone, but did your husband have any enemies?'

Edwina Bone opened her mouth to reply then seemed to change her mind. 'Someone who might have pushed him off?'

'I have to consider every possibility.'

She flipped her hands up. 'If anyone did, it would have been me.' She grimaced. 'Eric was a lovely man but when he got a bee in his bonnet he could drive a saint to distraction. He absolutely detested Chamberlain, said he should be put on trial as a traitor and shot.'

I smiled. 'I know a few people who might have agreed with him.'

'Quite so,' she told me. 'But Eric would rant about it for hours on end. Then there was the French. He was convinced they will turn tail and run the moment the Germans decide to attack. Oh, goodness, when he got the bit between his teeth there was no stopping him.' Mrs Bone folded her hands neatly in her lap. 'But enemies? None that would want to murder him.'

'He hadn't had any big arguments lately or got into money problems?'

Mrs Bone shook her head but did not expand on her response.

'So not murder, not suicide, not an accident,' I pondered.

'The last must be the most likely option,' Mrs Bone conceded. 'Perhaps he saw an injured gull and went to try to help it and slipped. He was very soft-hearted and couldn't bear to see anyone or anything suffering.'

'Your husband smoked a pipe.'

'What of it?'

'It wasn't on him, but just in case we come across it...' I watched a seagull hurl itself towards the window but wheel off just in time to avoid it. '...what sort was it?'

'A meerschaum carved with the face of a woman,' she said. 'Eric used to joke that she looked like Betty Grable.' She smiled sadly. 'He loved that pipe.'

'Why didn't you report your husband missing, Mrs Bone?' I watched her reaction to that carefully and her eyes fell, more in sorrow, I thought, than shiftiness.

'I didn't know he was.' Mrs Bone mulled that puzzling fact over before remembering her duties as a hostess and making a valiant effort to perk up. 'Would you like a cup of tea, Inspector?'

I would have loved a cup of tea when I arrived.

'Thank you, but I must be getting back to the station,' I declined regretfully. 'If you could just explain—'

She upped her bid. 'With a chocolate digestive.'

'That would be lovely,' I succumbed.

'Put the kettle on then.' Mrs Bone waved imperiously and I trotted off more obediently than Pooky ever did. I made a better cup of tea than she did, too, but Mrs Bone only had one biscuit left and I felt obliged to let her have it.

'If you could just explain—' I began again.

29

CHARLES DARWIN AND

THE LIGHTNESS OF LIGHTS

Tubby Gretham was hard at work and play when I arrived at the morgue. He had his hands almost up to the elbows inside the dead man's chest. The body had been sliced from neck to groin and the breastplate sawn through so that the ribs had sprung apart, holding the chest and stomach wide open.

'Betty,' he greeted me, with the happy grin of a man indulging in his favourite pursuit. 'You are just in time. Fill the sink for me.'

I went over. 'You've half-filled it already,' I observed. The porcelain bowl was stocked like a butcher's bin with a whole liver resting on glistening coils of intestines.

'Oh, just dump them on the draining board,' Tubby shrugged.

I hesitated. I am not especially squeamish but it was difficult to see how I could do it without being covered in slime and gore. There were heavy rubber gloves on a nearby table but one of those would not protect me much.

'Got a spare apron?' I asked.

'Oh, for goodness' sake,' Tubby tutted at my squeamishness. 'Just let me do it.' The doctor extracted his hands with a sucking squelch and marched over, sweeping up mounds of innards to plonk them on the drainer.

I chose a much-too-big glove. It's difficult getting a glove on with one hand without using my teeth to hold the cuff and I knew all too well what those gloves had been used for. I rinsed the clotted residue from the sink and turned on the tap.

'Now.' Tubby wielded the sort of knife that wouldn't look amiss in a slaughterhouse and deftly sliced through the windpipe, tugging it out like a thick root in a flower bed with accompanying rips. 'There we are.' He held up his trophy proudly, like a hunter posing for a photograph of something he has just slain. The windpipe was long and ridged down to two dark sagging spongy sacks. 'Heavy smoker,' he commented, 'but light lungs.'

'In what way?' I asked, hoping he didn't think that question as stupid as I feared it might be. Tubby was a kind man and an excellent doctor but he had little patience with fools who, in his opinion, formed a large majority of his fellow East Anglians.

'Good question,' he enthused, and I got that little glow I had when Sister Millicent read out my essay on Edible Toadstools. It was not my fault some of the girls got ill in the woods the next day. They can't have been paying attention to my descriptions. He marched over to the sink and turned the tap off. 'Now watch carefully.' He lowered his specimen into the sink, holding the pipe up and out of the water. 'Butchers do not call them *lights* for nothing.'

'The lungs float,' I said. 'So they must be full of air. So...' I tried to click my fingers but the gauntlet proved too much of a handicap and I ended up making the sort of pathetic flopping noise that Dodo can manage in one of her better attempts. '... he didn't drown.'

Tubby nodded approvingly. 'Just so. Fresh water can go into the bloodstream because of osmotic pressure.' That was something to do with solutes in solvents, I vaguely remembered, but decided to look it up later rather than show my ignorance. 'But saline stays in the lungs because it is almost exactly the same concentration in the sea as it is in blood. Which is why many scientists believe

124

that we came from the sea originally. Those who take the Book of Genesis more literally, however—'

'So he was dead before he was submerged,' I broke in before the doctor launched into a Darwinist diatribe.

Tubby sniffed at my rudeness. 'Quite so.' He lifted the lungs out and laid them on a steel table top. 'Let's take a look inside.' Tubby selected a hefty pair of scissors and snipped along the windpipe, the rings of cartilage parting to reveal the inside. 'Clean,' he said. 'Now come and look in his mouth.' He led me back to the body, white sunken eyes staring blindly like fish past its best. The mouth was open halfway, a thick grey moustache on the torn remnants of his upper lip. 'See?' Tubby took a spoon, bent up at right angles at the neck. He lowered it into the mouth like you might take honey from a jar but brought it out full of grey grit.

'Sand,' I said, because I felt I ought to contribute something.

Tubby tapped it into a glass jar. 'Looks like local sand to me.' He screwed the cap back on. 'But I have a geologist friend at London University. He should be able to be more definite.'

'Was there any in the stomach?' I asked.

Tubby shook his head. 'You missed me flushing that out.'

'Oh, what a shame,' I said, and he glanced at me sideways. 'Was there anything in it?'

'Nothing much,' Tubby shrugged. 'He'd had a spot of lunch a couple of hours before death. No alcohol.'

'So, if he didn't inhale or swallow any sand,' I clarified, 'it probably just got forced into his mouth as he was washed ashore dead.'

'Probably,' Tubby agreed.

I walked around the table. What empty husks we become in the end. 'Any idea on the cause of death?'

'Yes.' Tubby was slicing through a lobe of lung with that big knife again.

'And are you going to share that with me?'

'It's not conclusive,' Tubby warned. He was a highly intelligent man and that was his greatest vice. Where most people would be happy with a clue and the obvious explanation, Tubby would think up a dozen different theories and have to consider them all at length and then expound upon them at lengthier.

'Well, let's take it as a provisional diagnosis,' I suggested.

'Well.' Tubby wagged his hand side to side in a sort of don't-say-I-didn't-warn-you way. 'It's just a theory.' He lifted the dead man's head and there was a dent in the back of it – three or four inches in diameter and very roughly oval.

'Depressed fracture,' he told me, because it was his job, though I could have worked that out.

'Blunt object,' I said automatically, because we are trained to say that.

'Or damaged in the fall,' Tubby suggested. 'Although…' he paused thoughtfully.

'There are no rocks at the bottom of the cliffs,' I completed his sentence. Several lives would be too short for all of Tubby's what-ifs.

'Who mentioned cliffs?' he asked suspiciously.

'It's just a hunch,' I assured him and shook the glove off my hand.

'Ham sandwich,' Tubby said.

'And a pint?' I asked hopefully, because I was off duty in half an hour.

'No.' Tubby pointed to a bucket in the far corner and I went over. It was half-full of what looked and smelled like it was vomit, which, I supposed, was pretty much what it was – except that it had never been vomited. 'He had a ham sandwich for lunch.'

30

LYONS, A RABBIT AND SHEEP

t was windy and drizzly again and I didn't fancy a walk along the prom so I went to the Lyons tea shop in Mafeking Gardens. I had quite fancied a ham sandwich when Tubby first mentioned it, but I went off the idea when I saw what it had become.

I had curried meat and rice. I wasn't sure what the meat was and neither was the nippy – mutton, we speculated – but it was quite tender and tasty and not too hot. March Middleton, having lived in India, loved spicy food but I had been raised in a household where flavouring began and ended with salt and pepper. It was not bad value at eight pence washed down with a three-and-a-half-pence pot of tea, I reflected, especially as you were not allowed to tip the waitresses.

A well-dressed woman sat with her son, who looked like he was about four years old and was entranced by the smiling man on the next table showing him how to make a rabbit from a handkerchief – a lovely scene, except that I knew the man.

It was Simnal Cranditch and he had an unsavoury record, to say the least.

'Perhaps I could take your son across the road for an ice cream,' Cranditch was suggesting.

'Oh yes, please.' The little boy clapped his hands.

'That's ever so kind,' the woman grinned at them both.

I put down my knife and fork in a V – so that nobody would clear my plate, thinking I had finished – and went over. Cranditch was making his rabbit hop around the rim of his bowl of soup, much to the little boy's hilarity.

'Excuse me, madam, do you know this man?' I enquired and her smile soured.

'What's it to you?'

'I am an off-duty police officer.' I showed her my warrant card.

'Lord, we must be desperate.' She gawped at my pinned-up sleeve.

'I haven't done anything,' Cranditch protested.

'You haff,' the little boy insisted, 'you haff made a wabbit.'

'This man has criminal convictions for interfering with children,' I told her quietly.

'A sex fiend?' she shrieked. 'Why didn't you say? Why isn't he in prison?' She grabbed her son's arm as the manageress came hurrying over.

'Is there a problem, madam?'

'I'll say there is,' the woman stormed. 'Filling this place with dangerous preverts.' This did not seem a good time to correct her pronunciation, I decided, as the woman gathered her things, flinging stuff into her handbag and wrapping herself and her son in layers of wool. 'Come on, Grub, we're leaving.'

Grub? What sort of name was that for a child and was he named after a maggot or a meal?

'Don't trouble.' Simnal Cranditch got to his feet and slapped some coins on the table. 'I'm going.' His eyes bored into mine. 'Damn you,' he breathed. 'Well, you won't have to worry about me again. I'm off tomorrow.'

'Off where?' I said.

'Mind your own damned business.' Simnal Cranditch stalked out of the café.

'And you needn't think I'll be paying for this,' the woman hissed, sitting back down, arms folded defiantly.

'I think the gentleman has paid for you,' the manageress said in some confusion.

'I'm sorry,' I said to them both. 'I was trying to protect the child.'

'I'll protect my own son in future, thank you very much,' the woman sulked, and I refrained from observing that she hadn't been doing the best of jobs when I arrived.

I paid for my lunch and left. There was probably still another cup in that pot, I reflected gloomily, and made my way back up High Road East.

Georgie came hurrying down it.

'Oh, Betty – Inspector.' She waved a hand, knocking her little blue sideways hat even more sideways. 'They said you might be having lunch here. I'm so sorry, but he's wandered off again.'

I was beginning to think the tender-hearted shark might be right when he suggested Mr Orchard would be better locked away – or at least in a home where they could keep an eye on him.

'Any idea—' I began to ask.

'He's been talking a lot about going up the hill,' she told me. 'He used to go walking all over them with my mother but he isn't really up to it now.'

'Well, there are only two hills round here,' I told her unnecessarily. 'If you go back to the station, Constable Bank-Anthony should be there and I'm sure he will be delighted to accompany you to Fury Hill.'

'I'm sure.' Even in her agitated state, Georgie managed a faint twinkle at that thought. 'Thank you,' she said, 'and I will try to get somebody to look after him from now on.'

'I'll find Constable Box. He's on the town beat and he's not difficult to spot,' I told her. 'We'll go to the cliffs.'

I hated those damned cliffs and would much rather have

129

headed inland. It was just that Mr Orchard was much more likely to have a mishap on the steep and slippery tracks toward Jacob's Point and, if he had, I did not want Georgie to be the one to find him.

31

LOT'S WIFE AND THE RAT'S NEST

The House of Horrors stood at the top of Spectre Lane on Jacob's Point. It had enjoyed some success before the Great War with its depictions of murderers and their victims in an attempt to emulate Madame Tussaud's, but the plaster models were clumsy and suffered in comparison with Rafferty's Museum of Terrors in Anglethorpe, which had moving mannequins and a ghost train. Since we had discovered a genuine horror last September, the house had reopened to a ghoulish public, but the ravages of the weather, woodworm and dry rot soon led to it being boarded up again.

'When I think of tha' poor girl.' Box shook his great head sadly.

I tried not to think of her but it was impossible not to remember how I found her. She filled my dreams on many a troubled night.

'She is one of the reasons we do our job.' I paused to let my constable catch his breath. 'To bring her killer to justice.'

'Think we will?' Box looked at me doubtfully.

'One day.'

We both knew who had murdered the girl and it left a bitter taste that he still lived free and prospered.

We trudged on. It had been quite a nice day when we started off but the higher we got, the more a pleasant breeze became a gusty wind and it had brought a nasty thin drizzle with it.

At the top of the promontory there was a wonderful view of the River Angle estuary and the massive Martello tower across the water. It had been built to fend off Napoleon's armies and we could only hope it could perform that function against Adolf's barbarian hordes. There was an ack-ack gun fixed to the roof now. There had been no evidence of activity from the gunners on the day we were bombed but they had shown exemplary aggression towards a barrage balloon that had slipped its moorings in February and, spurred on by this success, brought down one of our battle bombers, killing all the crew on its way back to Norfolk the following night.

As usual, we had nothing to compete with that. St Alvery's Monastery stood out of sight in a depression ten yards back from where the land fell into the sea, but had not been in use since the last monk left some twenty-five years ago to minister to the sick and dying at Mons before becoming one of the latter. Now the site stood along a path strewn with razor wire and behind a high wall, topped with more of the same. *That should stop the Nazis from being able to pray,* I mused as I gazed towards it.

Our most impressive visible structure was a cairn on the slope maybe thirty yards from the edge. Nobody was sure how or why it was started but walkers would often add to the pillar of rocks with one from the many scattered about. They were flint, I thought, from Suffolk though not a local stone. Legend had it that they had been brought by a flock of eagles to help St Alvery build his first hermitage. I have my own opinion on the likelihood of this but I knew better than to argue with legends. I had been threatened with expulsion from Roedene Abbey for questioning whether they truly owned the foreskin of Jesus, especially as dozens of churches claimed to have it and surely the infant would only have had one?

The cairn stood about seven foot tall and had been named 'Lot's Wife'. Some said it went back to the days of the ancient magic and whoever touched it would be cursed. A person or persons unknown had made a wide circle of stones around the pillar as a warning to the unwary, unaware, it seems, that the unwary would be unaware of the dangers anyway. They were more likely to come a cropper in the ravine that ran from further up the slope, cleaving the cliff edge. In heavy rain it became a torrenting stream, but usually it was empty except for a few thorny shrubs and tossed-in rubbish.

'I become a copper,' Box began conversationally and apropos of nothing, 'for my mum is a wrong'un and I am determined to arrest her.'

The devotion of Suffolk folk to the present tense could sometimes be confusing but I managed to work that one out.

'And did you?'

Box kicked an old tin can aside.

'She do goo die while I am still trainin' so I never get the satisfaction. My father was a foreman.'

This was very chatty for Box. He was a man of few words as a rule and people tended to think this was because he had few thoughts but his still waters ran a little deeper than I had first given him credit for.

'Is that him?' I pointed.

'My father?'

'Mr Orchard.'

A man was sitting on Gabriel's Table, a long flat rock where Alvery was said to have stood with the intention of throwing himself off the cliffs before the archangel appeared with a sword of flame and forced him back from the edge. The celestial being commanded him in a voice of thunder which, legend has it, the whole town heard, to build a chapel there.

'Can't see from here with all this wet wind in my eye but he must be chill to the marrer,' Box commented.

'We'd better see if he's all right, whoever he is,' I said and turned off the grassy track.

At that moment, there was a howl. Even in broad daylight and chilled though I already was, it chilled me more. There was something inhuman in its long, high wavering pitch, something weird and unearthly cutting through the wind. Box stopped. He was not a nervous man as a rule but he twisted side to side uneasily.

'Wolf,' he declared without even the aid of an identification chart in the station, but I had not time to inform him that the last reliable sighting of a wolf in Suffolk was about seven hundred years ago and even the last unreliable one was long before either of us was born.

'Come on.' I sprinted off, stumbling and slithering but just managing to keep on my feet up the hill.

The man's head was tilted back now and, as it turned to the left, I saw his mouth agape even after the wail had dipped and died, carried past us by the Arctic wind gusting inland. I'm not a bad runner. I used to be good but then I used to be younger and have both arms. Box was like an ocean liner, stately in his movements and slow to come to a standstill but hopeless at acceleration.

He lumbered after me, gasping a helpful, 'Have a care, ma'am. He may be a mad maniac like in tha' film what's-its-name with what's-his-name.'

'I'll bear that in mind,' I panted as I approached the man. 'Hello,' I called and the head turned a little further. 'Mr Orchard?'

The head turned away to face out to sea again. I was almost upon him now and tried to stop but my brakes failed on the wet rocky ground and I skidded ungracefully on.

'Damn,' I breathed, sprawling over the table, stump flapping and good arm flailing and, with nothing to grasp, striking Mr Orchard firmly in the back.

Garrison Orchard let out a yelp. Compared to the howl, this was feeble stuff.

'Are you all right?' I asked, not sure if I was myself. My hand was barked and my stockings were shredded to reveal unattractively skinned knees. I got up to a kneeling position with as much decorum as I could muster, which wasn't very much at all.

'What?' Mr Orchard managed, suddenly rigid with shock.

'I'm sorry to startle you. Are you all right?' I crawled across the rock, trying not to put any pressure on my knees.

'What?' He cupped his right ear as I swung my legs around to sit beside him. 'Have you come to read the meter?'

'Use your hearing aid,' I shouted, pointing to my ears and then, for luck, to his.

'What?' We had come a long way for this conversation in conditions that, if they improved, could be described as *dismal,* and I was rather hoping for more.

'Hearing aid,' I bellowed and tapped the box.

'Just a minute.' He opened the box. It was about the size of a small portable radio and I recognised the contents as an acousticon, though not the latest model, and regretted my advice immediately. Garrison Orchard's hearing aid was a confusion of wires sprouting from the battery and into various Bakelite devices. 'Just another minute.' He reeled out a cord and tried to unravel it, reminding me of the one time my father took me fishing. I ended up with what a nearby proper angler described accurately as a *rat's nest* of line and got a hook caught in my ear, the one that Dodo shot a clipping out of in our pursuit of the so-called Suffolk Vampire. While I was pondering this, Mr Orchard was pulling jack plugs out and reinserting them, as far as I could judge, into the same holes.

'It's under the stairs,' he told me.

He had an earphone clamped to his head now and was looking more like Maggie at the exchange with every damp, blowy moment. 'What?' he repeated into a large brown electronic biscuit. 'Oh, this is for you.'

Garrison Orchard handed me the microphone and I turned it so the slots faced me.

'Are you all right?' I tried again.

Mr Orchard puzzled over that for so long I was beginning to wonder if I had spoken into the wrong part. 'Yes,' he decided eventually. 'Are you the man who sold me that lawn-mowing machine? It has never worked.'

I have been mistaken for a man on the phone occasionally, especially if the line is bad and I have to shout, but never face-to-face before. I occasionally worried about losing my looks but I hadn't realised I had already mislaid them.

'Why did you cry out?' I asked, and he cogitated this with the air of an innumerate child being given a problem in algebra.

'Did I?' He tapped the earpiece.

'Yes – as if you were in pain.'

'Oh no,' Mr Orchard told me. 'I have never even been to Spain. Have you come to measure me?'

'No. You know me, Mr Orchard. I'm Betty Church.'

'Why?' he puzzled.

'Georgina has been worried,' I told him.

'Dash it,' he muttered, ripping the headset off. 'Battery's dead.'

'I think we need to get you home,' I said as loudly and clearly as I could. 'Box.' I looked about to see my constable on his haunches a short distance away and nearer to the cliff edge than I would have liked to stand. 'What are you up to?'

'I think you need to see this, ma'am,' Box told me and I didn't need a great proportion of my detective skills to suspect that he was not talking about the scenery.

32

THE RULES OF ASSOCIATION FOOTBALL
AND A FLOCK OF EAGLES

left Mr Orchard sitting on Gabriel's Table and trying to pack his equipment away. Rather like soil from a hole, there seemed to be too much to go back in again. He pushed a coil of wire in one side and a loop popped out the other.

'What is it?' I went over.

Box pointed into an oval hollow in the ground about five foot by three, and there, between the larger rocks, was a bed of pebbles with a smooth stone about the size of a coconut nesting among them with fine ginger threads in a clump on its surface.

'Could be off a rabbit but tha' don't look like fur to me,' he said, sucking on his teeth, and I crouched beside him, accidentally clinking our helmets together.

Box looked shocked and shuffled aside.

'Have you touched it?'

'Not yet, ma'am,' Box replied. 'Do you want me to?'

'No.' I shot my hand out protectively and nearly overbalanced into my constable's lap, grabbing his shoulder to save myself.

Box sprang up, having had more than enough of my lascivious behaviour. I doubted even Mrs Vera Harrison's unmentionable unmentionables had caused him that much embarrassment.

'Found something interesting?' Mr Orchard appeared at my side.

'Tha' stone,' Box replied, the flapping of his cloak startling a pigeon that had been coming in to land. I wondered if it could be one of Sammy Sterne, the sweet shop owner's, birds. Because he still held a German passport, Sammy had been ordered to hand them all over before being interned as an enemy alien and I had a suspicion he had been less efficient in his task than the authorities had been in rounding up him and his wife.

'What stone?'

How come Mr Orchard could hear that when Box hadn't even raised his voice?

'The one shaped like a little football,' Box told him, though I thought it would have been better suited to a rugby pitch.

'A what?' Mr Orchard cupped his ear.

'Football.'

'Don't touch it,' I shouted, sticking my left arm out, forgetting briefly how deficient it was, but Mr Orchard was sidestepping me with an agility that did great credit to his decrepit frame. His foot hinged back and whipped forward with a skill Cliff Parker would have been hard-pressed to equal when he scored twice for Portsmouth in last year's FA cup final.

'No!' I yelled, scrambling after it as helplessly as Alex Scott, the keeper for Wolves.

'Goal!' Mr Orchard raised his arms in triumph, boxing me on the ear in the process. When I had time, I would ask people what they had against that part of my body. Sister Millicent was overly fond of clipping it in chapel.

I stretched forward and almost got a fingertip to the missile as it arced away, but I was all too aware how close we were to the cliff edge and I did not want to follow the rock as it flew over, rose gracefully, hesitated like it was thinking of coming back, then dropped like the stone it actually was.

*

We trudged back down the hill, Mr Orchard hugely buoyed by his sporting prowess, seemingly oblivious to a heavy downpour. He used to play in the North Suffolk Coastal League, he told us proudly.

'Then you will know Stubby Box,' Box said. 'No relation.'

'I do not believe he was my relation,' Mr Orchard pondered, his hearing apparently completely restored by his achievement.

We saw the old man home.

'Oh, thank you, and I am so sorry.' Georgie settled her father into an upright chair by the coal fire.

We left her to make him a cup of tea.

'There's blood on tha' stone,' Box said wonderingly.

'Not any more,' I reflected.

'Where d'you s'pose it come from, ma'am?'

'I would say it was human,' I said. 'I only wish I could have taken it back to the mortuary.'

And I would have liked a chance to inspect that hair more closely. I was almost certain that it was gingery.

'Was a good goal though,' Box ruminated as we made our way briskly back to the station.

'Rubbish,' I scoffed. 'He was miles offside.'

33

THE RIGHTNESS AND WRONGNESS OF RAIN

Dodo was quiet but I did not find that restful.

'If this is going to rain for ever—' she began.

'It isn't,' I assured her, though it had felt it might for the last couple of days and I wondered which chauffeured committee chairman had decided that policemen must never carry umbrellas.

'The *Daily Sketch* says it is, Boss.'

'The *Sketch* said we were in a new ice age in January,' I reminded her.

We crossed the road, Dodo looking left and right three times each way, though a glance would have told her there was nothing coming.

'If it is though…' She chewed her thoughts carefully. '…will we have to build an ark?'

'You can, if you like,' I said. 'I shall stay on *Cressida*.'

I was not sure that Captain Sultana's home would actually float but I was not going to fret about that just yet.

Dodo jumped, feet together, over the gutter, clutching at a redundant lamp post to stop herself skidding over.

'Behave,' I scolded just as Mrs Whitehouse came shuffling out of her house, carrying a wrinkled old shopping bag.

'Good morning, Aunty Josie,' Dodo greeted her.

Aunty Josie? I fumed silently, but Mrs Whitehouse accepted the title without a blink.

'Good morning, Dodo,' she smiled wearily. 'How are you?'

Dodo? This was going too far. Members of the public do not address officers by their first names. If an officer is in uniform on official business, his or her own mother should address him or her by rank – though, of course, mine never would.

'Where is Sylvia?' I butted in before they got even more familiar.

'At home in the kitchen where it do be warmer,' Mrs Whitehouse told me, 'playin' with her dolls. The ladies of the Women's Institute do collect them for her.'

'Is she all right to be left alone?' I asked and Mrs Whitehouse went to tap my arm before remembering it wasn't there.

'Course she is. She do be a sensible girl.'

Not so sensible as not to go diving for turtles, I thought.

'How has she been?' I asked.

'Oh, she's as right as rain,' Mrs Whitehouse assured me. 'Take it all in her stride, she do.'

'What is right about rain?' Dodo wondered and I was glad to note that it had taken umbrage and stopped falling.

'Take it better than I do, she do,' Mrs Whitehouse confessed. 'I'm in a terrible state when I learn what happen.' She shook her head sadly. 'Sleep so bad, have such bad dreams, my old doctor give me a draught to put in my cocoa, he do.'

'Do you mind if we go in and see her?' I asked and Mrs Whitehouse shrugged.

'She's glad of your company, I'm sure. The key's on a string.'

I had lectured members of the public many times about hanging the key inside their letter boxes or placing them under their doormats and been largely ignored, the general opinion being that these were ingenious hiding places. One of the few people to take my advice was Timothy Hart, a reclusive unemployed harpsichord restorer, whose front door was smashed down the next week because the burglar thought he must have something valuable to have taken such an extraordinary precaution.

'Oh, what a clever idea.' Dodo clapped her gloves. 'Then you can never lose it.'

Mrs Whitehouse plodded on, leaning over her empty bag like it was full of dumb-bells, and we went on to number seventeen. It was a nice semi-detached house, Victorian and, like most properties in Sackwater, a faded relic of the town's never-quite-achieved grandeur. The knocker was cast in the shape of a lady in frilly skirts over a crinoline but it was so worn by use that it looked more like a bruised pineapple now.

'Have you forgotten about the key, Boss?' Dodo enquired and then, like I wouldn't be able to hear her if she dropped a quarter of an octave, 'I hope the explosion did not explode part of my beloved Inspector's brilliant brain.'

'I don't want to startle her,' I explained and crouched to call through the letter box. 'Hello, Sylvia. It's Inspector Church and—'

'Dodo,' Dodo yelled in my left ear, because she hadn't damaged it enough last year.

'Constable Chivers,' I said firmly. 'We have just come to see you.' I was reaching inside to find the string when I saw a little shape come skipping out of a back room, along the long corridor towards me.

'I can reach the lock if I do stand on tipper-toes,' Sylvia called. 'I am tallerer than I look.' She stretched up. 'Perhaps I need a likkle stool,' she decided.

'I'll do it,' I assured her, fishing out the key and opening the door.

'Hello, Inspecterer.' Sylvia danced about me excitedly, ignoring Dodo. 'Come and see my friends.' Sylvia took me by the hand and led me, crabwise, down the hall with Dodo in the rear.

The kitchen was big and square and Mrs Whitehouse had been right about one thing. Thanks to an old iron cooking range it was much cosier than the unheated hallway. There was a sagging sofa against the far wall and six dolls were seated on it neatly in a row.

'Oh, I love dollies.' Dodo clapped her hands excitedly but the little girl narrowed her eyes crossly.

'These are *dolls*,' Sylvia said sternly.

'Oh, isn't this one pretty.' Dodo reached towards one in a pink frilly dress but Sylvia scampered in front of her to protect them.

'They are all pretty,' she said.

'What are their names?' I asked and Sylvia twisted her fingers shyly.

'It's a secret,' she whispered.

'Can I guess?' Dodo asked.

'I don't fink so,' Sylvia told her firmly and plonked herself down on the sofa, pulling at my empty sleeve for me to sit beside her. 'How did you lost your arm?'

'It got cut off,' I said, 'and then I had to have an operation to cut a bit more off when it went bad.'

'Inspector Church has a false arm for special occasions,' Dodo informed her.

Sylvia smiled like this was a lovely thing to have. 'Can I sit on your knee?'

'That would be nice,' I said, 'if you're careful not to bash my stump. It still gets a bit sore sometimes.'

Sylvia half got up and shuffled over to plonk herself down in my lap. 'What happended to your ear?' Her little forefinger ran around the jagged edge.

'I got a bit shot off by a very silly woman,' I said with a baleful glance at the culprit.

'A very clever woman who saved your life,' Dodo rejoined, with some justification for the last bit of that statement.

'Does that feel sore as well?' Sylvia asked.

'Only a bit,' I admitted reluctantly, because I was hoping

Dodo would feel guilty, but I was not sure this was something she felt very often.

Sylvia reached out and stroked my hair. 'Is that its real colour?' she asked.

'Very nearly,' I told her. 'I do lighten it a bit.' It was quite a bit, if truth be told, but I did not want Dodo going back to the station telling the men that.

Sylvia snuggled against me. 'You're very pretty,' she told me.

'Thank you,' I smiled. 'So are you, and your hair is lovely in its natural colour.'

Even in the dull light it shone like a halo around her face and I thought with a pang how I would have loved to have a daughter like her.

'What about me?' Dodo pouted and Sylvia turned this way and that to assess her. 'You are quite pretty,' she decided, 'but Inspecterer Church looks like my mummy.'

Sylvia combed through my hair and stroked my cheek and her big cornflower-blue eyes shone as they had the first time we met and I had given her some aniseed balls. I swallowed hard.

'I goo thinkin'.' Sylvia twirled a curl around her finger.

'About what?' I asked.

Her face was so intent and serious.

'Aunty Josie do say that people never change. Do you think that is so?'

'Well, I change my clothes every—' Dodo began but Sylvia raised a little hand.

'I am askin' the growed-up lady.'

'I believe they can sometimes,' I mused. 'I knew a very wicked man once who became almost a saint.'

'What sort of saint?'

'He sold everything to start a hospital for poorly children in Africa.'

'Oh,' Sylvia said thoughtfully and I was glad she had not asked why he was wicked because I would have had to make something up. Ritchel Coldman had killed a young woman in a jealous rage. Despite his confessions of guilt and readiness to die, Coldman was found insane and incarcerated but later pronounced cured and released.

'We had better get back to work,' I whispered and Sylvia's bow lips closed briefly.

'Do you come and see me again?'

'Of course I will.' I waited for Sylvia to shuffle off me. 'You stay here where it's warm,' I suggested. 'We can see ourselves out. You'll be all right by yourself?'

Sylvia knelt up on her cushion and looked straight into my eyes. 'But I am not by myself,' she told me and pecked me on the cheek. 'I have my f— dolls.'

I looked at her askance. Surely she had not stifled an obscenity? The Satins were a decent family, from what little I had heard, and Mrs Whitehouse did not strike me as a woman who cursed.

'We'll be back soon,' I promised.

'Perhaps I will bring one of my dollies next time or Archibald, my teddy,' Dodo said as she went back into the hall, and I refrained from objecting that Archibald was actually *my* teddy and that his real name was Mr Fluffly.

'Dolls,' Sylvia insisted, quite crossly this time. 'And by the by,' she added as I was about to close the door, 'you pro'lly don't know this but Dodo is a silly name for a lady policeman.'

Dodo opened her mouth, no doubt to explain about us being women not ladies, but I closed the door and touched my cheek and wondered what monster decided it would be a good idea for Sylvia Satin to be an orphan rejected by her own uncle.

'Why are you crying, Boss?' Dodo asked. I was not aware until then that I was. 'Is it because she made you confess to dyeing your lovely hair?'

'Something like that.' I blew my nose.

'Can I tell you something, Boss?' Dodo trotted at my heels, ever the faithful terrier, her helmet bobbing about on a mass of flaming red thatch. 'Just between ourselves, I don't use any bleach at all in my hair.'

'Your secret,' I assured her, 'is quite safe with me.'

'Only quite?' Dodo worried, but I pretended not to hear her.

It was starting to rain again.

34

THE PEARL FISHER AND PORCINE AROMAS

I called in on *Dr E J Gretham MB, General Medical Practitioner*, as his brass plate proclaimed. Tubby had his rooms on the ground floor of number eleven Pencil Street. The waiting room was lined with dark green wallpaper and nine bolt-upright wooden chairs – all, unlike my father's, occupied.

'You'll have to stand,' a middle-aged man told me from the discomfort of his seat.

He didn't look like he would be able to. His pipe-cleaner legs had not kept up with his hogshead torso and looked like they would snap under the strain.

'Quite right,' the woman possibly unfortunate enough to be his wife concurred. 'If you goo want to be treat like a lady, you goo learn to dress like one.'

This was a bit rich for somebody who had tied her rusty-grey skirt at the waist with a length of washing line.

'Hear hear,' chipped in another woman, younger but even scruffier. 'Women in uniform, it's an abdomination.'

'I might find it difficult to do my duty in a ball gown,' I objected.

'Oooh, hark at her,' the first woman sneered. 'Got a tiara too, I s'pose.'

The only time I ever had a tiara was when I played Cinderella going to the ball, the general opinion being that I was better suited to rags.

'No, I—' I began.

'Oh, she do go' a tongue on her,' broke in a wizened creature that might have been male or female in those brown corduroy trousers and straggly long straw hair.

I was not sure which *she* the creature was referring to, but from the grunts of agreement around the room it appeared to be me.

'So,' a lad in his teens and his father's cast-offs challenged. 'What you goona do abou' it, copper? Arrest us all?'

This might have been an attractive prospect if it wasn't for all the paperwork the act would embroil me in.

'Exaggerly the sort of thing we're fighting a war about,' another man contributed.

He looked young and fit but this wasn't the time to ask what contribution he was making to our lethargic crusade.

The door into Tubby's consulting room opened and a burly farmworker came out. He didn't have straw in his hair but he had brought all the aromas that breeding pigs generates so potently. Strange how expensive perfumes fade in a matter of hours, but an agricultural stench can linger for ever.

'Thank you, Doc,' he was saying. 'I tell them ou' there you dint be no quack and I do be right.'

'Next time, don't drink it. Just rub it on the sores,' Tubby told him and was forming the word *next* when he spotted me.

'Good afternoon, Inspector,' he greeted me. 'Come through.'

'Wha'?' came a general roar of incredulity.

'I was next,' at least four of them protested.

'You weren't not,' at least five of them argued.

'The Nazis don't need to invade, they've taken over already,' the young, fit but unenlisted man declared.

'Don't be daffy,' the possibly-the-first-man's-wife told them. 'She int got no appointment. She do come to arrest him.'

'I wish you would,' Tubby mumbled as he closed the door

after me. 'Fethershaw, the vet, has more civilised patients than I've been afflicted with. I assume this is police business.'

'Eric Bone,' I said. 'Constable Box found a boulder at Jacob's Point. It had what looked like blood and ginger hair on it.'

'Excellent.' Tubby clapped his hands together. 'Bring it to the morgue and we'll see if we can match it to the depression in his skull.'

'That's the problem,' I admitted. 'Garrison Orchard kicked it off the edge and into the sea.'

'I see,' Tubby said, as if that were the most natural thing that could happen to forensic evidence. 'What would you like me to do? My pearl fishing days are long gone.'

The image of Tubby diving off a cliff in a loin cloth was not one I wanted to dwell upon.

'I wondered if you could make a plaster impression of the dent to at least give me some idea of what the blunt object would look like.'

'I could,' Tubby agreed, 'but I shan't.'

'Oh?' I was so taken aback by his refusal that this was the best I could manage.

'Because,' Tubby grinned like the enormous schoolboy he was at heart, 'I have already done so.'

He marched over to his medical case behind his desk, unclipped the top and delved in for a pack of sandwiches in greaseproof paper, a slice of pie also wrapped, a black cloth-bound volume of the Treves and Wakeley *Handbook of Surgical Operations* and a lump of plaster with an arced surface.

'How did you get it so smooth?' I asked, turning it this way and that.

'Shaved his head.'

'And did you notice if any of his hair was already missing?'

'Couple of tufts,' Tubby told me. 'And I had a brainwave—Why are you groaning?'

'Just clearing my throat.'

'It occurred to me that, if this was a regular shape, I could extrapolate that curve. And so I took another impression, had a play with that and came up with—' Tubby delved into his bag again, like I do in mine when I am trying to find my brass Zippo windproof lighter. 'This.'

He thrust his creation into my hand so quickly I almost dropped it. It was a bit rough and had more than a few of Tubby Gretham's thumbprints over the surface, but it wasn't a bad facsimile of Box's find on the top of the cliffs, a flattened oval.

'Tubby,' I said. 'You're a genius.'

Tubby blushed with becoming modesty. 'Does it help?' he asked.

'It helps me wish I'd been a better goalkeeper,' I replied and Tubby wrinkled his massive brow but said nothing. 'And to confirm my suspicions that Eric Bone did not hit his head on a rock.'

'Eh?'

'The stone was in a hollow,' I explained. 'If he had tripped and fallen backwards he would have hit his head on all the surrounding stones first and they would have been covered in blood, plus the concussion would have been much larger and more irregular.'

'I think I know what you're saying.'

I hope I know it too.

'If Mr Bone did not hit his head on that stone, the stone must have hit him on the head and so...' I sprinted towards my conclusion. '...we are looking at a case of—'

'Murder,' Tubby broke in, somewhat to my annoyance because I had wanted to be the one to say it.

*

'She's accusing him of murder,' a voice hissed, and the woman in the rusty-grey skirt was trying to pretend she was kneeling by the door to tie her shoelaces – quite a trick when you are wearing wellington boots.

35

THE SKULL OF A GULL AND
THE SIGN OF SIMEON

U p we trudged again. When I was in London, I cogitated, nobody got murdered on wild vertiginous heights because there weren't any, especially on my patch in Bloomsbury. Victims were found conveniently in houses – though less often in their beds than people seem to imagine – or on the street. If they died in the river or in a drain and got washed into the river, they were problems for the Thames River Police.

'Ohhh, but it's ever so…' Algy moaned.

'Far,' Sandy whinged.

'And cold.'

'Pull yourselves together, you fairies,' Bantony taunted them and the twins bridled.

'Fairies!' they echoed indignantly.

'I'll 'ave you know, if we was fairies, we could 'ave…' Sandy began.

'Flown 'ere,' Algy finished, obviously feeling that the slight was on their lack of wings rather than manliness.

Dodo skipped ahead, twirling around excitedly. 'This is just like a school outing,' she burbled and, depressingly, I was inclined to agree.

I marched on before remembering that Bantony was behind me, looking up. 'Go ahead,' I ordered him and he grinned sheepishly.

Box was providing the heavy rear guard, plodding steadily and breathing hard.

The twins reached the top.

'Ohhh, but it's ever so…'

'High.'

'And scary.'

'Oh, you are a couple of silly-billies,' Dodo chided them. 'Let us see who dares go nearest to the edge.'

'No, you will not,' I bellowed. 'The edge is undermined in places and the only way to find out which is to tread on them.'

'Oh, we don't want to do…' Sandy assured me.

'That,' his brother said.

'If yow're frightened yow can 'old moy 'and,' Bantony reassured Dodo.

'Why on earth would I be frightened?' Dodo enquired. 'I *never* fall off cliffs.'

The sea was tossing about far below in that sort of restless way seas do when they are about to lose their tempers.

Far behind us I could just about make out Rivers, hobbling up the track, pausing only to massage the sides of his ribcage – a new addition to his repertoire – in case anyone was watching.

'What are we looking for, ma'am?' Bantony asked.

'Clues,' I told him. 'Box saw a boulder in this hollow with blood and hair on it. I am going to sort through the rest of these to see if there are any more like that. The rest of you spread out and look for anything you can find – blood, clothing, any sort of weapon … clues,' I ended lamely, because I didn't really know what to hope for.

'Grinder-Snipeses,' I summoned them, uncertain that that was the correct plural of their surname. 'You can search in the ravine.'

They clutched each other.

'Ohhh, but int that—' Algy began.

'Dangerous?' I butted in. 'Yes, it is very dangerous indeed. Now go and do it.'

'Right away, mam.' They saluted proudly, suddenly the plucky British heroes, shouldering the white man's burden and striding off with devil-may-care swaggers to certain death, or at least the risk of a few scratches from the bushes.

'And you go and help them,' I commanded Bantony, who was busily engaged in cleaning under a fingernail with the small blade of his penknife.

We spent two hours there but it felt like four. Dodo found a few rabbit droppings but I declined her offer to collect them. Box found a folded piece of paper under a large pebble and it flashed through my mind that this could be a suicide note, but it only said THE GIRLS OF CRANMER HOUSE, FELIXSTOWE COLLEGE WERE HERE MAY 7TH 1939, with a long double column of their signatures.

Dodo found an empty rusty sardine can – the one Box had kicked away when we were looking for Garrison Orchard – and an empty snail shell.

'It does not look quite right.' She showed me. 'But I cannot think why.'

'Really?' I sighed and glanced at the object in her cupped hand. 'Oh yes. It spirals anticlockwise. I don't think I've seen one like that before.'

'Is it a vital clue?' Dodo shuffled her feet excitedly, her helmet bobbing like a rowing boat on an ocean of red.

'Not unless you are hoping to find what killed the former occupant.'

'Not a blackbird,' Dodo decided, 'because they smash the shells on rocks, do they not, Boss?'

'They do,' I agreed.

'Do you think it could be lucky, Boss,' Dodo called after me.

Not for the snail, I thought, but called back, 'Could be. Why don't you keep it?'

'I do not quite understand that question, Boss,' Dodo yelled at my retreating back. 'Because I fully intend to do so.'

Rivers had found a slab of rock about four foot long with a mark on it which everybody else thought was just the natural pattern of the rock but he was convinced was the symbol of a secret society and had spent the best part of an hour bending our ears about *The Sign of Simeon*, an Ambrose G. Black story where whoever saw the sign would be murdered before the day was out.

The Grinder-Snipes struggled out of the ravine, bedraggled and bloodied but surprisingly cheerful.

'We 'ad a luvleh game of 'ide...'

'...and seek,' they told me, because they knew that was what I had sent them down there for.

'Did you find anything?' I asked.

'The skull—' Sandy announced dramatically.

'Of a gull,' Algy explained. 'Ooh, that rhymes, Lysander.'

Bantony emerged, immaculate as always.

'My toeses are frozes and so is my noses,' Dodo complained annoyingly but with some justification. The wind was never warm and now it was bringing a light but unwelcome rain. 'And my pingies are...'

'I think we have done everything we can,' I announced loudly, too exasperated to point out that policewomen have a great many things but none of them are *pingies*.

'What about my discovery, ma'am,' Rivers enquired, much energised by the thought of going home.

'You had better bring it with you,' I suggested, 'if you're sure it's a clue.'

Rivers glanced back at the slab. I doubted two men with a donkey could have shifted it far.

'Probably just a natural pattern,' he decided quickly.

36

THE TURKISH SLIPPER AND
THE SEALING OF THE CLUE

Georgie was standing in the lobby of Sackwater Central, leaning comfortably on the desk and chatting to Brigsy.
'Perhaps we could play a game of tennis sometime,' she suggested with a glance and a wink in my direction.

'Wellll,' Brigsy drawled uncertainly. 'I dint ge' much time for sports these day.'

'Oh, but I bet you used to be very sporty,' Georgie purred.

Her handbag was on her arm and there was a small cardboard box on the desk.

'I do play a bit of football when I'm a nipper,' Brigsy confessed.

'Hello, Miss Orchard,' I said. 'Your father hasn't gone missing again, has he?'

'Well, he won't get very far without this.' She took the lid off the box to reveal a brown brogue, curled up at the toe like it was thinking of changing into a Turkish slipper. The leather was scuffed and the lace had snapped and been retied. 'I was helping my father on with his socks when I spotted this.'

Peering over to where her perfectly manicured finger was pointing, I saw a wisp of something wedged between the sole and the upper. I lifted the shoe out carefully and held it under the green coolie shade light hanging over my sergeant's head.

'Got a magnifying glass?' I asked Brigsy.

'Nope.'

'Do we have one in the station?'

Brigsy shuffled the question around his face. 'Not tha' I know of. Never had no call for one.'

Something squirmed with embarrassment and I think it was me. There I was, an inspector in a police station that didn't even have the most basic piece of equipment. I knew my father had one on his desk but I could hardly go trotting home for it.

Georgie unclipped her handbag. 'Try these.'

'I didn't know you wore glasses.' I took them from her.

'Only for reading and only in private,' she told me with a smile. 'Oh, they rather suit you.'

Georgie's face became a blur but the shoe, when I held it close, went into sharp focus.

'Got an envelope?' I asked Brigsy. *And if you say* no *I shall have your head on a spike as a warning to whoever follows in your wake.*

'Two dozen,' he replied instantly, and I was about to cancel my order for an executioner's block when he said, 'Delivered fresh this marnin' they were 'cause we were clean out of them all week.'

'Give me one,' I snapped, and my friend coughed to suppress a laugh.

Brigsy flinched, a police sergeant with decades on the force suddenly a sensitive puppy, and I instantly felt guilty. It would probably come as something of a surprise to my men to discover that I don't like telling people off. We would all be a lot happier if I didn't have to. But you can't apologise for your tone. That would imply that you don't have the right to speak to your juniors as you please and the more a woman in authority respects a man, the less he respects her.

Brigsy drew one out of a pigeon hole like a card sharp dealing you an ace of spades when he knows you need a king for a running flush.

'Paperknife.' I knew we had one of those because the men, inspired by some Errol Flynn adventure, had held knife-throwing competitions and impaled the postman but, luckily, only in his sack of mail.

'Hold it open,' I said and put the shoe down to gingerly tease out the filament.

There was no doubt this was a hair. It even still had its root. And it looked distinctly gingery to me.

I dropped it in the envelope, handed Georgie her glasses back, sealed the envelope and wrote on it the date and *Hair sample recovered from Garrison Orchard's shoe.*

'Oh,' Brigsy remarked, 'just like a proper detective.'

For a second I thought the sergeant was being insubordinate in revenge for my snapping at him, but from his expression it was clear that he was deeply impressed.

37

THE LONELY HEADMISTRESS AND THE
GHASTLY MACHINES

We didn't have an office big enough to house everyone without playing sardines so I held the meeting in the lobby, standing in front of the desk with my fellow officers lined up on the bench seats.

Superintendent Vesty sat at the front to my right, bolt upright with his eyes closed. Something pulsed under the sunken skin of his forehead and I wondered, not for the first time, if there really was a metal plate or I was seeing his brain throbbing just beneath the surface.

Also on the front row but to the left was Sharkey, slouching with his arms folded, and I wished with childish malice that he would forget there was no back to his seat and topple backwards.

The others were scattered behind with Rivers right at the back like the schoolboy who doesn't want to be asked questions by teacher.

'Some of you know what this is all about.'

'I do,' Dodo piped up.

'But for those who don't, let me get you up—'

'Get up when the Inspector orders you to,' Vesty barked without opening his eyes, and the twins half-stood uncertainly before I motioned them to stay seated.

'Up to date,' I ploughed on. 'Last Monday, Constable Chivers and I came across the body—'

'I saw it first,' Dodo insisted.

'You did,' I agreed, omitting to remind her that she had thought it was a shop dummy. 'But we will get on much better if you all try not to interrupt.'

'Hear hear,' Vesty said, head falling forward and ballooning out.

'Is she going to tell him off?' Dodo whispered to Bantony.

'I can't hear you,' Bantony murmured. 'You'll have to sit closer.'

Dodo started to slide over.

'Stay where you are, Chivers,' I commanded. 'The body turned out to be that of a Mr Grevan Martin Eric Bone, a retired clockmaker known as Eric.'

'Not surprised,' Sharkey commented. 'Who the hell would want to be called Martin?'

Dodo waved her hand in the air. 'Is he allowed to use the H word, Boss?'

'Who the hell do you think you are talking to?' Sharkey exploded.

'Oh.' Dodo nibbled the tip of her thumb. 'I think I am talking to Inspector Church, sir.'

'She was too,' the twins chorused.

'Be quiet, the lot of you,' I snapped.

'You heard the ninspector,' Brigsy growled. 'Be quiet.'

'Thank you, Sergeant,' I began.

'And stop interjectioning,' Brigsy glared at the silent constables.

'It is—' I said, but the super awoke with a start.

'Keep up the good work,' he encouraged us and lowered his heavy head again.

'It is—' I paused, slightly disconcerted when nobody interrupted me this time. 'It is likely that Eric Bone was hit on the back of the head at Jacob's Point and pushed over the cliff. We know from

Mrs Bone that he habitually went out for a morning constitutional so that would have been on Saturday at about ten a.m.'

'So why didn't she report him missing?' Sharkey leaned forward but if he was hoping to floor me, he would need a better punch than that.

'Because she also went out on Saturday to visit a sick sister in Shanton Major and stayed three nights. Mrs Thurlong, a neighbour, was supposed to check on him. She had a key but when she found a note saying *Gone to see Sally*, she thought Mr Bone had written it and she locked up again,' I explained.

'Silly cow,' he muttered and I tried to tell myself he meant Mrs Thurlong or even Mrs Bone but certainly not me.

Brigsy half raised a hand before deciding that was beneath his dignity. 'Excuse me, madam.' He cleared his throat. 'How do we know it wasn't Sunday?'

'Two reasons,' I replied, glad that somebody else was paying attention. 'First, Mr Bone was a devout Catholic and always missed his walk to go to Mass on Sunday mornings. Secondly, the body had been in the water for longer than one day.'

'So, as Inspector Church told us, that means Mr Bone went missing on Saturday,' Dodo asserted fiercely, 'and we will all get on a lot quicker without all these digressions.' She caught Brigsy's glare. 'Except, of course, for Sergeant Briggs's pertinent point.'

'Who you callin' *pertinent*?' Brigsy demanded. 'Pertinent yourself.'

'Pert, at least,' Bantony murmured.

'Right.' I grabbed hold of the conversational steering wheel and hauled us back on track. 'I want all of you to go around as many houses as you can on the routes from here to the cliffs and ask people if they saw him. I have some copies of his photograph but they were taken a long time ago. Mrs Bone thinks it was before the Great War.'

'Will you be coming with us, Boss?' Dodo asked. 'Please say yes.'

'I am going to get some publicity,' I said.

'And I don't do footwork,' Sharkey muttered.

'You do now,' Inspector Vesty assured him, without even opening his eyes.

38

THE LONG LINE AND THE SHORT DROP

walked to the *Gazette* down Hardhart Alley past Simpson's Bicycles.

'Good morning, Inspector,' Timothy Simpson called out cheerily. He had worked in his father's shop, repairing and selling cycles, since he was a schoolboy, though he was still fresh-faced enough to pass as one at a glance. He had a bike resting upside down on the pavement with the shop door wide open. 'Solved any good crimes lately?'

'There are no good ones,' I told him, and he twanged a spoke like the string of a harp.

I had bought my first full-sized bike from Simpson senior with my Christmas money a long time ago and got Simpson Junior to repair it when I moved into *Cressida*.

I began to move off.

'Actually,' Timothy said, 'you can investigate a crime for me.'

'The crime of putting women in uniform?' his father roared with laughter from the shop.

'Haven't heard that one for hours,' I muttered.

'Shush, Dad,' Timothy scolded. 'No, I mean it, Inspector. Turn my back the other day and somebody goo swipe my oilcan, they do.'

'Oh dear,' I sympathised, but not very much. 'Come into the station and make a report.'

'Not worth the trouble.' Timothy spun the front wheel of the bike and got a spanner out of his overalls.

'Then it is not worth our trouble investigating it,' I told him.

'Fair enough,' he shrugged and went back to his work.

The offices of the *Sackwater and District Gazette* had stood in Straight Street, as the plaque over the red front door proclaimed, since 1870. It had been founded by Ean Gregson and passed on to his son Jorn who handed over the business to Porl, still the official owner but disabled by a stroke, so that his son had felt obliged to take the reins. At least Toby's name didn't look like a printer's error.

Carol, the receptionist, sometime columnist and sometime wedding reporter, sometime anything-else-that-needed-doing doer, told me to go straight into the office and so I did and only just in time.

Toby Gregson stood on a chair, a rope threaded through an old oil-lamp hook on the ceiling to form a noose tied tightly around his neck.

39

THE FOILING OF THE STRING FAIRY

stepped forward, not so close as to make him jump off but close enough so I could try to grab him if he did.

'Toby!'

Toby Gregson peered down at me. 'Oh, hello, Inspector.'

He was more correct than me in our forms of address but I had more urgent concerns.

'Oh gawd!' Carol called from behind me. 'Are you at it again?'

'What?' I puzzled. 'He makes a habit of hanging himself?'

I knew some people did strangle themselves for fun, including, March Middleton had told me, a former prime minister and a Roman Catholic cardinal, but Toby had always struck me as more down to earth than that.

'It's for my book.' His chair wobbled worryingly.

'The Condemned Man?'

'That's the one.' He laughed a bit awkwardly. 'You didn't have to worry though. The other end isn't tied to anything.'

'Take the noose off,' I said.

'It's perfectly safe.' Toby made to step forward and demonstrate how foolish my fears had been.

'Take… it… off.' I mustered as much authority as I could into that command.

'Oh, for goodness' sake.' Toby pouted but did as he was told, loosening the loop to lift it over his head. 'Happy?'

I had never been out with Toby except for a few drinks to discuss business but he had a knack of making me feel like we were an old married couple, sometimes in a cosy way but today I was definitely the nagging wife.

'Yes,' I said as he stepped down. 'Now pull the rope.'

Toby rolled his lovely Oxford-blue eyes and gave the rope a tug just above the knot.

'Oh shit,' he breathed.

The rope had jammed.

'But—' Toby managed.

'It was tangled around the leg of the desk,' I explained.

'Tangled?' Toby threw out his hands like a burglar claiming he's been framed after getting caught climbing out of a window with a bag of swag. 'I carefully coiled it under the desk so I didn't trip over it.'

'Well, the string fairy must have crept in and muddled it all up.'

'Trust you,' Carol remarked. She was a pretty girl but had a fondness for inflating her bosom with enough silk to supply a parachute regiment.

'What do you mean, *Trust me*?' Toby dragged his chair back.

'Well, I can't see either of us doing that,' she reasoned.

Toby had a comfortable office with two old leather armchairs but for some reason we sat upright either side of his desk.

'Coffee, please.' Toby struggled to re-muster his dignity.

Carol flicked her hair and went back downstairs.

'Are you all right?' I asked.

He was not a healthy colour.

'I feel so stupid.' Toby shuddered, sliding a triple-decker rack of paper-filled wire baskets to one side so we could see each other.

'It wasn't the cleverest thing you've ever done.'

'God, I could do with a drink.' Toby reached in his drawer and got out a full bottle of Johnnie Walker Red Label. 'Like one?'

'Love one,' I replied, 'but I'd better stick to the coffee.'

Toby considered the situation. 'So had I,' he decided and put it away. 'So, Betty, what brings you here?'

'A suspected murder,' I told him, accepting the Craven A cork-tipped that he offered me and the light from a shaky match.

'Are you all right to smoke those?' I asked.

Toby had had half a lung taken out for tuberculosis last summer and still got breathless more easily than he should.

'Doctor's orders,' he assured me, inhaling deeply. 'Clears the tubules.' He coughed gently. 'You said *murder*.'

'I said *suspected* murder,' I reminded him. 'Eric Bone.'

'The one you dragged off the beach,' Toby nodded. 'POLICE HEROINES GO WHERE BRAVE MEN FEAR TO TREAD.' He dragged his separated thumb and forefinger through the air to recreate his headline.

'That wasn't exactly fair on the royal engineers who also risked their lives,' I pointed out.

'Sappers don't sell papers,' Toby said, waving his cigarette loftily. 'Pretty policewomen with their shirts blowing up just enough to titillate the men without upsetting their mothers do.'

'For an alleged reporter, you are very good at not getting to the nub of a story,' I told him and Toby smiled ruefully. We both knew he would rather be playing jazz violin with his disbanded band.

'Whenever I've asked you about cases in the past, you tell me it's confidential.'

'Try me,' I suggested.

'You think he was... might have been,' he corrected himself before I got the chance, 'have been murdered?'

'We think he fell off the cliffs. Now this bit is just between you and me – he was hit on the head with a rock.'

I never liked revealing the method of murder. It was astonishing how many suspects would protest *I never shot, stabbed, strangled, drowned, poisoned, bludgeoned, suffocated or decapitated the old geezer* before they had been told how the victim died.

'That sounds quite murderous to me,' Toby whistled as Carol brought in two mugs of coffee.

'No biscuits, I'm afraid,' she said. 'Somebody ate them all.'

There was something in her easy familiarity I didn't quite like.

After a minor scuffle over who that someone might have been, Carol left us to it.

'We know Eric Bone left his house at about ten on the Saturday morning and his wife said he often walked to Jacob's Point,' I told him.

'And you want me to do a *Did you see this man* article?' Toby rubbed his throat, probably imagining that noose tightening around it.

'That would be very helpful.' I tried my coffee. It was better than anything I got in Howland's Café.

'To both of us,' Toby agreed. 'At the moment my front page is *Missing canary found safe.* Do you have a photograph?' He smiled. 'Of course you do. I can see it sticking out of your bag.' I handed it over and he piffed. 'Got anything more recent? A picture of the body, perhaps.' He perked up hopefully.

'After two days in the sea?' I objected. 'Think what your skin is like after a long soak in the bath.'

'Was he in any clubs or societies?'

'He played golf,' I remembered. 'In fact, he was the—' I stopped, exasperated by my own stupidity.

'Captain?' Toby suggested and I nodded. 'In that case, we will almost certainly have a picture of him giving a cup to somebody or opening a tournament, that sort of thing. Leave it with me.'

'Thank you,' I said sheepishly.

It was a sorry state of affairs when the man who wanted to be the next Stéphane Grappelli had to teach the woman who wanted to be the first female chief constable her job.

'No, thank *you*.' Toby toasted me with his mug. 'For giving me a story and,' he looked almost as embarrassed as I felt, 'for saving my life.'

'All in a day's work, sir.' I stood up and put my helmet back on.

He was one of the few men I had ever met who made me feel better just to be with him. It was a pity in some ways, I pondered as I fastened the strap, that I was supposed to be in love with Adam – wasn't I?

THE TANKS, THE TRAP AND
THE WRONG FORCEPS

The twins looked exhausted when they trudged back to the station, as well they might. I had sent them on a long footslog.

'We asked nearly fifteh…' Sandy flopped on to a chair in the back room.

'People,' Algy concluded, 'and that's ever such a…'

'Lot.'

'Fifty?' I echoed in disbelief and they nodded wearily.

'Forteh…'

'Eight,' Algy told me modestly, like he was telling us how many German tanks they had destroyed double-handed.

'Which works out at almost exactly seven an hour,' I calculated.

'Any chance of a cuppa?' Sandy asked in the tones of a man rescued from a fortnight in the desert.

Were they seriously expecting their inspector to make it for them?

'How the hell can it take you eight and a half minutes to ask someone if they have seen a man in a photograph?' I demanded. 'What were you doing? Cadging cups of tea?'

'Wellll…' they both said. 'Onleh a few.'

'Nine,' Algy admitted.

'Even so.' I whipped the photo out of my bag. 'Allow me to

demonstrate.' I held out the picture to an invisible member of the public. 'Excuse me, sir.'

'Or madam,' Sandy chipped in usefully.

'May I ask if you saw this man on Saturday?' I switched to a Suffolk accent. 'Le' me cogitate. No, I dint believe I do.'

'She changed voices,' Sandy remarked in astonishment.

''ow does she do that?' his brother marvelled.

'The point I am making is that the whole procedure, even given somebody who umms and ahhhs, takes one or two minutes at most.'

'Ohhh, but they 'ad to loook for their spectacles,' Sandy told me, to his brother's vigorous approval.

'All forty-eight of them?' I challenged.

'Yes,' they chorused.

'Except the man who was blind,' Algy assured me.

I stared at them. What on earth had I done in this or any previous life to deserve such a cruel and unusual punishment?

'Tell me the truth,' I commanded. 'What *exactly* have you been doing all day?'

'We wur asking people all day long,' Sandy vowed.

'Cross our 'earts,' – his twin crossed his own – 'Mam. But...'

They looked at each other and bit their lower lips.

'But what?' I urged, cross already because it was obvious they had done something stupid yet again.

'We lost the photy,' they both burst out.

'And so we 'ad to...'

'Describe 'im,' Algy mumbled.

'How did you manage to lose the photograph?' I asked sternly. 'And you, Sandy, will answer that question and you, Algy, will keep your trap shut.'

I allowed them both to mutter their indignant *Lysander* and *Algernon* before I poked a finger at Sandy to begin.

'It wur all Algy's fault,' he began loyally, and his twin gasped in pique. ''e asked me 'ow I could tell which way the wind wur blowing so I 'eld the photy up to show that it wur blowing outwards but it escaped my grasp and flew away like a kite out over the ocean. At least it proved I wur right but we couldn't gerrit back because we can't—'

'Swim,' Algy burst out, unable to restrain himself any more. They twitched nervously.

'You complete and utter twits,' I told them in a low voice so they couldn't go away and say I wur 'ysterical. 'Why on earth didn't you come back here for a spare copy?'

'We thought you might tell…' Sandy admitted.

'Uz off,' Algy whispered.

'At least you could have done your jobs,' I reasoned.

Was I really such a monster that they were terrified of me? I hoped not, because an officer should command by respect, not fear; but a part of me hoped they were.

We had three reliable and ten fairly reliable sightings of Eric Bone. He was quite a well-known character in town and he had been seen walking, unaccompanied and apparently unconcerned, in directions that would take him towards the cliffs. The last almost-definite sighting had him starting up Spectre Lane and there were no reports of anyone following him.

Four people, however, did mention Barnaby Mason. If Sackwater had been a village, Barnaby Mason would be the village idiot. He was what kind people would call *simple* and unkind people a *loony*. Barnaby Mason was born wrong. His neck had been crushed by excessive use of forceps. They damaged the muscles so that he always held his head to the left and the blood supply to his brain was disrupted. He suffered from blackouts and would sometimes stumble around the streets apparently oblivious to where he was or what he was doing.

Barnaby Mason lived with his mother and after she died, he lived alone. People were frightened of him and they made up stories to frighten themselves more. If he hadn't been in St Audry's Hospital for Mental Diseases in Woodbridge while the Suffolk Vampire Murders were taking place, I have no doubt he would have been many people's prime suspect.

But Barnaby was out now and people were looking at him distrustfully. I intended to have a word with Barnaby myself, if only to forestall any rumours that would doubtless arise the moment the murder was announced, but he hadn't been home when I called and he was not even on the list of suspects I hadn't had the time to start.

41

THE NEED FOR NORWAY
AND MORE THAN WORDS

When Captain Sultana lived alone on *Cressida*, he had rigged a water tank in the spinney for his daily shower. After I arrived, he and Jimmy constructed a wooden cubicle to protect my decency. Either they had miscalculated my height or run out of wood, but it only came up to my neck. Jimmy had managed to demonstrate that they could see no lower than that from the upper deck but I still felt a bit self-conscious knowing they could see me bobbing about with my shower cap on to protect my helmet-battered so-called hairstyle. The captain was discreet, I knew, but I had reasonable doubts about Jimmy.

The water came straight from the river and felt like it. In the winter I took out kettles of hot water or cadged baths at Felicity House, despite my parents' objections that I was emptying the supply they had heated for Dodo. Even in May when the air was comfortably warm, the River Angle was not. I had just finished drying myself when I heard a commotion.

Carmelo was shouting *Madonna!* And Jimmy confined himself to *Oh, for crying out loud!* Because he knew the captain hated swearing, in English at any rate. Their tones and the cries of disbelief told me this was not just them bickering.

I put on my dressing gown and the old tennis shoes I kept for those trips and hurried back to the boat and up the steps.

'Whatever is the matter?'

Carmelo had his head in his hands. Had another ship gone down? We had been losing far far too many of those lately.

Jimmy turned the wireless off, though he was not usually allowed to touch it. 'We're pulling out of Norway,' he told me in disgust.

'But I thought we were supposed to be counter-attacking,' I objected.

'That's what we were told.' Jimmy threw up his hands. 'But they counter-attacked our counter-attack and now we're running off with our tails between our legs.'

'So soon?' I asked, aghast.

The Germans had invaded less than a month ago and despite the Royal Navy and our mining of the sea, despite joint British/ French reinforcements, the Norwegian forces had been defeated in a matter of weeks.

'We need Norway for iron and to blockage Germany,' Carmelo groaned.

'At least it should distract Hitler from attacking France in the near future,' I suggested, because I didn't know what else to say. We only had words now, it seemed, and words do not win wars.

42

THE FALL OF BARNABY MASON

Rivers was on the desk when I arrived at the station and he looked distressed but not in his normal martyr-to-my-back way.

'What's happened?' I asked, awaiting a litany of despair over our military situation.

The newspaper hoardings had all blared the bad news for anyone who might have missed it.

Somebody was grunting in the cells.

'Old Scrapie has a suspect,' he told me unenthusiastically.

'*Inspector* Sharkey,' I corrected him. I didn't mind the men insulting Sharkey but I was not supposed to condone it. 'For the death of Eric Bone?'

'Tha's the one.' Rivers nodded grimly.

'Anyone I might know?'

'Mason,' Rivers said simply.

'Barnaby Mason?'

My constable nodded and from behind him there was a louder grunt and the sounds of a scuffle.

'What the hell?' I started off to the right of the desk.

'Old... 'spector Sharkey said not to be disturbed,' Rivers told me.

'I bet he did.' I raced down the corridor.

The noises came from cell six at the far end and I could hear a whimpering now.

'Stop lying, you weird freak,' Sharkey was shouting.

'Please,' was all I heard his suspect say, and then the sound of a slap.

The door was closed but crashed back when I flung it open. Old Scrapie was bent over a figure cowering on the floor. I could only see Mason's boots and trouser legs, one ridden halfway up his shin.

'I told you we were not to be disturbed,' Sharkey snarled without looking back.

'You told Rivers,' I conceded and my colleague spun around.

'You're not supposed to be here 'til nine,' he said accusingly, because my offence was much worse than his.

'It *is* nine,' I told him. 'Doesn't time fly when you are having fun?'

I put my back to the wall and tried to squeeze past but Sharkey was rising and put out an arm to block me.

'Are you all right, Barnaby?' I craned over that arm and it was obvious that he was not. There was blood streaming from both nostrils and one eye was already closing.

'Yes th-thank you, Inspector Church,' he stammered unconvincingly.

'You had a fit and fell over, didn't you,' Sharkey instructed him.

'Yes sir, I do believe I did.' Barnaby Mason touched his upper lip tentatively and winced.

'And I gave you a couple of taps to bring you round,' Sharkey said, slipping something brass into his trouser pocket.

'That's right, sir.' Barnaby was shaking violently as if about to start a genuine fit. 'Thank you very much.'

'Well, it sounds like Inspector Sharkey did you a good turn,' I observed drily, 'but I have medical training,' I lied, 'so I can take over now.'

'I haven't finished questioning him,' Sharkey objected.

'But he seems quite confused,' I pointed out, 'and you wouldn't want him to tell you anything he didn't mean, would you, Inspector?'

My colleague said something under his breath and it sounded like *for cough* but probably wasn't, and he was going to say something else but decided to spin around and barge past me through the open doorway.

'Can you get up?' I held my hand out to Barnaby and he took it warily. 'Come on, see if you can sit on the bed.'

Barnaby Mason tried to rise but his knees buckled and I just managed to twist him around so that he slumped on to the mattress. He was a stocky, powerfully built man and, in a fair fight, could have knocked six bells out of Sharkey, but my colleague was not a man to fight fair and Barnaby was not a man to fight at all.

'I told you I was not to be disturbed,' came down the corridor.

If Brigsy had been on duty, I reflected, senior officer that Sharkey was or not, he would not have stood by and let this happen.

'He say if I dint confess he do send me to the loony bin,' Barnaby wept. 'N-not the nice hospital where they make me better.'

'He won't be sending you anywhere,' I promised and raised my voice. 'Ring for Dr Gretham, Rivers,' I called, 'and if he's not there, ring for an ambulance. We need to get this man to hospital.'

'No, please.' Barnaby clutched my sleeve.

His hair was collapsed all over his face. I do not think it had been trimmed within living memory. The captain never cut his hair but he had it tied neatly back in a pigtail. Barnaby's thatch looked like something that needed scything before harvest festival could be celebrated.

'Just the Royal Albert Infirmary,' I reassured him, 'to get you checked over.'

And out of here, I thought.

'He say I do be locked away for ever,' Barnaby wept. 'But I dint do it, Inspector, I swear on my mother's grave.' He sobbed noisily. 'At least I dint think I did.'

You are a wicked bastard, *Paul Sharkey,* I reflected, *and this unhappy soul will not sleep easy until we find the real killer.*

43

THE SPECIAL SERVICES OF DORIS DRISCOW

Tubby Gretham rammed his stethoscope into his jacket pocket.

'Injuries inconsistent with a fall,' he told me as we stood over the bed.

Barnaby Mason had got into such a state that Tubby had been forced to sedate him.

'Sharkey says that Barnaby started punching himself when he was having a fit,' I told him without conviction.

'Was Barnaby wearing a knuckleduster?' Tubby asked pointedly as he ran a finger over a long red weal on Barnaby's cheek and another on the side of his jaw.

'No.' I eyed the injuries in disgust. 'But I know a man who was.'

'Can you report him?' Tubby asked quietly.

'I can,' I replied carefully, 'and I'm damned if I won't.'

The twins and Bantony were in the back room when I returned and Rivers was still on the desk.

'A word, Rivers,' I said and the men in the back room tipped their heads to listen in. 'In my office.'

'Have yow been a naughty boy?' Bantony jibbed.

'Pity you aren't so good at identifying the real naughty boys,' I told him and stepped smartly away.

'Shut the door,' I told Rivers. 'I think you know what this is about.'

'It's just a bit of fun,' he protested.

'Is it?' I demanded, without a clue what *it* might be.

'Well, I can't do much with my back,' he began and I groaned inwardly and outwardly. 'And Mrs Rivers won't go on top but Doris don't care what way she goo so long as she do get her five shillin'.'

Oh, for heaven's sake!

'Doris Driscow?' I checked. Doris See-You-Right Driscow had been notorious in Sackwater for decades. 'She must be over fifty now.'

'So am I,' Rivers pointed out.

'And what is this to do with me?' I sighed.

'Well...' Rivers coughed. 'Ohwa, you dint know, do you, ma'am?'

'You would be surprised what I know,' I said and thought, *You'd be even more surprised what I don't.* 'Just spit it out, Rivers, and get this over with.'

'Well, Sharkey...'

'*Inspector* Sharkey,' I corrected him.

'He do find out about Doris and say if I speak out 'gainst him, he goo tell on me.' Rivers looked all around like a hunted animal. 'Mrs Rivers goo skin me and feed me to the cat if she find out.'

'So Inspector Sharkey is blackmailing you to say that he never hurt Barnaby Mason,' I clarified in disgust.

Rivers looked at the floor and then at my feet before his gaze dropped again.

'That do be the length and breath of it,' he admitted nonsensically.

'What if I were to threaten to tell your wife if you don't tell the truth,' I suggested, and my constable shifted uneasily, eyes drifting as he calculated the risks.

'You dint goo do that,' he decided.

'Wouldn't I?' I tried to look him in the eyes but I would have had to lie on my back on the grubby lino to do that.

Rivers grinned lopsidedly and fleetingly.

'You int like him,' he said more confidently and I knew he was right.

'He beat up an innocent man,' I protested, but Rivers had no better side to appeal to.

'Did he, ma'am?' His eyes flickered up for an instant and I wasn't sure if he was questioning the beating or the innocence but at the end of the day it didn't make one jot of difference. If I ever had Sharkey on a hook, he was well and truly off it now.

I marched to his office and barged in without knocking, the effect of which was wasted by nobody being there. There was an unsmoked cigarette on the desk. I picked it up and slipped it carefully into the dregs of his tea but I would have to wait another time for the chance to really vent the steam I had just built up.

44

PSYCHIC PANDORA AND CRAVEN A

It was Toby Gregson who alerted me. We had gone for a drink to the Compasses. It was not my favourite pub and I objected to their 'no women' policy but we could sit outside in a shelter by the bowling green, which had now been ploughed up for vegetables – potatoes, I judged from the drooping leaves poking wearily through the soil.

We had met ostensibly to discuss the publicity for our murder enquiry but everyone likely to report anything of value had almost certainly done so by now. If truth be told, we enjoyed each other's company and it was nice for me to get out of my uniform (I was not supposed to drink in it in public), put on a dress and enjoy a not-too-bad pint of bitter with a man I had come to regard as a friend.

'I was trying to do a feature on the Windsers – no, not the royal family,' he chuckled before I could ask, because we both knew I was going to. 'Mr and Mrs and it's spelled s e r. It's their fiftieth anniversary next week and I wanted to do a feature – photo of them holding hands on the sofa and a bit of tosh about never a cross word. The way things are at the moment they'll take the front page. I can do another *Police are pursuing new lines of enquiries* but the public is fickle. I could always get Psychic Pandora, the clairvoyant, to polish her crystal ball.'

'Please don't,' I said. 'People believe her and if she says the killer is tall and dark with a limp, some superstitious idiots will ignore any short blond athletic men even if they interrupt them performing another murderous act.' I retraced our conversational path. 'So will they not cooperate?'

Toby supped his bitter appreciatively. 'Who knows?' He got out his cigarette case. 'I can't get hold of them.'

'Have one of mine,' I offered.

'One of your filthy constructions?' he said in mock horror. 'Not likely. I don't want to lose the other half of my lung.'

My roll-ups were a bit rough, I had to admit, but I preferred the stronger flavour, a taste I had acquired from my godmother.

'I could take umbrage at that,' I huffed, 'but I'll take one of yours instead.'

I slid a Craven A out from under the elasticated band and let him light it for me.

'How hard have you tried?' I asked.

'Been round three times when you'd expect them to be in – dinner and breakfast – and Carol has tried a couple of times and asked the neighbours but nobody has seen them for a week.'

'Where do they live?'

'Pheasant Lodge, Jaconda Road.'

'I'll get one of the men to look into it,' I promised.

'It may be nothing.'

'It usually is. Were the curtains closed?' I asked and inhaled deeply.

'No, and I peeked through the nets. There was no sign of them or a disturbance.'

'Why would you expect a disturbance?' My words came out in smoke signals.

'Not so much *expect* as *hope*.' Toby gazed into me, his eyes cobalt in the evening sun. 'Elderly Sackwater couple horribly murdered – sell a few copies.'

'You don't really mean that,' I told him and he snorted.

'Don't I? A good gruesome slaying does wonders for both our businesses.'

'The difference being we get blamed by you if we don't solve them,' I observed.

'And the police never try to blame the press if things go wrong?' he countered.

I clipped open my handbag and my purse and dealt a florin on to the wooden table.

'My round,' I said and Toby went off to get us two more pints.

I watched the dunes spiked with marram grass. There was a light breeze and the sand was swirling pale grey; the sun was low enough to dazzle but not enough for a beautiful setting. For some reason, I felt restless. I stood up and paced the weed-choked paved path around the old bowling area and as I turned the corner I saw Toby in the porchway, still with an empty glass in each hand. I was about to chide him for his slowness but there was something in the way he was looking at me, almost shyly I thought, but he didn't turn away and I suddenly realised I didn't want him to and Toby put the glasses on a low wall and came towards me.

'That,' he said, 'is the loneliest smile I have ever seen.'

'Perhaps you could keep it company then,' I said and, for no reason at all, I was in his arms.

45

THE SURGEON OF SACKWATER

W e never had that second drink and it became a standing joke between us that I never got my two shillings back either.

We walked, hand in hand and then arm in arm and then his arm around my waist.

'I still can't get used to how different you look out of uniform,' he told me.

'Better, I hope.'

'Different,' he repeated. 'You look beautiful both ways but ... softer in civvies.'

'My uniform is my armour,' I told him and Toby inclined his head to touch mine.

'But I don't think you are ever completely out of it.'

We left the path by mutual silent consent and trailed through the sand, heading towards the dunes. There were no mines on that stretch of coast, the military authorities being more confident than I was that tanks couldn't drive through sand dunes.

'Imagine we saw a crime now,' I said. 'You might want to observe it and wish you had your camera with you or, if it looked dangerous, you might think *What the hell?* And scarper. But I would have to do something about it. You never stop being a police officer and it's worse for a woman. I can't even get married.'

We skirted a high dune, the side scooped out as if by a giant spoon.

'You must see some awful things,' he said. 'I don't know how you stick it.'

'Because I can't pretend that those things will stop happening if I stop trying to deal with them.'

'Why you?'

'Because I can,' I said simply. 'People have died because of my mistakes and I will never forgive myself for those but I like to think I have saved more lives than I've lost.'

'You sound like a surgeon,' Toby said, but I didn't feel like he was mocking me.

'That's how Sidney Grice described his job once,' I recalled, 'cutting the cancer out of this world and sending the perpetrators to the next.'

'Can I quote that?' Toby asked.

'One day,' I said, and all at once I realised that I had said things to this man that could damage my career if he followed his. I had made myself vulnerable and it was the most wonderful feeling I had had in years – better than the roller skates I had for Christmas once, which seized up on Boxing Day because my father had bought them off a man in a pub.

It was only afterwards that I realised something else. We had never even kissed. Had he not wanted to? He can't have been too shy. Was he just being kind to me?

Kind to me?

'How dare you?' I startled a rookery of rooks as I pedalled furiously home.

46

THE TEETH OF HELL

Rivers was off the next morning with a bad back – or, more likely, a bad conscience – and the twins had been on nights. Brigsy was at the desk industriously polishing his reading glasses. He spent longer doing that than he did using them.

'Is he in?' I asked, and the disgust with which I said *he* left my sergeant in no doubt about who I was referring to.

'Sleepin' it off, I dare say.' Brigsy did his clever trick of rolling one eye up and the other down and the resignation with which he said *it* left me no doubt about what he was referring to.

'Not for long, he isn't,' I vowed, and I strode down the corridor and barged in without knocking.

This time, my surprise entry actually was a surprise. Sharkey was not sleeping it off as predicted but trying to drink it off. He had been slouched with his feet up on the mounds of paperwork on his desk, pouring a shot of whisky into his tea.

'Hell's teeth, Church.' Sharkey slopped his cocktail over his sleeve. 'You can't come barging in like that.'

'I am often struck,' I quoted Sidney Grice with great satisfaction, 'by how frequently people tell me I cannot do things that I have already done.'

'Eh?' Sharkey brought out a handkerchief, white and pressed and a great credit to his laundry. He mopped his wrist. 'Look, I'm not in the mood for any of your games today.'

He didn't look it, either. He looked more like an advertisement for the man who had yet to try Dr Mansell's Liver Salts – tie pulled down and collar not grubby but a bit crumpled, complexion grey with a hint of saffron around the jowls.

'Good,' I said, 'because I am not here to play any.' I whipped the chair away, not to sit on it but so I could plonk my hand on the debris of his desk and lean over him. 'If you ever attempt to question Barnaby Mason without the presence of at least two police officers, I will use the same blackmail on Rivers as you and—'

'Blackmail?' Sharkey looked genuinely indignant. 'Bribery maybe. I only said *If you keep your trap shut I'll see you right*.' He took a quick slug straight from the bottle.

Doris See-You-Right Driscow, I remembered.

'What the hell is so funny?' Sharkey recorked the bottle.

'You are,' I said, 'a bloody joke.'

I went back to the lobby where Bantony was unstrapping his helmet.

'Leave that on,' I commanded.

'But oy've com in for a brew,' he objected.

'No you haven't,' I corrected him. 'You've come in to go out again.'

'But I 'aven't 'ad anyfink to drink all day.'

'No time for that.' I marched to the door and wondered why the hell I talked myself into these situations. I was gasping for a cuppa too.

47

THE SLAUGHTERHOUSE OF PALMER

The sun was shining and the birds were singing, except for the seagulls who were assailing us with their horrible rusty-wheel shrieks. What could possibly be wrong with the world?

BRITISH TROOPS INVADE ICELAND, the newspaper board proclaimed.

'Is Oysland the enemy, ma'am?' Bantony asked, and for once I shared his puzzlement.

'As far as I know they are neutral,' I told him.

BELGIUM PUT ON HIGH ALERT, another board announced.

'Croypes! We're not invadink them too, are we?'

'I think the Germans are more likely to do that.'

'But Mr Chamberlain said that Hitler has missed the buz.' Bantony swivelled his head to watch a respectable young mother go past pushing a pram.

'Mr Chamberlain also promised us peace in our time,' I reminded him.

'Very noice,' Bantony murmured, probably to himself. He could hardly have expected me to comment on her shapely posterior.

'Stop staring,' I hissed.

'Oy was only thinkink what a beautiful … baby.'

And I know which baby you mean, as well.

We walked on past the railway station.

'Don't you ever think of anything other than women's legs?' I asked as we crossed the road.

'Course Oy do,' Bantony bridled. 'Oy think about their—'

'Anything other than women generally?' I broke in before he gave me an anatomical list, and Bantony mulled the question over.

'Women are moy main interest,' he conceded.

'Why did you become a policeman?' I asked and wished I hadn't, because I just knew he would tell me about how girls love a man in uniform.

'To foyght croyme,' Constable Bank-Anthony declared and I glanced across but his face was deadly serious. 'Oy 'ate croyme wiv a vengeance, Oy do.'

'Any particular reason?' I asked, wondering if some childhood incident had affected him so deeply.

'Because it's wrong.' Bantony's eyes flared furiously.

A cat shot across the pavement, making me stumble almost into the arms of my all-too willing constable.

'What did you do before you joined the force?' I asked, trying, not very successfully, to regain my poise. 'Apart from chase after girls.'

'They usually chase after moy,' he claimed with some justification. I had seen the way girls – and sometimes their respectable mothers – returned his ogles.

We turned off down Emery Lane, which wits, untroubled by dictionaries, used to change to Memery Lane until the council cut the sign right up to the first letter.

'So what *did* you do?' I asked again.

'Oy worked in Palmer's Abattoir,' he told me.

'But you're frightened of blood.'

'As a clerk in the office,' he said. 'I walked quarter of a moyle round the block every day to go in the back entrance but Oy could still 'ear the sufferinks of the cattle.'

'Sounds awful,' I sympathised.

'It was,' he agreed. 'Oy could 'ardly 'ear moyself chattink to the tea ladies or the toypists.'

I gave up and tried to console myself that if my constable had a one-track mind, at least he had a mind. We walked on, the terraces giving way to semis until we turned into Jaconda Road, where they became detached.

'Here we are.' We stopped.

'Not very grand for the name.' Bantony assessed it as critically as he might a woman's ankle and I found myself in agreement.

Pheasant Lodge was a nondescript one-storey bungalow pebble-dashed in a creamy colour and standing between Rose Cottage, which was blue and had no roses, and Dunroamin', which was pink and smothered in climbing roses.

'Has someone been swapping the names about?' I joked weakly.

'Oy don't think so, ma'am,' Bantony replied. 'The soyns are different soyzes and...'

'Joke,' I sighed, but Bantony took this as an invitation.

'I 'eard a good one by Big Hearted Arthur the other day,' he told me.

'No you didn't,' I insisted.

I couldn't stand Arthur Askey, that irritating little man with his irritating little song about busy busy bees going bzz bzz bzz. I opened the white picket gate and walked up the short path. The grass was a little overgrown but the hedge was neatly clipped. There were pansies in pots on either side and I couldn't work out if it was meant to be crazy paving or the slabs had been badly laid and cracked.

There was a bell push so I pushed it and heard the bell sound shrill nearby.

'No reploy,' Bantony said the moment I took my finger off the button.

'Give them a chance.'

'They've gone out,' he assured me.

I sort of folded my arms.

'And how, Constable Bank-Anthony, do you deduce that?' I challenged.

'Because of this.' Bantony held out a sheet of white notepaper folded in four. 'Oy found it under that pot.'

He jabbed a finger towards the pot in question like witnesses do in American courtroom scenes when they say *This is the man who murdered Morgan Katawalsky.* I unfolded the note. *GONE OUT BACK IN AN HOUR*, I read. I hate those notices. Cobblers are very fond of them and you never know if you'll have to wait ten seconds or three thousand five hundred and ninety. I crouched and poked a finger into the soil. Dodo would probably have asked if I was going to plant the note but Bantony had more sense.

'Are yow looking for the key, ma'am?' he asked, not unreasonably.

'I was checking how dry it is.' I pulled my finger out and stood up to show him the earth on the tip. 'Very.' I shook my finger but the dirt had become too fond of me to leave me that easily.

'So it hasn't been watered,' Bantony deduced. 'Allow moy, ma'am.' He whipped out a handkerchief as crisp and pristine as Old Scrapie's. Did they use the same laundry? I couldn't imagine either of them doing their own.

'No, thank you.' I struggled to unclip my bag and get my own hanky out without making anything else grubby but I was not going to give my constable an excuse to hold my hand.

I went to peer through the glass in the door but it was so heavily decorated with coloured leaves that I could make hardly anything out. Crouching to peer through the letter box, I saw a nice neat rectangular hall with coats on a row of pegs, umbrellas and sticks in an elephant's foot stand, a red mosaic-tiled floor, two closed doors either side and one straight ahead.

I went to the front left window – a pleasant front parlour with an upright piano. Through the right window was a dining room – a round table covered in a white lacy cloth.

'Is the side gate locked?'

'Oyl find out.' Bantony went along the right side of the house. 'No, ma'am,' he called and we went through – a small garden made private by privet, laid to lawn with low shrubs in the borders and a definitely crazy path winding to a little concrete fish pond. The inhabitants were alive but popping up to the surface with big O mouths, which I took to mean they were peckish.

There was one bedroom, the bed neatly made, and a kitchen with no dirty washing in the sink. A projection on the far side housed a bathroom, which Bantony assured me was unoccupied after he had balanced on a pipe to peer in through the small, high window.

'So no sign of Mr or Mrs C. Windser, no sign of a break-in or a struggle. All seems in order.' We went round to the front again. 'Let's try the neighbours.'

I went to Rose Cottage and left him to Dunroamin'. My knock was answered almost immediately by a shout of 'Because our surname is Rose', closely followed by the door being flung open. 'People are always asking us that,' a little man with round wire spectacles explained.

'Mr Rose?' I asked – stupidly, I realised immediately.

'You guessed,' he jeered.

'I am Inspector Church.'

'What happened to your arm?'

I held out my right hand. 'It looks fine to me.'

'No, the other one.'

One day I would scream *Oh my God! What have you done with it?* But today I only said, 'We parted company.'

'Yes, but how?'

'Amicably,' I told him. 'Have you seen Mr or Mrs Windser lately?'

'Who?'

'Your neighbours.'

'No.' Mr Rose made to shut the door but I was not going to be treated like a shady salesman so I behaved like one and stuck my foot against it.

'Is your wife at home?' I enquired, in the hope she might be more cooperative.

Mr Rose bobbled his head happily. 'I hope not. She's been dead eight years and before you ask…' – he wagged a forefinger in my face and I resisted an urge to snap it off – '…I didn't kill her.'

Don't be so sure, I told him silently.

'She killed herself,' he laughed merrily.

I rest my case.

'Do you have any idea where the Windsers might be?' I asked despondently.

'Presumably not at home or you wouldn't be asking,' he said helpfully, and I realised who this irksome little man reminded me of.

Bzz bzz bzz, I thought, but had no trouble at all in not using his other catchphrase, Ay-thang-yow.

'Goodbye, Mr Rose,' I sighed. 'I am sorry you have troubled me.'

'Don't you mean—' he called after me.

'What I say,' I said.

Bantony was lounging against a doorpost, his helmet tipped jauntily back, allowing his thick black hair to flop boyishly forward.

'Oy love dancing,' he was saying. 'Got the new Bert Ambrose last week only moy radiogram is broken.'

'You could come and play it on mine,' a woman was saying.

'Constable Bank-Anthony,' I called.

'Gotta go, madam.' He gave her a salute so casually that he might have been waving. 'But thank yow for yowr assistance.' He strolled over to me.

'Byeee,' the lady simpered.

'Yow know where Oy am if yow think of anythink else,' he called.

'Oh, I'm quite sure I'll think of something,' she giggled and wiggled her fingers and closed the door reluctantly.

'You do *not* use an official inquiry to seduce lonely housewives,' I scolded.

'Oh, trust me, ma'am, that one is never lonely,' Bantony smirked.

'And did she tell you anything useful – about her neighbours?' I tacked on as his smirk became a grin.

'Saw them walk out and leave the note last Tuesday,' he told me and sniggered. 'Knows it was Tuesday 'cause she 'ad the plumber round and it took 'im a couple of hours to see to 'er... pipes.'

Oh, for heaven's sake.

'Who did they leave the note for?' I wondered.

'Their daughter.' Bantony got out his notebook and flipped it open. 'Mrs Geramine Waggoner of twenty-nine Foster's Lane.'

He snapped his notebook shut and slipped it away without seeming to affect the line of his jacket.

Why... I wondered disconsolately as we waited for a truckful of ground crew to go past *...did the rubbish copper get all the information while I got practically none?*

The men were wolf-whistling.

'Give her one for me, mate,' a corporal mechanic yelled out.

'Oy certainly will,' Bantony called back and I took a sharp breath. 'Not,' he added too quietly and too late.

48

THE SWARTHY MEN AND
THE STRANGLED SKEIN

Sharkey had a new lead on the murder of Eric Bone. An anonymous letter claimed to have seen him struggling with two black men and being frogmarched up the hill towards the House of Horrors. We didn't have any negros in Sackwater so Old Scrapie decided that Lorenzo and Marco Bianchi, who ran the Napoli Restaurant in Germaine Street, would fit the bill. They were the swarthiest men he could think of and we might be at war with their countrymen soon, the way things were going, so it was obvious the Bianchis must have murderous intent. Being foreign, the brothers would doubtless be armed and dangerous and so he took every man on duty, leaving Dodo at the desk to catch up on her knitting.

'If you need me I will be at twenty-nine Foster's Lane,' I told her and she wrote out the address painstakingly.

'And where shall you be if I do not need you, Boss?' Dodo licked the nib of her pen. 'Oh but I mistook it for a pencil.' She screwed up her face.

'The same place,' I confirmed.

'So I did not need to pass my tongue over it,' Dodo huffed, looking all at once demonic with her hair ablaze, her eyes smouldering and a dark stain creeping creepily from the corner of her mouth across her face.

'Goodbye,' I said, shouldered my gas mask and left.

Twenty-nine Foster's Lane was a fish and chip shop when I was a girl but it was too successful for such a small location and had to move to a purpose-built-premises on the prom. Sometime after that it had been a wireless shop, which also moved on and up, and a book-keepers' office, which slowly wasted away. Now it sold wool and the woman behind the counter was very happy about it.

'This time last year we just about got by,' Geramine Waggoner told me, 'then with the war there's hardly a woman and a surprising number of men in the county who doesn't feel it their patriotic duty to knit, sew, make and mend. I've had one of your colleagues in quite a lot recently.'

I would take a large bet that it wasn't Sharkey or Brigsy.

'Constable Chivers?' I asked.

'That's the one, Dodo,' Geramine Waggoner laughed. 'She's a funny little sausage.'

There were a lot of things police officers were not supposed to be – too short, too young, too old, a convicted criminal or a certified lunatic, and I was fairly certain that list included being a funny little sausage.

'I thought she was a schoolgirl when she came in in her civvies,' Geramine told me. There was something schoolgirlish about her, too. You could easily imagine her playing lacrosse and ragging her chums. 'You could have knocked me down with a feather when I found out she was a policeman, I mean woman.'

I sometimes wished somebody would knock Dodo down with something.

'Have you been in contact with your parents recently, Mrs Waggoner?' I asked, and her laughter died as suddenly as if I had taken an axe to it.

'A week last Sunday,' she replied. 'Why? Has something happened?'

'I don't know,' I said. 'It's just that the *Gazette* wanted to contact them about their wedding anniversary but nobody has seen them since last Tuesday.'

'Really?' She picked up a ball of beige wool. 'They are such creatures of habit you could set your watch by them – church, whist club, shopping. Let me see. Today they should be playing bowls.' Her fingers dug in. 'Perhaps Daddy is ill. He has a weak chest.'

'They did not answer their door when my constable and I called round,' I told her. 'And we found a note saying they would be back soon but it looked like it had been there a while.'

'Oh dear.' Mrs Waggoner twisted the wool like she was trying to strangle it.

'Do you have any idea of where they might be?'

'None at all.' She looked me in the eye. 'Honestly, I'd tell you if I had. This isn't like them at all.'

She glanced down, realised what she was doing and laid the tangled remains of her skein on the counter.

'Do you have a key for the house?' I asked.

'Yes I do.' She made a half-hearted attempt to straighten the wool. 'Do you want me to go round and check?'

'That would be very helpful,' I said, 'but it might be better if I came with you.'

'You don't think anything has happened to them?' she asked in alarm.

'There's probably a very simple explanation,' I assured her, but didn't point out that simple explanations are not necessarily happy ones.

49

KNITTING FOR VICTORY AND
ST JOHN THE EVANGELIST

M rs Waggoner emptied her till, turned the *open* sign to *closed* and locked up the shop.

We walked along High Road East past Sammy's sweet shop.

'Do you have a Miss Prim as one of your customers?' I asked and Mrs Waggoner rolled her eyes.

'Unfortunately, yes,' she confirmed. 'The old biddy accused me of being defeatist because I said things didn't look very good.'

'It's not actually a crime to feel pessimistic,' I reassured her.

'I was talking about the weather,' she giggled and I joined in her laughter.

'Stop it, the pair of you,' an elderly man snapped. 'Cackling like crones in public. It is positively indecent.'

'Are you German?' Mrs Waggoner interrogated him, though his accent was cut glass.

'No, and further—'

'Did you hear that, officer?' Mrs Waggoner jumped in. 'He just said *nein, mein Führer*. This man is a storm trooper.'

'You are mad,' the man protested. 'You should be locked away.' He stalked off.

'I'm sorry,' Mrs Waggoner said, 'but I couldn't stop myself, pompous ass.'

'Good for you, Mrs Waggoner,' I said. 'I rather enjoyed that.'

'Please call me Gera,' she told me. 'Don't worry, I'll still call you Inspector. It's just I hate the name Waggoner almost as much as the man who gave it to me.'

I had some sympathy with that last sentiment.

'Does he have a bad front tooth?' I asked.

'No,' Gera puzzled. 'Why?'

'I was taken to dinner by an Attard Waggoner once and I ended up having to pay for us both plus a taxi to take him home because he was too drunk to walk.'

'Sounds like your Mr Waggoner was nearly as bad as mine,' Gera said.

'Are you still married?'

'In law,' she said, 'but separated, thank God. He slapped me once and I stupidly stayed with him. He did it again and I reshaped his nose with a statue of St John the Evangelist – or was it St Peter? He makes bronze religious images for a living.'

We arrived at the house and Gera hesitated. 'Will you open the door, please?'

I took the key and we went into the hall. There were four envelopes on the floor, all bills. Gera put them on a small cream-painted console table and we went around the bungalow. Everything looked spick and span.

'Do your parents have paper or milk deliveries?' I asked.

'They never read the paper and they cancelled the milk after a row with the dairy. I don't know how they manage without it.'

We poked about.

'No bodies under the beds or in the wardrobe,' Gera smiled weakly.

There was a thin pantry cupboard off the kitchen. I looked in a small sack hanging off a hook in the ceiling.

'These potatoes are past their best.' I showed her. They had sprouted and smelled musty.

'They would never let food go to waste like that,' Gera said in alarm.

'Do they have any friends they might be visiting or relatives who might be sick?'

'No, nobody I can think of.' Gera opened the butter dish. 'It's rancid.' She put the lid back on.

'Do your parents like walking?' I asked.

'They go for a stroll along the prom most days when the weather is good.'

'This may sound silly, but do they ever paddle in the sea?'

Gera snorted. 'It does sound very silly,' she agreed. 'No, they never go on the beach itself. Anyway, you can't now.'

'You can still get to the sea over the sandhills,' I pointed out, remembering my stroll with Toby.

'They're not the hiking kind.' Gera followed me back out into the hall. 'Oh, Inspector, what on earth could have happened to them?'

'I don't know, but I shall do everything I can to find out,' I promised, because it's the useless sort of thing we feel obliged to say.

50

DEAD MEN DRIVE AND
HITLER CATCHES THE BUS

went to Straight Street and was happy to see Toby light up when he saw me.

'So it wasn't just the beer,' he grinned. Carol had gone out on an errand. He stood up. 'I've never hugged a policewoman in uniform before.'

'And you won't this morning,' I laughed, though still feeling confused. 'This is official business.'

'Not even—?'

'Not even,' I assured him and sat on the armchair opposite his, not forgetting to pull my skirt primly over my knees.

'Must say I thoroughly approve of these material-saving measures.' Toby eyed me appreciatively.

My hemline had gone up a good ten inches while I had been stationed at Sackwater.

'Just wait until you men have to wear shorter trousers,' I threatened.

'That would not be a pretty sight,' Toby assured me, 'all those pallid hairy shins. We keep them covered for good reasons, you know.' He leaned back in his chair. 'So what's the official business? Any developments on the Eric Bone case?'

'Nothing,' I admitted. 'Nobody else has come forward except for the man who definitely saw Mr Bone driving a Lagonda at breakneck speed along the North Circular.'

'Don't think I'll bother printing that one,' Toby chuckled. 'It's your Mr and Mrs Windser.'

'I didn't realise I'd taken possession of them. What have they been up to then?'

'That's the problem,' I told him. 'We don't know.'

Toby leaned forward, the leather creaking under his elbow. 'Still not made an appearance?'

I shook my head. 'And their daughter has no idea where they might be. They were seen by neighbours last Tuesday, possibly going off for their morning constitutional along the prom, and never seen again.'

'You've checked the house?'

'Oh, I never thought of that,' I said and checked myself. 'I'm sorry, Toby. That sounded quite shrewish.'

Toby laughed. 'Whatever creature you might resemble, it isn't a bad-tempered rodent. But I'm a bit frightened to ask now... do you have a photograph?'

'Yes.' I brought it out. 'It was taken for their fortieth but Geramine Waggoner, their daughter, says they haven't changed much since then.'

Mr Colin Windser was an officious-looking man with hair parted just over his left ear and dragged across to the right in a way that proclaimed *Look everybody, I'm virtually bald*. He had a small moustache, not quite Chaplinesque or Führeresque but not far off. Mrs Netabery Windser had a little forage cap with a feather clinging miserably to her tightly permed grey hair. Her expression was severe and made all the worse by her trying to deform it into something menacingly pleasant.

'Gera, the woman who owns the wool shop?' Toby clarified.

'Don't tell me you've taken up knitting.'

'My mother is producing gloves at an industrial level,' he told me.

'So she expects the war to go through the winter?' I massaged around my stump very gingerly. It had been twinging intermittently for a couple of days now and I hoped I was not going to get any more bone fragments breaking off. Apart from the pain, I did not want to have to have it trimmed any shorter.

'This winter and God alone knows how many others,' Toby said grimly. 'Oh, haven't you heard?' He looked at me in concern. 'The Germans have invaded Belgium.'

And with perfect timing, the phone rang. Somebody wanting free advertising space for their social club.

It took Toby a long time to explain that while the club may be a charity, he wasn't, and I don't think he was too upset when the man said he would take his business elsewhere and hung up.

'I didn't know anything about it,' I said.

I don't know why I was so shocked. We knew the Germans were massing on the borders. We knew Belgium had declared a state of emergency. We were even aware that we and the French were at war with Germany, but I was still momentarily stunned.

'But why?' I began stupidly, because we all knew they couldn't drive straight through like last time. 'The Maginot Line…'

'Doesn't go across the Franco-Belgian border,' Toby pointed out.

I knew that really but we were led to believe that the line had almost mystical qualities.

'But they did this last time,' I remembered in disgust. 'So why are we letting them do it again?'

'I think the idea is to funnel the German Army into Belgium so we can concentrate our counter-attack with overwhelmingly superior forces,' Toby said, 'or so people who know more than me about these things tell me. They can't invade around the other end because the Ardennes forests form a natural barrier.'

'I hope so.'

'That's about all we can do,' Toby said.

The door closed downstairs.

'Only me,' Carol called up.

'Oh, yes please, with sugar,' I called down, to Toby's puzzlement. 'Sorry, I thought she said *Any tea?*'

'I believe you,' Toby smiled. 'Let me have a look at that photo.'

51

THE PERFECT MURDER OF MISS PRIM

I knew something was wrong the moment I entered the lobby and saw Brigsy's face and his hand on the desk flicking like I was being dismissed, but I was damned if I was going to be turfed out of my own station.

Brigsy was twitching his head now and mouthing something that looked like *Pru* or *pram*, but I realised too late I should have allowed myself to be ejected.

'Good afternoon, Inspector.'

I wheeled about and there she sat on the back bench, all in mauve with pale mauve hair, even the gas mask box on the seat beside her encased in a mauve cotton sleeve. If there was one sound I was coming to associate with war so far, it wasn't the drone of Hurricanes flying out to sea from Hadling Heath or the pumping explosions of ack-ack from across the bay or the whining false alarms of the sirens – it was the click-click-clicking of long fat sharp steel needles pumping out endless hairy yards of plain, rib and purl.

'Miss Prim.' I hadn't meant to snarl but I did and I didn't regret it. 'What do you want?'

I was not normally so rude to little old ladies but Miss Prim regarded herself as a sleuth, amateur only in the sense that she was unpaid, for in every other way her powers were superior to those of the professional force. If Miss Prim were to be believed, she had given us the solution to the Suffolk Vampire enquiries within hours of the very first death and all the other murders could have been prevented if only we had listened to her. She had also 'helped' with dozens of crimes, almost all imaginary, since then. It was Miss Prim who tracked down the man who stole Eden Eden's marmalade cat. The fact that Mr Eden never had a cat in no way tarnished the glitter of her success.

'Oh, Inspector.' Miss Prim's lips fibrillated with amusement beneath her can-opener nose and I just knew she was going to tell me it wasn't what she wanted; it was what I wanted. 'It isn't what I want; it's what you want,' she told me.

Elderly lady in fatal accident in police station foyer. I felt certain Brigsy would back my story of how she fell backwards and cracked her head, and with Tubby to perform the post mortem and a hasty cremation, even I would be unable to prove anything against myself.

'And what might that be?' I sighed.

'Wouldn't we be more comfortable in your office?' She treated me to a little teeth-worn-to-the-gums smile.

I was on the horns of a dilemma here. My office was a sanctuary from the vulgar herd but on the other hand I could polish her off in there without any witnesses.

'No,' I replied. 'My office is very uncomfortable.'

'I thought as much,' Miss Prim beamed stumpily. 'But you would never have admitted to such discomfort were it not for my trick question. That goes some way to explaining your general rundown and drab appearance.'

I had an axe in my office, I remembered. It had been left on the desk one morning and I had taken it in to stop the boy-men playing with it.

'What have you come to tell me, Miss Prim.' I folded my arms as best I could and glared down at her and Miss Prim tittered. She had strings of off-white saliva spanning her mouth like old wet cobwebs.

'I have come to offer you the benefit of my vast experience...'

Miss Prim began to recite the same litany that she always inflicted upon me.

I wonder what we'll have for dinner tonight? I cogitated.

'...and understanding of criminal psychology...'

Captain was cooking, so it would probably be *fenek*, as they called rabbit in Malta.

'...and extensive reading of who-did-its – I do so detest those who say *dunnit* – over...'

Roast or stew. I liked the stew and if Captain could still get pasta, he'd use some of the meat and juices to make a spaghetti sauce.

'The mistake you have been making...' Miss Prim was saying, and I tuned back in. She would still be talking tosh but it would be relevant tosh now. '...is in thinking that the body must have been washed in from the sea.'

'But how else do it have got there?' Brigsy asked, and I wished he hadn't. It implied that we valued her opinion, whereas the only thing we ever valued was her leaving.

'Have you considered the possibility of a tunnel?' Miss Prim enquired, her eyes behind her round wire spectacles a dull testimony to her intellect.

'No,' I admitted, 'because there isn't one.'

'Have you looked?'

'No, because I don't have time to waste looking for things that don't exist.'

'Seek and ye shall find,' Miss Prim quoted primly.

'Matthew chapter seven verse seven,' Brigsy chipped in, and I was so glad the afternoon was turning into a weekday Sunday school.

'An old smugglers route,' she suggested, 'or a way under the minefield for Hunnish invaders to creep through and murder us in our beds.'

If only they would.

'The best way to avoid that fate,' I advised her, 'is never to go to bed.'

'I never do,' Miss Prim countered defiantly.

'Why don't you have a look, Miss Prim?' I suggested unkindly and was rewarded with another titter.

'Oh, I suspect you are jesting with me, Inspector. You know I do not like to get sand on or in my shoes.'

'Oh, botheration,' Brigsy said loudly, 'I near forget to say. Superintendent Vesty do want to see you in his office immediately you do come in, madam.'

If I were filming an epic I would not have put Brigsy at the back of a crowd scene, but his monotone recital had the desired effect on the marvellous Miss Prim.

'Well, I'd better be off then.' She impaled her wool on the needles in a way that made me squirm for the ball, gathered her handbag, her shopping bag and her gas mask and bundled off like a beetle scuttling into its hole.

'Thank you, Brigsy,' I said. 'But I wish you'd thought of that ten minutes ago.'

'Sorry, madam, I clean forgot with her bein' here.'

'You mean the super *does* want to see me?'

Brigsy screwed up his eyes. 'Why else would I say it, madam?'

'No reason at all,' I said.

Brigsy mumbled something when I was halfway down the hall. I didn't catch it, but I caught its tone.

'I heard that,' I told him.

'Sorry, madam,' he called back. 'Oh blow,' he muttered, 'you do be in serious peril now, Brigsy boy.'

And I wished I had shouted, 'What did you say?' instead, because I might have been able to bully my sergeant into confessing but I couldn't admit that I was lying and now I would never know.

'Come,' Vesty responded to my knock. 'Ah, Church, have a seat.'

The superintendent sat at his desk closing a copy of Gertrude Jekyll's *Roses for English Gardens* that was probably nearly as old as me.

I perched opposite him.

'You wished to see me, sir.'

'Did I?'

'Sergeant Briggs said you did.'

'Then I must. Brigso, as I believe you call him, is not a man to play pranks, what?'

I was not so sure about that. Who else had the opportunity to swap the keys about in Sharkey's desk drawers so that he thought all the locks were jammed?

'Indeed not, sir.'

'Ah, yes.' Vesty clicked his fingers. 'I shall be taking some more time off in future.' He hadn't actually taken much time on lately but I nodded sympathetically when he explained. 'Been a bit run down lately.'

The super took a breath and I seized my chance to slip in an *Oh dear*.

'And I wanted you to be the first to know,' he continued. 'I am thinking of putting Inspector Sharkey's name down for promotion.'

52

THE REWARDS OF CORRUPTION AND THE
FRAYING OF HOPE

This was turning into quite a day for shock news and I was not sure which had stunned me the most. At least we had an inkling about Hitler's intentions but Vesty's had come completely out of the blue. Having survived a real bombshell recently, I could not describe this as one but I suddenly found myself clinging to the wreckage of my career.

A couple of lifelines dangled in front of me, though, and I snatched at the first.

'Only thinking, sir?'

'Indeed...' He almost let me touch that line before he whisked it away with '...very seriously.'

The second lifeline was looking worryingly frayed now.

'Why did you want me to be the first to know?'

Vesty put his elbows on his desk and his fingertips together.

'Because I wanted your opinion. I think I can guess what his would be.'

'Do you want an honest opinion, sir?'

Vesty interlocked his hands.

'Why would I want a dishonest one?' he asked reasonably. 'I could ask him for that.'

'That is exactly what you would get,' I leaped in. 'Inspector Sharkey is a deceitful and duplicitous man.' I wasn't quite sure, off the top of my head, what the exact difference was between those two qualities, but the second sounded especially damning.

'I am well aware of that.' Vesty rested his chin on his knuckles as if the weight of his head was too much for his neck. 'I am sure you know things about the blackguard that I do not, but I assure you, Inspector Church, I know things about him that would make your beautiful naturally blonde hair curl.'

'It is bad enough working with and often against Sharkey,' I said as calmly as I could. 'I cannot work under him.'

'Nor would you have to.'

'Then you would accept my resignation?'

Vesty unravelled his fingers, which seemed to be in one of the sort of complicated knots that Captain tried to teach me on long winter evenings. 'Like hell, I would.' He waved his right hand, relying upon the left to support his head. 'Pardon my expletive. The reason I am thinking of it is that they are looking for a new chief inspector in Felixstowe and we would be rid of him for ever – well, for the rest of my career at any rate.'

He took his left hand away and, to my irrational surprise, his head did not fall bumping on to the polished oak towards me.

'You cannot do it, sir.'

'Can I not?' There was more of a helplessness than defiance or assertion of authority in his question.

'No,' I insisted. 'You are an honourable man, Superintendent Vesty, and you cannot reward Sharkey's corrupt and incompetent behaviour in this way. Nor can you deceive them as to his suitability for the role. Nor can you inflict him upon another station. Nor—'

'Points taken,' Vesty butted in, somewhat to my relief because I had run out of *nors*.

My superior clutched his temples in frustration. 'Dash it all, Church, I was hoping you would talk me into it.'

'Neither of us would be able to look each other or ourselves in the eye,' I told him with more than a few twinges of regret.

After all that talk about honour, I supposed this was not the time to enquire if Felixstowe might be willing to consider a woman and, anyway, I had a meeting to prepare for.

53

THE CORPSES IN THE SWAMP

There was not as big a turnout as I had hoped for the meeting. Toby had advertised it in the *Gazette* and Gera had put posters up in several shops, but of the thousands of adults in the area with not much else to do, about forty turned up.

I stood on the low dais at the end of the Women's Institute and I didn't have to call for silence. They were huddled in sullen clumps on rows of wooden chairs, Gera sitting at the front alone.

'Thank you all for coming,' I began.

'Don't mind me,' Mrs Haghaw grumbled. 'She can thank all of you but she can't thank me.'

I – and thankfully everyone else – ignored her.

'As you may know, Mr and Mrs Windser have gone missing—'

'The King and Queen, gawd blesser, have gorn missing?' Mrs Dimmock howled in horror.

'Mr Colin and Mrs Netabery Windser,' I clarified.

'That's a dashed silly name,' commented a corpulent man in a striped blazer. 'Colin.'

'*Dashed?*' Mrs Stag mouthed in disgust. 'Mind your language, you fat-arsed fat arse.'

'You leave my husband's fat arse out of this,' Mrs Striped Blazer railed.

'I wish he would leave it somewhere else,' Mrs Stag retorted. 'He take up half my seat he do.'

'Move then.'

'Why should I? I was here first.'

Gera jumped to her feet and faced the audience.

'Please,' she cried. 'My parents have gone missing and—'

'Where did you leave them?' asked Mrs Haghaw, the fishmonger's wife.

'At home.'

'Then they should still be there.'

'But they're not.'

'Well, they should be,' Mrs Haghaw insisted. 'I int got time for folk who int where they should be.'

Gera tried again. 'I am desperately concerned. Nobody has seen them for a week.'

'Have you told the police?' enquired Mr Dradish, the curator of Sackwater Museum. 'I mean the proper police, not this woman.'

'I *am* the proper police,' I insisted and decided against explaining that I meant part of it.

'Well, part of it, possibly,' Mr Dradish conceded, and I resolved not to rush around the next time he called us out because somebody was demanding their money back.

'We are looking for volunteers to help search for Mr and Mrs Windser,' I announced.

'Int that your job?' demanded a greasy young man with two horrible waxy trickles from his snout.

'Yes, but we need help,' I tried.

'I thought we do come to meet the King and Queen, gawd blesser,' Mrs Stag complained.

'So do I,' declared a woman in something that looked like it had been cobbled from remnants of remnants. She had a hat on that you might store vegetable peelings in for the communal pig. 'Got dolled-up special I did.'

There was a general murmur of agreement and gatherings

of bags and gas masks and scrapings of chairs and buttoning of coats and Gera and I found ourselves addressing eight people.

'This is hopeless,' she lamented, close to tears.

'I'm missing Reginald Foort to be here,' declared a young woman with her hair in a checked turban.

How the hell could you miss Reginald Foort? Every time you turned on the wireless, if it wasn't some pretend upper-cruster patronising us in an over-clipped accent about how our men were giving the enemy what for, it was good old Reggie pumping 'Keep Smiling' out of his long-suffering Wurlitzer.

'I was told we were organising a party,' whined a girl who must have been all of fourteen – a classic example of lamb dressed as mutton in her twinset.

'A search party,' I clarified.

'Well, that's not my idea of a knees-up,' she retorted and tottered off on stilt-like heels to the fire exit then, finding it illegally blocked, through the back door marked *Private. No Unauthorised Personnel.*

'Do not despair of recovering your beloved parents, dear lady.' A tall bespectacled man arose from the back of the room. I had thought he was sleeping or dead – of natural causes, I hoped. 'For my troop shall come to your aid.'

'Are you an army man?' I asked and the tall man tossed his head. He couldn't toss his hair because it was trimmed to a sort of suede finish.

'Better than that,' he told me proudly. 'I am a Scoutmaster.'

'Boy Scouts?' I checked.

'Of course.' He tossed his spikes. 'We are trained to track and if anyone can find this couple's bodies, it is us.'

'Bodies?' Gera breathed.

I don't think the possibility had seriously occurred to her until that moment.

'Or us,' put in a tiny woman with masses of yellow hair tied up in not so much a bun as a home-made loaf.

'Don't be ridiculous,' the man sneered. 'You are girls and baby girls at that.'

'The Sackwater Brownies are more than a match for any of your boys,' the woman insisted with such fierce pride that I rather hoped she was right.

'How old are your Brownies?' I asked with a suspicion that the answer would be *not very*.

'Seven to ten,' she told me. 'But they have old heads on their young shoulders and if those mutilated corpses are to be found, my girls will do it.'

'Mutil...' was all Gera managed in her shock.

'This is ridiculous,' the Scoutmaster complained. 'We can't have silly little girls rooting about in sewers for rotting cadavers.'

The Brownie leader hesitated. 'We shall leave the drainage system to you,' she decided.

'Mind you,' the Scoutmaster conceded, 'your girls, being smaller, might more easily get along the pipes.'

Gera breathed hard, looking worryingly pale.

'Perhaps we could leave the drainage system for now,' I suggested hastily. 'As far as we know, Mr and Mrs Windser are still alive.'

'What? Out there?' The Scoutmaster pointed like *out there* was the sort of swamp I had read about in *Armstrong of the Amazon*, populated by leopard-skin-clad tribesmen with poisoned blow-darts.

'Oh dear,' Gera said. 'I think I need to sit down.'

'Oh,' said a man in a shepherd's smock, so loudly that some people ducked. 'And brin' some clothes – coats or unwashed shirts or the like.'

'Why?' I asked.

'Sent,' he said.

'Sent where?' I asked.

'Sent wherever it may be,' he explained confusingly, and then less confusingly, 'My dogs goo track by scent they do.'

54

JOLLY JOE HENDERSON AND
THE SHOAL OF PIRANHAS

Thirty-two people turned up at Sackwater Central Police Station the next morning, which was about twenty more than I had expected.

The Shark pushed his way through.

'What a bunch of deadbeats,' he commented loudly enough for several of them to hear.

'Are you coming to help, sir?' Dodo enquired brightly.

Old Scrapie looked down his nose. 'What do you think?'

'I think you are.' Dodo tried to look enthusiastic.

There was a button hanging loose on Sharkey's jacket and he needed someone to sew it. That someone was not going to be me. And he was not quite in need of a shave but he would be before the morning was out.

'Think again,' he told her and Dodo did.

'I think you are not,' she concluded with genuine enthusiasm.

Fifteen Scouts were there, looking very smart in their shorts, shirts and toggled neckerchiefs, their wide-brimmed hats and long staffs reminding me vaguely of Merlin. The Brownies looked very sweet in their miniature outfits but there were only three of them.

'Their mummies were not very happy at them being sent down sewers,' their tiny mistress explained. She made Dodo look quite big beside her and Dodo made many children look large. 'And Isabell had a party.'

'With jelly,' the smallest Brownie said, twiddling a ginger curl wistfully.

Teddy Moulton had come, not in his warden's uniform but in his bookshop uniform of brown corduroys and tweed jacket with a volume of Keats poking out in case he got bored.

Jolly Joe Henderson of Joe's Joke Shop was there and complaining that no refreshments had been provided.

'Want to sniff my flower, little boy?' he invited a child clutching his mother's hand, and before I could stop them the mother was storming off, dragging her wailing toddler, clutching his eye, out of the building.

The shepherd was there with his dogs – not collies, as I expected, or bloodhounds, as I had hoped, but terriers, three of them, baring their teeth and snarling at anyone coming within two yards of them.

'Shouldn't they be on leads?' I asked and the shepherd looked at me, appalled.

'You may as well chain up those mawthers.'

A mawther was anything from a small girl to an old woman, but he was pointing at the Brownies.

'You will do no such thing,' their leader assured me angrily, as if it had been my suggestion.

Gera handed the shepherd a brown paper bag.

'I brought a glove and a sock,' she told him, and the shepherd laid the bag on the floor. The dogs pounced.

'See how mustard they are?' he declared as they shredded the bag. 'They goo have the scent now they do,' he told us as they fought over a gentleman's black stocking. 'Have a good old sniff, girls,' he urged, every inch the proud father, watching them rip it apart before turning their aggression on to the glove, fingers torn off in their fight for possession.

'Will they hurt my parents if they find them?' Gera asked the shepherd.

'Nooooo, they are gentle as the lambs they tend.' He looked almost as wounded as he was about to be for, reaching down to pat their heads, there was a sudden blurred frenzy of snapping teeth and bloodied flesh. The shepherd let out a shriek, clutched his digits and ran from the lobby, the terriers lunging at his legs like that Greek bloke the goddess turned into a stag and set her hounds upon.

'That'll teach him,' a man in a trench coat said with great satisfaction.

'Actaeon,' I remembered and accidently said aloud.

'Action,' Teddy mis-repeated at the top of his voice, sounding more like a Hollywood director than an ARP man.

'Ready, troop,' the Scoutmaster commanded and his boys snapped smartly into two straight lines. 'Remember our motto.'

'Be prepared,' they yelled, except for a small boy at the end who piped out, 'Where a man has gone so far as to attempt suicide, a Scout should know what to do with him.' To scowls from his fellows but an approving nod from the master, who ruffled his hair and said, 'Well done, son.'

Not to be outdone, the Brownies were attempting to line up as well – not too difficult, I would have thought, when there were only two of them, the smallest one having asked Brigsy to show her the *powder room*, which, after some confusion and a whisper from Bantony in his ear, he did.

'Lend a hand,' they trilled, to their mistress's pride.

'Lend a hand,' the third Brownie echoed as she cantered over the lino to join them.

'A responsible job for responsible men,' Teddy Moulton

shouted, which I was not sure he was entitled to in his civvies, having got that from an ARP recruiting poster.

'Women of the Sackwater Women's Knitters for Victory,' shouted a young woman in rather a nice yellow coat. 'On the double, Lef-Right-Lef-Right.' At which all five of them tutted in exasperation and slouched after her.

'Constables of the East Suffolk Police Force, Sackwater Division,' Brigsy roared, 'Attennnnnnn Shun.'

Swallow me, earth, I prayed, but to my astonishment Box, Bantony, the Grinder-Snipes, even Rivers and even Dodo snapped instantly to attention.

'Quick march,' Brigsy bellowed and my heart pumped with pride as they made their way in perfect step to the door, until Box blocked the exit with his bulk, Dodo tripped and said *Owsy*, Rivers stumbled into her and said *Oh blimey! I've put my blinkin' back out*, the twins paused *After you Algernon – After you Lysander* like that blasted Claude and Cecil from ITMA, and oh I couldn't bear any more and was about to retreat to my office when I suddenly realised something rather important.

55

THE HUNT FOR HITLER

pushed through the milling mob of officers and civilians, elbowing Rivers and possibly putting his back back in again, though you wouldn't think it from his reaction. Out into Mulberry Road I rushed.

'Knock on doors and ask if they have seen anything. Ask if you can look in their sheds. If they say *no*, make a note of the address. One street per two people except the Brownies, who should stick together.'

But they were scattering. The man in a trench coat looked like he was heading for the Feathers, which was supposed to be closed for another two hours. The Boy Scouts were helping an old lady cross the road, nine of them holding up the traffic (consisting of Benny Bergman, the rag-and-bone man, with his donkey-drawn cart), one Scout on either side holding her arms, one carrying her shopping to the rear and the master leading all the way to the opposite pavement, asking, 'What does a Scout always do, boys?'

'A Scout always helps others,' they chanted.

'So does a Brownie,' the trio warbled back.

'Only more so,' their mistress chimed.

'Hello, nice police lady Church,' I heard at my side and I looked down to the shining blue eyes and golden-curled halo of Sylvia Satin.

Josie Whitehouse was holding Sylvia's hand.

'Sylvia want to come,' she explained and her ward nodded vigorously.

'And help,' she added.

'Well, that's very kind,' I said. 'Do you know Mr and Mrs Windser?'

'Oh, fiddlesticks to them,' Sylvia said sternly and those big blue eyes became flooded pools. 'I want my daddy.'

I pulled my lips hard together.

'Your daddy isn't here, darling,' I said softly.

'And tha's why we goo look for him,' Sylvia told me firmly, 'extra hard.'

'I have explained,' Josie Whitehouse told me softly. 'Daddy is in heaven, Sylvia.'

'No,' Sylvia told her calmly. 'People is happy in heaven and Daddy do never be happy without me.'

'He's watching over you,' Josie told her but Sylvia pulled her hand away.

'Then he must be very close,' Sylvia assured her. 'The vicar tell me he's in the next room.'

'He was quoting a poem,' Josie said hopelessly, and I wondered which room of the vicarage Reverend Heath was finding himself in now and whether he was being more careful with sharp instruments.

'Take her home,' I whispered to Josie and she grimaced.

'I'll try.'

'No, you won't,' I said firmly. 'You will do it.'

A young man came rushing up.

'Am I too late for the search?' he gasped.

'No, you can join it now, if you want,' I told him.

'Oh no.' He swatted the idea away. 'I dint want goo join it, I want to ask if they can keep an eye out for my boy too, while they're at it.'

'He's missing?' I asked with a sinking heart.

'Since yestdee mornin',' he nodded vigorously.

'But why did you wait so long?' I asked in dismay.

'I thought he might just come back.'

'How old is he?'

'Um, about three.'

'*About?*' I repeated in distaste for his cavalier attitude. 'Where did you last see him?'

'In the sand dunes. We do play and I do take my eye off him. I do try and look but it's gettin' dark. My wife is at her mother's. She'll kill me dead when she do find out.'

And who would blame her?

'What's his name?' I snapped and the man looked away.

'Adolf Hitler,' he said.

'You think that's funny?' I asked angrily. 'I have a missing couple to look for and you are very close to being arrested for wasting police time.'

'No, honest,' the man protested. 'We called him tha' for a joke. We goo try changing it to Winston but he won't come to tha' name.'

'This boy of yours,' I suddenly realised. 'Is he a dog?'

'Well, course he is – a sort of mixed-up spaniel.'

Normally I am sympathetic to lost pets and their owners. I know how distressing it can be for both.

'What I would suggest,' I said quietly in his ear, which had a lot of wax in it, I noticed, 'is that you go.'

'Go where?' he asked.

'Away,' I said.

56

CARNAGE AT TRINGFORD

The search found no trace of Mr or Mrs Windser but it was not entirely wasted. The Brownies let me down badly by finding a fairy ring and skipping around it with twigs for magic wands, but the Sackwater Women's Knitters for Victory recovered a lost tricycle that nobody had noticed was lost. There was great excitement when the Grinder-Snipes thought they had found the bench stolen from Sackwater Railway Station last year but it turned out to have been stolen from Tringford Model Village in 1910. The village had closed the following year after a cow trampled the high street, the church, the school, the pub and – every cloud has a silver lining – a whole crowd of Morris Dancers outside it into splinters.

The Scouts had the greatest triumph and disaster when they stumbled upon a conscription dodger hiding like something nasty in his mother's wood shed and arrested him, only to lose him when he asked them to turn their backs while he relieved himself and absconded. Their disappointment was tempered slightly when his mother admitted that he had never actually been called up because of his poor eyesight but she had wanted to keep him at home for company.

'I can't bear to think what might have happened to them,' Gera said sadly over a big pot of tea in the Lyons tea shop.

I recited my meaningless mantra. 'There may be a simple explanation.'

Tubby was in the corner trying to look inconspicuous as he tucked into a pork pie – he would be going home for dinner in half an hour – but the only place Tubby might have looked inconspicuous was in a den of grizzly bears. Even there, he would probably have stood out as the biggest and grizzliest of the pack, if that's what bears come in.

Gera finished her beverage, put fourpence on the table and left, but I was not going to pretend I hadn't seen Tubby.

'I missed lunch,' he assured me.

'Oh, Dr Gretham,' I laughed, 'don't ever commit a crime. You are the least convincing liar I have come across in my entire career.'

'Only,' Tubby wiped his mouth with his napkin, 'because I haven't had much practice.'

It was then that the door flew open and a young lad flew in.

'Do somebody goo ring for a doctor,' he told a nippy who was about to eject him. 'There's an old boy outside goo fallen over and he int getting' up.'

Tubby growled and rose magisterially to his feet. 'Nobody,' he roared, glaring around the room, 'and I mean *nobody* dare to touch that pie.'

57

THE MISTAKING OF DRUNKS FOR DRUNKS

followed Tubby out.

A small crowd was doing what small crowds do best – gathering. It stood in a circle, the perimeter thickening as more people gathered around it.

'Make way,' Tubby boomed, pushing through.

'Who you bargin'?' a dolphin-faced woman asked indignantly.

'You,' he told her.

'Don't you goo touchin' him,' she warned. 'We send for a doctor.'

'He *is* a doctor,' I assured her, following in Tubby's wake.

A man lay on his back. He was a long man and plump and probably rosy in health but right now he was a slate grey, clutching his chest and breathing in noisy convulsions.

'Call an ambulance,' Tubby commanded and knelt beside the man.

'I'll do tha',' the nippy volunteered and nipped back inside.

'Stand back,' I ordered the crowd. 'Give the man some air.'

Some people say that people gather round because of a natural desire to help. I put it down to nosiness because, when they do flock about, most people never actually try to do anything other than get in the way.

Tubby was taking the man's pulse and talking to him softly.

At first I thought somebody had cut the man's upper lip but there was no blood and I saw that it was a cleft and he must have been born with it.

'Does anybody know this man?' I asked and they shifted about guiltily as if I had accused them of causing his collapse. Most of them avoided my eye and a few of them did the other thing crowds are quite good at – melting away.

'He coom staggerin' and grabbin' hisself and he goo on his knees,' the youth declaimed to the crowd, who had now become his audience. 'And he shout *Get him away from me* he do and then he goo lay down.' The boy held out his hands, palms forward, like he was expecting a round of applause.

Tubby had unbuttoned the man's brown coat and jacket and waistcoat. He ripped open the shirt.

'Ohh, have a care,' the dolphin-faced woman cried, as if he had trodden on her corns.

Tubby put his ear to the man's chest.

'Be quiet, the lot of you,' he ordered and the dolphin-faced woman huffed.

'I do only be sayin'—'

'Shut up,' I snapped and she opened her beak but decided to do as instructed.

The man had gone limp.

'Dead,' Tubby announced and knelt up.

'If nobody knows him, you can all go about your business,' I instructed, but they were closing in. '*Now!*' I said and they did what this particular crowd didn't really want to do – drifted away.

Tubby got to his feet, a prolonged and lumbering business but he managed.

'What do you suppose he meant by saying *Get him away from me*?' I wondered.

Tubby dusted the knees of his baggy trousers.

'Probably nothing,' he said as I squatted on my haunches. 'The brain gets starved of oxygen when the heart isn't pumping properly. People get confused, they slur and they stagger. They're often mistaken for drunks. My father was, when he had his fatal heart attack. Mind you, it was unusual for him to be sober.'

'His shirt looked very crumpled and rucked up before you set to work on it,' I commented.

'Probably trying to tug his collar open to breathe better,' Tubby proposed.

'What about this?' I turned the dead man's head to show Tubby the left side of it.

'Nasty blow to the ear,' he confirmed. 'But he may well have fallen and bashed it.'

I checked for identification. Ronald Strap, aged fifty-nine, a fertiliser manufacturer from Ipswich.

'Maybe,' I agreed and stood up, declining the offer of Tubby Gretham's hand.

58

TODAY'S THE DAY THEY'RE NOT HAVING A BEARS' PICNIC

There were sniggers as I entered the station lobby and I was not in the best of moods already. It had not been a good journey with the night's rain flooding the track in muddy puddles that my bicycle wheels sprayed all over me, forgetting that they had mudguards to stop them doing that, and I was filthy before I was halfway there.

'Shall we 'ave a teddy bears'...' Sandy was asking.

'Picnic?' Algy chipped in.

'What a charming idea,' Dodo beamed.

'And can I bring my dolly-wolly?' Bantony asked to snorts from Rivers.

'I do not think dolly-wollies go to teddy bears' picnics,' Dodo told him gravely.

'In my office... *Now*,' I snapped, arm outstretched towards Dodo like a painting of the grim reaper.

Dodo wrinkled her nose in that sweet way she had.

'What is, Boss?' she asked innocently.

'You are,' I told her and before she could tell me that she wasn't, I added, 'within one minute or you are in trouble.'

She was in trouble anyway so I hadn't put that very well.

'So I will not be in trouble if I go straight there?' Dodo asked hopefully.

'You will not be in trouble for not being in my office if you are in it,' I told her, the wind somewhat out of my sails.

'I shall go there immediately then, Boss,' Dodo promised and trotted obediently down the corridor.

I glared at the men.

'What?' Bantony flopped his hands like a centre forward disputing a penalty with the referee.

'I will deal with you later,' I said, and was pleased to see him pale ever so slightly.

Do this, I told myself and knew that I didn't want to but knew that I had to.

I burst into my own office and the door struck something.

'Ouchy-wouchy,' Dodo said, rubbing the back of her head.

And with that one expression, my resolve was stiffened to the sticking point as Lady Macbeth sort of nearly said, if I remembered correctly.

'Do you know what that was?' I asked.

'Painful as a piano,' she told me.

'It was the very last time you say *ouchy-wouchy* or *owsy-wowsy* or any of those infantile phrases you come up with,' I told her.

'But what do I say if I am hurt, Boss?' Dodo asked plaintively, 'because I very often am.'

'You can say *ouch*,' I said. 'You can even use a mild expletive like *blast* or possibly *damn*.'

'I don't like to swear.'

'You don't have to,' I conceded. 'Why are you still rubbing your head? It can't have been that painful.'

'It comforts me, Boss.'

'You are not here to be comforted,' I informed her. 'You are here to be a police officer. Stop it.'

Dodo took her hand down reluctantly and asked, 'Are you cross as a cucumber with me, Boss.'

233

'Stop using silly silimes.' I struggled to untwist my tongue. 'Similes,' I corrected myself. 'No, Constable Chivers, I am not cross with you.' The look of relief that flooded her face made me feel like I was about to drown a kitten that was purring trustingly on my lap. 'I am absolutely furious with you.'

'But—'

'Shut up and listen,' I snarled. 'You are a disgrace, Constable Chivers. You are a disgrace to the East Suffolk Police Force. You are a disgrace to that uniform. Stop snivelling.'

'Sorry, Boss.' Dodo blew her nose noisily. 'But you are upsetting me.'

'Good,' I retorted. 'You are a disgrace to Sackwater Central Police Station.' Dodo opened her mouth to respond but I was getting into my flow now. 'I told you to shut up and listen,' I reminded her. 'You will not speak again until I tell you to.'

'Not even if I see that your hair is on fire and want to warn you?' she quavered.

'Shut *up*!' I yelled and Dodo's paper-white complexion paled to whatever is whiter than paper-white. 'Have you any idea how hard I struggled to get where I am?'

'Am I to answer that?' Dodo trembled.

'Yes.'

'I think I have a teensy-weensy idea.'

'No you do not,' I insisted. 'You do not have a teensy-weensy anything. You have a bit of an idea or an inkling, if you prefer, but that is another baby phrase that you will never utter in front of other people ever again.'

'Not even your parents, Boss?'

'They are not people,' I conceded. 'You have no idea how many battles I fought even to get into the police force and to hold my own every day against men who were determined to destroy me.'

'They wanted to murder you?' Dodo gasped.

'I am talking about my career.'

'That was not very clear,' Dodo whispered to the lino.

'And stop talking to objects about me in my presence.'

'Oh, but I never do that,' she told the chair.

'I have spent my entire adult life with stupid men, intelligent men, uneducated or educated men who are absolutely convinced that all women are witless and weak,' I told her, 'and I have struggled every step of the way to prove that we are not and what do you do? You turn up and prove beyond any doubt that we are. You are a disgrace to womanhood,' I told her coldly. 'Women campaigned, went to prison and even died to get us the suffrage men thought us too foolish to deserve and you betray them every time you open your silly, little girl mouth. You are an embarrassment to the force and to me personally.'

Dodo went a bit wobbly and I hoped she wasn't going to faint because you can't keep shouting at someone who has swooned.

'Why,' I demanded, 'do you do it?'

'Um,' Dodo put her thumb to her mouth and I slapped it away.

You're not supposed to strike a fellow officer but then fellow officers are not supposed to drive you to distraction and beyond.

'Daddy took me to a psychiatrist once,' she confessed. 'Well, lots of times, really.'

I never really got used to hearing Chief Superintendent Frederick 'Fido' Chivers referred to as *Daddy*. The man had become an almost legendary figure in East Anglia since rounding up the Woodchip Boys of Lowestoft and foiling a plot to eviscerate the Bishop of Dunwich on the feast of St Polycarp. Chivers and his wife had taken Dodo from an orphanage where she had been placed after her father was hanged. They adopted her and then Mrs Chivers died.

'And the doctor said that I was juvenile because I was trying to recapture my childhood.' Dodo was trembling all over.

'Give me your hands,' I said.

'Are you going to hurt me, Boss?'

'I think I have hurt you enough,' I said and took both her hands in my one. 'But I did it for a reason. You have become a laughing stock and you deserve better than that.' I looked into those big prize-winning pansy eyes. 'You have had your childhood, Dodo, and it was appalling.' Many people believed Dodo had witnessed her natural father murdering a man. 'Why on earth would you want to cling to that? You are a young, healthy woman and it is time to start behaving like one.'

Dodo quivered. 'I want you to be proud of me, Boss, and my father too.'

'So do I and so does he,' I told her, 'but most of all we want you to be proud of yourself.'

'Oh.' Dodo put her thumb up but realised and whipped it away. She was shaking badly now. 'I never thought of it like that, Boss.' She wrinkled her nose. 'Do you mind me calling you *Boss*?'

'No,' I assured her. 'I like it.'

'Policewomen do not cry, do they, Boss?'

'Not in front of the men,' I confirmed, 'but they do in private.'

'Is this …' Her voice broke.

'It's private,' I assured her and Dodo Chivers crumpled into noisy, breath-stealing sobs. 'Come here.'

I put my arm around my constable, held her close and let her tears subside to sniffles.

There was a knock on the door.

'Go and look through that filing cabinet,' I urged and after she had blown her nose again, I called, 'Enter.'

Brigsy poked his head through. 'Sorry, madam, but the men int sure if they're taking Chivers on the beat today.' He lowered his voice. 'I was out the back but I hear the end of it and I've given them a bloody good talking to.'

'That was well intentioned,' I replied, 'but from now on, Constable Chivers will stand up for herself.'

'Thank you, Sergeant Briggs, I am sorry to delay them,' Dodo said quite steadily, though still with her back to him, 'but I shall be out in a moment.'

Briggs left and Dodo took a breath and then a few more.

'Thank you, Inspector,' she said with a not-too-bad salute.

I heard them down the corridor. 'And are you going to bring your magic wand?' Rivers mocked her, clearly immune to Brigsy's warning.

'Do you know what, Constable Rivers,' Dodo told him. 'For a man who is old enough to be my father, you need to start growing up and developing a proper backbone.'

'I am surprised at the pair of you, being cruel to Constable Chivers,' I reprimanded the Grinder-Snipes later that day and I genuinely was. They were a couple of weedy nitwits but I never had them down as malicious.

The twins looked at me and then at each other in unfeigned astonishment.

'But 'ow, Mam?' Algy asked.

'It wurn't uz who put that worm in 'er 'elmet,' Sandy vowed.

I hadn't heard about that but I said magisterially, 'I am fully aware of that. I am talking about making her look foolish about the picnic. It's not like you to be cruel.'

They gave each other ever-so-hurt glances.

'Oh but, mam, we wurn't being…' Sandy set the ball rolling.

''orrid,' Algy said. 'We thought it would be a luvleh…'

'Idea,' they both said and I just didn't have the energy to haul them together or singly over the coals at that moment. Lord knew I had tried in the past.

59

QUASIMODO AND THE CONFESSION

t was lunch hour. At least, it was lunch hour for Brigsy and Bantony. It was lunch two hours for Sharkey and it was bedtime for the twins, who had been working the night shift, and for Rivers, who was laid up.

'I doubt anyone has had so much trouble with his back since Quasimodo,' I said to Dodo, who looked at me blankly. 'You do know who that is?' I asked.

'Of course I know who Rivers is, Boss,' Dodo huffed. 'But who—' Dodo jumped and to give my constable her due, she tried to stifle the yelp that escaped her throat.

I jumped too, partly because she did and the police are supposed to show some solidarity but mainly because I was taken by surprise as well. Neither of us heard the door open or the man coming in or the door closing after him. Barnaby Mason just sort of materialised at our shoulders.

'Mr Mason.' I managed to heave my heart back down my gullet. 'You surprised us.'

'And not in a nice way,' Dodo qualified my remark.

'I do coom hand myself in,' Barnaby announced, since apologies were clearly not required.

Barnaby scratched his head like an old dog with especially thirsty fleas.

'What—' I began, but Barnaby had come to say something and he was not going to be deflected by anything I had to contribute.

'For murder,' he recited, deadpan and very loudly, gazing up

– as far as his neck permitted – and through me into the distance, like a very bad actor trying to make himself heard in the gods.

'Who—' I began.

'That is a serious crime,' Dodo informed him severely, and I supposed at least she hadn't told him it was naughty.

'I know tha', miss.' Barnaby's head dropped even further sideways until it almost rested on my constable's shoulder.

'I am not a Miss,' she told the newcomer and edged away.

'Who—' I began again.

'It is no laughing matter,' Dodo scolded, obviously mistaking his twitching grimace for a grin.

'Who—'

'I know tha', missus,' Barnaby assured her.

'Nor am I a Mrs.' Dodo patted her upper arm as if it had stripes or coronets on it.

'Who—'

'I am a Woman Police Constable.'

'Sorry, Woman Police Constable.' I had a feeling that Barnaby was reconsidering his decision to confess all and I knew that once he clammed up you could not separate his lips with an oyster knife.

'You are wearing odd shoes,' she told him.

It hardly seemed worth me saying *Who* so I just made a little *Huh* sound for old times' sake.

'Sorry, Woman Police Constable.'

'Why on earth did you murder someone?' Dodo stood back, probably overpowered by the fragrance of his breath. 'Pooey.' She covered her nose with her hand to dispose of the *probably* part of my thought. 'Sorry, Boss.' Dodo realised she had used a forbidden word.

'I dint know, Woman Police Constable.' Barnaby was starting to turn away.

'Mr Mason,' I called, cutting off Dodo's *Huh* before she churned out some other irrelevancy. 'Who did you murder?'

'Oh, I was just about to ask that,' Dodo pouted, because immaturity is like tuberculosis. You can cure it, if you're lucky, but not all at once and you can never be one hundred per cent certain that it won't recur.

'The man on the beach,' he answered. 'Mr Bone.'

60

THE SHUTTLECOCK SLAYINGS AND
THE SILVER GHOST

Dodo took another step back, uncovered her nose and opened her mouth.

'Do not say anything,' I commanded. I had not forgotten how we were on the brink of getting a confession out of Father O'Graffic that it was he who stole his own collection money when Dodo revealed that the man he thought had seen him was blind.

'Are you not supposed to tell the suspect that, Boss?' Dodo crinkled her brow.

'No,' I replied. 'The suspect can say as much as he likes, provided,' – I tried to fix Barnaby Mason in a gimlet stare but his head was bobbling about too much – 'that it is true.'

'I was only going to ask—'

'No you were not,' I said firmly. 'You are going to man the desk and I am going to take Mr Mason to the interview room.'

'Oh, but where is that?' Dodo asked excitedly.

It was a fair enough question because we didn't really have one. We had a corridor of hardly used cells to the right of the desk and one of offices to the left. At the end of the second corridor was Superintendent Vesty's domain. He had knocked three rooms into one and put in a door at his own expense to access his rose garden. Before that on the right was Sharkey's office and then mine. On the left were two unused rooms that I had never bothered with but must at least have a desk and chairs.

'Interview room one,' I said airily. 'Come this way, Mr Mason.'

Nobody told me the room was full of stuff that looked like it belonged on Benny Bergman the rag-and-bone man's cart – old pots and pans, a rolled carpet, an empty bookcase with no shelves. I slid a badminton racket out of the way with my foot.

'Ah, this is being used for storing evidence,' I bluffed unconvincingly.

'Oh yes.' Barnaby Mason nodded in recognition. 'The Shuttlecock Slayings.'

This was a new one on me but a police officer can't admit to knowing less about crime than a confessed murderer.

'Indeed,' I murmured. It was a word Sidney Grice used a lot and I found it increasingly useful when I had nothing relevant to say.

'Come with me, please.'

I guided him into the next room, which mercifully had the furniture I required and nothing else.

'Now.' I sat facing Barnaby Mason across the desk and brought out my notebook and pencil. 'Let's get this straight, Mr Mason, before we have a formal interview and take a statement. Are you confessing to murdering Eric Bone?'

Please say no *because I know in my heart you didn't do it and I don't want to send you to Broadmoor for life.*

'Yes,' he said simply, placing his hands palm down and flat upon the desk like we were going to have a séance. 'I am.'

'But why?'

'Because I do it.'

'No.' I opened my notebook. 'I mean why did you kill him?'

Barnaby squirmed in his seat like a schoolboy who needs to be excused.

'I dint really know.'

'Did you know Eric Bone?'

'No.' Barnaby mopped his brow with an empty hand then,

deciding he should expand on that statement, added, 'I dint know Mr Bone.'

'Where did you kill him?' I pressed.

'At Jacob's Point near to the cliffs.'

'When?'

'Last Sat'day aatanoon 'bout halfway through I'd say.'

This would tie in with Tubby Gretham's find of a partly digested ham sandwich in the dead man's stomach but everything Mason had said so far could have been let slip when the men were asking for information. There was one thing, however, I had given them very strict instructions to keep quiet about.

'H—' I managed before he was off again.

'I'm true sorry, Woman Police Inspector Church, but I can't be more precise for the time for you see my watch do be in for repairs and I've the jeweller's ticket from Frosby's which I brought with me as proof of my statement.'

'Perhaps later,' I demurred, but Mason had an odd sleeveless cardigan-cum-waistcoat garment on with at least a dozen pockets either side and he was emptying the contents on to the desk – bent nails, burnt matchsticks, an unwashed milk-bottle top, a torn cigarette card with a cricketer's lower half visible but the name scratched out.

'The winder goo loose, it do, and I can't wind it and I fear dust or water or a small brown ant do get in and stop the works working. It int especial valuable but it do be of sentimental—'

'How—' I yelled, much louder than I had intended, and Barnaby Mason froze. If we had been playing musical statues he would have won hands down. 'How did you kill him?' I asked more calmly and closed my notebook in preparation for releasing him and advising him to have a check-up with Dr Gretham at the earliest opportunity.

'I int proud of it,' Barnaby Mason muttered.

This did not exactly answer my question but I know when a man is about to close down and Barnaby Mason already had his hand on that pole they use for lowering the shutters.

'What happened, Mr Mason?' I asked quietly and I wasn't sure he had heard me at first. He swallowed loudly and tossed his head about in a violent corkscrew motion that would have dislocated my neck if I'd tried it.

'It do be awful,' he cried and there was real horror in that voice and on that face, his lips peeling back and half-closing repeatedly in distress. 'He's staggering abou' with a terror on his face. I dint know why and I dint think he know where he is gooin'. And he fall to his knees. He trip up, I think. I creep up behind. He dint hear me with the wind blowing in strong from the sea and I punch him on the side of the head and—'

'Hang on.' I interrupted his account. 'You punched him? With your fist, you mean?'

Barnaby picked at his lower lip.

'Yes.' He picked at his upper lip. 'Or is it a rock?'

'Which?' I pressed. 'This is very important.'

Barnaby puzzled it over, wiggled his left little finger in his right ear and puzzled some more.

'A rock,' he decided. 'Yes, definite. I pick up a boulder and bring it thwacking down and he fall forward but he goo get up again, holdin' his head and moanin' and he scrumble over the edge. Scream he do and then, a long time gone and far away, I hear the splash. Must of fallen straighten in.'

We did some clutching – Barnaby Mason at his head and me at some straws. 'And what did you do with the stone?'

'I drop it in a hollow,' he told me mechanically, thus blowing the last few straws away.

'But why did you do it?' I asked in genuine shock. I had known him as a harmless eccentric since I was a little girl. I had got angry with people who tried to have him committed to an asylum.

Barnaby Mason started to cry, big noisy hiccups with tears dripping down his ticking cheeks.

'I swear by my Lord Jesus,' he managed between sobs, 'I dint know. It was like as I was somebody else.'

Barnaby's nose was running. I handed him my handkerchief and he tucked it up his sleeve unused.

'Oh, Barnaby,' I sighed at this pathetic figure, an innocent baby brought into the world as a monster by a man who now lived in a mansion with servants and drove a beautiful old Silver Ghost.

Mr G would have ridiculed me for acting on my feelings – Aunty M told me he could be very cutting about those – but Mr G was dead and gone and I had a living man in front of me.

'I'm going to let you sleep on what you have told me,' I decided, 'and we will talk about it tomorrow before you make an official statement.'

'Sleep?' Barnaby cried. 'How do I ever goo sleep again?'

But when I checked on him half an hour later, Barnaby Mason was curled up in his bed, snoring like a hippo.

61

PRIMROSES, HEDGES AND
THE HURTING OF FLIES

Tubby Gretham came.

'Had my first case of self-inflicted gunshot wound of this war so far,' he told me, knocking the ash from his pipe mainly into my metal wastepaper bin but partly on to the green cracked lino floor.

'Anyone I know?' I lit one of my self-rolled cigarettes and drew the smoke deep into my lungs, savouring the moment briefly.

'Farmer by the name of Ted Trinder – no relation of Tommy, though he acted like a clown.' Tubby scraped out the tarry remnants with his old penknife. 'Tried to shoot his big toe and blew off half his left leg. Lucky to be alive.'

'But he would be in a reserved occupation,' I objected, and Tubby snorted.

'Most upset when I pointed that out to him,' he said and hinged the knife shut. 'Silly so-and-so.'

'At least the Ministry of War won't prosecute him for evading a duty he never even had,' I pondered. I picked a strand of Gallaher's off the tip of my tongue and wondered what, if anything, had happened to the man in his mother's wood shed.

'Constable Chivers summoned me,' Tubby said as he brought a bulging leather pouch out of his shapeless Harris tweed jacket. 'But then you know that. She seemed very sensible. It was quite unnerving.'

'She's trying hard,' I said.

He selected a plug of tobacco as carefully as you might decide which biscuit you wanted from a large assortment, then slipped the pouch away. 'Did you have to be cruel?'

'A little.'

Tubby nodded slowly. 'She tells me you have a man in custody.'

'Barnaby Mason,' I told him and Tubby raised his big brown eyes.

'What's he been up to now?' He sniffed the plug like a wine waiter with a cork.

We both remembered how Tubby had had to sedate Barnaby when he was rushing up and down High Road West, claiming to be a tree and panicking about his leaves blowing away.

'This time it's serious,' I told him. 'Barnaby has confessed to the murder of Eric Bone.'

'And was he persuaded to do so by Inspector Sharkey?' Tubby asked carefully.

'No. He came in voluntarily and only I have interviewed him.'

'No.' Tubby frowned – at least, I think he frowned behind his dark brown, slightly grizzled moustache and beard – in disbelief. 'A fly is more likely to hurt Barnaby Mason than he is to hurt it.'

'He went into quite a lot of detail,' I told him. 'He described creeping up behind Eric Bone and striking him on the back of the head with a rock.'

'Did he, by George?' Tubby rolled the tobacco between his massive paws.

'And he even remembered dropping the stone in a hollow close by.'

'Did he, by Jupiter?' He fed the shreds into the bowl and tamped them down with a dark orange fingertip.

'With all due respect to your fellow officers,' Tubby began cautiously, for we both knew that when people say *With all due respect* it means they are likely to show none, 'is it possible that any of them – the name of Inspector Sharkey springs to mind – told him this?'

He struck a foul sulphurous match.

'They were given very strict orders not to tell anyone all the details,' I replied with as much confidence as I could muster, because Old Scrapie would not feel bound by my instructions.

'Hmm,' Tubby hmmed, puffing on his old briar pipe and filling my office with clouds of smoke that would do credit to the Royal Scot. I could hardly taste my cigarette in competition with that.

'I honestly don't think they would have given away that much information,' I said and resolved to find out which officer had spoken to him. Box and Bantony were fairly sensible but goodness knew what Dodo or the Grinder-Snipes would let slip without realising.

'Probably not,' Tubby conceded.

'Anyway, only you, I, Box and the Orchards know exactly where the stone was found. Mr Orchard won't remember and I can trust the others.'

Neither Box nor I were going to go about bragging that we found a probable murder weapon and lost it.

I went to open a window.

'Feeling hot?'

'Something like that.' I didn't like to tell him his tobacco made Captain's Navy Cut seem bland.

'Tried evening primrose oil?'

'No,' I said more snappily than I intended. I may have been a spinster but I was not a dried-up old spinster yet. 'Will you examine him?'

'Has he been injured?'

'No, but I'm hoping you'll think he isn't fit to stand trial.'

Tubby reclined in his chair, the front legs rising six inches and the back spindles squeaking worryingly.

'If you want him certified, you'll need two doctors.'

'Will Dr Hedges do it?' I asked.

'Give him a triple brandy and he'll do the Highland fling,' Tubby remarked tartly but justifiably. He stood up, to his chair's great relief as it creaked back into shape. 'Perhaps I should take a look at him first.'

Tubby held the door – I didn't mind him doing that because we were friends – and lumbered after me back along the corridor.

'Tea's a long time coming,' he grumbled to Brigsy, who was occupied in sharpening a pencil, a delicate and complex operation that seemed to occupy a great deal of his time.

'Oh?' Brigsy looked at me questioningly as it was news to him that he was expected to have made any.

'Yes, please,' I told him. 'And Dr Gretham has two sugars.'

'Three,' Tubby corrected before we went down the other corridor.

62

THE CRIMSON TRAIL AND
THE RETURN OF THE SNAIL

For reasons I did not enquire into, Dodo had taken it upon herself to guard cell three and stood rigidly to attention outside the door.

'Oh, please do let me out,' Barnaby implored her. 'I dint like it in here.'

'Well, you should have thought of that before you went gaga,' she scolded, as if going mad was a personal choice as foolish as taking a trip to Skegness.

Oh Dodo, I thought, *We have such a long way to go.*

'Open the door,' I instructed and Dodo seemed about to comply when she decided that she would concentrate on dropping the keys instead.

'Oh, Dr Gretham,' – Barnaby came to the observation hatch – 'do you come to cure me so I goo home?'

Tubby cast his eyes down and said sadly, 'I've just come for a chat, Barnaby.'

'Oh, how kind,' Barnaby said, so like a hostess receiving flowers from her guest that I half-expected him to follow it up with *You shouldn't have.*

'Stand against the wall with your hands up, Prisoner Mason,' Dodo rapped and Tubby chuckled.

'You won't cause us any trouble, will you, Barnaby?'

I snatched the keys off my constable.

'Ouch!' Dodo sucked her little finger and I was only glad she hadn't said anything more babyish. 'You twisted my pingie,' she complained and my gladness shrivelled like a grape into a raisin. 'I mean my finger,' she corrected herself, but the damage was done.

I unlocked the door.

'Now then, Barnaby.' Tubby bowled into the cell, quarter-filling it with his bulk. 'What's this all about?'

I couldn't even see our prisoner behind that bear of a man but I heard very clearly, 'I kill him, Doctor, I do. I'm sorry.'

'Who told you how he died?' Tubby demanded, stepping somewhat out of his remit as medical assessor.

'No one, Doc, honest.'

'Remember how you thought you were the Aspic Killer of Merthyr Tydfil?' Tubby pressed.

I listened in surprise. The capture of Ekriel Coy, the real Aspic Killer, had been an early success for Sidney Grice, who kept Coy's mummified claw in a bottle on his desk.

'I'm confoosed then but I know I do this. The inspector she'll tell you, I tell her all about it.'

This was the most rational I had ever heard Barnaby and I could not see anybody having him declared mentally unfit in that condition.

Gretham raised his voice. 'Who are you covering up for, Barnaby?'

'Nobody, Doc, I swear it.'

'*Doctor* Gretham,' I said quietly to remind him of his role.

'What?' he asked over his shoulder. 'Oh yes.' He put his black bag on the bed. 'I shall just give him a quick check-up.' He bent over and inhaled noisily. 'You don't smell of drink.'

'I never drink, Doc, I dint never – only that once.'

That once had lasted quite a few years, as I recalled.

I stepped outside to give them both a bit of space. It was a small cell, designed for two men at most. The trouble was, Tubby was also designed for two men at least.

Sharkey came marching towards us. 'Briggs says you've got that cretin Mason in there. Give me five minutes and I'll get a confession out of him.'

'I will give you no minutes and this man came in voluntarily,' I told him.

Tubby came out behind me. 'Well, that completes my thorough physical examination,' he lied to me pointedly, 'and I can confirm that your prisoner has no cuts, bruises or abrasions.'

'Good,' Sharkey snarled and slunk away, disappointed at not getting a chance to practise a bit of good old-fashioned police work.

'Have you searched him for razors or anything he might harm himself with?' Tubby asked me. There was a resigned air about him now.

'The sergeant do that,' Barnaby answered for me. 'He even take my waistcoat away, he do.'

'He had lots of bits in the pockets,' I explained and a terrible thought struck me. 'Have you still got that shell, Constable Chivers?'

'The one—' she began.

'Yes,' I butted in.

'The one—'

'Just say yes or no.'

Dodo ground her lips crossly. 'I was only going to ask—'

'Yes or no,' I snapped, suddenly the prosecuting council demolishing a witness in the box.

'Yes, but I was—'

'Give it to me.'

Dodo reached into her jacket pocket and handed it over and I stepped back into the cell.

'Now, Mr Mason. I want you to look at this very carefully

and tell me if you have seen it before.' I held the shell up between my thumb and forefinger.

'Yes,' he said. 'It's my lucky snail shell.'

This could be the unluckiest good-luck charm anyone has ever had, I mused.

'Oh, I thought it was mine,' Dodo grumped.

'Are you absolutely sure?' I pressed, hoping to shake his certainty.

'I can be,' he answered.

'How?' I asked.

'I carve my initials inside.'

I held the shell up to the bare electric light bulb. It was more of a scratch than a carving but the letters were there unmistakeably, *BM*.

'You see!' he pointed excitedly. 'I tell you it's mine. Where'd you find it?'

On your way to the gallows, I thought but only said, 'On Jacob's Point.'

'What more proof do you want?' Barnaby folded his arms in satisfaction.

Only a man would want to be right about something that could put a rope around his neck.

'I can't certify him in that state of mind,' Tubby puffed. 'He shows every sign of being completely aware of what is going on. Ninety per cent of my patients are less compos mentis than he is today.'

'What, then?' I said. 'You know as well as I do that most of the time he has no grip on reality.'

'I have to make my judgement on how he is when I assess him,' Tubby pointed out reasonably. 'If he deteriorates while he's here, give me a call and I can take another look at him. Other than that, he is unlikely to go through a trial and not show signs of mental disturbance.'

'If he can be persuaded to plead not guilty,' I pondered. 'Otherwise he'll be in and out in no time.'

'That, as you know, is out of our control.' Tubby checked his watch. It was probably time for a beer and/or a snack.

'You knew his initials were inside that shell, did you not, Boss?' Dodo asked over a cold bitter tea.

'Of course,' I assured her shamelessly.

'Then why did you give it to me?'

Good question.

'Because I knew you would look after it.' I turned my attention back to my mug.

Oh what a tangled web we weave, I ruminated, *when first we practise to be a superior officer.*

Brigsy stood behind his desk, rubbing his arm through his shirt sleeve.

'Try to take his prints,' he told me, which explained the black ink on his face and collar, 'but he do panic – just like when we want to take his photo. Try to bite Mr Gregson, he do and...' – He rolled up his left sleeve to show me an impressive bruise – '...succeed with me.' He pulled his sleeve down. 'I can get the men to hold him still for the prints, if you like, but he'll probly get damaged in the process.'

'I'll see if I can persuade him later,' I promised and forgot all about it.

63

MARCH COMES IN MAY

rang March Middleton.

'I know this isn't very scientific,' I told her, 'but I just don't think it smells right.'

'You must trust your nose,' she told me encouragingly. 'The solution to a crime is like an egg. If it smells bad, it is. I am at a loss to know how to advise you, though,' she continued less encouragingly. 'You are a highly intelligent woman, Betty, but the trouble is you are telling me what you see and that may well not be what I would see. It is rather like listening to one side of an argument.'

'I don't know what else I can tell you.'

'One moment.' I heard Aunty M grunt and rustle about. 'Now,' she said, 'While I am looking something up, tell me about your own life.'

'I think I have fallen in love,' I told her, remembering guiltily that I had still not written that letter.

'It was obvious you were falling out of love with Adam,' she said, and I could almost see her eyes light up with interest. Some people survive on food and money. March Middleton survived on gin, cigarettes and gossip. 'But you only *think*?'

'It's a very strong think,' I assured her.

'Then you shall have to tell me all about him … Twenty past nine.'

'I'm sorry?'

'So am I, dear. I was trying to read my Bradshaw's and if I catch the twenty past nine tomorrow morning, I can be at Sackwater station in time to be collected for lunch.'

'You are coming here?' I asked in disbelief.

March Middleton had not come to Suffolk in decades.

'The sea air might do me good,' she told me, 'before my operation – just a small procedure on my eye.'

I wasn't sure that any procedure on the eye could be small.

'But where will you stay?' *Cressida* was hardly suitably equipped for an old lady and my godmother was by now nearly eighty.

'Well,' Aunty M debated, 'I know your present home is not suitable, though I should very much like to visit it. I detest British hotels. The waiters are almost as sycophantic as their customers – they are both so busy vying to impress each other. Not with your – forgive me, dear – appalling parents either.'

It occurred to me, and not for the first time, that I had never actually been told how my parents had even become acquainted with March Middleton, let alone persuaded her to be my godmother.

'I wonder,' Aunty M continued, 'if Dr Gretham might be willing to give me a bed. It would only be for two nights.'

Willing? Tubby Gretham held March Middleton more in awe than he did his monarch, or Mr Henry Gray of *Anatomy* fame. His proudest possessions were the volumes of her books she had signed for him.

'I think he can be persuaded,' I told her.

'What? When?' Tubby was thrilled and horrified. 'But I haven't cut the grass or the hedges.'

He danced on the spot.

'You never cut the grass or the hedges,' Greta, his wife, reminded him, rinsing her old brown pot in hot water.

'Have we any clean bedding? Does she prefer to sleep in a

north- or south-facing room? What kind of gin does she like?' Tubby ran his fingers through his heavy beard and unruly hair. 'I need to go to the barbers.'

'I've been telling him that for weeks,' Greta said, spooning in the tea leaves. 'Only don't go shaving that beard off again. We don't want to shock her with your ugly mug.'

'How does one greet her?' Tubby paced around the long pine table.

'You curtsy,' I said.

Tubby stopped at the end of the table.

'I am never quite sure when you are joking,' he said.

The station was busy, girls waving goodbye to troops, farm boys in uniform – or *clodhoppers* as they were known locally – trying to look nonchalant about going to France to fight the Jerries but wide-eyed with poorly hidden apprehension. I doubted many of them had ever left the county before.

Two girls used often to be seen waving boyfriends off but the scraggy one had joined the Land Army, I had heard, and her scraggier friend was in the maternity wing of the Royal Albert Sackwater Infirmary.

Rufus Verdigris, the disgraced ex-accountant, was there, prowling the platform in search of ladies getting grit in their eyes from the smoke, but according to Alan Baker, the porter, Verdigris had not been lucky for weeks now.

The train pulled up and Mr Trime, the station master, strode out, splendid in his three-piece suit, wire-framed spectacles and deluxe moustache.

'Seeing off?' he asked after we had greeted each other.

'Meeting,' I said as the windows began to slide down and hands reached out to turn the handles.

A tall, well-constructed gentleman clambered out of the nearest first-class carriage and held up his hand. It was taken by a white glove and the tiny lady stepped daintily down to the platform.

'Aunty M,' I cried, forgetting my official status and rushing to kiss her.

'Inspector.' March Middleton winked, not forgetting my official status. 'How splendid you look.'

Aunty M seemed to get tinier every time I saw her and I was fairly confident I had stopped growing.

'Careful with those,' the gentleman was instructing two other gentlemen, who were struggling out with three suitcases and depositing them on the courtyard.

'Thank you so much,' Aunty M smiled prettily.

'It has been a great privilege to have travelled with you, ma'am,' the tall gentleman assured her. The other two nodded, one said 'hear hear', and all three of them bowed and returned to their carriage.

'Is she royalty?' Mr Trime whispered.

'Sort of,' I told him, for March Middleton was simultaneously the most unassuming and most regal lady I had ever met.

'Perhaps you could arrange to have my suitcases sent to White Lodge,' she told Mr Trime.

'I'm sorry, madam-ma'am,' he replied uncertainly, 'but we don't deliver luggage.'

'Oh, but surely you can just this once,' my godmother cajoled Mr Trime, slipping a coin into his hand.

If anybody else had offered the stationmaster a tip, especially not of paper money, he would have been outraged, but Mr Trime gazed at that half-crown in his palm as if it were six months of his salary and he glowed.

'Oh, thank you very much, ma'am. I shall see to it immediately.' He slid the coin into his waistcoat pocket and patted his stomach.

'Does madam require any transport?' What? I had not been able to get a taxi since the day I came back. Joe Paradise had not been working since the sea air got to his suspension and there were no other services. 'Because my nephew has a hearse, if it wouldn't distress you to travel in the front of that.'

'Oh, I shall be in one of those quite soon enough, thank you,' Aunty M told him. 'It is a lovely day. I am sure we can perambulate.'

And so we walked.

'What foul creatures these Nazis are.' Aunty M tapped a newspaper hoarding.

BRISTISH TROOPS PUSH GERMENS BACK AT it read, but the bottom corner of the notice had been torn off.

'Do you think we can beat them?' I asked.

'With that spelling, possibly not,' my godmother smiled. 'But with Winston in charge, yes. He's a bumptious fool, an appalling tactician and a worse strategist, but he will stiffen the resolve of the nation. We are a bloody-minded people – how else did we manage to subjugate one quarter of the planet?' I knew that my godmother did not approve of the British Empire. She had lived in India and loved the country and its people too much to see them in chains. 'And if we are determined not to surrender, we shall not,' she concluded.

'You are sounding quite like Mr Churchill yourself,' I laughed and Aunty M chuckled.

'Some say he is too old but he is thirteen years younger than I.' She paused for a second and breathed in. 'Le tabac,' she murmured.

'Would you like a cigarette?'

'I would love one,' my godmother said, 'but I would not like you to be associated in public with such disreputable behaviour.'

'I'm not sure people worry about women smoking in public any more,' I reassured her, though I never smoked on the street in uniform. 'What would you like for lunch?'

'Any rag-bone,' Benny Bergman hollered from his donkey cart.

'Fish and chips and a good glass of best bitter,' she told me, her pace – already fast for such a little elderly lady – picking up at the idea of the latter.

64

WILFRED OWEN AND
THE THREE COLOURED THREADS

After a good lunch, I took Aunty M to Sackwater Central Police Station. I hadn't really wanted to because I was afraid they would show me up or fail to be impressed by my visitor, but she wanted to go and what my godmother wanted to do, she generally did.

Brigsy was at the desk, slouched over a *Daily Mail* and puffing on his foulest pipe, but he put both down, sprang to his feet and saluted very smartly to our guest.

'It is a honour and an privlidge,' he told her as she took his hand.

'How lucky you were,' she told him. 'I assume you got your gas mask on just in time.'

'But...' Brigsy gaped like people don't in real life but he did. 'I int never told no one here 'bout tha'.'

'The old burns on the side of your neck and scalp are typical of mustard gas,' she pointed out. And I had always thought he just had blotchy skin and was going bald patchily. 'And that slight rasp in your voice. I assume you got a whiff of it.'

Brigsy chewed his lips. 'Many a good man got more than that, ma'am,' he recalled unhappily.

How come he could call her *ma'am* but despite my repeated instructions always got me wrong as madam?

'Obscene as cancer, bitter as the cud,' she said – incomprehensibly to me, but Brigsy was not so easily confused.

'"Dulce et Decorum Est",' he nodded wisely. 'Wilfred Owen.'

So now he was an expert on poetry, this man who could hardly spell *register* in the register? And now they were chattering away about his allotment and he was making her, but not me, a big mug of tea in my big mug.

Sharkey came out of his office, sniffing about like a shabby fox from its lair.

'Ah, the famous Miss Middleton.' He shook my godmother's hand and if she disliked the ironic way he said *famous* as much as I did, Aunty M didn't show it as she extracted her hand and clipped her spectacles over her ears.

'Inspector Sharkey.' She returned his gaze steadily. 'Oh, you poor man.' Sharkey blinked. 'Do you love her very much?' she enquired solicitously.

The Shark stiffened. 'I don't know what you are talking about,' he said in a way that made me think he did. 'And what's more, Miss Middleton, in this case, neither do you.'

'I am sorry if I have offended you, Inspector,' Aunty M said. 'I was talking about Abigail, or, as you call her, Abi.'

'What the hell do you know about that?' Sharkey breathed, clearly rattled.

'You need not worry, Inspector,' my godmother assured him, 'I shall say no more about it.'

'You've said a-bloody-nuff already,' he fumed and stalked back to his den.

'Don't mind me if you want to say more, ma'am,' Brigsy urged our visitor.

March Middleton crinkled her eyes.

'If truth be told, I do not have any more to tell you.'

'Now I *know* you're a witch,' I marvelled.

'Mr G thought my ladies' club on Huntley Street little better than a coven,' Aunty M recalled. 'But there was no magic, Inspector. There were three very short different coloured threads on Inspector Sharkey's jacket,' she told us. 'And where else would you pick those up other than a seamstress's premises?'

'But how did you know her name?' I objected. 'I know we went past Abigail's Dress Shop and I think I heard a customer calling her Abi as she left but there must be a good half-dozen seamstresses in business in the town centre alone.'

'I doubt many of them wear Le Tabac Blond perfume,' she reasoned.

'I thought you wanted a smoke.'

'I did and I still do.' Aunty M flicked open her father's old gold cigarette case. 'They are Turkish,' she told Brigsy. 'Would you like to try one?'

'Don't mind if I do, thank you, ma'am.' Brigsy lit all our cigarettes from a Swan Vesta and sucked in appreciatively. 'Lord,' he coughed slightly. 'Stronger than my black shag, they are.'

'So Abi wears Le Tabac Blond by Caron,' I recapped. 'And that isn't cheap.'

'And I could smell it on your colleague the moment we shook hands,' she told me.

'I could only smell cigarettes, whisky and coal tar soap.'

My godmother piffed. 'If you had spent hundreds of long Sunday afternoons being badgered to differentiate between different scents, you would have detected it,' she assured me. 'Mr G always told me I had destroyed my olfactory senses by smoking.'

It was not often that Uncle G, as I called him, was wrong.

'So he was human after all,' I said.

'Very nearly,' Aunty M conceded.

'If I might ask, ma'am,' said Brigsy, puffing away contentedly, 'why did you say 'spector Sharkey was a *poor man*?'

'Does he strike you as a man who is happy in love?' March Middleton asked simply, and all three of us knew the answer to that.

65

ZULUS AND THE ECSTASY OF ONIONS

March Middleton arrived at the station the next morning looking, unusually for her, slightly dishevelled.

'Do not tell Tubby…' – she straightened her blue bonnet – '…but I was less frightened being chased by the Wild Man of Wilmslow down Scafell Pike than I was by his driving.'

'He is a bit erratic,' I laughed. 'And I think he's quite excited meeting you.'

'Oh, it was so embarrassing.' Aunty M touched her cheeks. 'When he came out to greet me, he did a sort of curtsy.'

'Oh, he didn't!' I curled up inside and probably outside as well.

'Did you play a prank on the poor man?' Aunty M fixed me with a stern eye.

'I didn't think he'd take it seriously,' I protested and she chuckled.

Brigsy appeared with three teas. I had my mug back but Aunty M had the bone china cup and saucer that were, until now, for the exclusive use of our superintendent, not that he had been around to use them much lately.

'I do be wonderin' how you get up to Jacob's Point,' he declared to my godmother. 'It do be too narrow for a car and it do be a long old walk, it do.'

'And you think I am too old for that?' she challenged, adding much to his relief, 'Because I am.'

'And I dint s'pose you ride a horse,' Brigsy suggested.

'The last time I tried that was after the war,' Aunty M told him.

'You dint mean the Great War?' Brigsy checked.

'Nor the second Boer War,' she assured him. 'Nor the first, come to that.'

'The Crimean War?' Brigsy guessed.

'The eighteen fifties?' my godmother cried in mock outrage. 'Just how old do you think I am?'

'I wouldn't answer that,' I advised.

'The Zulu War,' she told him. 'Eighteen seventy-nine.'

She would have been seventeen then, I calculated.

'When you be a baby,' Brigsy responded with clumsy but well-meant gallantry.

'And that,' Aunty M cocked an ear, 'sounds like my transport now.'

I never quite understood it. My hearing is good, I am told, but March Middleton, I sometimes believed, could hear a hair fall off your head – cruel training by her guardian, she had told me.

I went to the door and there, on the forecourt, it was – Benny Bergman with his donkey cart. He had brought wooden steps and helped my godmother up them to perch on a thick fur rug with her respectably skirted legs hanging over the lowered front board, her carpet bag sitting on her knees. She had not brought her gas mask and refused to borrow Brigsy's, insisting that it did not match her pale blue outfit.

'Oh, this is luxury,' she laughed as Benny, climbing up beside her, took the reins and clicked his tongue.

'Goon boy,' he urged his steed and off they set with me walking easily alongside.

'What is he called?' Aunty M chatted as he crossed the High Roads junction.

'Onion,' he told her and she laughed delightedly. 'Oh, it was a donkey called Onion who took me from my home in Parbold to the railway station on my very first trip to London.'

And it was worth the extra shilling I had given Benny just to see the smiles that wreathed my godmother's face.

66

THE RAVEN AND THE RAZOR

t was a steep climb to Jacob's Point and Benny had to dismount and lead his donkey up the track, taking a long detour around Spectre Lane, which was much too narrow for the cart.

'Now,' Aunty M said, 'show me where you found the rock.'

I took her up to the hollow.

'It has all been disturbed,' she observed.

'The men were looking for any other stones that might have blood or hair on them,' I explained.

'But they did not find any.'

'I feel so stupid letting Mr Orchard kick it away,' I confessed.

'Did I ever tell you how I found the cut-throat razor I had good reason to believe was used to slaughter the Underwood family?' Aunty M asked, but did not wait for an answer. 'A raven swooped and snatched it from my grasp and I never found it again.'

'Truly?' I asked. She had not told me that before.

'Truly,' she assured me. 'It was not my finest moment when I had to explain that one to Mr G.'

I sighed.

'I'm afraid you have had a wasted journey, Aunty M,' I apologised. 'There won't be very much to see now.'

'If nothing else, I thoroughly enjoyed the ride,' she consoled me, 'but we have hardly started looking yet.'

'For what?' I asked.

'An excellent question.' March Middleton rotated slowly. 'So, if Barnaby Mason did hit Eric Bone and drop the stone more or less immediately, Eric Bone must have been standing somewhere around here.' She swept her parasol over a small area between us and the cliff. 'Hold my hand, dear.' Aunty M dropped her carpet bag to the ground.

'Are you all right?' I asked in concern.

'Perfectly,' she assured me. 'The breeze is quite bracing.' She walked towards the edge.

'Take care,' I warned as she got close to it.

'But what can possibly go wrong?' she asked, pulling me along with her, 'apart from me slipping and dragging you over or an undermined section of land giving way, plunging us both to our doom?'

My godmother might greet the prospect of death with a light heart, I reflected, but I could not do so. She slid her feet carefully through the short grass until she was within six inches of a hundred-foot drop into the ocean.

'If I feel myself falling, I shall let go,' she promised.

'No, you will not,' I vowed. 'I have a sworn duty to protect the public.'

I had to raise my voice above the wind now and, while it flapped at March Middleton's dress quite violently, it did not have the temerity to lift it.

'Even dotty old ladies?' she laughed.

'Even them.'

My godmother put her free hand on top of her bonnet and leaned terrifyingly forward, so far that I felt my grip slipping.

'Aunty!' I cried in alarm and she straightened up, twisted towards me and stumbled back down into what would have been my arms before I had my mishap.

I stepped back, almost tumbling over my own feet before steadying us both.

'Watch yourselves, ladies,' Benny called out. He had been instructed on no account to leave his donkey.

'I do not want Onion eating evidence,' Aunty M had told him.

'Well, that was exhilarating,' my godmother puffed as we headed back to the hollow.

'And did you see anything?' I asked, breathless myself with the sudden activity.

'A vertiginous drop,' she informed me. 'With no ledges, so that Mr Mason's account of Mr Bone falling straight into the water has some elements of veracity.'

'Oh, good,' I said. 'Well worth risking our lives for.'

'I have taken greater risks for less benefit,' she assured me, smoothing the lines of her dress. 'Now.' She perched for a moment on the edge of Gabriel's Table. 'Two matters occur to me. First, let us consider Constable Box. He is a worthy and likeable man but would you describe him as acutely observant?'

'Hardly,' I said.

'This lost stone,' Aunty M pondered. 'Was it absolutely caked?'

'No,' I recalled. 'There was only a light smear of what was probably blood and perhaps a dozen at most shortish hairs.'

'Then what, I wonder,' my godmother considered carefully, 'drew your constable's attention to it?'

'It was big and round,' I said.

'Fascinating,' she murmured in all sincerity. 'How would you describe the other rocks in this hollow?'

'Apart from the five big boulders, the rest are small and fairly flat,' I said and, in a rush of memory, 'It was also a more flinty colour.'

'Flinty!' Aunty M cried as if I had solved the entire case, though obviously I had not. 'Pertaining to a sedimentary cryptocrystalline species of quartz. Flint is common in Suffolk, is it not?'

'Very,' I agreed. 'Many cottages are built from it and a lot of good-quality flint was sold from the Brandon area for muskets.'

'And yet,' she continued. 'Sackwater rests on sandy soil and loose limestone, which is why the cliffs get eroded. How did all this flint get here?'

'It was brought to build a small monastery in a dip just beyond that brow.' I pointed. 'There is more natural shelter there but the last monk left twenty-five years ago.'

'A monastery.' Aunty M perked up. 'I should like to visit that. One is forced by desperation to take more interest in spiritual matters in one's dotage.'

'It is all wired off,' I told her, 'so that Nazi paratroopers can't establish a foothold there.'

'How fortunate we are that the Germans do not have any wire cutters,' March Middleton mused.

'What was the other thing that concerned you?' I asked, not sure why the first mattered.

'If you were to sneak up on somebody standing here,' she questioned, 'how would you set about it? You could not be sure he would not turn at any moment and spot you foolishly creeping.'

'Well, you would probably take as much cover as you could.' I surveyed the scene. 'But there isn't much of that. I suppose the nearest thing you could crouch behind would be that cairn.' I pointed. 'They call it Lot's Wife – from the Bible,' I explained stupidly, for Aunty M knew her scriptures cover to cover.

'And it is made of...'

'Flint,' I replied, feeling more the obtuse child with every word. 'So Barnaby crouched behind the cairn, selected a large flint and then crept up on Eric Bone.'

'Possibly.' Aunty M repinned her bonnet to her thick greying hair. 'Shall we take a look?'

67

LOT'S WIFE AND THE TOMB OF TUTANKHAMUN

We made our way down the hill perhaps twenty yards to the cairn, a pillar about seven feet high and three wide on a small natural mound.

'Well, it would certainly give you cover,' I agreed.

'Did your men look around it?'

'Yes, I think so… yes. The Grinder-Snipes had a look,' I recollected.

'They are the ones from Parbold, I believe,' my godmother mused. 'I hope they are more sensible than their father.'

'Unless he is clinically moronic, they are not,' I told her ruefully, for I didn't like criticising my men, even to her.

'Oh, poor you,' she sympathised. 'Did they crouch behind it?'

'I don't think so … No, I'm sure they didn't. In fact, they didn't even touch it, in case it was cursed,' I recalled in despair.

'Wonderful.' March Middleton clapped her hands.

'Is it?' I mumbled.

'Indeed,' she assured me. 'Mr Bergman,' Aunty M called over. 'Will Onion stand still if you come over here and, if so, could you do so, please?'

Benny looked at her quizzically for a second and she chuckled softly.

'Onion? Oh yeah, he'll stand all right. Standing is what he's most fond of doing. Trotting is another matter,' he told her as he came up the slope.

'You are quite a solidly built man,' March Middleton observed.

'Not quite the same as Lot's Wife here, but you will have to do. If you could kindly stand here bolt upright, please.'

'Righto.' Benny looked askance at this eccentric old lady but did as she requested.

My godmother stepped a little way up the hill.

'Now, Inspector, if you could crouch behind him as if to conceal yourself from someone at the top of the hill.' She viewed me critically. 'You would have to get closer than that.'

I edged nearer, wobbling on my haunches.

'Thank you, Inspector. You may stand now,' Aunty M told me. 'Well done, Mr Bergman. If ever we produce a dramatic entertainment featuring a cairn, the role is yours for the asking.' She smiled playfully. 'If I might ask one question, did the inspector touch you at all?'

'Well, yes,' Benny replied, 'but only to steady herself as she got up. There weren't nothing in it.'

My godmother snorted in amusement. 'I was not trying to imply any impropriety. Thank you, Mr Bergman, you may return to Onion now.'

Benny narrowed his eyes as if he thought he might have been the butt of a practical joke, but said nothing as he went back down.

'Probably thinks I am mad as a hatpin,' Aunty M said quietly.

'So what was all that about?' I asked, the same thought as Benny's having crossed my mind.

'I wanted to demonstrate to my own and your satisfaction that you would find it extremely difficult to hide behind that cairn without touching it. You no doubt tried quite hard not to for the sake of decency but if you had no such constraint, you would have laid hands on it probably many times.'

At my godmother's beckoning, we went back to the pillar.

'Some of those stones have been turned,' she commented. 'See how some have lichen on top and some do not, though I would bet a gallon of London Dry that they do underneath.'

'Are you talking about fingerprints?' I asked and she inclined her head a fraction. 'But we have had heavy rain since then,' I objected and March Middleton clicked her tongue.

'You would be astonished how durable a dab can be,' she informed me. 'Why, I found a good set on the statue of a cat that had been untouched for three thousand years in the tomb of Tutankhamun and,' she hurried on before I could object that it would have been dry, 'on a hammer that had been thrown into the Serpentine four years prior to discovery and recovery.

'If Barnaby Mason hid here and sorted through the stones, as seems possible, he does not have your natural grace. Indeed, he strikes me as a rather clumsy fellow, in which case there must have been dozens and dozens of fingerprints.'

My godmother unclipped her carpet bag and produced a jam-jar-sized pot with two brushes and I did not need telling what they were for.

'Yes but—' I began to object again.

'Darling.' March touched my left elbow gently. 'We only need one.'

68

THE INEXHAUSTIBLE JOY OF
ALWAYS BEING RIGHT

hate fingerprint hunting. Even in good conditions you rarely get clear lines. People tend not to press their fingers carefully on to knives or guns. They move around and smear them and half the time when you think you've found a good dab, it turns out one of your colleagues couldn't keep his mittens on for five minutes.

March Middleton held out a white cotton glove, open so that I could slip my hand in.

'I am confident you have calculated that you are taller than I.' She did a passable imitation of Mr G's precise tones. 'So I shall start on the ground floor and you can start in the attic.' My godmother got stiffly to her knees and carefully turned the nearest stone. 'Lichen,' she showed me with obvious satisfaction.

Even someone who is always right gets pleasure from being right yet again, I pondered with more than a twinge of envy.

We dipped our brushes.

'This is one of Mr G's formulations,' Aunty M told me, 'and better suited to outdoor use as he added a fine oil to stop the powder blowing away. I believe he took out a patent.'

There is more of an art to dusting for fingerprints than people realise. You have to make sure to coat everything but if you brush too hard you will wipe the print away. For a long time we worked, me silently, my godmother humming contentedly – something from the music halls, I think. 'My Mother Was a Mermaid by the Sea' was one of her favourites, but this sounded a bit more light-operatic. She fell quiet for a while after that and then started off again with 'You Can't Take Your Donkey on the Bus'.

'I just don't think I'm going to find anything,' I said after being treated to 'Who Stole the Sweet from My Sweetheart?' and 'Polly of Petticoat Lane'.

Aunty M broke off from her work. 'Neither do I, dear. Your area is much too exposed to the elements, but you never know.'

I wanted to say sometimes you do know and I knew that she was wasting my time and her own, but then my godmother said, 'Aahh,' and I knew that *Aahh* from days of old.

'Found something?' I asked and Aunty M held up a stone carefully by the edges. It had four marks that might have been prints on it. I could see a few waves and whorls on one but the middle part was blank and the others were too smeary to make out any detail at all.

'What a pity it's smudged,' I tutted, but March Middleton was getting to her feet with the aid of my empty sleeve.

'Is it, dear?' she asked serenely. 'I am not quite so sure.'

69

GIN AND THE UNCARVED STONE

S harkey was on the prowl when we got back to the station. 'Her again.' He spoke literally over March Middleton's head, with all his trademark charm. 'Just remember she is not allowed to interview the prisoner.'

'Nor have I any intention of doing so,' my godmother assured him.

'I am seeking Miss Middleton's professional opinion,' I replied.

'Professional?' he mocked. 'Gifted amateur maybe.'

'Miss Middleton,' I began indignantly, 'has—'

'No standing whatsoever in this force or any other,' the Shark interrupted me.

'But…' I began, but I knew he was right and my godmother had no right even to examine our evidence.

'You are correct, of course, Inspector,' she told him. 'And I would no more dream of going against protocol than I would divulge the intimate details of your life last night.'

Sharkey shifted uncomfortably. 'I haven't got time for this,' he said and barged out of the front door.

Aunty M took me by the arm. 'If we may adjourn to your office, Inspector Church, I am almost exhausted and would appreciate an opportunity to recuperate.'

'Dohhhaw,' Brigsy moaned as I led her to my room. He had been hoping for some juicy gossip.

'Go on, spill the beans,' I urged, the moment I had shut the door.

My godmother's face was inscrutable.

'None to spill, I fear,' she told me. 'But his jaundiced eyes and haunted expression led me to suspect that he had had a distressing time.'

'I'm not sure he ever has a happy one.'

'Now, dear,' March Middleton said. 'Somebody will have made a record of Barnaby Mason's fingerprints, I imagine.'

'Brigsy tried,' I told her, 'but Barnaby struggled too much and we didn't want to hurt him.'

'Then might I suggest that you take a look at Mr Mason's right index finger.'

'Well, I can,' I said doubtfully, 'but there wasn't much of a print to go on.'

'That is exactly what I am hoping,' March Middleton told me. 'And now, I must sit down awhile. My ancient frame is protesting at the unaccustomed exercise I have compelled it to perform this day.'

'Have my seat,' I urged. 'It's a bit more comfortable.'

'Oh, no, Betty.' Aunty M waved a hand. 'I know my place.'

She lowered herself wearily on to the spare chair, her carpet bag on her lap.

'Shall I take that for you?' I offered.

It looked heavy.

'You most certainly shall not.' My godmother clutched the handle, prepared to resist any attempt to snatch it from her. 'Now, where are you?' She unclipped the two catches and dipped inside. 'Here you are.' She brought out her father's gold cigarette case and silvered hip flask. Sidney Grice had shot them both once in the Midland Grand Hotel and the scars of repair were still visible fifty-eight years later.

I left her to take off the dented cap and pour herself a generous gin.

'What are you up to now?' Old Scrapie asked suspiciously as I returned to the lobby.

'I am going to look at Barnaby Mason,' I told him.

'And?'

'Just look,' I said. 'You can come too if you like.'

Sharkey sniffed loudly. 'Seen him before,' he said and drifted away.

'I'll come with you, madam,' Brigsy volunteered. 'He's been a bit troublesome lately.'

I followed him to the cells and he unlocked the first one.

Barnaby was asleep and snoring on his back on top of the bed, his right hand hanging loose over the side. I took it in mine, uncurled the fingers and bent over to inspect it.

'The light int very good,' Brigsy commented, standing to one side so as to block it even more, but I had seen enough already.

I let go.

'Sleep like a babe, he do,' Brigsy commented fondly, as if Barnaby Mason was his favourite child.

I stepped out and Brigsy locked up behind us.

'What?' Barnaby shot up. 'No, please.'

'Try to rest,' I said through the viewing window, but I could hear him whimpering again.

'Did you get a look?' Aunty M was puffing on a Turkish.

'Yes,' I said, 'and the middle of the index finger is scarred so badly – by a full-thickness burn, I would think – that it has no print.'

'Just a few lines around the edges?' Aunty M flicked her cigarette into my ashtray and, seeing my nod, continued, 'I thought as much. It would be difficult to smudge the middle of a print while leaving the perimeter so clearly defined.'

'I suppose so,' I agreed – glumly, because I felt stupid again but mainly because things looked very bad indeed for Barnaby Mason. 'Looks like we have all the proof we need.'

'Do we, dear?' Aunty M drained her cup.

'More than enough for me to have to charge him, at any rate,' I said.

'I fear so,' my godmother agreed, 'but let us hope, not enough to convict.'

'You don't think he did it?' I looked at her quizzically.

'The evidence weighs very heavily against him,' March Middleton said glumly, 'but as a highly experienced senior police officer recently said, *It doesn't smell right.*'

I arrested Barnaby Mason – I would have been in dereliction of my duty not to – and he took it disconcertingly calmly.

'It int like this is really happening,' he assured me.

'I'm afraid it is,' I assured him.

'Oh please dint be afraid.' He looked at me with real concern. 'At least nobody got hurt.'

70

THE MEASURE OF A WOMAN

I pulled my chair round to sit next to Aunty M, both of us facing my filing cabinet as if it was a cosy fireplace. The actual fire in my office was rarely lit because it never drew properly and almost choked anybody foolish enough to try – which was me most recently, on three separate occasions.

'Thank you for your innocent deception.' Aunty M lifted a loose tress of hair from my cheek and placed it neatly over my ear. 'Oh, and do not even attempt to deny it.' She chuckled softly. 'Onion, indeed! I heard Benny Bergman call him Kuni when we passed him on the road as we walked from the railway station, and his puzzlement when I asked if Onion could be left unattended, before he remembered his white lie, was a treat to behold.'

I remembered her laughing now.

'Are you ever deceived?' I wondered.

'Many times,' my godmother replied, and a sadness came over her, 'and sometimes cruelly.'

'I hope your operation goes well,' I said.

'There is little to lose,' she assured me. 'I am completely blind in it now but I believe that removing the lens should give me light and the ability to distinguish unfocused shapes at best.' She chuckled. 'At worst I will end up like Mr G, with my eye in a case by my bed.'

It embarrassed me to think how this elderly lady could see more with one eye than I could with both.

'I can't thank you enough,' I began, but March Middleton patted my hand. She was never very comfortable with praise.

'I have two pieces of advice for you,' she said, 'and I do not suppose you will thank me for either of them.'

'That sounds ominous,' I worried.

'You must write to Adam,' she began.

'It's difficult.'

'All the more reason to do it.'

I exhaled. 'I shall,' I promised.

'And you should wear your arm, dear.'

'It's not very comfortable.'

'Sidney Grice went through agonies to wear his prosthetic eye,' she recalled, 'but then he was much more vain than you.' She stroked my hand. 'The trouble is, it becomes the measure of you. You may be the best police officer in the country. You are certainly one of the best I have ever met.'

I swallowed. Aunty M was not a lady to dish out false praise.

'But,' she continued, 'you will be remembered for two things – for being a woman, which you can do nothing about, and for only having one arm, which you can. You deserve to be remembered for more than that. If that bloody-minded Douglas Bader can fly aeroplanes with two artificial legs...' March Middleton's voice faded away.

'I will try again,' I promised.

My godmother squeezed my good arm. 'I must go.' She held on to me, more tightly than she needed to for balance.

'I shall miss you,' she said, letting her hand rest on mine.

'And I you,' I told her. 'I hope, when this is over, to be able to visit you.'

'Over, darling?' Aunty M sighed. 'Oh, but it shall never be that.'

We went through the lobby.

'Oh, Sergeant Briggs,' March Middleton said. 'I went this morning to stock up on some cigarettes for my journey home.'

'Oh yes, ma'am?' Brigsy asked in polite puzzlement.

'And fell into conversation with Mr Lawringe, the proprietor,' she continued. 'He told me you had shown interest in a particular briar pipe.'

Brigsy had not so much shown an interest as pressed his nose to the window like a child at a sweet shop every time he passed Lawringe's on his way to or from work.

'A king of pipes but a bit pricey for me, ma'am,' he frowned.

'But when I went past later, it had gone,' she continued and Brigsy's face fell even further.

Even if he could not afford it, he liked to drool over the prize and dream.

'Weren't me, ma'am,' he assured her. 'Mrs Briggs would skin me a-life, she would.'

'Oh, I know it was not,' Aunty M assured him. 'Because it was me and I should like you to have it.'

She placed it on the desk top in a polished mahogany box.

'But I int not got any-nothin' tu-to give you, ma'am.' My sergeant stumbled over his words in confusion.

'But you already have,' she assured him. 'You gave me a warm welcome and that is something money cannot buy.'

'Blimey – excuse my befouled language, ma'am, but I dint know what to say.'

'Goodbye will suffice,' Aunty M replied, and she turned me towards the door.

'Goodbye, ma'am,' Brigsy said, more stunned than when a

shelf of weighty procedural manuals had fallen on his head. 'A proper gent, you are, a real and proper gent.'

Hempson's the Undertakers had never been less busy. Nobody else had died for weeks except a Miss Vibernam, whose cousin, a funeral director in Saffron Walden, came at a very un-funereal pace to whisk her body away for interment. March Middleton had taken up the suggestion of Mr Trime, the stationmaster, and the funeral director had diversified to become her official chauffeur.

Mr Randar Hempson, the owner, came within ten minutes of being summoned. He wore his full black mourning suit and waistcoat. It was not right to be seen driving a hearse in casual attire, he asserted, placing his highly brushed top hat on the seat between them.

'As long as I am not expected to wear a shroud,' my godmother said with mock gravity.

'What time is your train?' I asked.

'I hope to catch the six-twenty in the morning,' March Middleton grimaced, 'if I survive Tubby's lift to the station.'

I didn't like to tell her how his last car had ended up upside down in Tringford village pond.

'If I'm not too late I'll come up the hill to see you this evening,' I promised and kissed her goodbye.

'Please do,' she said. 'Then we can get a proper game of poker going. Greta is a lovely lady but her face would have made her a fortune on the silent screen – she is so expressive – and Tubby cheats but he is so bad at it that it does him no good at all.'

I laughed and closed the door, but Aunty M wound down the window and indicated for me to come closer. I bent towards her.

'The greatest gift my godfather ever gave to me was when he

said he loved me.' Her voice trembled. 'And I should like to give that gift to you.'

And I was about to reply when she tapped the glove box and the hearse glided away.

I did not want to cry but I wanted a few minutes to myself. It didn't seem a lot to ask, but apparently it was.

71

SARDINES AND THE MISSING BOY

had not even finished waving when a woman in her mid-twenties came rushing up.

'Oh, officer, help me,' she panted, her face flushed over a cheesy complexion.

'Whatever is the matter?' I asked in concern, for she was obviously beside herself with anxiety.

'It's Wally,' she sobbed, 'my little boy. He was playin' in the front garden and now I can't goo find him anywhere.'

'You had better come in,' I told her calmly, for in nine thousand, nine hundred and ninety-nine times out of ten thousand, the child turns up unharmed within the hour.

'You must help me look for him.' She twisted her head wildly, her black-plaited hair working slightly loose from its moorings of tortoiseshell combs.

'We will,' I promised, 'but we need a few details.'

'Details?' she cried. 'I haven't got time for paperwork.'

'Neither have I,' I assured her. 'Come inside.'

I put my arm on her back and guided her into the lobby.

'Now.' I sat beside her on a bench and was just about to ask her name when Brigsy called, 'Hello, Maude Green. What's the trouble?'

'It's Wally, Sergeant Briggs.' She jumped to her feet. 'He's goo gone, he do.'

'When? Where from?' Brigsy came around the side of the desk.

'From our front garden. I just pop inside to hang the washing out the back and when I do come back he's goo and gone.'

'How long ago was this?' I pressed her.

'I dint know.' She flapped her hands about like there was a swarm of bees around her head. 'About one hour ago.'

'Where do you live?' I asked.

'Tw … tw,' she managed.

'Twelve Jackson Road,' Brigsy answered. 'Maude is my sister's cousin.'

I didn't have time to consider why she wasn't also Brigsy's cousin. Jackson Road was a nice respectable area, I knew, semi-detached houses set back from the pavement, with well-tended frontages. I had been to Jeremy Flotchett's birthday party at number nine once, before discovering that his parents were out and I was the only guest and it wasn't his birthday at all and he wanted to play sardines.

'Where have you looked?' I asked, *and please don't say everywhere.*

'All over the house. I thought he might come in and play hide and seek on me. Up and down the road I goo. Over to the playground. He love it there, he do.'

'How old is he?' I asked.

'Five,' she wept, 'and only just last week.'

'The best thing you can do is go home, Mrs Green,' I told her. 'The chances are that Wally has got bored and will be home now, worrying where you are.'

'Oh, you think so?' Maude Green asked, a ray of hope lighting her face.

'Almost certainly,' I assured her. 'There's a phone box just around the corner from you, isn't there?'

'Corner of Foremost Road,' she agreed.

'Ring here as soon as you get back to let us know if Wally is there,' I said. 'The operator will put you straight through.'

'He'll be sittin' on the doorstep, he will,' Brigsy forecast, 'I do believe.'

'Oh, I hope so, Uncle Frank.' Maude Green clutched her handbag to her chest and I gave up trying to work out their relationship.

'He's a nice boy, little Wally,' Brigsy told me when she had gone. 'No trouble at all as a rule.'

''You know what children are like,' I commented. 'They wander off somewhere, get bored and go home.'

'Do that myself, I do.' Brigsy nodded gravely. 'Mrs B don't care for it, though.'

'You wandering off?' I queried.

'No, me gooin' home,' he said glumly.

We sat a while, the near silence broken only by Brigsy vigorously clearing his throat every now and then as if to make an important statement, but there was none forthcoming.

'While I think of it,' I said, 'why did you call Miss Middleton *ma'am* but you always call me *madam*?'

Brigsy tugged a tuft near the back of his head.

'Do I, madam?' he enquired. 'I never really thought about it.'

I looked at the phone. Maude Green was only a few streets away. She should have been back by now.

There was something else I had been meaning to tackle him on.

'Know anything about all that junk in the office?' I asked, and Brigsy chewed the lead end of his pencil thoughtfully.

'Yes, madam,' he told me. 'I know it do be there and I know for a fact I dint know why it do be there.'

'Perhaps somebody would like to clear it away,' I suggested.

'Dint know who that somebody might be,' Brigsy puzzled, and even though we were expecting it, the phone made us both jump.

72

A FLUTTER WITH SISTER FRANCIS

B rigsy preened the smudge on his upper lip and lifted the receiver like this was a delicate and dangerous procedure. 'Sackwater Central Police Station,' he announced and then for good measure, 'Sergeant Briggs speaking ... Oh hello, Maude.' I knew from the drop in his voice there was no good news. 'Have you tried next door? ... Aunty Paula? ... What about Mrs Payne?' Brigsy ran through a list of perhaps a dozen people. 'All right then, Maude. You goo home like the n'inspector say and wait there for him.' There was a long pause. 'Well, someone has to be there,' he said sensibly. 'I'll hang up in case we get any news... No, I mean good news...' This disjointed conversation continued for perhaps another couple of minutes before he replaced the receiver and looked at me for instructions.

'I expect by the time they get here it'll all have blown over, but we need everyone we can get hold of,' I decided. 'The trouble is, only Dodo is on the phone.'

'I'll ring her,' Brigsy said. 'Then I goo to the convent. I've a good idea Old Scrapie is there.'

'At the convent?' I queried in disbelief.

'Sister Francis do run a poker school this aatanoon, I do believe,' he told me, 'and the Shark do like a flutter, he do.'

I would have to tell Aunty M about that if she ever returned.

'I suppose we do need him,' I moaned.

'He's our most experienced officer,' Brigsy pointed out, 'and the only one as can drive with Superintendent Vesty being off. He can round up some of the others.'

'Don't they have a phone at the convent?'

'They do,' my sergeant conceded, 'but they'll deny he do be there.'

'We need a search party,' I said, ignoring his rising eyebrows. 'A proper one this time.' I organised my thoughts. 'You go. I'll ring Dodo. She might be able to get Rivers on the way.'

Brigsy usually moved like a rusty Meccano man but today he was Johnny Weissmuller diving into the river to save a maiden from the statically grinning jaws of a rubber crocodile. This was one of the rare times I regretted having so few officers. Normally I thought we had at least four too many.

My mother answered the phone, 'Yes?' Whatever happened to *Good afternoon, Mr Church's dental surgery*?

'I need to speak to Dodo.'

'She's off duty,' my mother said. 'Who is this?'

Why did she do that to me? She knew damned well who it was. 'Inspector Church,' I said. 'And this is an official emergency.'

'Right,' my mother said. She clunked the receiver down on the table and I was not sure if that was a *we'll-see-about-that-then* kind of *right* or a *right-away-ma'am* kind of *right*, which would be a first – and it was.

'Constable Chivers speaking,' Dodo said, remembering my lecture about formality.

'A child has gone missing from Jackson Road. We need everyone at the station as soon as possible.'

'I was just on my way to Sackwater Ladies' Sewing Circle,' Dodo told me.

'Well, I'm sorry but you'll just have to miss it,' I stormed, after all the talks we had had about maturity and responsibility.

'I just thought,' Dodo said quickly as I was drawing breath for my onslaught, 'that if you were thinking of organising a search party, there are about thirty of us.'

'That is a very sensible suggestion,' I said, 'and perhaps someone could fetch Rivers. Sergeant Briggs has gone for Inspector Sharkey.'

'I'll be as quick as I can, Boss,' Dodo said.

I put the phone down, looked through the station directory and dialled again. I needed a friendly magistrate.

73

VULTURES, PENGUINS AND HARRIDANS

Dodo had not exaggerated the numbers of her sewing club. Thirty-two ladies all anxious to help had answered her call. Not to be outdone, but being outdone, Sharkey had brought his fellow poker players – Mr Swan the mayor and *the penguins*, as we had called them at Roedene Abbey. Six Sisters of Fortitude – all worthy women, no doubt, but hampered by having taken vows of silence. Brigsy had rounded up five members of his darts club and eight of his bowls club. Bantony had brought nine ladies. I did not ask where he had come across them but they ranged from a professional lady – a vet – to a professional lady in a very different occupation. Box had brought Mrs Box, a tiny lady with a nervous smile and not at all the harridan he claimed to be terrified of. Josie Whitehouse came. She had left Sylvia at home, she told me. And Toby arrived, camera and accoutrements around his neck, as usual.

'Vulture,' a young woman with no visible means of chewing spat at him.

'Mr Gregson has come to help,' I assured her.

'And – who knows? – you might get your picture on the front of the *Gazette*,' Toby teased her.

'Oh, hardly,' the woman simpered, petting her hair up with the flat of her hand and pouting with an expression that reminded me of a catfish I had seen grubbing along the bottom of a tank in London Zoo Aquarium.

I had learned many things from my last experience of

organising a search party – including not to summon the Boy Scouts or Brownies and to draw up a proper plan. We divided the area into sections starting at Jackson Road and working ever outwards, and I handed out lists of street names to everyone.

'You will go in pairs to each house,' I instructed, 'and ask if they have seen Wally. He is five years old and Mr Gregson of the *Gazette* has printed copies of the photograph taken last week on his fifth birthday. You are to ask if you can look in their gardens and if they refuse, tell them you will return within fifteen minutes with the police, who will have a warrant not only to do that but also to enter their houses. One of you will stand at a safe distance nearby and the other will hurry here. Mr Cunningham-Draper, the magistrate—' I pointed to the heavy-framed gentleman installed, to Brigsy's indignation, behind the desk. '—will take all the necessary details.'

'Bit heavy-handed,' objected a young man with horn-rimmed glasses and a floppy fringe. 'What next, the stamp of jackboots along the promenade?'

'The safety of a child is at stake,' Dodo told him fiercely, 'and if you are not willing to help find him, you might like to call on his mother and explain exactly why.'

Several *hear-hears* greeted her little speech, including a silent one from me.

'Didn't say I wouldn't,' he mumbled.

'Where *is* his mother?' one of Bantony's ladies asked. I was almost sure I had seen her mugshot in the station records. 'Why isn't she here helping?'

I wanted to say *She has gone to have a perm* but I had a feeling some of them might believe me, so I stuck with, 'I have advised her to stay at home with her sister and await developments.'

'You nun ladies—' Brigsy handed some paper and pencils to

the oldest one, who wore a bigger crucifix and so was probably in charge. '—will have to write messages to people.'

'Oh, bad cess to that,' the probably Mother Superior said. 'We are allowed to speak in case of emergency and I would say that this is one.'

'Oh, thank the sweet baby Jaysus,' another nun breathed. 'I was beginning to wonder if I'd lost my voice.'

'Is that a Cork accent?' the next one asked, suddenly animated. 'I hail from Ballyarthur.'

'Ballinrush.'

'Away with you!'

'And I'm from Boolakelly,' another announced delightedly.

'No way! Born and raised in Carriganleigh, I was.'

A little one with the face of a cherub eyed all her sisters in wonderment. 'Oh, bloody hell,' she groused, 'I've spent seven years with a bunch of fricking Paddies.'

74

THE RABBIT AND THE FIRE ENGINE

A few people saw Wally. They noticed him because he was a pretty little boy. Two women from Arthur's Fish Shop watched him skipping down High Road East towards the sea and both of them were convinced he was alone. A retired vicar spotted him on the promenade and thought that he waved to somebody but didn't see who.

There were, of course, several less reliable sightings. A plumber saw Wally boarding a bus in Tennis Court Lane but the conductor was adamant that no unaccompanied child had done so.

It was starting to get dark and we were running out of time and ideas. I rang White Lodge and Tubby answered. Aunty M had gone to bed with a headache, he told me. She had been getting a lot of those lately, she had admitted. Tubby had urged her to get this investigated and she had promised she would, when her eye was better. I said to let her sleep. There was nothing she could do anyway. I had just wanted to talk.

It was Rivers who found our first concrete clue, not because he was the cleverest or most observant officer but because he had stopped for a rest and sat on a bench and happened to glance down and see a child's toy lying in the gutter. Dodo and I took the little stuffed rabbit to Maude Green's house. Her husband was in France with the 1st Battalion, Suffolk Regiment and her sister had gone to find someone to look after her own children.

'Where did you find it?' she asked anxiously, sunk down in a new green armchair.

'On Benjamin Road,' I told her. 'Near the old pumping station.'

'But what would Wally be doing there?' She ran her hands all over her face.

There was a nearly full bottle of gin on the sideboard. I was not one to frown on that and Aunty M would have heartily approved, but I was surprised she had it on view to visitors.

'I was hoping you might have some idea,' I said. 'Does he ever play in that area?'

'No, why would he? It's a rubbish tip.' She played with her hair.

I knew some more adventurous boys liked to explore it as the fence was broken in a few places, but Wally was probably too young for that.

'Does he have any friends in that area?' Dodo asked. She was sitting on the arm of Maude Green's armchair now and holding Maude's left hand.

'Certainly not,' Maude Green bristled. 'They are very rough children there.'

'Are any of his other toys missing?' Dodo asked.

'What? Well, his fire engine, of course.' She was running her hands through her hair like she was checking for nits.

Fire engines were very popular toys since the bombings began and people saw the newsreels, especially among children who preferred to play at helping people rather than killing them.

'Why *of course*?' I enquired and Mrs Green snapped her fingers at me like I was an idle garçon.

'Because it isn't here.' She didn't actually add the word *Stupid* but it lay heavily on every syllable.

It was difficult to take offence, though. I could smell the gin on her breath and I couldn't blame her. God alone knew what that woman was going through and God alone knew why.

'I need to get back to the station,' I said. 'Would you like Constable Chivers to stay with you, Mrs Green?'

'What?' Maude Green closed her eyes and shook her head wildly. 'No. My sister will be back soon.'

'I can make us a nice pot of tea,' Dodo tempted her, which would have been a unique event since she usually got something wrong – not boiling the water, not letting it brew, leaving it to stew, not enough milk or mainly milk.

'Thank you...' – Maude Green rubbed her right temple – '...but I do rather you goo out there lookin'.'

We gathered our helmets and gas masks and handbags.

'You will find him?' Maude Green asked, because people always do and this is where I had to say *We will do everything we can*. I was not even sure those terror-clouded eyes were focusing on me but I stood erect and, looking into them, said steadily, 'Of course we will.'

75

HARLOCK AND THE LOST TRIBES

We gathered outside the old pumping station, me and Dodo, Sharkey, Box and Bantony. I clicked my torch on and it cut across the weed-strewn concrete yard like a searchlight.

'Oy 'ope there aren't any ARP men about?' Bantony said and, summoned by the magic of those words, Warden Harlock came dashing up the road screaming, 'Put that bloody light out!'

If it had been Teddy Moulton, I could have dealt with him – we had been sort of friends since we were children – but Harlock was a very different prospect. He had reported Mrs Vine for lighting a candle in church after dark in memory of her husband and she had been fined four pounds, which was four pounds more than she could afford, by a magistrate anxious to prove that being called Hess did not make him one of those fifth columnists we kept reading about.

'We are looking for a little lost boy,' Dodo explained.

'I don't care if you are looking for the lost tribes of Israel,' Harlock shouted, straight into her face.

'You will not speak to my officers like that,' I told him, which was a stupid thing to say because he would.

'Shall Oy beat the shit out of 'im, ma'am?' Bantony offered.

This was a tempting prospect. Harlock was a big man but most of his bulk was lard and Bantony used to box before he started to worry about his looks, and I was confident that Box would live up to his name and lend a hand.

'I don't think so,' I declined regretfully. 'Now, Warden Harlock—'

'If you don't put that light out in ten seconds, I will charge you under the Defence of the Realm Act,' Harlock said, and I clicked my torch off. There was no point in wasting the battery and there was no point, no matter how much I detested the man, in aggravating the situation.

'Do you have any children, Mr Harlock?' Box demanded furiously.

'No I bloody don't,' Harlock replied, 'and I'm not going to risk the whole town getting bombed for the sake of one brat.'

'Warden Harlock is right,' Sharkey said. He had been quiet up to then but I could rely on him to become more loathsome in a crisis. 'We mustn't break even the smallest regulation, whatever the reason.'

Since when did you become so sanctimonious, you… Words failed me even in my thoughts.

'Quite right, Inspector,' Harlock said.

'Especially with regard to petrol rationing,' Old Scrapie said brightly. 'Well, of course.' Harlock suddenly had the air of a man on the ropes. 'But I get extra coupons for my work.'

'Enough to take you to Manchester and back two weekends in a row?' Sharkey smiled amicably.

'Well, we all bend the rules a little.' Harlock tried to rally but only succeeded in delivering a body blow to himself.

'Precisely.' Sharkey put an arm over his new chum's shoulder and for a moment I thought they were going to have a cuddle, but then I saw my colleague's arm was tightening around the warden's neck. 'So why don't you piss off and leave us to bend a few of our own?'

Sharkey released his grip and Harlock stumbled sideways, rubbing his throat.

'You'll take a tumble one day, Sharkey,' he warned, lurching away down the road.

'Not when I've got good friends like you,' Sharkey mocked the vanishing figure. 'And even better information about them,' he mumbled to himself.

I had never felt like kissing my fellow inspector before and I didn't feel like it now, but if we had been in a pub, I might have bought him a double.

'Thank you,' I said, for probably the first time. 'But how did you know about that?'

Sharkey scratched the side of his nose. 'Let's just say I know a dressmaker who knows a few other dressmakers who know where they can get extra supplies.'

I wondered how many other black market scams my colleague was turning a blind eye to but there was no time to think about that now. The warden had wasted enough of it already and night was falling fast. I turned my torch on again and the others, having been instructed to bring proper torches, rather than the silly almost-blacked-out things we were supposed to use routinely, followed suit and then me through a gap in the tall link-wire fence where the posts tilted inwards.

The yard was about one hundred feet square and littered with rusting bits of machinery. There was a stack of old iron pipes in one corner and we shone our lights down each one. They were about two-foot diameter and a child could easily have crawled down any of them.

'Oh yuck!' Dodo shrieked and jumped back, frantically brushing something off her sleeve.

The men laughed and Dodo looked at me shamefacedly.

'Sorry, Boss,' she mouthed and I let it go. She was trying very hard, I knew.

'Was it a spidery-widery?' Sharkey mocked.

'I did not know there was such a creature, sir,' Dodo replied with great dignity. 'Perhaps you have one in your home.'

Old Scrapie snorted and trained his beam all around the yard. 'Go and look inside that boiler, Bank-Anthony,' he commanded, 'and you, Box, check behind those cable reels.'

Strictly speaking I was in charge of this investigation but this was not an occasion for bickering over the chain of command.

'Stand still!' I barked. 'I heard something.' And the men froze. 'Wally,' I called into the night. 'We are here to help you. Can you hear me?'

But only a distant dog answered my voice and then a rustle and a rat shot out from under a collapsed packing crate and over my foot. I recoiled and very nearly said something that sounded like, but wasn't quite, Dodo's *yuck*.

76

LOCKS, CHAINS AND DRAINS

Bantony and Box rejoined us, having found nothing of interest.

'Well, he's not out here,' I conceded. 'Can we get inside?'

The pumping station was a one-storey building, the height of two. It had tall arched windows but all of them were barred over. The wooden double front door was padlocked with a heavy chain but the leaves pushed open a few inches when I tried the handle.

'I might be able to squeeze through,' Dodo volunteered.

'And how would you get out again?' I asked.

'I might be able to shoulder it down,' Box proposed dubiously.

'Or I can nip back to the station for an axe,' Bantony suggested, but Sharkey shouldered the constable aside.

'Let me have a look.' Sharkey went down on his haunches. 'Shine a light on it, someone.' And, being the nearest to him, I did. Sharkey humphed a couple of times. 'Hardened steel. Never cut that.'

He fiddled inside his jacket and I heard a rattle. 'Hold that light steady,' he snapped, flicking through a chain of keys. Only they were not ordinary keys. Some of them looked more like things my father used to scrape teeth or dig out bits of broken roots. Sharkey fiddled about and tried a couple of picks. Sidney Grice was an expert lock-picker. He tried to teach his god-daughter but she was never very good at it. She tried to teach me and I wasn't bad but I had twice as many digits then.

'Come on, you bastard,' Sharkey cursed, his pick seeming to

jam. 'Whole bloody thing's rusty.' And I thought he was pulling the pick out and giving up when there was a loud and very satisfactory click and the lock hinged open.

We looked at each other. This was something that at least merited a round of applause. If he had been nicer he would have got one, or even a slap on the back.

'Good,' I said and stepped away while he pulled the chain out of the handles and the double doors swung apart.

'This remoinds me of a n'orror film.' Bantony looked around himself uneasily.

'What? *Death of the Daft Brummie*?' Box suggested. 'I'd pay good money to see that.'

I stepped inside. The floor was stone-slabbed so there was no risk of dry rot. The room was plain, all the pumps having been taken out when the building fell out of use, and with the high windows it had a distinctly churchy atmosphere to it.

'Well, he ain't in here,' Box observed.

There was something on the floor and I made my way towards it.

'Watch yow step, ma'am.' Bantony grabbed my empty sleeve and yanked me back. 'Yow nearly fell down the drain.'

I recovered my balance and saw that he was right. There was a gaping hole in front of me and just beyond it, on its side, lay a little wooden fire engine.

77

THE DEEP, DARK WATERS

caught my breath.

'Thank you, Bantony.'

'Don't want you fallin' down any more holes, we don't,' Box reminded me, as if I would ever forget.

Sharkey walked to the edge and pointed his torch down. The hole was rectangular, about three foot by four.

'Hope the little so-and-so didn't fall down that,' Sharkey muttered. About a yard down it was full of water.

'How deep is it?' I wondered.

'Straight down maybe fifteen feet,' Box said authoritatively. 'It's a sump well.'

'What is it for?' Dodo enquired.

'It's a reservoir,' Box told her. 'Pumps dint like to run short of water. They overheat and seize up. The water flow through the supply pipe might not be steady, 'special in summer.'

'How d'yow know all this?' Bantony asked.

'Dad work here 'til it close, he do.' Box looked about like he was expecting to see his father and maybe in his mind's eye he actually was. 'Foreman. He shew me round a foo time, to give me the taste of it but it int a taste I like so I goo Bury St Edmunds and join the force.'

'So where does the supply come from?' I asked.

'In-pipe near the top,' Box explained. ' 'bout this big.' He held his hands as if strangling somebody, possibly Bantony. 'Drain from Perry's, it do.'

Perry's Pond filled from the sea. It was built around the turn of the century as a boating lake and had been quite popular in Edwardian times for owners of small sailboats not suited to the open ocean.

'And there's an out-pipe at the bottom same size as them outside but there's a sluice over that.'

'So, if Wally had fallen in here, he would still be in there?' I said grimly.

'Unless he goo full under,' Box confirmed. 'There's a second chamber connected by one of those big pipes so a boiler man's lad can swim down and into it if he need to repair the sluice. Too tight for most men.'

'Like a sort of U-bend,' I clarified and Box nodded. 'But you'd have to be a good swimmer to get down there,' I pointed out. 'Bodies don't sink like stones.'

'Tha's true,' Box agreed, 'but the pipe from the pond do flow good and strong so the current would carry you under. Got a handkerchief, Bantony?'

'S'pose.' Bank-Anthony handed him a folded square of pressed white cotton. 'And Oy want it back – properly laundered.'

'Just want to demonstrate.' Box tossed the handkerchief into the drain. It swirled and was sucked away.

'Oy said Oy wanted it back,' Bantony protested.

'You did,' Box agreed. 'But I never say you do get it.'

'Why didn't you use your own?'

Box shrugged. 'Dint want to lose it,' Box said simply and Sharkey roared with laughter.

'Whoy yow—' Bantony began.

'So, it's possible Wally could be in the second chamber alive?' I asked firmly.

'If he's down there,' Box conceded. 'Dog fall in once and get into the chamber.'

'Did it survive?' Dodo asked.

'' 'til the day it die,' Box confirmed.

'Can we get it drained?' Sharkey asked.

'Not without openin' the sluice and floodin' the second chamber,' Box pondered. 'Or gettin' a big-boy pump to empty it and that take a good long while. We dint know how much air is left in there or if it's gone foul.'

'So...' – Dodo knelt to fiddle with her shoelaces, as if they mattered at the moment – '...the boiler man's lad would just swim to the bottom and turn right and go up into the chamber? Is there any light in there?'

'Bit through some airbricks in the day,' Box said, 'but this int in the day.'

'Can you see in through them?' I asked.

'No, ma'am.'

'How big is the second chamber?' Dodo kicked off her shoes.

'Never been in there.' Box held out his hands. 'How long is a piece of string?'

'Seventy-nine units,' Dodo assured him, because I had once told her that as a sort-of joke.

She started unbuttoning her jacket.

'What are you doing?' I asked, though I feared I knew the answer to that. 'You are *not* going into that sump.'

'But I am the only one small enough, Boss,' Dodo reasoned. 'I often wondered why God made me so tiny. Perhaps it was this.'

'And so yow could have such a trim little figure,' Bantony smarmed, and Dodo smiled nicely.

'Are there any comments you would like to make about Inspector Sharkey's figure, Constable Bank-Anthony?'

'What?' Bantony looked repelled. 'No.'

'Then kindly do not make any about mine,' Dodo said, word

perfect. I had coached her on that and a few other retorts. 'Please turn your backs, except for Inspector Church, of course.'

Dodo handed me her jacket and unbuttoned her skirt. She did not have stockings on but had painted her legs black and made quite a good job of it. I would ask her what she used later – if there was a later.

'I can't let you do this,' I protested, but took her skirt and folded it while she was undoing her shirt.

'Will you explain to Mrs Green why we let her boy die?' She pulled her arms out of her sleeves and handed me her shirt.

'Don't let her do it,' Bantony begged, his head twisting sideways.

'Do not dare to turn around,' Dodo told him.

'We don't even know he's down there,' I reasoned.

'He could be,' the Shark chipped in, back, it seemed, to his evil ways.

'Precisely.' Dodo was pulling her chemise over her head.

'Are yow trying to prove yourself as good as a man?' Bantony demanded.

'No.' Dodo thrust her chemise at me and, thank goodness, stopped there. 'I am proving myself better.' In uniform, Dodo looked diminutive. Out of it she was miniscule. She leaned forward and whispered in my ear, 'This is not the way I intend to die, Boss.'

I should have taken hold of her there and then and explained that we are not always given the choice, but I didn't. I don't think I really believed Dodo would do it. She was such a silly wimp as a rule.

Dodo sat on the stone floor and swung her legs over the edge.

'No,' I said. This had gone far enough. 'I absolutely—'

'Let her go.' Sharkey spoke over me and as I stepped sideways to argue with him, Dodo slid forward to balance on the edge, took a deep breath and let herself drop heavily into the water.

'Goodness!' she cried out. 'This is as cold as a cauliflower.' Dodo bobbed a moment in the beam of my torch, said, 'Sorry Boss,' took a deep breath, put her head under and kicked her skinny legs, splashing me head to foot before she disappeared into the dark water.

78

THE PRAYERS OF THE POLICE AND
THE BITING OF TONGUES

stared down, the light from my torch dancing wildly in Dodo's wake.

'Come back,' I whispered.

'Please, God,' Bantony reinforced my sentiment.

'You can all turn round now,' I said, staring helplessly down.

The black waves slopped against the brick sides of the sump.

Box, I noticed, was mouthing something and making the sign of the cross. 'Lord,' he said aloud. 'I wish I dint tell her, I do.'

I wished he hadn't too but I couldn't even remember Pooky's nonsense about wishes.

I looked at my watch. She must have been half a minute now but I had forgotten to time her from the start. Even half a minute is a long time to stay submerged in icy water and especially when you're doing vigorous exercise.

Another twenty seconds ticked agonisingly by and, excruciatingly, another twenty.

'Well,' Sharkey said flatly. 'She's either dead in the sump or she's through to the chamber and who knows if she's alive there or will even find her way back?'

People talk about biting their tongues figuratively but I bit mine literally.

Another minute went by, and another, and I stopped timing.

Oh God, I know you can do all the mean things. You've

proved that time and time again. Just this once be as kind as they say you are. This probably wasn't much of prayer, I reflected, so I added a heartfelt *please*.

The water swelled, rose and broke and Dodo crashed through the surface, gulping and choking frantically, her hair collapsed into a soggy mass. Her skin looked blue in a way you never really believe skin can go.

'Give her your hand,' I shouted at Bantony, ramming him in the back so hard he nearly toppled in on top of her.

'SSSorry, Boss,' she gasped. 'He's…'

'Dead,' Sharkey contributed.

'Not there,' Dodo managed, thrashing wildly now.

Bantony was not quite as tall as Box but he was a great deal more lithe. He dropped face down, shuffled up to his waist over the edge and leaned far into the hole, Box pinioning his ankles to stop him sliding further.

'Take moy hands.'

'N-n-not until you close your eyes,' she clattered.

'They're closed now.'

'If you o-open them, I will break your blasted jaw,' she vowed and I saw Bantony's shoulders tense as he took her weight. *Blasted* was strong stuff for Dodo, the strongest I had ever heard her use.

'Pull me up,' he shouted and Box and Sharkey took a leg each and hauled.

'Careful,' Bantony yelped. 'Oy've only 'ad these trousers a week.'

'They are very s-smart,' Dodo assured him as her head emerged through the floor. 'I noticed on the wa-way here.'

Bantony grinned, got to his knees and heaved her up.

'Eyes closed all men,' I commanded, having glimpsed how translucent her wet underwear had become, and I took off my jacket.

'You'll need mine too,' Box said.

'And moyne.' Both men handed their jackets over and it wasn't until much later that I wondered how they had known I was taking mine off.

79

FALSE HOPES AND THE HEAVINESS OF GIN

dried Dodo as best I could with the jackets and got her dressed again. At least her teeth stopped clattering and her skin returned almost to its usual tint of white.

Sharkey drove her back to Felicity House and I rather hoped my parents would launch into him as they would me for bringing her home in that state.

I had given Dodo my jacket first so I got it back, just-used-towel-wet and as crumpled as the newspaper you throw away after your fish and chips. I did think about going to the station and changing it but decided it was more important to keep Maude Green informed. I just wished I had something to inform her about.

A big woman with a stubbly chin came to the door. She had a nose to match her bulk but the nostrils looked like they had been sealed at birth and nobody had troubled to unblock them. She breathed heavily through her white-flecked lips.

'I'm Maude's sister, Violeth Took,' she introduced herself and took me straight through. Maude leapt out of her chair.

'Have you found him?' she demanded, striding towards me. 'Is he all right? Where is he? Where's my baby?'

'We're still looking,' I said, being careful not to say I was sorry first in case she thought I was about to break even worse news. 'I'm sorry.'

'Is that it?' Violeth asked furiously. 'Is that why you came – to raise false hopes?'

'I promised to keep your sister informed,' I said as she pushed her face unpleasantly close to mine.

She was a hefty woman who might have been a useful prop forward in her time, whenever that was. She looked so much older than Maude that she would not even have passed as a young mother to her.

'Informed of what?' she asked aggressively, though not without reason.

'And also…' I bypassed the question because I didn't have an answer to it, and produced the fire engine, wrapped in my handkerchief, from my handbag. '…to ask your sister if she recognised this.' I held it up and Violeth reached out. 'Please don't touch it,' I said hastily.

'What is it?' Maude Green rushed over with grasping hands and I whisked it away.

'What is this, some kind of game?' She pulled a plait of her hair loose so that it swung over her face like a back-to-front ponytail.

'We might need to check it for fingerprints,' I explained.

'Fingerprints?' she repeated in confusion. 'Do you think my little Wally stole it?'

Her breath was heavy with gin and I saw that the bottle, nearly full when I came earlier, was almost empty now.

'What on earth for? I have never seen it in my life before and why do you keep calling my mother my sister?'

'Because she—' I started to explain.

'Oh, it's a common mistake.' Mrs Took waved a hand dismissively. 'Most people think we are sisters.'

'So this is not Wally's toy?' I double-checked.

'Of *course* it isn't Wally's fire engine,' Maude Green shrieked at me. 'I found that in the kitchen. What the hell does that matter?'

Dodo could have died because of what you told us, I thought, but only said, 'We have to follow all possible leads, Mrs Green.'

'Then try following some proper ones,' Mrs Took told me and I bit my tongue yet again, but figuratively this time.

I put the fire engine back in my bag.

'I shan't come again unless I have definite news or there is something I need to ask you,' I promised.

'So is that it?' Violeth cried. 'You are leaving my poor daughter to sit and go demented with fret?'

'No, I am going out to keep searching,' I said.

She jabbed me in the chest because you are allowed to poke police officers about as much as you like.

'Coming here dressed like that.' She prodded my creased damp jacket again. 'It's an insult.'

'Why did you tell me you were her sister?'

'Mother. I said *mother.*'

'Then you have a serious speech impediment.' I thought back. 'And Mrs Green said her sister was coming back.'

'And so she is, when she can get somebody to look after her stinking snot-nosed brats.'

It occurred to me that Mrs Took was referring to her own grandchildren.

She lowered her voice. 'Have you even spoken to him?'

'Who do you mean?'

'Simnal Cranditch, of course,' she told me contemptuously, 'the old pervert who's been hanging around the street.'

80

AFTERNOON TEA WITH SIMNAL CRANDITCH

blinked, not a normal hardly-aware-of-it blink. It was an effort to stop my eyes rolling in disbelief.

'Simnal Cranditch has been loitering around here?' I repeated incredulously. 'You mean just around this house or the street or the area?'

'Up and down the street, he is.'

'For how long?'

'Ten minutes sometimes, five others, I s'pose. I dint have a stopwatch.'

I doubted she had a toothbrush either. Her teeth were blackened with decay and her gums were growing over them.

'For how long has he been coming here?'

''bout a week.' The gin was the only fresh thing on Violeth Took's breath. 'I dint carry a calendar.'

'Why didn't you tell us?'

''bout the calendar? What for?'

'About Simnal Cranditch.'

'Why dint you know?'

'I'm surprised your daughter didn't mention it.'

'She dint know. Think she int goh nuff to worry on?'

'I didn't even know he was still around,' I ruminated, because I hadn't seen or heard of him since he had told me he was leaving.

'Well, don't tha' take the last ginger biscuit from the ginger biscuit tin?' Violeth Took folded her arms untidily, like when you can't get a deckchair to close properly. 'What's the point of having a police state if you don't keep a track on everyone?'

I would debate that another time over a glass of mouthwash, I decided.

'I don't suppose you know where he lives?'

'Course I do.' She tossed her head, not a hair of it shifting with the movement. 'Take aatanoon tea with him every mornin', I do.'

They say sarcasm is the lowest form of wit but Violeth Took had cleverly removed the wit element completely.

'Well, thank you very much,' I smiled politely. 'It is not often I meet a member of the public who is so abhorrent.'

If she took offence I would claim she had misheard me, but Violeth Took grinned malodorously and said, 'I do my best.' And ruined even that by adding, 'Sergeant.'

Sharkey looked as drained as I felt when I returned to the station and, to be fair to him, he had been on duty since the night before.

'Did Chivers get back all right?' I asked.

'Dodipops?' he grinned and I shrivelled in the core of my body. He would never let me or her live that down. 'Yes, they were going to put her to bed with hot water bottles and Ovaltine.'

They had never done that for me, not even after my father let me fall into a wintry North Sea, not even when I had the Spanish 'flu.

'And a story,' he smirked, but then his face was serious. 'Lovely couple, your parents,' he said in apparent sincerity. 'Gave me a mug of tea with a good shot of Glenmorangie.'

Glenmorangie? That was my single malt and I had been saving it for a special occasion – if ever I had one.

'Invited me for Sunday lunch,' he said dreamily.

'And are you going?' I asked warily.

'Oh, of course.' Sharkey took on his usual Sharkey tone. 'They've hardly begun to tell me about your childhood.'

I went back to *Cressida*. Captain had fallen asleep in his armchair by the stove. Had he been waiting up for me? I let him slumber and went to my cabin. My arm in the jar of formalin was starting to look withered. Tubby had warned me it wouldn't keep well because the hospital hadn't bothered to inject it with the preservative. My false arm hung on a hook on the wall. It was an ugly device of metal rods in a copper sleeve connected at the wrist to a steel claw. The fingers were all designed to bend on hinges that I could loosen or tighten with little screws. It was lighter than my first prosthetic limb but it was still an unwelcome weight. My stump slotted into a cup that was supposed to mould around it but the end of my arm had shrunk more since the limb was made and there was not much between my bone and skin, so I padded the socket with handkerchiefs. The whole thing was attached by leather straps, which I buckled over my shoulder and around my chest, just under my armpits. It was at best uncomfortable, at worst painful, but I had told my godmother I would try and so I would. I had kept my other promise, to write to Adam, and had been feeling bad about it ever since.

81

THE SECRET COFFEE AND
THE SPECIAL EDITION

pswich Police came for Barnaby Mason. They hadn't wasted much time; coppers love a good murder. With any luck, they get photographed taking the accused to court.

'He's a card,' one of them laughed. 'Thought I was the King come to knight him.'

Keep it up, Barnaby, I prayed. With a lot of luck, he could be back in Woodbridge in a matter of weeks. The last time he was there he had confessed to strangling the Pope's wife.

I didn't so much call off the search for Wally as let people decide when they had had enough. The Sisters of Fortitude lived up to the name of their order except for the young one, who had gone off to the Compasses to dispense with at least one of her vows.

'Ah, we had a grand time,' the Mother Superior assured me. 'And don't you go fretting over that poor wee nipper. We'll pray for him.'

'Thank you,' I muttered and wondered why they hadn't prayed for and ended the suffering of all the other children in their wonderful world.

'Remember oh gracious Virgin Mary,' one of them started off.

I hadn't realised she had meant there and then but the others were joining in and imploring their mother's help and I knew they meant well and were sincere and I bowed my head and said *Amen* at the end and wished them all a good night.

The twins were on patrol that night but there was little they could do. You can't knock on innocent people's doors or root around their gardens at two in the morning.

I sent Brigsy home and went to the cells. For some reason, cell five had the thickest mattress so I used that, taking the keys with me just in case one of the men thought he would play a jolly jape. It was more comfortable than the old camp bed I had used in the past. I took off my jacket and shirt, unstrapped my arm, laid it on the stone-slabbed floor, put my shirt back on and lay down.

My mind was racing with thoughts of little Wally. Even in the happiest of outcomes, if he had just wandered off, got lost and taken shelter for the night, he would be terrified. I didn't like to think of the less happy possibilities but I had to consider them all. I had put out instructions to seek Simnal Cranditch and bring him in for questioning. And almost all the volunteers had said they would come again the next day, some even promising reinforcements of friends and family.

Toby was issuing a special free edition of the *Gazette* to come out first thing in the morning and had printed hundreds of posters to put up in shop windows and anywhere else that would have them. I wondered how he could afford that. The paper was in enough financial difficulties as it was.

It was hopeless trying to sleep. I got up, reassembled myself, and made a strong black coffee from the jar I hid in my desk because it was expensive and I didn't want the men nicking it. Then I rolled a cigarette. I was very proud of how I could do that one-handed but tonight I was getting strands all down my sleeve. It took half a dozen attempts to get a flame on my brass Zippo lighter – a present from Adam, I reflected guiltily. The flint was almost as worn down as me.

I sat at my desk and finished my cigarette while poring over a map of the town. I thought I knew Sackwater but there were back streets and alleys I was not sure I had ever been along. I had a stack of papers from people listing which streets they had been down and which houses they had not been able to access because nobody had answered the door.

Mr Cunningham-Draper, the magistrate, had had a quiet day. Only two people refused to cooperate, an unemployed man who turned out to have an illegal sugar beet alcohol still in his kitchen and Cunningham-Draper's wife, who was outraged at the infringement of her liberties but changed her mind after he rang her up.

There were two definite sightings of a little blond boy near the tennis courts but it turned out to be a little blonde girl wearing a hat.

I pencilled over the map the streets or properties that had been done and circled any remaining. What now? I chewed a cheddar sandwich and tried to think, struggling to keep my eyes open, but it had been a long day and eventually even the caffeine and the nicotine and my worries about Wally could not overcome my tiredness.

Adam came back with two open bottles of Hopleaf and we sat in the shade and watched the boats in the harbour, the painted eyes on their prows bobbing up and down. I rolled the bottle, wet with condensation, over my forehead.

'How on earth do people work in this heat?' I asked.

'Most don't.' Adam read the label. He did that every time and I never knew why. He had funny superstitions about doing things in the same way every time. 'That's why they get up at half-past four.'

I took a drink and leaned back, kicking off my sandals, and Adam took my hand. It was so nice not to be having to tell him yet again that of course I loved him but I did not want to give up my career, especially when he was abroad on secret missions most of the time. I could never bring myself to say that I didn't want to be a widow with a child and an army pension. Adam became impatient and, in the end, deeply unpleasant when I did try to discuss it and I had come to the conclusion that the regulation might be a blessing and that I would have to tell him so, if ever I managed to get in touch.

There was something wrong with my beer. It tasted of cheese.

'Lord, madam,' Brigsy said. 'Have you been up all night?'

I jolted awake and tried to look like I hadn't just jolted awake. 'Yes.' I looked about me blankly.

My half-drunk coffee sat beside the ashtray, proof of my deceit.

'No milk?' Brigsy enquired. 'I do tell Rivers to stock up.'

'No,' I said, 'I had it black to keep me awake.'

I reached for the mug. Cold black coffee would have suited me fine but my sergeant beat me to it.

'Allow me, madam.' He sniffed and I knew my guilty secret was about to be exposed. 'Oh, tha' dint smell right at all,' he tutted. 'I'll make you a fresh one.'

82

THE SOUNDINGS, THE ROUT AND THE MOB

I went to what the captain called *the head* and freshened myself up as best I could in the cramped facilities. There was no *Ladies* in Sackwater Central, of course, because the idea of a female police officer was farcical. Prisoners of either sex were given a jug of cold water and had to use the pots in their cells. There was no competition among the men over who had the privilege of emptying those.

Sharkey was standing behind the desk, leaning over Brigsy and mingling his cigarette smoke with Brigsy's pipe, and since there were no constables around to set a bad example to, I lit one of my own.

'If he got enticed into a car,' Sharkey was saying, 'he could be anywhere by now.' He looked and sounded genuinely upset by that prospect as he looked up.

'It's a pity this isn't Felixstowe,' I commented.

Being an active port, Felixstowe was a military zone and everybody going in or out had to have additional identification and their movements recorded.

'Any volunteers been in yet?'

'The sewing circle,' Brigsy told me, 'with Dodo.'

'Is she all right?'

'She say so,' he replied, 'but she look worse than you, madam.'

How splendid to be the standard against which all afflictions are measured, I thought.

'The nuns have been,' Sharkey told me. 'I sent them off to The Soundings.'

The Soundings was where the so-called Desolation Tree stood and where my childhood friend Etterly had last been seen. I still had nightmares about what could have happened to her.

'Do they really play poker?' I asked and he grimaced.

'Ruthlessly,' he replied. 'They don't cheat – at least I don't think so – but they are inscrutable and will bleed you dry.'

'I've started a new list of other places to search,' Brigsy said and handed it over.

We were spreading out and would soon be in rural areas.

'Has anyone been in contact with Wally's mother?' I asked and they clicked their tongues.

'Not me,' they chorused, very Grinder-Sniperly.

'I suppose I'd better,' I said without enthusiasm. It was not that I had no sympathy for Mrs Green – my heart ached for her – but I knew that I had no hope to give her, and I did not especially want to have another chat with her mother.

I set out down Tenniel Road on to High Street East.

ALLIES PULL BACK, a poster informed us. Not in headlong retreat then? The speed the German troops were heading across France, even given the limited information we were receiving, did not sound like an orderly withdrawal. It sounded like a rout.

I was about to turn left when there were sounds of a commotion to the right towards the sea. I was too far back to see the actual water but the tops of the funnels of a battleship slipped across the horizon, heading south towards God only knew what perils. The fuss was on dry land, however; a large group of women were marching up the pavement and it sounded like they were having an argument, though not, I saw as we walked towards each other, with one another.

The women were surrounding someone who was struggling and behind them all came Dodo, holding a child's hand. I glimpsed the hair as the crowd parted and before it mixed together again and for a blissful moment I thought it was Wally; but then I saw that it was Sylvia and that Sylvia was crying.

There were about twenty women in that group and it looked like more were joining them. A couple of men tried to get involved.

'Hands off, he's ours.' An angry lady smacked them away and I recognised her as Miss Thrompingale, the Sunday school teacher.

Another woman was lashing at somebody with a furled umbrella.

I stopped and was relieved when they did too. Being trampled by a mob was not high on the list of experiences I craved.

'What is going on, Constable Chivers?' I demanded, since she was the one at least nominally in charge, and the crowd parted in a manner reminiscent of when Moses made a path through the Red Sea.

'This man—' Dodo pointed to the figure being dragged by two burly women I recognised from Twinkles the Florist's, their arms locked through his. '—was trying to abduct this little girl.'

'No,' Sylvia sobbed, 'he was going to be my daddy.'

A woman behind the man took a good fistful of his yellow hair and hauled it back to raise his head but I knew even before I saw that face that this was Simnal Cranditch.

83

THE MAN WITH CERULEAN EYES

P eople always expect criminals to look like their crimes. They think that murderers will have cold stares or that swindlers will have crafty eyes – whatever they might be – and that all criminals are ugly or even deformed. How easy my job would be if any of that were true. The trouble is, I had come across many a sinner who looked like a saint and some of the most disreputable-looking people I have met have led completely blameless lives.

Simnal Cranditch was one of the best arguments against those delusions that I have come across. Far from being a drooling hunchback, he was a well-built man and verging on handsome. He had a thick head of sandy hair and cerulean eyes. He had a strong square jaw with good teeth and might have had a nice smile in happier circumstances. He took care over his clothing, always clean and well-pressed, his shoes highly polished and a neatly knotted striped tie from some school or college he claimed to have attended.

'Mr Cranditch,' I acknowledged him. 'I've been wanting to talk to you.'

'Inspector Church.' He addressed me through a cracked and bloody upper lip. 'Are you arresting me and if so, on what charge?'

'Shut your gob,' snarled Henrietta, an ageing nippy from the Lyons tea shop, with a good stinging slap to Simnal Cranditch's cheek.

'Of course not,' I said, because with the wind in the right

direction I can detect a man who will demand a brief from thirty yards. 'I just want a chat – or would you prefer I left you with the ladies?'

Simnal Cranditch licked his upper lip gingerly.

'Okay, I'll come, but I want a doctor.'

'You'll need one in a minute,' vowed one of the Twinkles florists.

'You can let go of the gentleman now,' I said, 'and I'm sure he is very grateful for your assistance after his unfortunate accident.'

'What accident?' he demanded.

'The one you'll have if you don't behave.' An elderly lady whacked at him with her walking stick but caught the Sunday school teacher on the side of the head.

'You stupid old biddy! You nearly put my eye out.'

'Why don't you take Sylvia to the station? You can use my office,' I suggested to Dodo. 'Come along, Mr Cranditch. Let's get you inside.'

And keep you inside, I thought, *for as long as possible.*

I grabbed his sleeve with some distaste. The outer man was like any other but it was knowing what lurked inside that truly repelled me.

84

THE SHAME AND THE SLEEPWALKER

Brigsy and Sharkey were still behind the desk.

'Cranditch,' they said, more like the twins than ever, though it was not too difficult to tell them apart.

'Mr Cranditch had a nasty fall,' I told them, 'and these ladies kindly brought him here.'

I had had some difficulty in persuading the sewing circle to stay outside. They would get their chance to make statements later, I promised, but we did not have the manpower to record twenty or so excited accounts at present.

'Please go home and write everything down,' I had urged, with a mental note to make sure their efforts ended up on Sharkey's desk.

'I want my brief,' Cranditch muttered with a spray of blood.

'What?' Sharkey put a hand to his ear.

'He dint speak very clear, do he?' Brigsy commented.

'Mr Cranditch said he is tired and would like to rest in a cell and please could we lock it as he is a sleepwalker.'

'Somnambulist,' Brigsy told me as if I had asked him a crossword clue. I was astonished he even knew the word.

He came round the desk.

'I've tried hard to persuade him but he refuses to see a doctor,' I continued.

'I bloody—' Cranditch began.

'Yes, you are,' Brigsy agreed, 'and if only you would listen to Inspector Church, we could get you some help.' He took a hold of Cranditch's shirt and jacket collars from behind and twisted them. 'Better walk quickly, sir, while you still can.'

Our visitor choked and put both hands to his neck.

'Come along, sir.' Brigsy gave him a shove. 'Wouldn't want you to fall and smash your face on the floor, would we?'

'Chivers said he was trying to take that girl,' Sharkey breathed furiously. 'And you can bet your life he took the boy.' He clenched his fists. 'I know your views on my methods of questioning, but give me five minutes.'

'It's not how we do things,' I objected.

'If that child is still alive, he will be witless with fear,' Sharkey predicted huskily. 'God knows what that sick bastard has done to him.'

'Wait there.' I hurried to the cell just as Brigsy was about to lock it.

'Where's the boy?' I demanded and Simnal Cranditch leered up at me.

'How would I know?' he sneered and I spun around.

'Don't lock the door,' I told Brigsy. 'Mr Cranditch has a visitor.'

'My brief?' Cranditch brightened briefly.

'Someone who will advise you to cooperate,' I replied and marched down the corridor.

I am not proud of what I did – looking back, it was the most shameful episode of my career – but I did it to try to save a little boy. I don't know if the end justifies the means but I do know that if Wally Green had been the child I longed for, I would have done much worse.

'Well?' said Sharkey.

'Don't mark him,' I said, 'because he *will* get a lawyer and a doctor.' Sharkey's face fell. 'You wanted five minutes,' I continued. 'Well, you just take as long as you like, Inspector.'

I went to the men's room to wash, but mainly to stop myself

shaking. I had a mirror in my handbag but I didn't want to see the face I had at that moment. I might not recognise it or, even more frighteningly, I might.

85

THE RAT AND THE WHIPPET AND
THE ICE CREAM MAN

Dodo was down on her haunches and holding Sylvia's hands when I went into my office, but Sylvia was crying again and trying to pull away.

'Did the man hurt you or frighten you?' I asked.

'Of course not.' She pulled her very crossest face. 'He was a nice man and he goo take me for a nice walk.'

Sylvia stamped her foot.

'He is a horrid man,' Dodo told her.

'Dirty liar,' Sylvia cried. 'He was goo get me an ice cream, a double one.'

'Have you ever seen him before?' I asked, crouching too.

'Course I have,' Sylvia wept. 'He stand outside our house lots of times.'

'Do you know his name?' I asked.

'He said I could call him *Daddy*,' she sobbed and I closed my eyes.

Could Cranditch have known that Sylvia Satin had lost her family? It would have been in all the papers. And he would have calculated that she would be missing her father dreadfully and looking for somebody to fill at least a part of the gap. A bit of me hoped that Sharkey was doing a good job but a lot of me was feeling sick about it already.

'Has nobody told you not to talk to strangers?' I asked.

'Course they have.' Her big blue eyes glittered furiously. 'Aunty Josie is always bothering me about it. She even wented out and tell him to goo away or she do call a policeman.'

'And did he go away?'

'I should say so.' Her eyes opened even wider. 'He scarperded like a rat from a whippet.'

That sounded like an expression she had mislearned from an adult.

'So how did you meet him today?' Dodo asked.

'I am still cross with you.' Sylvia tossed her head. 'You should have arresteded those horrid ladies.' She turned her face up to me. 'He tell me the other night when he threwed stones at my windows – just likkle ones so as not to break the pane – that's what you call the glass. He said, *Come down to the prom – that means promdenade – and I'll buy you a big lolly.* So I did and there he was, only I prefers ice cream.'

Sylvia took a big breath.

'Did Aunty Josie not ask where you were going?' I asked.

'Oh, but she was asleeped.' Sylvia batted her eyelashes. 'She is very old and always sleepy.'

There was a tap on the door.

'Thought you might like this.' Brigsy put a tumbler on the desk.

'Lemdonade.' Sylvia clapped her hands. 'Oh, thank you, General. I have a small headache in my head and I am ever so thirsty in my mouth.'

She let go of Dodo and trotted to the desk. It was a big glass and she needed both hands to hold it. 'Oh, lovely.' Her pouting upper lip dipped birdlike into the surface and she sipped noisily, swilling the drink around her mouth. 'Rather warm and a bit flat' was her verdict.

86

ROUGH JUSTICE AND
THE RIGHT TO BEAR ARMS

B rigsy was back at his desk when I came out of my office.
'Do my best,' he told me in hurt tones. 'Had to go down to the Feathers for that.'

There was a whimper coming up the corridor from the cells.

'Had to have a quick half while you were there as well,' I remarked.

I could smell it on his breath.

'Couldn't just go in and ask for a lemonade,' he sniffed. 'Be a laughing stock.'

'It was a kind thought,' I assured him. 'What's happening in there?'

I heard a sharp cry of pain.

Brigsy rolled both eyes outwards – the first time I had seen that trick – and said, 'I do believe they have a disputation, madam. 'spector Sharkey do think Cranditch is double-jointed and Cranditch do think he int. 'spector Sharkey is very keen to prove his point.'

From the cries coming towards us, it sounded like Sharkey was trying very hard indeed.

The door swung open.

'Superintendent,' we said in unison, though not perfectly because Brigsy said *Superintendent*, and Vesty wandered in.

'Thought I'd pop round and see how things are going,' he told us. 'Good, good.'

'How are you feeling, sir?' I asked, but his head was cocked, listening to something else with a wisp of the wistful smile of a man who thinks he has heard a nightingale on a balmy summer's evening.

'What's going on in the cells?' He rubbed his brow, making the skin over his metal plate bunch up like an unmade bed.

'Would you like a nice cup of tea, sir?' Brigsy slapped a few papers about noisily but he could not mask the sharp cry of pain and the, 'I don't know, I swear it.'

'Don't you, by George,' Vesty said and he strode down the corridor.

I hurried after him.

'Now then.' Vesty flung open the door. 'What's going on here, Inspector?'

Sharkey – who had Cranditch pinned against the wall and was holding his hand in a way that might easily have been misinterpreted if it was not for the expression of agony on the prisoner's face – jumped back. 'Just questioning a suspect, sir.'

'Torturing me!' Cranditch cried, holding his left hand up limply.

'Torture, by jingo!' Vesty stormed.

I had never seen our superintendent so angry. He was usually such an urbane man he would hardly have tutted if you set fire to him.

'What's he accused of?'

'Kidnapping that little boy and caught in the act of kidnapping a little girl,' I explained guiltily.

'Wally Green?' Vesty enquired. I wasn't aware he had even known about the case. 'Organised a search for him on the golf course yesterday but no deuced good.' He tugged his right ear lobe. 'Found a few lost balls in the rough, though.'

'And he won't tell us where Wally is,' Sharkey said furiously. I don't think it had occurred to him that both our careers had probably just ended.

'Well, torture is no way to set about it,' Vesty tutted. 'Not the done thing at all.'

He slipped a hand into his jacket over his breast, like Napoleon posing for a portrait.

'No, sir.' For the first time ever, I found I could not look my superior in the eye.

'Shall I tell you how we interrogated the Hun in the war?' Vesty motioned for Cranditch to sit on the bunk and settled beside him.

Oh Lord, not another rambling anecdote, please, I prayed, and the Lord was clearly in no mood for one either.

'Quickly and painlessly,' Vesty said.

'You're a gentleman, sir,' Cranditch gasped gratefully.

'Indeed I am,' Vesty agreed, pulling his service revolver out of its holster. Cranditch jumped. 'Now, you blighter,' Vesty said sternly, 'open your mouth.'

Cranditch stared at the weapon in disbelief. 'What?'

'*Öffne deinen Mund,*' Vesty yelled and Cranditch gaped.

'You're mad.'

'Now.' Vesty rammed the barrel between our prisoner's lips. 'Where's the child, you Jerry schweinhund?'

Cranditch choked and tried to grab the gun but his fingers hurt too much and he gave a choking scream.

'Speak, you filthy cabbage-eater,' Vesty yelled.

'I don't think he can, sir,' I suggested and Vesty turned his head, eyes wild and forehead pulsating.

'What?'

'With that in his mouth,' I prompted.

334

'What? Ah, by George. Wondered why that Kapitan wouldn't tell us anything,' he reminisced. 'When he was such a snivelling coward.' Vesty pulled the barrel out, grabbed Cranditch's neck and pressed the muzzle to his temple. 'Where is the boy, Fritz?'

'I don't know,' Cranditch trembled, and I saw a dark stain on the front of his trousers.

'What do you think I should count from?' Vesty's finger blanched on the trigger.

'I think three is traditional, sir,' I suggested in fascinated horror.

'Last chance, you wurst-munching sewer rat. Where is he?' Vesty raged. 'On the count of three, I fire.'

'Oh God no, sir. I don't know. I swear it on my life.'

'Too right you do,' Sharkey assured him grimly.

'*Eins*,' Vesty began.

Sweat was pouring down Cranditch's face and his shirt was distinctly damp.

'*Zwei.*'

'Oh sweet Lord Jesus, I would tell you if I knew.'

Cranditch was almost as wet as Dodo had been in that sump.

'*Drei*,' Vesty said with icy calm and Cranditch toppled as limply, though less bloodstained, as if our superintendent had pulled that trigger.

'What do you think, Sharkey?'

'He's sh— soiled himself,' Sharkey observed. 'Any man would rather risk prison than get his head blown off.'

'Unless he has killed the child,' Vesty conjectured with a shudder, 'and knew he would face the hangman if he told us.' He slipped his revolver back into its holster. 'What's your opinion, Church?'

'I don't think he knows, sir. He didn't even have the sense to make something up to buy time.'

'Are you allowed to carry that, sir?' Sharkey asked.

He looked as dazed as I felt.

'Indeed.' Our superior jutted his noble chin. 'The Vestys were granted the right to bear arms in perpetuity by Good King John in eleven ninety-nine for protecting him against an assassination attempt by the third – or was it the second? – Baron – or was it the Earl? – of—'

'I think he's coming round, sir,' I said before we got the whole family tree, though I had never seen a fainted man in less of a hurry to recover.

'What'll we do with him, sir?' Sharkey prodded our crumpled suspect with his toe.

'What exactly has he done?' the super asked.

'Caught talking to a little girl and offering to buy her an ice cream,' I said weakly.

'Hardly criminal offences.' Vesty stretched his right earlobe. 'Better let the blighter go.'

Dodo took Sylvia back to her home where, I was told later, Josie Whitehouse had not even known her ward had gone out. I would have words with Josie, I vowed. Anything could have happened to Sylvia while the woman who was supposed to take care of her dozed in her armchair by the fire.

87

CUT GLASS AND CAPRICORN

When Chamberlain declared war on our behalf, Superintendent Vesty had fortified his office, at first with piles of books but later with sandbags, not because he was a coward but because he was determined to resist a German invasion to the bitter end.

Now, with our army in retreat and the threat of invasion never more real, he had decided to place his faith in the Royal Navy and cleared everything away. Not even a scrap of paper was visible on his enormous oak partners' desk.

The superintendent waved Sharkey and I into two chairs at a rather nice inlaid square coffee table and pulled out a filing cabinet drawer.

'Shall I bring you some tea, sir?' Brigsy had offered, but the super batted his sergeant and the idea away with the back of his hand and poured three very generous Irish whiskeys from a cut-glass decanter.

'Not for me, sir,' I declined, unheard.

Vesty joined us and put down the glasses in a row like he was going to do the pebble under a cup trick.

'Don't worry, Church, I'll drink it for you,' Sharkey offered, ever the martyr.

'Damned beastly business,' Vesty said, downing his without even a pretence of tasting it. 'What have you done so far?'

'Well, I organised a search party,' the Shark began.

'As part of mine,' I put in, childishly perhaps, but if this case had a successful outcome, I did not want our super issuing statements thanking Old Scrapie for taking charge of the operation.

I ran through what we had done while Vesty poured himself a larger shot but mulled on it more slowly this time.

'Seems to me,' our super meditated when I had finished, 'that if he is not where you have looked, he must be somewhere you have not looked.'

'Good point, sir.' Sharkey raised his glass in salute and I was only surprised that it did not slip out of his greasy grasp.

'So where haven't you looked?' Vesty fired the question at me and the Shark settled back to enjoy my response.

Most of the Far East and hardly any of North Africa, I wanted to answer, but I slid my glass away and said, 'I have made a map showing houses where we were unable to question the occupants and we have sent our volunteers to try again today. There are also some public buildings – churches, the town hall—'

'Tarka!' Vesty cried, slapping a hand to his forehead in a way that always alarmed me. What if the plate had corroded and broke or became dislodged?

The Otter? I wondered briefly if our superior was having another of his turns.

'I'm sorry, sir?' I queried.

'Sir Tarka Capricorn,' Vesty explained impatiently. 'Master of the hunt.'

'Excellent idea, sir,' old oily mouth grovelled. 'He must have dozens of servants who can help.'

'And hounds,' I realised. Why the hell had I not thought of that when we had that fool of a shepherd with his horrible terriers looking for Mr and Mrs Windser? 'That are trained to—'

'Follow scents,' Sharkey butted in, because, of course, he had realised all along.

'It's well worth a try,' I agreed, 'but we have the unsolved murder of Eric Bone, the disappearances of Mr and Mrs Windser and now little Wally Green.' I hesitated. 'Don't you think it's time we called for extra help?'

'No, Inspector Church, I do not—' Vesty chucked back his second drink and slumped slightly sideways.

'Quite right, sir.' The Shark reached out for my drink but I changed my mind and whisked it back, slopping some on the table. 'We don't want outsiders coming in stealing all our thunder.'

'If we had any thunder to steal, I might agree.' I rounded on him because I couldn't round on the superintendent.

'—I think it is long overdue.' Vesty finished his response and his drink. 'See to it, Sharkey, and you, Church, go home.'

'But—' For a moment I thought I was being suspended.

'Come back fresh in the morning,' the super said. 'No use to me if you're both out of action at the same time.'

'Very good, sir.' I knew it made sense but sometimes you need someone else to make sense for you.

We stood up and Sharkey hurried off importantly.

'Is that revolver actually loaded, sir?' I asked, eyeing the bulge in his jacket uneasily.

'Of course.' Vesty tapped over it affectionately. 'But what that disgusting specimen didn't notice was that I never cocked the hammer, though you would have spotted that immediately.'

'Indeed,' I said faintly. I knew you had to cock single-action revolvers but not double, but I didn't know how to tell the difference.

Adam had given me some lessons on a firing range, mainly in order to demonstrate what an excellent shot he was, and he had been most aggrieved when we found, to my surprise, that I wasn't too bad either. Dodo was surprisingly handy with a gun, as she had demonstrated when she clipped my ear from thirty foot.

I went back to *Cressida* and wondered how much longer I

could call her home. I had only met the captain because of my relationship with his son, Adam, and it felt increasingly like I was living there under false pretences.

88

MAP-READING AND REMORSE

Sharkey was still making phone calls the next morning, telling his rival at Anglethorpe how he had decided we needed more manpower.

'Of course, I am in overall charge,' he was telling them while staring directly at me, and I raised my eyes in despair.

Short of snatching the phone off him and yelling *No he isn't*, there wasn't much I could do to dispute his claim.

I went to my office and pored over the map. If Wally had been taken, he could, as Sharkey had pointed out, be anywhere in the country by now; but if he had just wandered off, where would he have gone? Assuming the sightings on the promenade were accurate – and there were enough of them, all stating he was alone and walking towards the north end – where would he be heading for?

Most children would have gone in the opposite direction, towards the pier. Even though it was closed, it still held a fascination for youngsters. The last sighting was past the end of the beach, near the miniature jetty where they set up a Punch and Judy show in the summer season. I rather hoped the war would put a stop to that so-called entertainment. That vile squeaky man beating up his baby never failed not to amuse me.

From here, the way swung to the left and up Steep Hill back into town or forked to the right up another incline towards Jacob's Point. Wally would be tiring by the time he reached there. His little legs would have come quite a way. If I was a child, I would be more tempted to take the little sandy track between, which sloped down towards the fishermen's cottages. I circled it on the map but my pencil snapped.

'Oh, for heaven's sake.' I snatched up my pen. It was my map and I could ruin it if I wanted to.

I went back through the lobby.

Sharkey was still on the phone. 'Just a second, Sergeant.' He covered the mouthpiece. 'Hang on, Church, and I'll give you your instructions.'

My what? I took a breath.

'Sorry, this is urgent,' I lied and scooted through the door.

If nothing else, I needed some fresh air. I felt nauseous. I had set my scruples and professional integrity aside and sunk to the level of Sharkey, a man I loathed and despised, in colluding with torture. And for what? We had had to let the suspect go when we might normally have detained him longer and were further away from finding Wally Green than ever.

I cycled over the forecourt – wishing for the umpteenth time that somebody, other than me, would weed it – and out on to Tenniel Road. This was normally quiet, but today a group of airmen slouched, hands in pockets, puffing on their pipes, which made them look very grown-up indeed. They straightened up as I cycled towards them.

'Keep those legs pumping, darling,' called one of them, a youth dressed as a flying officer, and he pointed to his groin with a crude gesture. 'Want to find out what this is for?'

'No,' I muttered. 'But I bet you've often wondered.'

I rode on, leaving him to be astonished that I had not accepted his kind offer.

An armoured car was hurtling past the end of the road.

'The Jerries are that way,' a youth shouted, pointing towards the coast with great hilarity.

Josie Whitehouse came rushing along. She had no coat or hat on and her apron was still tied around her neck and waist.

'Oh, In-insp-spector,' she panted, grabbing hold of a telegraph pole for support. 'Heh-hel—' She fought for breath, her whole torso heaving up and down.

'Try to be calm,' I told her, which sounds like the most useless advice you could give anyone in a crisis but, surprisingly, it usually works.

'Soh-sorry.' She tried hard to take my advice.

'Catch your breath and use short words,' I advised. 'Now – what has happened?' I asked slowly to focus her attention and give her a chance to recover from her run.

'I need heh-help,' she managed.

'Is Sylvia all right?' I asked.

'No,' she gasped. 'Sylvia… Sylvia… is missing.' Her words came out in a rush now. 'I int see her since last night.'

dismounted from my bike, aghast.

'But she's a little girl,' I said in disbelief. 'Why have you waited until now?'

'I dint know 'til now,' she told me. 'Her bed int been slept in.'

'But surely you put her to bed normally?' I looked into Josie Whitehouse's eyes but they shifted uneasily away.

'I get so tired,' she told me. 'That Dr Hedges he goo give me too many strong pills and I do have a sherry or two – just for my nerves – of an evening.' She bridled against my unspoken disapproval. 'Well, I do have to have something.'

There was no point in remarking that Sylvia, who had suffered far greater traumas, had to get by without the benefit of drugs or alcohol.

'When did you last see her?' I asked.

'It must've bin 'round six on the clock.'

I glanced at my watch. 'That was fourteen hours ago.'

Josie nodded miserably.

'I mean to come in before anyways,' she said hesitantly.

'Why?' I watched her closely.

'Tha' man—' she told me.

'Which man?' I hardly needed to ask.

'The one you let goo.'

'Simnal Cranditch?'

She nodded. 'He goo past last night and wave to the upstairs window. I was gooin' to come this marnin' anyway.'

I could hardly look at her, this woman who had been entrusted with something so precious, something I yearned for, and treated it so carelessly.

I made a snap decision and it wasn't the right one. I suspected that then and I knew it later, but my judgement was bad at the time. The trouble was I cared, and desperately. They were children and it was up to me to protect them.

'Go into the police station,' I ordered Josie Whitehouse, 'and tell Inspector Sharkey and Sergeant Briggs what you have told me. Tell them I said to raise a full alert.'

Mrs Whitehouse hesitated.

'Int you comin' too?' she asked uncertainly.

'I want to check something first,' I told her. 'But I'll be back in about half an hour. Hurry, woman.'

I got back on my bike.

For the first time in years I panicked. *Oh please not little Sylvia too. Hasn't she been through enough? In the name of God, when does this stop?*

And something in my head replied, *You have to make it stop, Betty Church, or it never will.*

AL JOLSON AND THE THREAT OF INVASION

I went to the end of Tenniel Road, turned right down High Road East and looked up. Three ships were heading south towards Felixstowe. The one at the front had two tugs towing it and looked like a chunk had been blown out of the stern, but it was still floating high in the water. I put my head down and pedalled for all I was worth.

I don't think I had ridden so fast since Georgie and I fled two boys from St Joseph's School and tried to pretend we weren't disappointed that they didn't catch up. I hardly glanced at the traffic as I whizzed left along the prom. Luckily it was fairly quiet, though I saw another armoured car coming towards me. The soldier sticking his head out of the top was in camouflage with his face blacked-up like a bad Al Jolson impersonator.

Two jeeps came by as well. Was this the start of the much-prophesied invasion? I didn't have time to worry about that.

At the end of the prom I dismounted and raced, pushing my bike a little way down the sandy track, leaving it behind a large gorse bush. My left arm was coming slightly adrift and rubbing. I was tempted to take it off and leave it there as well but it would take too long. Also, there are people who will steal anything, if only for the scrap value, and it had been hard enough to get a false arm that was anything approaching comfortable.

I rushed down the track. The cottages at the bottom were really just sheds where sea fishermen could store their equipment, but they had been painted a couple of years ago in different pastel colours and I could imagine any child might be attracted to them.

A young man was scraping the underside of an upturned rowing boat with a metal spatula. The double doors of his shed were open and I could see right into it. He paused and eyed me warily. There were tea chests and packing crates stacked high inside, no doubt something smuggled and valuable enough for him to risk putting out to sea and returning through that minefield, but I had other things to worry about.

'Good afternoon,' I greeted him, trying to control my breathing as I had urged Josie Whitehouse to do. 'I'm looking for a child, a little blonde—'

'Up that way.' He pointed hastily to where the track wound up again.

'When?'

The fisherman was trying to close the right-hand door casually behind him but was failing dismally with the casual part.

''bout five minute ago.'

'Are you sure?' I wondered if he was just saying it to get rid of me.

'Positive.' He stepped in front of the opening but I had seen all I needed to – a label saying 'Teachers', and I was willing to bet it was not educational equipment. 'I just saw her going over the ridge.'

'Her?' I double-checked.

'That's right,' he said, 'with her dad, I suppose he is. Pretty little thing. Remind me of what's-her-name...'

'Shirley Temple,' we said together.

'I don't suppose you've seen a little boy recently, five years old, also got blond hair?'

'No I int.' He slid the bolt across without looking at it because

347

some people have a theory that if they don't look at something, you won't either. It doesn't work. 'How many bleedin' kids you lost?'

'Just the two,' I told him, but didn't bother mentioning the missing Windsers or the murdered Eric Bone or the possibly murdered Reverend Heath. I would save my breath for the ascent.

trotted up the dune. The sand was too soft to run full pelt and my feet slid down almost as fast as I stepped up – that flying officer would have been most gratified to see how my legs were pumping now – but I managed to scramble to the top without taking a single spill.

Down to my right was a boardwalk where the fishermen would once have dragged their craft into the sea, but now it was wired over. I didn't have time to wonder how the young fisherman/smuggler managed. To my left and above me was that damned House of Horrors and beyond that I saw her, Sylvia Satin, holding a man's hand, and he seemed to be dragging her up towards the cliffs.

I cupped my hands as best I could because the false one had been knocked sideways and the fingers didn't want to curl over.

'Let her go,' I yelled as loudly as I could. 'This is the police.'

For a moment I thought Sylvia had heard me because she shaded her eyes with her free hand, but the man was still pulling her up. I caught his profile.

'Oh shit!' There was no mistaking that strong-jawed profile belonged to Simnal Cranditch. 'Stop!' I almost screamed. 'Police! You there, Cranditch, *stop*!'

But they had disappeared over into a natural dip before the final ascent.

I turned around.

'We need help,' I shouted back down, but the fisherman had

locked his shed and I thought I glimpsed a shadow as he scarpered through the pines.

I rushed up the hill but you get out of practice with hills in Suffolk. Apart from Jacob's Point and Treacle Hill, there wasn't much to break the flat bleakness for as far as the eye could see.

Every thirty or forty yards I paused to get a bit of oxygen back inside me before I pressed on up.

Near the top I thought I heard a shout, a man's voice I would have said, certainly not Sylvia's.

'Sylvia!' I shouted. 'I'm coming.'

If you hurt her, you bastard… But I couldn't even imagine what I would do.

I took as deep a breath as I could and forced myself on to the edge of the dip. There was no sign of them there. Could they really have crossed it and gone up the other side so quickly? And if so, to where? Only Lot's Wife, Gabriel's Table and the sheer drop of the cliffs lay ahead. They could not have disappeared.

The ravine was to the left. Perhaps he had dragged Sylvia into that. I yelled her name again but heard nothing and was about to run on up the final stretch to Jacob's Point when I heard a sobbing. I swerved towards the ravine and looked over the edge.

Little Sylvia peered up. She had blood on her dress.

'Oh, nice police lady Church,' she cried. 'I know you goo come. Help me, please.'

92

LIFE AND DEATH IN THE RAVINE

S ylvia was kneeling on a smooth boulder ten or fifteen feet down the ravine and a few feet below her, right at the bottom and face down, was Simnal Cranditch.

'I think he's deaded or worse,' she told me, her little face drained with fear.

'It's all right, Sylvia,' I said. 'Step away from him, darling.' I was afraid he might be faking unconsciousness and waiting for a chance to attack me and leave her undefended.

The side was steeper than I thought but I managed to grab hold of a bush and step cautiously down.

'Are you hurt?'

Sylvia patted her dress. 'I don't think so. Thank you very much for asking.'

I let go of the branch and half-clambered, half-slithered to the bottom, accidentally stepping on Cranditch's legs as I came to a halt, but if he minded, he wasn't going to admit it. I knelt partly on and partly beside him and pushed my fingers into his neck. Not only was there no pulse but his head lolled so loosely and at such an odd angle that it was obvious his neck had been snapped by the fall.

'He's dead,' I told her, 'but he was a very bad man.'

'No,' Sylvia said. 'He was a lovely man and he was going to take me to the church.'

'The monastery?' I queried and Sylvia nodded.

'He said that sweet little boy was there and wanted somebody nice to play with and that—' Sylvia stuck her chin out proudly. '—is me.'

93

THE STONES OF ST ALVERY'S

Hope and fear flooded my mind at those words. He may have been lying about Wally being there and he may have been lying about Wally being alive but this was a chance and, with nothing else to go on, I snatched at it.

It should have been easier getting up than it had been getting down – I could see the footholds and stretch up to a shrub and then the tree hanging over the edge – but I had Sylvia to worry about now.

'Can you climb on my back?' I asked. 'I won't be able to hold you, though.'

'But you have your arm back.' Sylvia prodded it with inquisitive fingers.

'It's not real, though,' I told her and crouched. 'Hop on.' Sylvia put her arms around my neck and snuggled up. 'Hold on tight,' I warned and stood slowly.

'But not so tight as to stringle you,' she said and I laughed.

'No, not that tight.'

Sylvia was heavier than I had expected but it was not too much of a battle to get out of the ravine and kneel on the grass to let her down.

'Are you all right?' I asked, looking at her. The blood on her dress must have come from Simnal Cranditch.

'Oh yes, thank you,' Sylvia smiled, though still a bit tearfully. 'Though I do feel a bit shakened up.'

'We'll get a nice doctor to have a look at you when we get

back,' I promised and Sylvia took my hand, even managing a couple of weary skips.

She had some long, scabbed scars on the backs of her wrists, I noticed.

'How did you get scratched?' I asked.

'A pussycat,' she told me.

'A horrid pussycat with big claws,' I sympathised, but the scars looked too wide for a domestic cat to me.

Had somebody hurt Sylvia? I would find out later.

'Wally will be very glad to see us,' she chatted.

'I hope so,' I said and we walked on, the cliff five yards to our right.

Anglethorpe was spread out across the bay below, guarded by their Martello tower, and I was pleased to see their pier had also been cut in two, though a great deal more tidily than ours. Half a mile inland, the estuary bent south. High above the bend rose Fury Hill, crowned by Treacle Woods, and below, hidden by that promontory, *Cressida* sat on Brindle Bar, tucked into Shingle Cove.

The sea heaved far below, slopping sulkily against the soft east coast and chilling the wind that bustled up over it. We pushed on a few more yards and there, straight ahead of us in the depression known as Jacob's Bowl, stood the black flint walls of St Alvery's Monastery – the chapel still intact, the low monks' refectory and dormitory buildings roofless now from a century of storms and a quarter of a century of neglect. A local farmer, it was said, had taken the great oak beams to construct a barn.

'I don't know how we can get in,' I said.

A forest of razor wire rolled in massive bales from the cliffs to our right, across the old stone track in front of us, to a ten-foot-high flint wall on our left. Sooty Sweep and his team of sappers would have been hard-pressed to force a way through it.

'The man said there is a gate behind some bushes,' Sylvia told me. 'Do you think Wally will be all right?'

'I hope so,' I said again but no less fervently.

There was a natural hedge of high gorse but it was easy enough to push my way through if I ignored the scratches and Sylvia was small enough to crawl under the spines until we reached the wall and made our way along it. Were it not for the wire coiled along the top in lethal blades I could have scaled that wall with ease before my mishap, but now I was glad to see that, just as Sylvia had forecast, there was a gate. Built of wide wooden boards, it guarded an archway. There was no lock on the outside and when I tried it, the gate swung inwards with a creak but not very much effort at all.

To our right was the graveyard – perhaps two dozen stones, none recent and some so close to the edge I couldn't help but wonder if any of the monks' coffins had slid away with the landslides, reburying their occupants a second time at sea.

The chapel stood side-on twenty foot before us, oddly proportioned, I felt, the roof low for its length and the high narrow windows starting just above ground level. It had no tower or spire and the simple stone arch on the roof where the bell would have hung was empty. There would be good scrap value in a church bell, I imagined. A brick had fallen out of the arch, I noted, and I wondered how long it would be before the structure collapsed through the roof.

The door was on our left, partly to be on the most sheltered side and partly so that worshippers faced east, towards Jerusalem.

'Now, Sylvia,' I said firmly, 'if you just wait here for a minute, I'll go and check that it's safe.'

'Oh, please don't leave me,' she begged, grasping my jacket.

'I'll only be a minute, darling.'

Sylvia smiled tearfully. 'I like it when you call me that. You'll be a perfect mummy.'

I swallowed hard. 'I can never be that, Sylvia.'

'Of course you can,' she laughed at my silliness. 'Oh!' She twisted her head. 'Is that you, Billy? I'm coming, dear.'

Billy it? That was her brother's name. A slip of tongue, I assumed. I hadn't heard anything but Sylvia slipped her hand from mine and, ignoring my calls, trotted to the back of the church.

94

THE IRON RINGS AND THE DARK CURTAIN

hurried after Sylvia and would easily have caught her if I hadn't slipped on a mossy slab stone.

'Sylvia, wait,' I yelled uselessly.

I managed to stay on my feet but it cost me a vital couple of seconds and she was out of reach now, standing on a stone platform raised about eighteen inches from the ground. One of the great studded oak doors at the back of this platform had a more human-sized door cut into it. It had a ring handle and Sylvia grasped it in both hands, twisting hard. The little door opened inwards and Sylvia disappeared after it with me in close pursuit.

It was gloomy inside as the windows were bricked up, and I couldn't see her at first. I nearly fell but Sylvia called out *Mind the steps, Mummy* and I glimpsed her far below and saw that there was a flight of steps heading steeply down. I hadn't thought to bring a torch – why would I, in daylight? I followed cautiously but the treads were dry and I realised that was why the front door was well above ground level – to stop flooding.

We were in a sort of underground porch now and Sylvia was pulling at a wooden beam. It had been wedged to stop the door opening outwards. There was a rectangular viewing hole in the door, about eight by four inches, but it was closed from the inside.

'It's ever so heavy,' she puffed.

'Let me.' I pulled the beam away. It was actually quite light but then she was actually quite little.

'There we are,' I said and Sylvia danced about excitedly. 'Now you must wait outside until I call you.'

'Ohhhhh.' Sylvia sucked her thumb.

'I must make sure it's safe.'

'Just on the stairs then…' – She negotiated more skilfully on her behalf than Mr Chamberlain had ever done on ours – '…so you can see me.'

She trotted up and sat on the bottom step, her elbows on her knees and her face in her cupped hands.

I grasped the ring handle and turned. The latch inside lifted easily. Somebody must have oiled it. I pulled the door open and the stink hit me immediately.

'Is Wally there?' Sylvia called down from behind me. 'Hello, Wally, I'm Slyvia and I've come to play.'

The light was a little better and I could see inside quite clearly.

Wally certainly was there. He lay on a pew on his back, his blond hair glinting in the light from the high windows and his sunken eyes closed. But he was not alone. An old man sat upright two pews in front of him and, lying on the floor, in a nearby aisle, looking up at the ceiling, was an elderly woman.

Not one of them got up or even glanced over for, as far as I could see, they were all dead, and I was about to warn Sylvia not to come in when a shadow crossed the floor and joined the new darkness that flooded the room. I turned just in time to see the door slam and hear the beam bang against it and I knew it was pointless but I twisted the handle and rammed the woodwork, hurting my shoulder but not affecting the door one little bit.

'Run, Sylvia, run!' I screamed.

'But why would I want to do that, Mummy?' came the muffled but happy reply.

95

WAKING THE DEAD

hammered on the door. There didn't seem much else I could do but then I remembered the viewing panel, slid the catch back and hinged the little door open.

'Sylvia,' I called through it, 'is there anybody else there?'

'No, Mummy, just us.'

'Good, then you can let me out now.'

'I would so like to,' Sylvia said slowly and I glimpsed the top of her head. 'But you would certainly run away.'

'I could take you home,' I suggested.

'But my home was blown up,' Sylvia reminded me.

'To Aunty Josie,' I said and Sylvia giggled. It might have been a contagious laugh in other circumstances.

'Aunty Josie is horrid and smelly and she's not really my aunty and she was late for my party.'

'She'll be worried about you,' I said as Sylvia jumped backwards side to side, like she was playing hopscotch. At least I could see her now.

'She doesn't even know I'm out,' Sylvia assured me. 'She's always asleep.'

'That's because she can't sleep at night because she is so worried about you,' I told Sylvia and she blew an invisible smoke ring.

'Aunty Josie can't sleep at night because I don't put her medicine in her cocoa,' she confessed, 'but she sleeps in the day because I put it in her elevenses tea.'

'But why?' I asked, though I feared I knew the answer.

'So I don't get stopped from going out.' Sylvia nibbled the end of her hair.

'Don't do that,' I said automatically.

'Sorry, Mummy,' she said, and she pulled the soggy tress out of her mouth.

'You do know I am not really your mummy, don't you?' I checked, and Sylvia wrinkled her nose in a very Dodoish way.

'Well, not yet,' she conceded. 'But you are very pretty like my mummy and kind and you have blonde hair out of a bottle like hers.' I opened my mouth to protest about the last bit but Sylvia chattered on, 'And you call me *Darling* and you have two arms now and you told me people can change so you could just change a big bit and be her.'

I trod on something and heard it snap – a meerschaum pipe *carved with the face of a woman*, Mrs Bone had said. *Eric used to joke that she looked like Betty Grable.*

Not the only one to look like a film star, I reflected wryly.

'Did you bring all these people here?' I asked and Sylvia nodded energetically, as if I had asked if she had been a good girl and made her own bed.

'And more,' she said.

'Mr Bone?' I asked gently.

'Was he the funny man with the wonky nose?'

He looks a bit like Sylvia Satin's daddy, I remembered Dodo saying, *only much older and yuckier and with a bent nose.*

'Yes, well, he was very naughty.' Sylvia wagged a finger sternly. 'I told him to go in but he wouldn't and he ran back up and said he needed air and sat on a rock and kept making stupid noises.'

'He was frightened of being trapped,' I told her.

'Well, he should have told me that before I trapped him.' Sylvia threw out her hands.

'How did you get him to the church?' I wondered.

'He was walking on the path and I ran up and tugged his coat and said...' – Sylvia put on the little girl's voice I realised now she had abandoned – '...*Come quick, very old man. My likkle sister is hurted*. And he followed me and went in a bit of the way but then he went all funny and said...' – She put on a big deep voice that wasn't very big or deep at all, really – '...*I'm sorry. I want to help but I need to breathe.*' Imitation over, Sylvia returned to her older girl's voice. 'And he ran out and sat on the big flat rock doing lots of breathing.' She mimicked his panting.

'So what did you do?' I asked her.

'Well.' Sylvia put her hands together. 'I told him *Stop that noise and come back in* because that's what Daddy used to say when I played too noisily in the garden. But he kept doing it and so I went to the big pile of stones and hid and said *Come and find me* but he just kept on being silly. He was nearly as bad as the next man and I had ever such a bad headache so I got a nice big round stone and I crept up behind and *bashed* him on his head to make him be quiet.' Sylvia nodded, as if encouraging me to give my approval.

'Then what happened?'

'Well, he jumped up and held his head and dappled like Granny when she has been to the Feathers and I said, *Look out you big ox* but he kept going and so he felled over the cliff.'

I hadn't heard *dappled* for a while but I knew it mean *staggered* and Sylvia's use of the word only emphasised how much she had abandoned her Suffolk accent.

'What did you do with the stone?' I questioned her.

'There's a hollow in the ground full of pebbles like a giant bird's nest,' Sylvia recalled. 'And the stone looked like a big egg so I put it in.'

'Do you know what happened to him after that?' I asked.

'Well, he must have swum away because Aunty Josie said you and that silly Dodo girl found him asleep on the beach.'

'Mr Bone was dead, Sylvia,' I told her and she smiled.

'Nobody really dies,' she assured me. 'The vicar told us that and it says on one of the gravestones *Not Dead But Sleeping*. I can read, you know. I'm not stupid.'

Unfortunately, I thought sadly, *you are not.*

Sylvia put her fingertips together.

'So what did you do next?' I asked, but before she could answer I let out a yelp.

Just like a dream I used to have when I was a child, something horrible and clammy had grabbed hold of my hand.

jumped sideways and twisted round. It was Wally Green – risen from the dead, it seemed – tugging on my hand and looking up at me. He put a straight index finger to his cracked lips and I slammed the hatch shut.

'Wally!' I whispered. 'Are you all right?'

I've asked some good questions in my time and some stupid, and that one fitted comfortably into the latter category. Wally looked awful. His eyes were hollowed and rimmed black and his face was grey. He tugged on my sleeve.

'You goo be quiet,' he whispered. 'She come back, she do. First time I run up and she do get very cross and slap my face and shout *Why aren't you asleep yet?* So I do pretend to be asleepin' next time.'

'I was talking to you.' Sylvia's voice came faint but angry through the door.

'Just a minute, darling,' I called and lowered my voice. 'Are any of the others still alive?'

Wally shook his head, his blond hair dark with dirt and cobwebs. 'The lady move the next time Slyvia come and Slyvia push a coat over her face. She come awake proper and start moanin' and tryin' to push her off but she's too sick to do much. The lady move her feet like she do be runnin' but she dint get nowhere. She make squeaky noises and then she stop runnin' and goo all quiet and floppy.'

Oh dear God!

'And Slyvia say *That's better*,' Wally continued in an odd monotone, 'and come and have another look at me. I hold my breath and she open my eye but I keep it rolled up and she lift my arm and I make it goo floppy.'

'That was clever of you.'

'Do you goo tell Mummy that?' Wally beamed. 'She say I'm a loggerhead.'

'Open the hatch,' Sylvia demanded.

'You had best,' Wally counselled.

'Why, what can she do?' I wondered, and Wally trembled.

'She can goo leave us here.' He burst into tears, choking back the noise with his mouth buried in the crook of his sleeve. 'I dint want goo die,' came out muffled.

'What's going on?' Sylvia banged on the door.

Wally nodded and shuffled off to the side as far as he could go, his sobbing almost under control by the time I opened the hatch.

'This has gone on long enough, Sylvia,' I said firmly. 'You have to let me out now.'

Sylvia rolled her big blue eyes and humphed.

'That's what they all say.' She shook her golden locks, the light from behind making them glow like a halo. 'But I'm Slyvia and I don't have to do anything I don't want.'

Sylvia pirouetted, put her nose up in the air and walked with great dignity back up the steps.

'Come back, darling,' I called, but she had what Suffolk folk call *a petty on* and was in no hurry to take it off again.

'Shan't.' She kicked the top step and trotted outside.

'Don't close the door,' I shouted – uselessly, I knew, but I had to shout something.

'Shall,' she yelled back and slammed it shut.

*

Wally came back and took hold of my hand again. His skinny legs looked like they were about to give way under him.

'Come and sit on my lap.' I perched on the end of a back pew and he clambered on to my knee.

'Are you a real policeman?' he asked. 'And have you come to rescue me?'

'Yes, I am,' I confirmed. This didn't seem the time or the person to debate genders with. 'And we've been looking for you.'

'You should of looked here first,' he advised mildly and closed his eyes.

Perhaps I should have tried to make him keep them open, but that would have seemed cruel and what would have been the point? It wasn't like reinforcements were on the way. The only people who had an inkling of our whereabouts were Sylvia and a man with a shed full of contraband, and I didn't think either of them was going to summon a constable in a hurry.

97

RODENTS AND THE ELEVEN APOSTLES

looked about. Were it not for the circumstances and, Wally excepted, the rest of the congregation, this might have been a pleasant chapel.

The lower half was underground and lined with granite blocks and the upper was traditional Suffolk flint, which explained the odd proportions from the outside – possibly, I conjectured, because there might have been an old fort there before Anglethorpe built a better one and the Angel Gabriel wisely counselled St Alvery to use the existing foundations.

The windows went most of the way up the above-ground section and the small glass leaded sections were very largely intact, with only a few panes cracked or missing.

The altar was marble – a table on a solid rectangular plinth, with carved pillars bearing the faces of what I assumed were apostles, there being five to one side and six to the other, Judas having been erased from the records.

There was a slab of differently grained stone about two-foot square set in the centre. It had been smashed diagonally and the edges chipped away so much I could get my fingers into the gaps and lift. Beneath the slab was a cavity and for a glorious moment I thought it might lead down and out of there but it was only about nine inches deep and empty. I remembered that many old altars had relics inserted into them – the bone of a saint being an especial favourite. This would have been removed, I realised, when the church was decommissioned, but I was surprised it had been done so destructively.

Above the altar dangled a chain where the crucifix would have hung but that had been removed, presumably also when the church was abandoned.

Behind the altar were niches in the walls with statues of other worthies – Jesus, Mary and Joseph being prominent. There was a long central aisle and side aisles ending in little side chapels. The fact that there were only eight rows of pews, when there was room for at least twice as many, indicated that there had never been much of an attendance.

Wally was fast asleep. I laid him on a pew. It had a solid back and I hoped he wouldn't roll off. There were no kneelers so either the monks brought cushions or knelt on the cold stone floor to mortify their flesh. The pews were bolted down and there was an oilcan on its side under one of them. That at least solved the theft from Simpson's Bicycles, though it wasn't a crime that had weighed heavily on my mind.

It was chilly in the chapel, which explained why the bodies were not in a worse state than they might have been. At first sight, Mr Windser didn't look too bad. Still easily recognisable with his combed-over hair and toothbrush moustache, he was sitting upright at the central end of a pew near the front, in a tweed jacket, head back a little like he was engrossed in a sermon from the ornate wooden pulpit. But his eyeballs were concave and opaque white and his skin had blistered and ulcerated and was oozing slimily. He smelled decidedly unpleasant and I thought about moving him out of view but I was not sure that he would not start to come apart if I tried to drag him, which would have been even more horrible for little Wally.

Mrs Windser had a nice blue dress on – not quite summery, but it was not quite summer. Her grey perm looked more like a

Brillo pad than hair now. She lay on her back, her hands clawed like she was still trying to pull little Sylvia's hands away, which was a more likely cause than a cat of the scratches on Sylvia's wrists. Her eyes were closed, which, knowing how she died, puzzled me. I would have expected them to be bulging and staring. I was crouching for a closer look when Mrs Windser moved. Her stomach rose like she was taking a breath and sank down again. This was not possible. Nobody could spontaneously recover from such advanced changes of death. And yet her stomach rose again. It joggled up then side to side, reminding me of a sack of kittens I had seen left on the promenade once. The space between two buttons opened and a furry nose poked out, but this was no kitten. A button flew off and a rat scrambled through the rip. The rat saw me and bared its teeth, long, yellow and sharp. I jumped back and so did the rat, turning a scaly tail to burrow back into Mrs Windser's abdomen. As far as I was concerned, it could stay there. I didn't like the idea of it eating the unfortunate woman but I liked the idea of delving into a corpse's stomach even less and I had no idea how many other rats were lurking inside her. I shuddered. Given a choice, I would rather face a rabid dog than a filthy, vicious, sewage-eating rodent.

I moved on, walking as quietly as I could in my regulation boots, partly so as not to wake Wally and partly because it seemed disrespectful to clatter about.

There was another elderly man, in dark blue trousers with light stripes, but I did not recognise him – probably a visitor to the area, I conjectured, as he had not been reported missing. He was quite plump with very sparse white hair, wispy as a dandelion clock, and he was curled on a pew like a tramp in the park, his mouth open and his tongue projecting black and swollen, like a toad I ran over on my bicycle once. As far as I could see, the rats had not got to him but I had no intention of looking too closely.

The chapel, I estimated by pacing around it, was about sixty foot long and thirty wide. There was a door near the south-east corner, which probably led into a sacristy, but it was solid oak and locked. I worked my way up and down the floor. It seemed unlikely that there would be a crypt in a half-buried building, especially as I had seen the graveyard, but you never knew. An abbot might merit an under-church tomb and that might have an exit of some sort. But the mottled stone slabs seemed solid and there were no rings inserted to lift them.

The windows might have been the best bet but they were barred and even if they weren't, I doubt I could have squeezed through the narrow slits. Where was Sidney Grice when I needed him? He had invented a walking cane with a built-in blowtorch, which he was very proud of until it went off spontaneously on official business and set fire to 12 Downing Street in 1879, an incident officially blamed on an unswept chimney.

I went back to Wally. He was still asleep but breathing quite regularly. His cheek, when I touched it, felt cool but not chilled.

A small mongrel lay on its side, its mouth agape too, and looking like it was resting after a long hot walk, except that those projecting ribs were completely static. This must have been Adolf Hitler, the *sort of mixed-up spaniel* the man had asked me to search for.

A shadow crossed Wally and I looked behind to see a small figure going past a window and then the next, towards the west end of the church. Wally did not stir when I gave him a gentle shake to warn him and I prayed he had not sunk into something deeper than sleep.

I hurried to the door, slid back the catch and opened the panel just in time to see the inset door at the top of the steps opening and Sylvia coming back down, jumping from one step to the next with both feet at once.

'Be careful, darling,' I called out, concerned not just for her safety but for ours. If anything happened to Sylvia, how on earth would we ever get out?

'It's all right, Mummy,' she trilled. 'I hardly ever fall over.'

She stumbled and I held my breath, but she giggled and kept on running to the bottom.

'That man is still sleeping in the ditch,' she told me chattily.

'Sylvia...' – I took a breath – '...there is a difference between being asleep and being dead. When you are dead, you don't wake up again in this world.'

Sylvia thought about that. 'Yes, you do,' she decided.

'How did he fall in?' I asked.

'I shoved him,' Sylvia said, bunching her skinny arms up to show her stringy muscles. 'I'm a lot stronger than I look.' She knotted her brow. 'But then he grabbed my dress and I fell in with him.' She screwed her mouth up angrily. 'He could have ripped it.'

'But why did you push him?'

'Because he said he would tell you we were coming here,' she said simply, 'and then the police would come and take everyone away and I would have to start aaall over again.'

Sylvia flopped her arms in exasperation at the very thought.

'You said Mr Bone was nearly as bad as the next man,' I remembered. 'Was that the old man in the striped trousers?'

'He was very troublesome.' Sylvia wagged a finger like it was my fault. 'He kept running about and making noises like Rusty when Mrs Edwards up the road played her violin.'

'Howling?' I asked, and Sylvia threw her head back and imitated the cry.

She sounded more like a cockerel than a dog but I got the message. When Box had thought he heard a wolf and I had thought it was Garrison Orchard, the man in the striped trousers must have been trapped a few hundred yards away, terror-stricken and wailing for the help I should have given him.

'Oh, sweet Jesus,' I whispered.

If I had had the sense I was born with, I would have investigated that cry and saved the man and everybody after him who had died or was about to die because of my stupidity.

98

THE HAYSTACK MAN AND
THE DAMNED GOOD SPY

steadied my thoughts. There would be plenty of time for self-recrimination afterwards – if there was an afterwards.

'How old are you, Sylvia?' I asked.

'How old do you think I am?' she challenged.

'Well, I would have said about five when you came to the police station looking for your button,' I began, and Sylvia giggled.

'Everybody thinks that because I'm so little for my age.' She frowned momentarily. 'But I am nine now.'

I avoided the subject of what had happened on her birthday.

'But you spoke in such a young way,' I pointed out.

Sylvia tossed her golden curls.

'Grown-ups are kinder if they think you're still a baby,' she explained, 'and they trust you more.'

'And you've lost your accent.'

Sylvia smiled beautifully.

'Daddy wants me to be a star.' She simpered and *Shirley Temple* flashed through my mind. 'So he paid for me to have elocution and acting lessons.' Sylvia performed an elegant curtsy before reverting to her native tongue. 'But Bath Street boys goo think you do be a turn-up-nose if you dint goo talk Suffolk.'

A *boy* in Sackwater could be anything from one to a hundred and was not necessarily a male.

'You learned your lessons well,' I complimented Sylvia.

She smirked and spun a complete revolution on her toes.

'I think I shall go and play now,' she announced.

'So have you gathered everybody here yet?' I asked as she half turned, and Sylvia stuck her hands on her hips.

'Think about it,' she challenged in a way an adult must have instructed her once. 'I still haven't got a daddy.'

'I know your real daddy died in the bomb,' I said, watching her closely. 'Was the next one going to be Mr Bone, the man with the wonky nose who... fell over the cliff?' I suggested as tactfully as I could, and Sylvia dipped her head slowly. 'And then the man in the striped trousers who howled,' I continued. 'What was his name?'

'I don't think he had one.'

Sylvia puggled about in her ear with her little finger and inspected the tip.

'So the one after that was Simnal Cranditch,' I guessed, hoping there weren't any others I didn't know about, 'the man in the gully?'

'Yes.'

Sylvia was not having much luck with her replacement father, I reflected gloomily. He had already died three times.

'How did you find out about this place, Sylvia?' I asked.

'Daddy brought me,' she remembered happily. 'The filthy Hun hurt his leg in the war and he couldn't climb so he lifted me on to the wall and put me down on a rope to open the gate. It was stuck hard but I bashed it with a hammer he threw over. He said he would bring oil next time.'

'But why did he come here?'

'Uncle Danny told him there was treasure inside the altar.'

That would explain why the slab was smashed. A monk would have taken much greater care, especially as he probably hoped to return.

'And was there?'

'No,' she sniffed. 'Daddy said we would come back with more tools – but we didn't,' she concluded sadly, then immediately perked up with, 'but I did.'

'So you brought the oilcan?' I checked.

'I borrowed it from the bicycle shop,' she declared proudly.

'Were you never frightened of any of these men?' I wondered, and Sylvia giggled.

'But why should I be scared? They are all my daddies or my Uncle Danny.' She screwed her nose anticlockwise. 'Except a nasty man with a cut lip,' she remembered. 'He tried to make me go down an alley with him and when I wouldn't he started to drag me but a nice man with a haystack head came and boxed him on the ear and said *You goo leaf her alohan*. He followed me a few times after that to be sure the man didn't try again.'

The *nasty man*, I realised, must be Ronald Strap, who had collapsed with a bruised ear and died outside the café. That was probably why he had gasped *Get him away from me* as he lay dying. Haystack nicely described Barnaby Mason's hair and the scene Sylvia had just described would explain why he had spoken about punching a man on the side of his head. While Barnaby hid behind the cairn where we found his fingerprint and snail shell, he must have witnessed Sylvia hitting Eric Bone on the head. Barnaby had been intending to protect the killer from her victim. Little wonder a man who was so anxious and confused about everyday life muddled up these traumatic events in his memory.

'He was a nice man,' Sylvia recalled fondly, 'but he got too frightened to come with me after a bit.'

'He saw you hit Mr Bone,' I told her.

'Oh, and he didn't split on me.' Sylvia clasped her hands to her cheek. 'I *knew* he was nice.'

'How did you get Wally here?'

Sylvia giggled and shuffled about.

374

'I told him there was a party with lots of jelly and chocolate cake and his mummy had asked me to bring him.'

'But why did everyone say he was walking alone?'

'Oh, that's easy-peasy,' Sylvia threw her hands in the air. 'I pretended to be a German spy and he had to follow me to my secret base.'

You'd make a damned good spy, at that, I thought. Many so-called grown-ups would not have planned so carefully or executed their plans so skilfully.

'Anyway,' Sylvia confided. 'I have another daddy in mind now and I know you like him lots already.'

'Who?' My mind raced – could she have seen me with Toby or Tubby or Jimmy or the Captain? Brigsy had been nice to her when I first arrived back in Sackwater, offering a tin of buttons when she had *losted* hers, but I smiled to think how she had called him a tosspot for a misunderstanding. Sharkey? I stifled a laugh, perhaps a little hysterically.

But Sylvia only tapped her nose. 'Wait and see,' she said and she skipped up the steps and away without another word.

99

THE BAPTISM OF BEES

Wally was stirring and I hurried over and sat next to him. He struggled up with a start, almost gibbering in terror, but managed a weak smile when he saw me.

'How have you managed without anything to eat or drink?' I asked, popping him on my knee.

'But I do have had things to eat,' he told me. 'There was my ration of sweets and Mummy give me hers and the horrid girl give me some and…' – He pointed to an iron chest at the back of the church – '…I find a box of cangles.'

'You ate them?'

'All of them.' He snuggled closer. 'Except the strings.'

Church candles were beeswax, I remembered, so I supposed they would have more nutrition than the normal paraffin wax, which were probably not very good for you. They must have been sitting in that box for a quarter of a century by now, though.

'That was clever of you.' I stroked his hair. 'But what did you drink?'

He pointed to the baptismal font. 'I find water in that but there int much left. I goo stand on our gas masks to get it.'

He had made a little platform, I saw, out of the boxes and they had all sagged and one had split under his weight, but they had served their purpose.

'Does it taste all right?' I asked and he screwed up his face.

'No, it's nnnyucky.'

'Is your tummy all right?'

'Not very,' he told me. 'It goo hurt.'

The world was going haywire, I thought. Not only were we hell-bent on slaughtering each other again but a five-year-old boy had shown more sense than the three adults who had died there and a nine-year-old girl had outwitted the lot of us.

'Let me have a look at that water,' I said and went to the font.

There wasn't much of it and what was left was a horrible duckweed green. There was a cup on the edge of the font, probably used for pouring water over indignant babies' heads. I skimmed the surface but I would have had to throw half of it away to get anything approaching clear. I got out my handkerchief and Wally came over to watch. His walk was worryingly stiff and unsteady.

'I thought we might be able to filter it a bit,' I said, scooping up as much as I could in my handkerchief and holding it by the corners over the cup.

'I hope your mum dint tell you off for making it dirty,' Wally said anxiously and I laughed.

'She probably would,' I told him, 'if she still did my washing.'

'Is she too lazy?' he asked.

'Very lazy,' I confirmed.

'And smelly?' he giggled.

'Like a farmyard,' I said, and almost dropped the cup in our helpless laughter.

Tommy Handley would have given a thousand pounds for an audience like us. Tubby Gretham might have diagnosed hysteria and given Wally a very mild sedative and me a very large Scotch.

'It's a bit very slow,' Wally said, licking his dry lips with his dry tongue.

I sniffed my filtrate – a bit stale, but better than the residue in my handkerchief.

'Try that.' I handed it to him. 'Roll it round your mouth first.'

Wally downed my effort in one and handed the cup back.

'Same again please, landlord,' he said, and we both almost expired from mirth. 'And the same for you,' he said, but was suddenly serious. 'There's some for you, int there?'

'Gallons,' I said, looking at the couple of cups of slime in the bottom of the font. 'But I think I'd rather have a cigarette.'

I know you're not supposed to smoke in church, but then you're not supposed to imprison people or murder them in church either and I needed a cigarette. I got out my tin with its three compartments for tobacco, papers and lighter. It was really designed for holding dental instruments but I had a better use for it.

'Coo, that's clever.' Wally watched me sow the tobacco and roll it all in my right hand. 'Will you learn me how to do that?'

So, having nothing better to do, I put him back on my lap and did.

Wally wasted quite a bit of tobacco and ripped a few papers but he was so intent on his task I believe that, for the best part of ten minutes, he forgot how dreadful his situation was.

Afterwards, I rocked him gently and tried to think. If there was no way out, was there anything I could say to persuade Sylvia to let us out or trick her into coming in?

Wally drifted off. A black rat appeared, sniffing around my feet. I kicked out and missed and Wally woke, startled.

'Just got a cramped leg,' I told him, my hand up to shield the view as the rat shrugged and ambled away.

'Your arm feels hard.' Wally tried to nestle sleepily into my prosthesis. 'And why are you wearing...' – he yawned – '...a glove?'

'Well,' I began, but Wally's eyelids were falling again and he was immediately sound asleep. His mouth fell open and I saw his tongue, dry as a thick slice of old ham, and his little pinched, pallid face and I knew that if I didn't get him out of there soon, Wally Green would die.

100

THE RETURN OF THE SHADOWS

tried to stay awake but they say even a condemned man falls asleep the night before he is to be executed so, cold and uncomfortable as I was, I lost the battle, only to be confronted by my father smiling fondly as he took my hand and my mother saying, 'Sit there with your mug of hot chocolate, darling, while Mummy makes you a big plate of bacon and eggs.' And even in my dream I knew this must be a dream but also that the next bit wasn't.

'They is just in there,' a little voice said.

'Good girl,' a man said. 'Gorr, what a stink.'

I shot up and Wally clutched my gloved hand, the edge of the cup digging into my stump. I winced and signalled to remind him to stay quiet. Wally covered his mouth. The room, strangely lighter, was filling with shadow again.

'What the hell?' I shook myself.

'What the hell?' Sharkey's head turned towards me and then back to the door and he rushed to grab the handle and throw himself against the woodwork. 'Very funny,' he yelled, hammering on a panel in a way that made me think he didn't find it amusing at all. 'Now let me out, you brat, before you get in serious trouble.'

If ever a man knew how to sweet-talk a little girl, it was not Inspector Sharkey.

I put Wally down and ran to the door, pushing my colleague aside to yank open the hatch.

'Sylvia,' I called. She was standing on the steps. 'You do not want this man for a daddy. He's horrible.'

'But people can change,' she quoted and I wished to the bottom of my heart that I had never dispensed that paste pearl of wisdom.

'Not that much,' I assured her. 'I hate him.'

'Mutual,' Old Scrapie muttered. 'What the hell is going on?'

'Oh, but Mummy...' Sylvia shrugged theatrically. 'You're always saying you hate Daddy but you don't really.'

'I do,' I vowed.

'I can't keep finding daddies,' she argued, not entirely unreasonably.

'Hang on a minute,' I told her. 'Daddy and I need to talk.'

I shut the hatch and whispered, 'She can hear loud voices.'

'What the hell's going on?' he hissed. He swivelled about. 'Shit me! Are they all dead?'

'The little boy isn't,' I said. 'So watch your language.'

Wally came unsteadily over. 'Have you come to save us?' He tugged at Sharkey's jacket and, apparently, his heart strings, for he ruffled Wally's hair in that way that children hate adults doing and said, 'Course I have, sonny' and I had an idea of how he might help to do that.

'She thinks I'm her mother,' I explained quietly, 'so if she thinks you are hurting me, she might try to save me.'

My colleague nodded quite enthusiastically at that idea. 'So, if I start knocking you about...'

'*Pretending* to,' I insisted.

'All right.' He slipped his hand into his pocket.

'If you bring out that knuckleduster, I'll stick it up your... nose,' I threatened. 'You had better keep out of sight, Wally.'

I lifted my right leg and slapped my calf loudly. 'Ouch!' And again. 'Ow, no, stop it!'

'What's happening?' Sylvia called.

'He's beating me,' I cried. 'Help me, Sylvia.'

'Take that,' Sharkey clapped his hands, 'you cow.' He used that last word with great relish and we were doing quite well, I thought, until the viewing panel swung open. I must have forgotten to slide the catch back on.

I glanced over and saw Sylvia standing on the fourth step, trying to peer through the opening. If I could see her, I reasoned, the chances were she could see us and Sharkey must have realised that too for he took me, firmly but not too roughly, in both hands around the throat.

'Stop it,' Sylvia shouted. 'You'll hurt her.'

I made a few choking noises.

'Hurt her?' Sharkey jeered. 'I'll f— flipping well kill her.'

I coughed and Sharkey squeezed harder.

'Leave her alone!' Sylvia shrieked, and I was beginning to wish he would because I could feel my larynx starting to creak.

Sharkey was entering into his role with gusto now and shaking me quite violently. Two could play at that game. I grabbed hold of his hair and tried to yank but it was generously Brylcreemed and my fingers slid through too easily, flopping it over his face as I pulled away.

Sylvia was dancing about in agitation. I leaned towards Sharkey's ear.

'When I hit you the third time, pretend to be knocked out,' I whispered.

'Die, you stinking bi—' he yelled, changing the word at the last moment to 'biddy' but, with less concern for our young audience, flinging me about in a remarkably convincing manner.

My turn and I had three shots for free now. I swung back my arm and slapped Old Scrapie as hard as I could across the face. It made a good solid contact and I was gratified to see him flinch but not so gratified to feel his grip tighten. I pulled my hand back, made a fist and lashed out. I meant to clip his ear but he pulled away and I caught him, Joe Louis style, with a terrific right hook under the jaw. I felt my knuckles crunch, but I am not sure Sharkey felt anything at all. He fell, Max Schmeling style, to nothing so forgiving as a canvas, but rather the hard stone-slabbed floor.

'Bloody hell,' I breathed and I was about to call out to Sylvia to come and help me tie him up when Wally, overcome with excitement at the bout, yelled, *Hooray for you, missus!* and Sylvia, who had been rushing towards us, paused and wrinkled her brow.

'I smell a fish,' she said, and I only wished half the men under my command had her nose.

'Help me, Sylvia,' I cried too late.

'Wally can do that,' she told me matter-of-factly and trotted back up the stairs. 'You'll never turn into my brother, Billy. You're just not good enough,' she screamed and rushed away.

'What the—' Sharkey massaged his jaw and sat up groggily.

'I think she's going to try to find a new little brother,' I said, 'when we have all... quietened down.'

'We int bin very noisy,' Wally pointed out but Sharkey knew exactly what I meant.

101

THE LIVING AND THE DEAD

Paul Sharkey struggled to his feet but it was well after the count of ten and an actual rather than just a technical knockout, I noted with some satisfaction.

'Bloody hell.' He rubbed his face gingerly.

I massaged my neck and my fist.

'I'm sorry,' I told him, 'but you were actually strangling me. I didn't realise you had such a weak jaw.'

Sharkey huffed and felt the back of his head, which had bounced off the floor.

'Bloody hell,' he muttered again, 'We must have looked like…'

'Louis and Schmeling,' I filled the pause for him.

'Punch and Judy,' he refilled it for me.

The blurred figure of Sylvia rushed away past the windows and Wally came out of his corner.

'Sorry,' he said meekly.

'For what?' Sharkey demanded.

'You getting hurt,' I explained quickly.

'Hurt?' Sharkey laughed. 'You must be joking. I went down because I was worried you might get injured.'

Wally sniffed once and then a dozen times, chest heaving and breaking into sobs. 'Now we int never getting out of here.'

'Course we will, sonny.' Sharkey reached down for a quick ruffle but Wally jerked his head away. 'What about the windows?'

'Solidly barred, I've checked them all,' I assured him.

'That other door?'

'Bolted, and the floor is solid.'

'Bother,' Sharkey spat with such vehemence it sounded like an obscenity.

'How did you know I was here?' I asked.

'You missed my briefing so I guessed there must be something really important,' Sharkey said.

'Quite so,' I breathed.

'So I checked your office and saw the map on your desk. The fishermen's cottages were circled in ink and I knew you wouldn't ruin a good map for no reason, a stingy old bag like you.'

'*Old?*' I fumed. 'I'm younger than you.'

'Women deteriorate, men mature,' he told me, and I was about to retort that I had never met a man yet who had matured past the age of twelve, which wouldn't have been fair or true, when I remembered we had more important things to worry about.

'So you went to the cottages...' I prompted.

'And that little...' He swallowed whatever profanity he had in mind. '...girl came running down the hill and said to come quickly because a police lady was injured.' Sharkey rubbed the back of his neck. 'What the hell is the matter with her?'

'Apart from being severely concussed and losing all her family in that bombing?' I reminded him.

'Well,' Sharkey waved a hand at us all, the living and the dead, 'she seems to have acquired a new one.'

'That,' I agreed, 'is exactly what she has done.'

102

RUST AND SHIRT TAILS

'If only we could find a window with the bars weakened enough to force,' I said in frustration.

I poked about with my nail file.

'Going to saw through the bars?' Sharkey sneered.

'Just checking,' I explained. 'They're corroded a bit at the bases.'

'And in another fifty years they'll be rusted all the way through, I daresay,' Sharkey grunted.

'But I'll miss school,' Wally said in dismay. 'Mummy will baste me.'

'Mummy will give you a big hug and a kiss,' I forecast.

'Yuck,' Wally said. 'That's soppy.'

'They're corroded!' I said.

'I think we have already established that,' my colleague snapped.

'Yes, but it's because they get damp,' I realised. 'The stone sills are a bit stained too.'

'Oh, dear,' Sharkey said in mock concern. 'If only you had your old maid in to clean them.'

I ran a finger over the window and the tip came away slightly shiny.

'There is condensation on the glass,' I said.

'What are you suggesting?' Sharkey asked in exasperation. 'We lick it off?'

'It wouldn't do any harm,' I said, 'but then it wouldn't do

much good. We need something to soak up the condensation – handkerchiefs, ties, that sort of thing – nothing too big or it will just wick the water away. It will build up more when it gets colder at night.'

'It do get cold,' Wally confirmed as I unknotted my tie to lay against the bottom of the glass.

'Oh, why not?' Sharkey groaned. 'We have nothing else to do.' He took off his tie and brought out two handkerchiefs. 'One for use and one for show,' he explained. 'Neither used.'

I took off my stockings and shook my head in despair. Even in this situation, it was obvious where Sharkey's thoughts lay.

'Socks,' I urged.

We laid out our few scraps.

'What else?' We looked about and at each other.

'Got a penknife on you?' I asked.

All men have penknives. They never use them unless they smoke pipes or can't find a pencil sharpener, although Toby unblocks his typewriter with his when his *g* and *h* jam together.

Sharkey brought one out, an ivory-handled one, so worn he had probably had it since childhood – *so, a few weeks*, I thought unkindly.

'Shirt tails,' I said and pulled mine out at the front.

Sharkey hacked and ripped with gusto before turning with less enthusiasm to his own. I cut off his back shirt tail for him, trying not to think about what had made it so warm.

'If this doesn't work, you owe me a new shirt.'

'I'll get Abi to repair it for you,' I promised.

'You keep away from her,' Sharkey threatened. 'I know what women are like when they get together.'

'Oh no, Inspector,' I assured him. 'I do not think you know what we are like at all.'

'What's that supposed to mean?' he challenged gratifyingly uneasily.

'If I told you that,' I smiled as sweetly as my parched mouth allowed, 'I doubt you would ever sleep at night.'

103

THE SHARK IN THE MOONLIGHT

t was getting dark and Wally was not exaggerating when he said it would be cold. There was a damp chilliness in those subterranean stones that seemed to seep into my bones.

'We should snuggle up for warmth,' Sharkey suggested.

'I'll just snuggle up with Wally, thank you,' I decided.

Sharkey scowled. 'Please yourself.'

I took Wally on my lap and pulled my jacket as far as I could around him. He popped his thumb in his mouth but instantly pulled it out again.

'Mummy say it's for babies,' he admitted.

'Mummy won't mind you doing it tonight,' I promised.

It might help make his mouth a bit moister.

'Do you think it's just for babies, mister?' Wally asked anxiously.

'Course not,' Sharkey assured him. 'I suck mine all the time.'

And to my surprise, my colleague slipped a grubby thumb into his own mouth and slurped on it appreciatively.

'That was kind,' I mouthed as Wally nodded off.

There were times in the last few hours, I reflected, when Old Scrapie had seemed almost human.

Sharkey paced, his leather soles clicking on the stone as he went up and down the aisles. He stopped alongside me.

'Smoke?' My colleague held out a crumpled packet, flicking the base with practised skill to make two cigarettes project.

'Thanks.' I took one and Sharkey tapped his cigarette on the box before he struck a match, the flare making me realise how dark it was getting. 'At least it's a clear night and a full moon,' I commented. 'Wally was so hungry he ate all the candles.' Senior Service, not my favourite but I sucked the smoke in greedily.

'I could make a taper out of your notebook pages.' Sharkey blew smoke in my face. 'Only it wouldn't last long.'

'Why mine?'

'Mine has important information in it.'

'And I suppose mine doesn't.'

He took a long drag. 'There you go again, starting an argument when I'm trying to be friendly.'

'I appreciate the cigarette,' I said, and refrained from adding *but not the insult about my work*.

Sharkey put a boot up on the end of my pew, giving me a non-tantalising glimpse of one of those pallid hairy shins Toby had talked about. Now that was someone I would have willingly snuggled up to, I ruminated.

'You and me got off on the wrong foot,' he said, and for a moment I thought he was referring to the one just under my nose.

'We certainly did,' I agreed. He had thought I was a sergeant and treated me and my sex with contempt.

'But I'm prepared to let bygones be bygones,' he continued with the magnanimity that only wrongdoers can dispense.

'Are you?' My tone was meant to be cutting but my fellow officer remained unscathed.

'We should go for a drink when this is all over.'

The idea of a drink was heavenly. The idea of sharing it with him was not.

'That would be nice,' I purred, 'just you and me.' Sharkey nodded approvingly until I continued, 'And Brigsy and Bantony and Chivers and Rivers and the Grinder-Snipes.'

Wally's eyelids flickered. 'And Uncle Tom Cobley and all,' he murmured sleepily and closed them again.

I laughed and for once Sharkey laughed with me and I nearly said, 'Perhaps we should,' but I still hadn't forgiven him and I would never forgive myself for what we did to our suspect.

'Here.' Sharkey took off his jacket and rolled it up. 'You can't hold him like that all night.'

'You'll freeze.'

'You'll care?' For the first time I could remember, my colleague made me smile and I resisted making a truthful response.

I laid Wally gently on the pew with a glance back at Colin Windser staring at us with milky eyes, his face glistening in the moonlight, his jaw dropped and lips parted like he was about to join in the conversation. He would never be doing that again in this world with his wife or Gera.

'Isn't he frightened of them?' Sharkey followed my gaze.

'I think he's too busy trying to survive,' I said.

'He's a fighter,' Sharkey nodded approvingly.

I got up and stretched.

'Ever wanted kids?' Sharkey asked with a glance at Wally.

'Never,' I told him. 'Have you?'

'Chr-ipes, no.' He tossed his fag end down and pulled his foot away to stub it out.

And I looked into those eyes, peering tenderly through the gloom, and wondered which of us was the worse liar. Sometimes my body ached for the lack of a child.

'Of course, I could have one any time if I wanted.' Sharkey got out another cigarette but didn't offer me one this time. 'But you must be much too old for it now.'

And I resolved that I would arrange to go for a drink with Sharkey after all – somewhere far away and romantic – if only so that I could stand him up.

104

LIZZIE AND THE LIZARD

strode about the chapel, reflecting how bizarre it was to be in the company of a child, three human corpses, a dead dog and a man I loathed but might soon be dead with. I was determined to outlast Sharkey, though. The thought of dying in his arms, with him telling me what weaklings women are, would surely keep me going long enough to hear his last breath. The thought that really gnawed at me, though, was that little Wally Green was almost certainly moribund. The amount of water we could hope to collect for him would hardly be enough to moisten his tongue; there was nothing for him to eat and he was weakening fast. I was only surprised that he had lasted so long, but Wally had what March Middleton referred to as *spirit*. In fact, she had given a cat that name when it survived a similar ordeal to ours.

Sharkey went and laid on his back on a pew in the right-hand side chapel.

'There'll be no sleep tonight,' he forecast, and he took a swig from his hip flask. He didn't offer me any of that, either – and within a few minutes he was snoring, making the same horrible gargling noise my mother used to make during the sermon after a few Christmas Eve sherries.

A fat rat sauntered over Sharkey's chest and I do not believe he realised what he had sleepily brushed aside. The rat scuttled off in search of meat that would put up less resistance.

I went back and sat, shivering, next to Wally. His cheek felt warm – too warm, I thought – and his breath was worryingly soft on the backs of my fingers. Was this his last night? I held his hand and decided to keep a vigil. Unlike my colleague, I was not able to sleep anyway, but I must have nodded off eventually because I didn't see Sylvia pass the windows or hear anything at all until there was a tap on the door.

'Enter,' I croaked automatically before realising I wasn't in my office and that Brigsy wasn't bringing me a nice big mug of tea.

'I just come to talk, Mummy,' Sylvia piped up.

Wally half-smiled without opening his eyes. There was no point in disturbing him. What would I be waking him for?

I pulled my jacket back up over his shoulders and got up to go over to the hatch. Sylvia stood on the fourth step up. She was in a different dress – red, with a red ribbon in her hair. I preferred the blue, myself. I cleared my throat but still sounded hoarse.

'Hello, darling.' I might as well stay on the right side of her. 'That's a pretty dress.'

Sylvia wiggled her nose.

'Which do you prefer?'

I knew this was a trick question. Women do it to men all the time. If they say *this one* we say *what was wrong with the other* and if they say *the other* we say *don't you like this one?* If they say *I like them both the same* or ask us which we think, we know they are dodging the question. It's a game we all play.

'The other one,' I gambled, in the hope she would think I was at least being sincere.

'So do I.'

Wally was still asleep, or unconscious – I could see his chest rising and falling – but Sharkey was struggling up stiffly, his face unattractively bristly, and I signalled to him to shush.

'Would you like to have a chat?'

Sylvia sat on a step. 'We just have,' she said simply, and cupped her chin in her hands with her elbows on her skinny knees.

'Would you like to talk about the day you fell in the pond?' I asked.

'Maybe,' Sylvia replied coyly.

'You didn't really fall in accidently, did you?' I said teasingly and Sylvia shook her golden hair.

'I jumped in,' she admitted with a giggle, 'and it was blinking cold.'

'You wanted to rinse your dress, didn't you, darling?'

Sylvia said nothing so I continued, 'Because you had blood on it.'

'Only a bit,' she conceded.

'But it didn't wash off properly, did it?' I smiled. 'So you threw it in the fire.'

'You're very clever,' Sylvia said. 'I suppose it comes from being in the police.'

If the job did come with brains, I reflected, most of my colleagues had forgotten to collect theirs.

'And it was Reverend Heath's blood, wasn't it, Sylvia?' I asked, as mildly as a mother might ask how her daughter got a smudge on her face.

Sylvia nodded. 'I went to see him and he took me in his office and I told him I wanted to see my mummy and daddy and my brother, Billy little and Rusty my dog and Uncle Danny and Aunty Mabel and Uncle Horace.' She counted them off on her fingers, all seven of them. 'But he said I couldn't and I said *but I want to* and he said *they are asleep* and I said *I won't awaken them* and *which room are they in* and he said *it's a room you can't go in yet* and that he didn't mean to make me to cry.'

I didn't mean to upset her, Reverend Heath had told us just before he died.

'But what is the point of not meaning to do something and doing it anyway?' Sylvia demanded. 'It made me so cross I got the knife and poked him with it to make him take me to the room but he pushed me away and hurt my tummy and he tripped over the rug and bashed the knife on the floor and it stuck right in.'

Sylvia rolled her eyes in exasperation.

'What happened then?' I asked, hoping she would say she tried to help the vicar.

'Oh, he coughed a bit and closed his eyes,' she shrugged, bored with the subject already.

That would explain why the vicar had only appeared after I had seen Sylvia with Lizzie Longhorn. He had passed out and when he came to, in his weakened and confused state, he may well have had trouble opening the front door lock that I had had to fiddle with.

'Did you climb out of the window?' I asked, remembering the blood on the sill, and Sylvia nodded.

'I think you are a nicer mummy now. You don't shout at me.'

'Didn't the gardener see you?' I asked and she looked genuinely puzzled.

'What gardener?'

And then I realised what I should have realised at the time. The reason Gervil Fisher had only a small pile of pruned branches near the rhododendron bush was that he hadn't actually been there anything like the two hours that he claimed. For the sake of fiddling his wages he had obstructed what could have been a murder investigation.

'She was a very nice lady, the one who had the turtles,' Sylvia recalled fondly. 'She will be a kinder aunty than that one.'

And Sylvia's eyes swivelled to her left as if she could see through the door and to the body of Netabery Windser, who had been suffocated to replace Mabel Satin but was, apparently, unsatisfactory now.

'Will be?' I breathed. 'Oh God, help us all.'

'Hell's teeth,' Sharkey muttered after Sylvia had trotted away. 'How many people is she going to collect?'

'I don't think she'll ever stop voluntarily,' I speculated. 'I think she enjoys the game.'

'Some bloody game,' he muttered, brightening as he remembered, 'I told you he tripped.'

'But you destroyed the evidence that might have backed your theory,' I reminded him. 'And you didn't say she had stabbed him first.'

The Shark sniffed and I went to look at Wally. His lips were very cracked and reddened. His face felt hot and dry.

'Hello, miss,' he greeted me weakly.

'Check your socks,' I told Sharkey, and he glanced down before remembering but, to be fair to him, I think we were both losing our powers of concentration.

He took one sock from the sill.

'Quite damp,' he said and brought it across, wringing it carefully over the cup. 'A few drops,' he said and went to get the rest of our things.

There wasn't much for all our efforts. Sharkey lifted Wally's head and put the cup to his lips.

'Drink up, sonny,' he said, letting the water trickle into Wally's mouth.

'Oh, lovely,' Wally whispered hoarsely.

I folded his handkerchief and laid it on Wally's brow.

'Couple of drops on my fingers.' Sharkey ran them over Wally's lips and I saw a cracked red tongue flick out like a lizard.

I made my handkerchief into a cylinder.

'Pop that in your mouth,' I suggested. I went to put the things back on the sills and for the first and last time in my life, I had an almost overpowering urge to suck one of Sharkey's socks.

105

THE DISMANTLING OF BETTY CHURCH

paced around.

'There must be some way out of here.'

'You'll find it, lady,' Wally assured me and I wished I had his faith.

'What if we smashed the furniture and made a bonfire to burn the door down,' Sharkey suggested, but rejected his own idea immediately. 'Nothing to smash it with and we'd probably die in the smoke.'

'Fires is highly dangerous,' Wally chipped in. 'Mummy say Uncle John's budgie die in one.' And his eyes welled up, whether at the thought of her or the bird I wasn't sure.

'That door is wedged with a wooden beam,' I remembered.

'I know it b— blinking is,' Sharkey retorted with more restraint than I had ever witnessed in him before. Perhaps I should borrow a child to be with me whenever my colleague was around.

'So, if we could dislodge that beam...'

'How?' Sharkey demanded. 'The door's jammed too solid to shake it loose and there aren't any knot holes to push anything through.'

'And our arms aren't long enough,' Wally chipped in.

He was looking very bleary now.

'Of course they fu—' Sharkey snuffed out the fuse just as his temper was about to explode. '...aren't,' he ended mildly.

'Mine might be,' I said.

'What the hell are you talking about?' my colleague demanded, fuse aglow again, but I was too busy struggling out of my jacket.

'Turn around,' I said.

'You're not going to strip off like Chivers?' Sharkey asked with unconvincing casualness.

'Not quite that far,' I told my colleague. 'Turn away.'

Sharkey shrugged and did as he was told. Wally sat on the end of a pew and watched me curiously as I unbuttoned my shirt and tugged it down, followed by my chemise.

'My mummy hangs those on her washing line,' he told me.

'Most ladies do,' I told him.

'Didn't know you were a lady,' Sharkey sniped.

'Only in the presence of gentlemen,' I told him, though I took his point after all my protests about not being one. 'And I don't know very many of those.'

I unstrapped my leather harness and the relief was instant. You can push chronic discomfort to the back of your mind but it's always lurking there like a monster in the shadows. My stump was raw, despite my padding the cup, and a metal clasp had dug deep into my left shoulder.

Lord, what wouldn't I give for a lovely soak in a hot bath now?

'Have you got something to drink?' Wally asked.

'Nothing for little boys,' Sharkey said quickly – too quickly – and he made a great show of swigging from his hip flask, but I had seen the way he was holding up the reflective surface.

Oh, good grief.

I took off my arm and pulled my clothes back into place.

Wally was watching me open-mouthed.

'Cor!' he gasped in awe. 'Can you do that with the other one?'

'I'm afraid not,' I said to his great disappointment, and tugged off the glove. 'But I expect this man can unscrew his head.'

Wally laughed. 'Like a beetle drive.'

And even Sharkey managed a smile as he inspected my false arm.

'Thought it might be wood,' he commented.

'Some are, but steel is stronger,' I said, 'and the fingers bend better.'

'And why would that matter? You don't actually do much with it,' my beloved colleague pointed out.

'I am about to do a great deal with it, I hope,' I assured him, and I put my arm on a long low table that was probably once piled with missals and hymnals but now lay clothed in cobwebs. 'Give me your penknife.'

He dug into his trouser pocket and thrust the knife towards me.

'I can't unhinge the blade one-handed,' I said, so he did, muttering, 'Not the only thing you can't do, by a long chalk.'

'She's got a good left hook,' Wally told him admiringly.

It was a right hook, actually, but I wasn't going to quibble over that.

Sharkey slapped the knife into my hand, narrowly missing severing one of my last five digits, and I returned to my hand, bending the fingers and turning the blade in the screws to tighten them.

'And she can roll fags,' Wally told him, but got no response from my colleague.

I loosened the shoulder straps as much as I could but it was obvious at a glance they would not be anything like long enough.

'I need your help, Wally,' I said. 'Do you think you could take the straps off those gas masks?'

'I certainly can.' Wally brightened at having something useful to do.

I can't pretend he scampered over to the font but his legs looked a little less unsteady as he sat on the floor beside them. The buckles were too stiff, though, for his weakened little fingers.

'Can you show me how to do it?' Sharkey went over and crouched beside him.

'They are very stiff,' Wally warned.

'I'll do my best,' Sharkey promised and I felt a wave, if not of affection, then at least of less loathing wash over me. 'How do I do this one?'

'You pull that end through,' Wally told him and he settled back to watch his pupil at work.

It didn't take long and soon they were back, Wally proudly holding out their prizes and Sharkey steadying him with a hand behind his back.

'We need to join them all together,' I said, and Sharkey grudgingly obliged while I pointed out which clip I wanted attached to which strap. 'And your boot laces, please.'

'Why not yours?' he demanded.

'Because yours are longer.'

'I can do my own laces, nearly,' Wally told me proudly.

'So can Inspector Sharkey,' I told him.

'That's a scary name.' Wally edged away from my colleague.

'But he's a lovely cuddly man,' I lied.

'He dint look it,' Wally said, and I laughed.

Sharkey huffed indignantly and went down on one knee. Wally nudged my leg.

'He's gooin' pop the question,' he whispered.

'Of course I will marry you, dear Old Scrapie,' I said, taking the laces from him.

Sharkey got back on his feet.

'Glad you can still make a joke of things,' he grumped.

'So am I,' I agreed. 'Now, if you could tie one lace through that last hole and the other lace around my wrist and then knot them tightly together.' I held the result up to the door. 'Perfect,' I said, with a great deal more confidence than I felt.

106

FISHING FOR FREEDOM

There was no sign of Sylvia when I opened the hatch and peered out.

'Here goes.' I pushed my false arm through the opening. The widest bit, where the socket for my stump was, got stuck, but with a lot of wiggling I managed to force it through.

'Coo, that's a clever trick,' Wally grinned delightedly. 'Are you goon post yourself through the door?'

'Just my arm,' I told him, lowering it carefully by the straps.

'Will it goo run and get help?' he asked excitedly.

'I am hoping it will open the door for us,' I told him. 'Have you heard of a grappling hook?'

'Is it like a fishin' hook?'

'Yes, but bigger.' It was more difficult than I expected since I had to stand on tiptoes to reach fully through the hatch and struggle to sweep my right arm out sideways, but I managed to swing the false arm gently to my right and heard it hit the door. 'I bent the fingers into a sort of claw, so I'm hoping I can get the hand round to the other side of the beam…' I hit something again but the arm swung freely back. 'And pull it away.'

'Cor!' Wally clapped his hands, not doubting for a moment that I would succeed.

'Oh shi—' Sharkey was finding this non-swearing business difficult. 'She's coming back.'

'She is, too,' Wally called out in terror.

I glanced back and saw Sylvia's little shape bobbing past a stained-glass window at the far, western end of the church.

'Pull it back in,' Sharkey instructed. 'You can try again later.'

'It'll never get back through the hole,' I objected. 'I had enough trouble pushing it from this side.'

'She goo kill us.' Wally clutched my skirt.

'She can't hurt us,' I reassured him.

We all knew what she could do, though, but it was Wally who said fearfully, 'She might leave us here.'

I swung my grappling iron again and hit woodwork again.

'She's still coming,' Sharkey warned.

'Make her goo away,' Wally begged him.

'How?' Sharkey demanded.

'You're a copper,' Wally said quite reasonably, and I was glad he hadn't given me the task of sending Sylvia packing because I had no idea either.

It was difficult to tell, but I suspected I was either hitting the door or my side of the post, whereas I needed to hit the far side of the post to catch it with my metal fingers. I swung the arm further away from the door in the hope of arcing round the post.

Sharkey ran to the window.

'Hello,' he bellowed and banged on the glass in the hope of distracting Sylvia. 'Da-sh it. She's still coming,' he told me, 'and over halfway now.'

My arm clattered against something but failed to engage with whatever it was.

'It's bloody useless,' Sharkey said encouragingly.

'Shall we use your arm instead?' I suggested, swishing the strap again.

'Second to last window,' Sharkey told me, filling his new role as commentator with great professionalism.

I could feel the arm swinging madly now and waited a moment to try to steady it.

'Last window,' he said, 'she'll be here any second.' Because I needed, more than anything else in the world at that moment, to be panicked. 'Hurry up,' he urged.

'She's doin' her best.' Wally defended me loyally and tugged on my skirt again. 'You are, aren't you?'

'My very best,' I assured him with another desperate swing as there was a rattling at the top door.

'Hooray,' Wally cheered. ''Cause your best do be best, police lady woman.'

'Well I can't—' I began reluctantly as the door swung inwards and Sylvia stood silhouetted in a rectangle of light, Shirley Temple made terrifying.

'She's here,' Sharkey breathed, though I was the only one who could actually see her.

'What are you doing?' Sylvia shrieked.

I tugged and the arm engaged on something. The beam? I yanked harder, but whatever my fingers had latched on to was not giving way.

'Just waving to you,' I lied, utterly unconvincingly, and gave another tug.

Nothing.

'No!' Sylvia screamed. 'You goo tryin' to escape.'

Elocution lessons all forgotten now, she started down the steps.

'Pull harder,' Sharkey yelled, nearly deafening my left ear, and I hauled as strongly as I could and thought I felt the beam shift and heard it scrape on the flagstones, but I only seemed to have wedged it tighter.

'I'm trying.'

And Sylvia was halfway down when my makeshift hook fell

away, metal scraping uselessly against the stone floor, and she had reached the bottom step and leaped to grab the arm while I was still frantically reeling it back in the hope of the one last go that I knew I would never get.

107

THE GREAT WHITE HUNTER

S ylvia snatched at my artificial arm.

'I will never let you out now, never!' she shrieked with petrifying venom.

Oh God!

'Your f— flipping bootlace has snapped,' I shouted at Sharkey, because he should have had the foresight to have bought laces that withstood the weight of a steel-framed arm and two people heaving at it.

I drew my right arm back in and bid a fond farewell to the left.

'No, it hasn't. The knot came undone,' he pointed out, because that made everything all right.

'Got it!' Sylvia waved my prosthesis in a triumphant little dance, the straps tangling round her feet.

'Be careful,' I warned with a stupidity that bordered on insanity, but Sylvia wasn't listening. She skipped sideways and tripped even more sideways and fell further sideways yet and the wooden bar clattered away as she stumbled over it.

I grasped the iron ring handle and heaved it around and the latch lifted. With one push the door swung open, only eighteen inches maybe but that was all I needed, and I was about to slide through when Sharkey leaped, side on, shouldering the door in best/worst police style and sending it – and, with a sickening thud, Sylvia – flying backwards.

I rushed out.

Sylvia Satin lay crumpled on the floor, her neck twisted,

horribly reminiscent of how Simnal Cranditch's had been. Sharkey strode proudly to her side, standing over her like a hunter with his first lion.

Wally Green came out more timidly.

'Cor!' he said, much impressed. 'You've killed her, mister.'

'Hope so.' Sharkey prodded Sylvia in the stomach with the toe of his laceless boot.

'Don't do that again,' I told him furiously.

'She didn't feel it.'

'It's a question of respect,' I said, not that that would mean much to him.

'Respect?' Sharkey laughed bitterly. 'She was a murdering—'

'Bitch.' Wally supplied the word my colleague was looking for just before his little legs crumpled and he collapsed into Sharkey's arms.

108

THE VICTOR AND THE VICTIMS

S harkey picked Wally up and cradled him in a tender action I never thought I would see him perform.

'Poor little chap,' he cooed. 'All been too much for him.'

'We need to get him to hospital,' I said, and my colleague nodded.

'I'll take him and ring the station from there for backup.'

'Could you also ring the *Gazette* and get Mr Gregson to come and take some pictures of the bodies?'

One day we would have our own photographer but I was more than happy to see Toby doing the job and he was becoming inured to the sight of corpses, after the first time when he had nearly fainted down a staircase.

'Mr Gregson,' Sharkey snorted. 'Funny way to speak of your lover.'

'It would be if he was,' I agreed, and knelt on a cold slab by Sylvia's limp form.

'Don't disturb the body,' Sharkey warned as I touched her neck.

'Get a doctor,' I said. 'She still has a pulse.'

Sharkey eyed Sylvia's limp form with loathing.

'What's the rush?' he said.

'She's a child,' I said, and he snorted contemptuously.

'A child of the devil maybe.' He turned up his lips. 'Sylvia Satan would be a better name for her.'

'She is not a monster.' I stroked Sylvia's golden curls from her eyes. 'She was a lovely, happy little girl before that bomb fell. She lost her parents, her younger brother, her uncles and an aunt, even her pet dog. Did she have to lose her legs before you would see her as a victim of war?'

Sharkey started up the steps with little Wally Green.

'I'll be quick as I can,' he said.

109

FLEUR AND THE CROCODILE AND
THE MAN FROM TAUNTON

Harrold Schofield came to the hospital, but just as she was when I first met him, Sylvia was in a sedative-induced deep sleep.

'Oh, you poor child,' he said, but I was not going to be fooled by any crocodile tears this time.

'Was she really that impossible to look after?' I asked coldly.

I had not forgotten what Josie had told me, that he only wanted his niece for the money he believed she would come into.

'Yes,' he replied simply. 'It was dreadful. She cried the whole time about wanting to come back here and get her family back together. I tried to explain but she wouldn't listen. She complained of terrible headaches but when I took her to the doctor's she said it was because I kept hitting her about the head. He took me to one side and threatened to involve the police if anything happened to her. He more or less implied that he had his suspicions about Oscar, the little boy I was guardian to.' Harrold Schofield's voice cracked with emotion. 'I adored that boy. He was like a son to me and I thought – I hoped – that Sylvia would be like a daughter. I could never have children of my own – being unmarried.'

I didn't like to point out that I knew a great many men who were not married but had children, though I knew what he meant and I believed then that he was a fundamentally decent man.

'Your relationship seemed strained at the funeral,' I commented, and he tugged at his shirt collar like it was suddenly choking him.

'I know she's only a child but she's a manipulative little devil,' he told me. 'All the way to Sackwater she kept telling me that she was going to tell everybody that I beat her, and that Fleur, the woman I employed to look after Sylvia while I was about my business, starved her and locked her in cupboards.'

'Was that why you didn't like her talking to people?' I asked and he nodded.

'That and the way she kept speaking to strangers, inviting them into my house. Usually Fleur or I managed to put a stop to it, but once I came in from the garden to find a tramp sitting in my armchair, having helped himself to a good cigar and a large whisky and soda.'

I laughed. 'I'm sorry. That's not funny.'

Harry smiled. 'It is if it happens to somebody else.' He ran his hands backwards over his soft brown hair. 'It got worse after the funeral. All the way home she screamed and screamed and tried to get out of the car while I was driving. I only just managed to drag her back without crashing or driving us into a ditch.'

'I didn't realise it was that bad.'

'Oh, it got worse,' he assured me. 'She took to creeping into my room and standing by my bed. I would wake up and see her there, just staring.' He shuddered. 'Gave me the willies, it did, the look on her face. It was pure malevolence. I tried not to make a big thing of it and I was damned if I was going to let a child frighten me into locking my bedroom door.' Harry cleared his throat. 'Then the last time she did it, she had a carving knife – high over her head. She brought it right down into the pillow by my head and I still don't know if she missed on purpose or I moved.' He looked at the angelic face on the bed beside us. 'I was reluctant to send her to a home – we've all heard stories about those – but

Josie Whitehouse had already written to say she would always have Sylvia for holidays or longer, if I wanted.'

'Did you tell her about the knife?' I asked.

'That, and everything,' he assured me.

Sylvia stirred, nestling deeper into her pillow.

'But she said I must be exaggerating or being cruel to Sylvia to make her behave that way. I thought perhaps it was because she missed her home town so much and maybe I was unkind to take her away. So, God forgive me...' – Harry pinched the bridge of his nose – '...I brought her back but I had no idea...' He couldn't bring himself to say what had happened.

'Of course you didn't.' I pulled the blanket up to Sylvia's neck. 'It was kind of Mrs Whitehouse to take her in, though.'

'Kind and lucrative.' Harry saw my puzzlement. 'I paid her good money to care for my niece,' he snorted. 'And a fine job she did, letting her go out and about at will.'

'Sylvia was giving her sleeping draughts,' I explained, brushing a curl from Sylvia's eye that was making it flicker.

'Oh, hell,' Harry said. 'I caught Fleur napping a few times and sacked her in the end.' He exhaled through his mouth. 'I shall have to put that right.' He clicked his tongue. 'It's about the only thing I can put right now.'

There might be something else Harrold Schofield could do, but I would have to make a few calls first.

It was a simple task to identify the body of the man who was the substitute for Sylvia's Uncle Horace. His name, as his papers indicated, was Frank Smith, a fifty-year-old travelling salesman for agricultural machinery from Taunton in Somerset. I had thought him much older than that, but death flatters nobody with its ravages. He had failed to attend a meeting with Arthur, Marquis

Stovebury, and had been written off as unreliable. He was a married man but estranged from his wife and children, who were used to going for months without hearing from him and would probably never have reported him missing at all. His funeral back in his home town was very sparsely attended, I believe.

The funerals of Mr and Mrs Windser were delayed until Tubby had performed their post mortems and the coroner released their bodies. They were buried at St Hilda's cemetery, not very far from the family Sylvia had hoped they would replace. There was a good turnout – 'More than could be bothered to help look for them,' their daughter, Gera, commented bitterly as we watched the so-called mourners wash her sandwiches down with copious quantities of her tea.

110

THE MONSTER AND
THE VOICE FROM THE GRAVE

Mornette Pegsy was behind the desk at the Royal Albert Sackwater Infirmary when I called back in. She was a nice girl who used to help in her parents' grocery shop when she was little and was always scrupulous in making sure she weighed everything properly, much to the annoyance of her mother, who used to slip the wrong weights on the scales if you weren't paying attention. Morney had always wanted to be a nurse and I was glad to see that she loved her work and to be told that the patients adored her.

'Good morning, Inspector.' She gave me a lovely smile. 'Are you here to see the children? Wally will be thrilled. He talks about you all the time and how you beat up Inspector Sharkey.' She giggled.

'It wasn't quite like that,' I chuckled, but I was perfectly happy for that rumour to circulate. 'Is Sylvia awake yet?'

The two had been put in opposite wings of the hospital, partly so that Wally would not have to see his kidnapper and partly because his mother, Mrs Green, and grandmother, Violeth Took, had made unveiled threats against her. For that reason and to stop Sylvia escaping, we had had a police guard outside her room night and day.

'She was earlier,' Morney told me, 'but she had a very bad headache so the doctor gave her some more sedative. Her grandmother will be disappointed if she doesn't wake up.'

'Grandmother?' I queried in puzzlement. We had been told that all her grandparents were dead.

'Yes, she only arrived about five minutes ago.'

'Thank you, nurse,' I said. 'I think I'll go and have a word with her first.'

I hurried down the corridor. Was it possible that there had been a mistake and that Sylvia did have a relative other than her uncle? Another, less savoury explanation also occurred to me. I ran.

Rivers was in a chair, slumped with amazing flexibility for a man with his allegedly unbendable spine, his helmet on the floor and his chin on his chest. I kicked his boot. 'Wake up.' And rushed into the room, the door flying open to crash against the wall. The woman inside had her back to me but I knew that tall, elegant figure with the unnaturally auburn hair before she had even spun around to face me.

'Mrs Bone,' I said, and was taken aback to see that Edwina Bone was crying, her powdered cheeks broken into deltas by the tracks of her tears.

She had a pillow in her hand.

'I came to kill her,' she said, shocked by her own words, and I was relieved to look over to see Sylvia slumbering peacefully on her back. 'After all the wicked things she did to my Eric. He was such a gentle, kind man.'

'That was why she did it,' I explained. 'She wanted him to be her daddy.'

'And that poor little boy and all those others?'

'She was trying to get her family back.'

'I looked at her,' Mrs Bone continued, 'and she was just a pretty little girl, but then I remembered how she must have used those charms to lure my husband. He would have been terrified to go into that place but he tried to make himself help her, that wicked little monster.'

'The loss of her loved ones and the bomb—' I tried to explain, but Mrs Bone was not listening.

'I lifted her head and slid the pillow out from under it and laid her head down again and I took the pillow in both hands and was about to press it over her face when I heard a voice.' Mrs Bone looked at me, as if she had just seen me. 'It was Eric,' she said in wonderment. 'I heard him loud and clear. He said *No, Eddie*. Nobody else called me that. I dropped the pillow on the bed and was just about to put it back under her head when you came.'

'Eric and your son...' – I whizzed through the card index of names in my brain – '...Peter would never forgive you.'

'Do you believe in God, Inspector Church?' Mrs Bone raised Sylvia's head and slipped the pillow underneath.

'Oh course,' I assured her. This was no time to parade my sceptical agnosticism.

'Then pray that I die soon,' Mrs Bone said, in much the same tone that she had instructed me to make a pot of tea. 'Goodbye, Inspector.'

She pushed past me to the door.

It went through my head that I could have charged her with attempted or intent to murder but who would have been the better for that?

'Goodbye, Mrs Bone,' I said, then I straightened Sylvia's sheets, brushed her golden hair from over her right eye and went back into the corridor to give a confused Constable Rivers the biggest dressing-down of his wretched career.

That done, I went to see Wally, who was sitting up in bed playing with a wooden train on a wooden tray.

'Lady policeman Church,' he grinned happily. He held out his arms and I leaned over to give him a careful hug.

I didn't see the woman sitting in the corner at first but I heard the click-click-clicking of her needles.

'Oh, Mrs Green, hello,' I greeted her, with more warmth than I felt. 'Wally looks so much improved already, doesn't he?'

'S'pose,' she said, and I wondered what her reason for stinking of gin was today. She didn't look especially in a celebratory mood. 'Bet you went to see the bitch first.'

I ignored that.

'How are you feeling, Wally?'

He slipped his hand into mine.

'Much more better,' he said. His eyes were still ringed black and sunken and his lips were still cracked but his tongue, when I glimpsed it, was no longer like dried ham.

'I give him what for,' Mrs Green told me grimly. 'Gooin' off with strangers on all the times I tell him not to, mitherin' me and his gran half to death.'

'I'm sure he didn't mean to,' I assured her in as measured a tone as I could manage. 'Anyway, I told you we'd find him, didn't I?' I said brightly.

Mrs Green snorted. 'Took your bleedin' time.'

'I shall come back later, if that's all right,' I said to Wally, not wishing him to witness an example of police brutality, and he tugged me down to kiss me on the cheek.

'Don't goo mind her,' he whispered moistly into my ear. 'She's articled.'

111

THE WIND AND THE SAND

Toby and I went for a drink and I insisted on paying for the first round. I drank mine quickly and he had hardly settled into his pint before I had finished mine and was saying, 'Shall we walk?'

Toby raised his glass. 'What's the hurry?'

'I feel restless.' I stood up while he gulped his beer down and trotted after me, around the vegetable-bowls pitch and across the road into the dunes.

'Hey.' He took hold of my good arm. 'What have I done?'

'It's what you haven't done,' I told him and I shook myself free.

I hate women who do that – get into huffs instead of coming straight out and saying why.

'Is it something to do with the way I've been reporting the case?' he asked. 'I've tried not to be sensational but it's a sensational story however you write it.'

'No,' I said. 'You've done a very good job – a damned good job, when I think what the rest of the press have been up to. We were lucky Sylvia Satin wasn't lynched.'

'What then?' Toby struggled to keep up with me, which wasn't fair because he was still recovering from his semi-lungectomy.

I stopped.

'Why have you never kissed me?' I demanded, and Toby laughed.

'I'm sorry.' He caught his breath. 'But you sounded like a wife scolding her husband for not cutting the grass.' He turned to look at my profile. 'I didn't think you wanted me to.'

'What? Why?'

'Well, I was going to, before you started telling me how your uniform is like a suit of armour and how you could never marry.'

'I didn't mean it like that.'

'How did you mean it?'

'Oh.' The wind was suddenly out of my sails. 'I don't know.'

'And you have a man risking his life in the services while I stay safe at home seducing his fiancée.'

'I am not his fiancée,' I said. 'I told you he had asked me to marry him.' I didn't tell Toby how Adam had tried to bully me to the altar. 'I turned him down and, what's more, I have written to him – to his regiment anyway. I don't know if he'll get it.'

'Saying what?'

'That I cannot continue our relationship. I didn't mention you because it doesn't make any difference to how I feel about him. Anyway, I didn't know if there was anything to mention.' A gust blew sand in my mouth and I got out a handkerchief to try to get rid of it.

'Oh, for crying out loud, just spit it out,' Toby said with uncharacteristic impatience, so I twisted my head away and did. 'Also, I wanted to have my final check to make one hundred per cent certain I am clear of the bug,' he said, and I took his hand.

'You are, aren't you?'

'Yes, and healing well.'

'Thank God.'

'I suppose so,' Toby nodded. 'But I'd thank him even more if he hadn't invented that blasted bacillus in the first place.'

I chuckled and got some more sand in my mouth but decided to learn to live with it.

'Anyway,' Toby continued, 'I could be asking you exactly the same question. Why have you never kissed me? Or are you suddenly a weak swooning girl waiting for the big strong man to sweep her into his arms?'

'Well, it seems more romantic,' I admitted shamefacedly.

'Beside which,' Toby faced me, 'I don't even know if I'll enjoy it.'

'You cheeky...' I laughed, but I never got the next word out because he had taken my face in his hands and was kissing me very softly and then not quite so softly and then hard and for quite a long time. 'So how was that?' I stroked his face and saw the tenderness in his eyes.

'Gritty,' he said and kissed me again.

112

THE GOOD AND THE BAD AND THE WEIGHT

We stood on the deck after dinner. The captain had washed and I had done my best to dry. It would be another week before I got my repaired arm back. It was crow time and the birds wheeled black around Treacle Woods, croaking hoarsely as they returned to their nests. The rabbits were all in their cages and the hens back in their runs. I had seen a rat earlier on and we had set traps.

'I let Sharkey beat up Simnal Cranditch,' I burst out.

'Madonna,' Captain breathed. 'Why?'

'We thought he had kidnapped Wally Green.'

'And now?'

'He was a disgusting man,' I said, 'but he had no part in that crime and I can do nothing to make amends.'

'And now?' Captain repeated.

We stood shoulder to shoulder, watching the water darken.

'I am deeply – deeply ashamed.'

'You did a bad thing,' Captain said gravely, 'but show me someone who has not.'

'You?' I suggested, because he always seemed like a man troubled by what he had been through, but at peace with himself.

Captain tapped his pipe out over the side and cold ash swirled away in the late evening breeze.

'I have done terrible things – terrible.'

'In war?' I asked and he inclined his head. 'All men do terrible things in war.' I put my hand on his, so leathery still after years at sea.

'Do you not fight a war,' he asked, 'every day?'

'It doesn't make what I did right,' I objected, clutching Cressida's rail much harder than I needed to.

Captain put his pipe in his mouth and blew through the stem.

'You did a bad thing,' he repeated at last, 'and if you did not think so, you would not be the woman I care for.'

It was then I knew that I could not keep doing this – living with him on the strength of a lie.

'I am not sure I can stay with you any more,' I began before faltering.

I wanted so much not to hurt him, this man who had taken me for a daughter, who had, more than once, taken my part against his own flesh and blood when Adam had tried to bully me into marriage.

'Because you do not love my son?' he asked.

'Yes. I don't think I do any more.' It surprised me how matter-of-factly I could announce that after all my years of protest to Adam and Captain and myself.

Captain sucked on his empty pipe and chewed that information over.

'Is it that newspaper man?'

'How did you know?'

'Ah, Betty,' Carmelo said. 'You have the weight of the world on your shoulders but I see it lift a little when you speak of him and I see it fall back heavy again when we talk of Adam.'

'I'm sorry,' I said.

'Why can you not—'

If he was going to ask me to forgive and forget and give his son another chance, I could not bear to tell him how many of those Adam had thrown away.

'What?' I broke in, because I didn't want to hear it.

'—invite him for dinner?' Captain continued. 'He sounds like a good man. I hope he likes rabbit.'

'The way you cook it, how could he not?' I asked.

'*Qalbi.*' *My heart.* Captain turned towards me and I towards him and we wrapped each other as best we could in the warmth of what love we had.

113

DR SECRET AND THE GLADIATOR

S ylvia Satin was, as expected, certified as suffering from juvenile psychosis and March Middleton was, as I had hoped, able to have her transferred to Queen Matilda's Mental Health Hospital in Surrey, which was run as a private sanatorium rather than a correctional institution. St Audry's at Woodbridge had a reputation for an enlightened approach to treatment but Sylvia would have been in the company of extremely disturbed adults there, whereas Matilda's specialised in treating children. Harrold Schofield helped to pay for his niece's upkeep but he never visited her there. As soon as Sylvia had settled, I went to see her.

'Sylvia has made marvellous progress,' Dr Secret assured me. He was a consultant and so, presumably, a mature man but he looked like he was taking a day off school. His clothes fitted but he seemed awkward in them. 'She fully understands what she has done and completely accepts that it was wrong. She even told me she must have been mad but I explained that she was bereaved, concussed and confused.' Dr Secret flashed me a grin that could have sold tooth powder by the barrel. 'I am convinced that, in time, she will be perfectly able to re-enter society.'

She would need to change her name first, I thought, and thanked him.

All the patients at Queen Matilda's had their own bedrooms and were allowed a few carefully selected personal possessions. Sylvia had little left from her old life but wanted nothing, not even her dolls. It was only then that I recalled wondering if she was about to swear when she said *f— dolls,* but I realised she had been about to say *family* and that was her first attempt to retrieve them.

When I arrived, Sylvia was sitting at a little wooden table, her hair golden in the sunshine, drawing a picture. At first, I thought it was a house, but as I peered over I saw that it was a church with a low roof and long narrow windows, all the lines drawn straight with a ruler. I was surprised by the amount of detail. She had even remembered the missing brick in the empty bell arch.

Sylvia broke into a dazzling smile and put down her chewed red crayon to jump up and greet me.

'Inspector lady,' she cried, wrapping her arms around me in such a big hug that any observer would have thought we had parted the greatest of friends.

'How are you, Sylvia?'

She let go and danced around me.

'I am very well indeed, thank you,' she told me with a happy laugh. 'They are lovely people here. The nurses are so kind and Dr Secret is just like my daddy.'

I took Sylvia's hand and tried to get her to look at me.

'You do know that he isn't, don't you, Sylvia?'

'I'm not that silly.' Sylvia gave her lovely light contagious giggle. 'Of course I know it. He's much too young for you, Mummy.'

I walked from the hospital to the bus stop. It was a warm, sunny day and I found it difficult to believe that eighty miles away, our men were dying in flight from the German onslaught. A solitary Gloster Gladiator buzzed a few hundred feet over my head. I knew that Jimmy's Hurricane squadron was being held in reserve but surely we were not relying in the meantime on biplanes to save us from invasion?

It was only a few months since I had come back to Sackwater. We were at peace then and had no serious crimes on our books when Shirley Temple crept into the station, all golden curls, looking about her like a babe lost in the woods.

'I've losted my button,' she piped up timorously. 'My mum will kill me dead or worse.'

And as the little girl held out the lower edge of her cardigan with a trembling hand for me to see the torn thread, her big, innocent, anxious cornflower eyes brimmed with tears that melted my heart away.